CITY
UNDER
SIEGE

ALSO BY R.J. PRESCOTT

The Hurricane

The Aftermath

The Storm

City Under Siege

CITY
UNDER
SIEGE

USA TODAY BESTSELLING AUTHOR
R.J. PRESCOTT

City Under Siege
By R.J. Prescott

Copyright © 2018 R.J. Prescott
All rights reserved.
First Published 2018 by R.J. Prescott

Print ISBN : 978-1-9999038-1-7

Interior Formatting by Leigh Stone

Editing by Hot Tree Editing and Clare Reay

Cover Design by Sarah Hansen of Okay Cover Creations

PROLOGUE

Sarah

Three Months Earlier

The utilitarian metal clock, its ticking painfully loud against the silence, reminded me of the antiquated time pieces that hung on the walls of almost of my high school classrooms, and in most every office I'd ever been in. Absently, I wondered if they weren't part of some cruel joke. Inviting pupils and employees alike to witness time slipping away within the four walls of their confines. It was these kinds of useless meanderings that helped me to bear the indeterminable wait without completely losing my shit. And I'd been close.

So very close.

Painfully near to screaming at the top of my lungs for as long as I could. The only thing that held me back was the knowledge that doing so would almost certainly lead to an immediate bullet through my brain. I didn't want to die.

When it came down to it, nobody ever really did. The instinct for self-preservation was stronger than most of us knew, and in the end, maybe that was all some people had left. But not me. The torrent of emotion raging inside me was so much stronger than a simple will to survive. In the beginning, there was only fear. But once the adrenaline had subsided, and the reality of my situation sank in, I found the ability to see past the terror and panic. To feel other things. Frustration. Helplessness. Rage. Pain.

In those final hours, I lived through all the stages of grief. Denial. Anger. Bargaining and depression. Now, finally, I was at acceptance. I accepted what was going to happen, and I hoped my life had meant something. That in the end, my actions had changed somebody else's life for the better. I had been brave when bravery wasn't the easiest choice, and for that I had some measure of peace. And then there was Tom. When I pictured his face, my heart wept. It was the cruellest of tragedies to be ripped away so soon from the person it had taken me a lifetime to find. But the real tragedy would've been to never have loved him at all. And in my darkest hour, he was here with me.

As I watched the clock hand tick over into one minute past midnight, making it officially the twenty second of January, I was struck by the irony. I was born on the twenty second, it was likely that I would die on the twenty second, and my only glimmer of hope had been that the twenty second Special Air Service would save me. I was past that now though.

After hours and hours of complete silence, voices were raised and doors slammed in a flurry of activity. Eventually, the door to my room flew open. A gun was pointed at my head while my captor screamed at me in a foreign language. Seeming to realise I didn't understand, he gestured with his weapon for me to get up. The weight of the explosive vest strapped tightly to my chest made standing painful. But I knew from experience that not doing as I was told would lead to more discomfort. Apparently, I wasn't moving fast enough for his liking. Grabbing me by my upper arm with a bruising grip, he dragged me into another larger room off a narrow hallway that was filled with his associates.

Gone was their icy control reserve of earlier. In its place was panic and unrest. The men argued heatedly between themselves, often pointing a gun in my direction as they spoke. My eyes wandered absently around the room as I tried to block out the noise. All of the windows I'd seen had been covered with closed blinds. The shafts of light piercing through the slats served as a reminder of the world that existed outside of this prison. Through the doorway, I could see part of a long window across the hall. The dark cloth draped across it had partially slipped. I understood then how the mind could play tricks, because a dead man stared back at me through the glass. It didn't matter that he wasn't real. What mattered was that the last face I'd ever see wouldn't be looking at me with eyes filled with hate. Closing my eyes against the pain, I felt a single tear track slowly down my cheek, before the world exploded. After that, I felt nothing at all.

CHAPTER ONE

Sarah

As I watched both coffins lower slowly into the ground, I felt as though I was made of stone. Like any other statue in a graveyard filled with effigies, I stood in solemn tribute to the last of my immediate family. Rain pelted down mercilessly over the crowd of London's finest, most of whom were completely unprepared for the brutal Yorkshire weather. My aunt Elizabeth told me it was ridiculous to have Dad and John buried here, and didn't I care how much I inconvenienced their friends by making them travel all this way from London? It was on the tip of my tongue to tell her that I didn't give a shit about any of them, but Dad wouldn't have wanted that. So I said nothing and replied by booking the funeral anyway. If she had her way, there'd be a state procession that ended at St Paul's Cathedral.

Despite what you might think, I didn't drag everyone two hundred and fifty miles just to piss off Dad's sister. I did it so that in death, they'd feel free. Like I did, standing on the Yorkshire moors with the wind in my face, remembering my mum dancing around with John and me like a crazy person. Dad's family might come from money, but Mum had been a down-to-earth northern lass through and through. She'd been Dad's moment of madness, and he had loved her like no other until the day she died. But cancer was such a cruel, merciless bitch. Not content with taking lives, she also stole the spirit of those she left behind. One day my beautiful, free-spirited, effervescent mum was teaching me to cartwheel through the long grass, and less than eight months later, she was gone, and with her the soul of her beloved. Dad was never the same after she passed. In his loss, his sister stepped in to help raise us and guide him as to the example he should set. Cottage holidays on the moors and Lake District gave way to cocktail parties on yachts in Monaco as she finally had him living up to the Tatem name. Eventually, even John and I drifted apart. With ten years between us, I was sent to an all-girls boarding school to finish out my education, and following John's graduation from university, he joined Tatem Shipping and fell into the vapid wormhole of life as a shipping magnate.

As for me, I did everything I could to disappoint them. In contrast to John's feng shui, minimalist monstrosity of a house, my eclectic flat was filled with textures, colours, and light. Sketches, paintings, drawings, and doodles were scattered haphazardly around potted plants and wild flower-filled jam jars. I'd refused Dad's offer to help me find something "a bit more up market" and instead relished in the beauty of the fact that I was paying my own way. Standing on my own two feet without a penny of my family's money, doing something I knew Mum would've loved. I illustrated children's books, and every once in a while, I had the privilege of contributing to charity books that benefited Great Ormond Street Children's Hospital. Maybe I wasn't setting the world of business and commerce on fire, and I'd certainly never be making the society pages, but I was happy. Or at least I was until that cold September day when the phone rang and didn't stop.

Aunt Elizabeth had been the one to tell me that my father and brother had been on their way to a board meeting together, when they'd been involved in a tragic accident. Apparently, a truck jumping a red light had ploughed into the side of their town car, killing them almost instantly. For hours I'd sat there, too numb to shed a tear until I worked out how long it had been since Dad and I had spoken last. Honestly, I thought it hurt him to even look at me. He was kind and generous and spent every minute of every conversation we'd ever had trying to buy me things. But I was my mother through and through, and every moment we spent together made it harder for him to bear. The older I became, the more I reminded him of everything he'd lost. So, I embraced her memory while Dad and John did their best to forget it. I guess we all dealt with grief in our own way. But the distance between us didn't make this moment any less painful. In fact, it felt like losing Mum all over again.

The priest said one last short prayer over their graves, and the crowd of strangers I barely even knew scurried away like insects.

"Sarah, if you're going to be travelling in the family car with me, we need to leave now. It isn't appropriate that we should be the last to arrive at the wake," Aunt Elizabeth remarked.

"Surely people won't begrudge us a few minutes to say our goodbyes," I reasoned.

She sighed deeply, as though I was an obstinate child unnecessarily testing her patience.

"Sarah, I understand that you've led somewhat of a cosseted life. Despite my advice, your father humoured your bohemian leanings and indulged you in all of your artistic nonsense. But I'm afraid you no longer have the luxury of selfishness. The time for that way of thinking is over. Like it or not, you are now the head of Tatem Shipping and you must act accordingly. A great number of the people here are shareholders. How do you think share prices will be affected if they see you as anything other than a strong leader? Of course, I will be able to school you in social etiquette, but you must stop pandering to your emotions for the sake of the company," she said, stunning me speechless for a moment.

Rather naively perhaps, I'd hoped that the younger version of myself had somehow villainised her. That she'd come over to offer me a hug, or some words of comfort in our shared grief. I was disappointed, but not surprised by the confrontation. Her manipulation and meddling had worked with my father, but she was about to learn that they wouldn't work with me.

"Aunt Elizabeth, I appreciate that you were close to my father, and that he regularly sought your advice on many matters, so please don't think that I mean this disrespectfully, but I don't really care how many shareholders are here or why they came. I don't care about my outfit or my timekeeping or even my etiquette. Tomorrow I'll do whatever needs to be done. Today, I'm saying goodbye to my family," I replied.

Turning my back, I walked closer to the graveside and closed my eyes as I inhaled the scent of fresh rain. Elizabeth snorted indignantly, but I could hear the sound of her footsteps as she walked away. Regardless of what happened, neither of us had the luxury of turning our back on one another permanently. She was a board member who held valuable company shares. If it was up to me, I'd liquidate the company tomorrow, but thousands of livelihoods depended on Tatem Shipping for employment. There was no way I was cut out to do this forever, but to a certain degree, she was right. Without a Tatem at the helm, share prices would plummet, and everyone from the little guy paying his mortgage to my richer than Onassis aunt would be ruined. So I made a deal with my conscience. I would stay for a few years until the stability of the company was assured, and then I'd wash my hands of the Tatem name for good. I looked out across the bleak, unforgiving beauty of the moors, the wind whipping away my tears before they could fall, and I felt nothing but despair. Because if the last few days had been anything to go by, the next few years would be interminable.

"I'm sorry to disturb you Miss Tatem, but there's a Mr Vasili Agheenco here to see you," Victoria said. She'd been Dad's secretary since he first started at the firm, and I was sure she felt his loss as much as I did. In the weeks that had passed since the funeral, I'd been drowning in everything I didn't know. Bombarded with information I had no idea how to interpret and decisions I had no idea how to make. Each of the board members had their own vision of the company's future and were little to no help at all. But in the middle of the quagmire, Victoria would appear with a cup of tea and a few desperately needed chocolate biscuits. I was pretty sure that she was shielding me from the worst of things. I was sailing alone in the dark, and without her I'd be rudderless. Yet, despite all of my pleading, she still wouldn't call me by my first name.

"Does he have an appointment? I wasn't expecting to meet with anyone this afternoon," I replied. Hoped was more like. I didn't think I could take one more meeting with an over-opinionated director or nervous stockholder.

"No. He doesn't have an appointment," she replied nervously. "But Mr Agheenco doesn't make them. He didn't come in often, but when he did, your father would always see him."

"What aren't you telling me?" I asked anxiously. Victoria was completely unflappable. Her edginess about this guy made me feel uneasy.

"To be honest, there's something about him that scares me. When he came by, your father would send me out on some meaningless errand, and by the time I'd get back he was gone. I tried to talk to him about it a few times, but he would always change the subject. I don't know what it is about him, but he seems so...uncivilised," she explained.

I sighed deeply and contemplated what to do. I couldn't imagine Dad having continued associations with someone dangerous, but her reaction made me uncomfortable. I could try and postpone, but with things being as unstable as they were, I didn't want to risk offending a potential client.

"It's all right, Victoria, I'll see him. But would you mind staying in your office while he's here?" I asked, and she nodded as she left. Hers was a connecting room that led from the end of a hallway into Dad's. Tatem Shipping had modern offices in a number of cities, but Dad had kept the London head office in the original, listed, turn of the century building in which his grandfather had founded the company. The many rooms and anterooms didn't lend themselves to modern, open-plan office working, but I agreed with his decision. In a world that was dreary and humdrum, this antiquated building had character.

A sharp knock at the door preceded Victoria with my visitor.

"Miss Tatem, this is Mr Agheenco," Victoria said, holding the door open. Rather rudely, he waved his hand to dismiss her, and wearing a small frown, she closed the door with a quiet click. Knowing she was close by to call security if needed made me feel a little easier, but only when I was in his presence did I understand why she'd been so unnerved.

"I have heard a great deal about you, Miss Tatem, but nobody told me how beautiful you were," he remarked. Dressed sharply in what looked to be an expensive tailored suit, his salt and peppered hair neatly trimmed, there was nothing outwardly to suggest that he was anything other than a respectable business man. His impeccable English, even heavily laced as it was with an obvious Russian accent, suggested that he'd been well-educated. He had a slight build and was perhaps only around five foot ten, but it was his eyes that made him so terrifying. Cold, empty eyes that undressed me from across the room. Without invitation, he sat himself in a leather chair and made himself comfortable in a way he'd clearly done before.

"Thank you for the compliment," I replied politely. "How is it I can help you today?"

Surprising me, he barked out a laugh.

"Straight to the point, just like your father. I like that. And not one for flattery either. I see I will need to work harder to fall into your good graces," he said, leering at me as though "good graces" was code for bed.

"You sound as though you shared a close association with my father. Do you mind if I ask the nature of your relationship?" I asked, taking a seat behind Dad's desk. For weeks I'd sat bowed over the aged, worn oak, trying to connect with a man I barely knew. He was gone and never coming back, but regardless, the furnishings around me all felt like his. Perhaps the time would come to make the office a little more my own, but I doubted it.

He steepled his fingers and stared at me for longer than was comfortable. Trying to conceal my anxiety, I looked him in the eyes with as much steel as I could muster and waited for his response. His appearance lent him an air of civility, but it was a paper-thin veneer that did little to conceal his contempt. Given his behaviour so far, I imagined his distain was less of a personal loathing and more a dislike of women in general.

"You have found yourself at the helm of one of your country's oldest family-owned shipping companies, but how much do you really know about it?" he asked, finally.

"If you're looking for some history as to the background of the company, our website is a wealth of information. My family has been dedicated to the business of shipping for generations. It's what draws new clients and investors to the company every year, and it's our impeccable levels of service that keep them," I replied, having memorised the shit from a pamphlet in an attempt to navigate my way through trade meetings and negotiations with potential new clients.

"You know next to nothing about this company, because that is the way your father intended it. The truth is that Tatem Shipping is a failing enterprise and has been since your country joined the European Union."

"I'm sorry to have to contradict you, Mr Agheenco, but the quarterly accounts tell a very different story. Our profits last year are a matter of public record, as are the many years before that, and I'm reassured that they all say the same thing. Joining the European Union opened up a number of opportunities for trade partnerships, and inevitably, those partnerships expanded into shipping. Joining the Union was a turning point for the growth of our business," I disputed. The truth was that I was woefully out of my depth already. The bullshit I was feeding him, whilst true, was part of the crash course in Tatem Shipping I'd been given by advisors to the board in a vain attempt to bring me up to speed.

"To a degree, that is true. But before that occurred, your firm found itself mired in European shipping laws and red tape, the likes of which it had never seen. After four generations and two world wars, your father, the great Charles Tatem, was on the verge of allowing his family's legacy to crumble. With a pretty wife and two young children, his heart was not in it as you say, but his pride would not see the company destroyed, so when my organisation approached him about an arrangement mutually beneficial to both parties, he was very amenable to the idea," he explained, as he continue to peruse me, somewhat condescendingly.

"So that is how you knew my father. You were a client of his?"

"In a manner of speaking," he said, cryptically. "The relaxation of the borders in Europe meant the opening of a whole new market for my import business. But, given that my companies are all Russian, our shipments were still heavily targeted by customs officers and Border Force. To overcome this problem, our merchandise was concealed within legitimate shipping containers, all of which had the correct paperwork, and was extracted at the other end."

"So you're a smuggler?" I asked, rather naively, making him chuckle.

"If you want to romanticise the arrangement, I suppose that's one way of looking at it."

"And what exactly is your merchandise?"

He narrowed his beady eyes and stared at me calculatedly. "You should think very carefully before you ask questions like that. For many years, your father was happy in his ignorance. He had a good life with your mother, and I was making him very rich. You too could have the same life, but now you are asking to open Pandora's box, which you will never be able to close. If you choose to know, I will tell you, but make no mistake, you will have to live with the consequences."

"Thank you for your concern, Mr Agheenco, but I'm quite sure that I want to know."

"Very well, Miss Tatem," he said, with a smirk. "But please remember that it was your choice to sour what could have been an amicable relationship for us both. You wanted details and particulars, so here we are. For nearly ten years, Tatum Shipping has successfully transported a great many things from my country. In the early days, it was tobacco and alcohol. When the market demanded it, the nature of our shipments changed, and we found it much more profitable to bring stockpiles of weapons from the former Soviet Union into Eastern Europe," he explained, casually picking invisible lint off his suit as though he wasn't making the bottom fall out of my world. "While this is still our main source of income, we also move drugs, human cargo, endangered animals, and anything else that will bring a profit."

"Human cargo? You mean to tell me that my family has been helping you traffic women and children?" I whispered, barely able to contain the bile from creeping up my throat.

"You Westerners are so narrow-minded," he replied, with a smile, obviously amused by my horror. "You breed cattle your entire lives, horses, cows, pigs, sheep. They are born purely for the purpose of their use. You raise them, crammed together in tiny pens, then slaughter them when you need to. But when the cattle walk on two legs instead of four, your sensibilities are offended. You complain when you hear that these people are being used for forced labour, but you will happily buy goods at the lowest price on the market. These days everyone wants cheap, and they don't care about the human cost as long as they don't have to hear about it. Our transit links supply surrogate mothers, arranged marriages, organ donation, cheap labour, and yes, sexual labour as well. You may want to vilify my organisation, but what we do is simply supply and demand."

"You can't seriously expect me to believe that my dad and brother turned a blind eye to this? That nobody else on the board knows about this!" I protested.

"Why would they know? Shipments are made through legitimate shell companies, and the cargo manifests are all in order," he responded, smoothly.

"What about customs officials? Surely these containers are searched. It really can't be that easy to do what you're suggesting."

"Containers are randomly checked, but in the event that we can't conceal the freight, an official can always be bribed or intimidated. We do own the ports after all. But you are right in a sense. It isn't nearly as easy or straightforward as I'm suggesting. A venture of the size at which we operate takes planning and cooperation. It's an undertaking that's been mutually beneficial to my associates and the Tatem family for quite some time."

"I'd like you to leave," I said, shaking as I stood. "If Tatem Shipping has somehow been involved with this, there is no way Dad or John knew about this. Your association with my family is over. Please don't come here again."

He sighed as though I were a petulant child who needed

scolding as he fastened the buttons on his suit jacket.

"Miss Tatem, without my business, there simply is no Tatem Shipping."

"If that's true, then so be it. I'm not prepared to give up years of my life to saving a company that traffics in human misery. I'd rather see it go under," I sneered. Moving to walk past him, I hoped to show him the door. Too late I realised that turning my back on him was a mistake. Before I could even register what was happening, he grabbed hold of my throat and slammed me hard against the wall. The force of the blow to the back of my head had me seeing stars, but worse still, he squeezed so hard that I couldn't breathe.

"You seem to be under the misapprehension that I am asking you to continue our arrangement. There is no choice for you to make here. There is no doing the right thing. Quite simply all I ask is that you continue to play the part of the dutiful heiress. You will be the figurehead for the company, keeping those stockholders happy and the share prices stable. I will be sending in some of my own employees to work alongside your executives, making sure that business continues as usual, and you will sign anything that they put in front of you. In return, you'll lead a life of wealth and privilege," he said.

I clawed at his hand, gasping for any breath of oxygen that would keep me conscious.

"Do yourself a favour, Sarah. Don't make the same mistake your father did. He started listening to your brother and grew himself a conscience. Now he is no longer a problem, and if you defy me, you won't be either," he warned. Pulling me forward slightly, he slammed my head against the wall once more before dropping me to the floor. I coughed and spluttered between filling my lungs with air.

"Now, why don't you take a few days to think over what I've said. Speak with your accountants and get a picture of how deeply ingrained my business is to your company. Mention the name Kornax Limited to him. Once you've had some time to think about it, you'll realise how people rely on your cooperation to pay their mortgages and feed their families. In time, any guilt you might feel will pass, I'm sure. But one last word of warning. Should you feel a burning need to pass on the details of our relationship, to say the board members, a best friend, even your fucking priest, don't. There are so many ways to feel pain that are worse than death, and I will introduce you to them all."

He crouched beside me and ran the back of his fingers gently over my cheek.

"You are so beautiful. The lesson will be my pleasure. Now, I have some business in the capital, but I will be back soon enough. As long as you've been discrete, I don't see why our next visit should be anything less than cordial." He stood over me and, like the monster he was, relished the sight of my pain at his feet.

His head turned as a quick knock sounded at the door and it flew open. A nervous looking Victoria clutched at the handle.

"I apologise for interrupting you," she said.

"Not at all. Miss Tatem appears to have choked on something. Perhaps you'd be so kind as to get her a glass of water," he said.

Victoria looked nervously towards me where I was still struggling to breathe normally. "Miss Tatem?" she asked.

"It's all right, Victoria," I reassured her, my voice scratchy and coarse. "Water would help." She nodded and disappeared, knowing then that I was sending her on the same kind of mundane errand that my father did.

"Until next time, Sarah," he said, and strode nonchalantly out of the door, closing it gently behind him.

Using what little strength I had left, I crawled towards the waste bin and vomited until there was nothing left.

CHAPTER TWO

Sarah

More than once that day, I'd questioned the sanity of my decision, but as the taxi pulled up next to me, I knew it was too late for regrets. When the Ministry of Defence said they were sending a car, I somehow expected something a little more clandestine. Perhaps a black four-wheel drive with tinted windows. My choice had been a little easier when I imagined myself protected by James Bond and his secret service associates. In reality, these people were still part of the same government of civil servants who took five months to rectify the misspelling of my name on a tax form. Perhaps I was setting unrealistic expectations.

"Taxi for Miss Tatem?" the driver said. I nodded and climbed inside. He whistled along to the radio but didn't try to make idle chat, and for that I was grateful. My stomach was in knots as it was, and I didn't think making small talk would help. Most of our journey was spent sitting in traffic, an inevitability in central London at any time of day.

"Here we go, love," he said, pulling up in front of chrome and glass monolith that stretched high above us.

"How much do I owe you?" I asked, reaching for my purse.

"That'll be a fiver please," he replied. There's no way that the fare would be that cheap, so I figured that paying him must be for appearances sake. My hand shook as I passed him a note, and I'd barely closed the door behind me before he shot off, leaving me behind to stare up at the building. A chill ran down my spine as I imagined who might be staring down at me through the glass. Plucking up my courage, I pushed my way through the large door and walked up to the reception desk, feigning a confidence I didn't feel.

"Hello," the receptionist said, smiling warmly. "How may I help you?"

"Hi. My name is Sarah Tatem. I'm here for an appointment," I replied, with as much of a returning smile as I could muster.

"Good afternoon, Miss Tatem. I believe that you're expected on the eighteenth floor." She indicated to the bank of elevators behind me.

"Thank you," I replied, with a nod of acknowledgement. My body on autopilot, I followed her directions, and all too quickly, I was delivered to a meeting I was nowhere near ready for. The smell of fresh paint struck me, before I realised that all the chairs stacked along the corridor were in protective wrap. Opening up the main door to the floor, I could see that the whole place was an open-plan office space, newly furbished and almost ready for occupation.

"Ah! Sarah! You made it. It's a pleasure to see you." Simon Masterson was my government liaison, and while he didn't exactly give me the warm and fuzzies, from our telephone conversation, he certainly seemed to know what he was talking about.

Three days ago, after I stopped vomiting and reassuring Victoria I was fine, I visited our accounts department like Vasili had suggested. Without telling them why I wanted the information, they confirmed that contracts with Kornax Limited were the cornerstone of our business. He'd been right. Without him, Tatum Shipping would cease to exist. It took me all of ten minutes to decide what to do, and that ten minutes had been spent vacillating between ways to try and salvage the livelihoods of our employees and wondering how it was that my dad and brother could ever live with themselves for what they'd done. Fear and shame drove my decision, but having made it, knowing who to trust was a minefield. Reporting what I'd learned was the only decision I could live with, but even I, in my naivety, knew that organised crime gangs had corrupt police officers on the payroll. Eventually, I settled on the London Metropolitan Counter Terrorism Hotline. Vasili had mentioned arms sales, among other things, so I figured that counted as terrorist activity. Apparently, the government agreed. Within thirty minutes of leaving my name and details, I was contacted by an officer who connected me with Simon. We had spoken a couple of times since then on the telephone, though today was the first time we'd met in person.

Striding energetically towards me, and seeming significantly more enthusiastic about the meeting than I was, he held out his hand. As I shook it, he laid a second hand on top of mine like we were old friends. The gleeful gleam in his eye was no doubt caused by the valuable connection to Russian gang members operating in the country that I presented. While I appreciated his experience in these matters, I didn't appreciate the pretence. I gave him something he needed, and in return did my best to sail my father's legacy out of the shadow of malady and corruption it had been mired in while he'd be at the helm.

"Hello, Mr Masterson. I'm happy to be here," I lied. "I must confess, I'm not sure how it is I can help any further. I've told you absolutely everything I can think of I'm afraid. At the very least, I'm sure I've given you enough financial information to arrest Vasili Agheenco, and I've already agreed to testify against him."

"You have certainly been most helpful, and of course we are very grateful to you for coming forward, but there are ways that you could help us further. Before we get into that though, there is someone that I'd like you to meet." He pushed his glasses further up his nose, something he had a habit of doing every few minutes like a nervous tick. I dreaded the thought of hashing out my dirty secret once more, but followed him resignedly to a meeting room, partitioned from the main office by floor-to-ceiling opaque glass.

"May I offer you some tea or coffee?" Mr Masterson asked, as he pulled out a chair for me to sit.

"Tea would be nice, thank you," I replied, wanting the warmth of the cup around my icy-cold hands, rather than the drink itself. He smiled in reply and busied himself preparing my beverage. A small silver urn sat next to a wooden box of tea and bone china cups on a long mahogany end table at the top of the room. It matched the large oval boardroom table at which I sat, surrounded by luxurious leather chairs, the only bits of furniture that appeared to have been unwrapped.

It took me a moment to realise we weren't alone. From across the room, I was being watched. My observer perched casually against the windowsill, his strong, tanned forearms crossed over his chest. Until that point, I didn't know it was possible to be both attracted to a person and simultaneously scared shitless of them. He was the complete antithesis of every male I'd ever known. Dad had been a soft man. Soft hands, soft belly, and a soft backbone as it turned out. There wasn't a thing about this soldier that wasn't hard as nails. I was almost positive that was what he was. He practically screamed military.

Shaved short on the sides, but longer on top, his thick black hair fell naturally into artfully dishevelled spikes that begged to have hands running through them. He was too far away for me to tell the colour of his eyes, but they were dark.

Piercing.

Assessing.

Sharp.

Eyes that missed nothing and took in everything. His strong jaw was clean shaven but as granite hard and sharp as his cheekbones. Everything about him, from his size to his demeanour, called to the primal core of me. The one governed by millions of years of predetermination to choose the most dominant, the most alpha male in the pack. Some might say it was the need to feel protected that attracted me to him. I'd concede that in a world that left me feeling alone and vulnerable, inside of his strong arms seemed like a pretty tempting place to be. But what I felt at that moment was pure, unadulterated lust, tinged with the smallest amount of fear that even imagining a fantasy of myself with a guy like that was a bad idea. My gaze fell to his plump, full lips, and seeming to sense the direction of my thoughts, the side of his mouth lifted in a slight smirk.

"Here you are, Sarah," Mr Masterson said, placing a cup of tea down in front of me and interrupting my ruminations.

"Thank you." I looked down to wrap my hands around the delicate bone china. To my absolute mortification, I could feel colour flood my cheeks as I blushed with embarrassment. Keeping it together in front of my liaison had been challenging enough so far, but this guy was in a different league. The vain, shallow part of me wanted to impress him, not air my family's dirty laundry in his presence.

"Sarah, I'd like to introduce you to Lieutenant Tom Harper. Lieutenant Harper leads a Special Projects team in our military counterterrorism unit," Mr Masterson said, indicating towards the soldier.

"It's nice to meet you," he said. Pushing off the ledge, he made short work of the distance between us and held out his hand. At around six foot four, I had to tilt my head to meet his gaze as I placed my small, pale palm into his. Heat shot through me at the contact, and the slight narrowing of his eyes told me that I wasn't the only one to feel it.

"You too," I replied nervously, knowing that was the understatement of the century.

The introduction over, he pulled out the chair next to mine and sat down. It all happened rather fast, but before he released me, I could have sworn the he rubbed his thumb gently across mine. Perhaps it was simply wishful thinking. While I wanted to seem calm and professional, I was flustered. I'd never met a man so unapologetically male before. There was no softness to his edges, no social proprietary in the intense way he inhabited my space. Although his looks added to the package, it was the penetrating look in those big eyes, I could see now were brown, that had me captivated. Being this close to him was both terrifying and exhilarating.

"Firstly, I'd like to thank you for coming forward. For someone in your position, it would have been very tempting to think first of your company's interests and to hide your family's involvement in this matter. To speak up and risk your own personal safety and the reputation of your business takes a great deal of courage," Mr Masterson said, his hands clasped in front of him on the table.

"What happened to your neck?" Lieutenant Harper asked randomly. His voice was deep and clipped, as though he was straining to conceal his anger. Subconsciously, I reached up to rub it and realised my scarf had slipped, exposing the ugly purple bruising that had been a gift from Vasili.

"The Russian who came to my office choked me and threw me against the wall when he warned me not to do what I'm doing."

His jaw clenched even tighter as he stared intently at the damage. A few tense seconds passed before Mr Masterson coughed uncomfortably before continuing with his sales pitch. I could tell that's what it was. With his slicked-back hair and sharp suit, he looked more like a politician than the security specialist I knew him to be. Still, he'd taken me seriously so far. I could only hope that he could protect me from the fallout if the fact of our meeting ever came to light.

"I understand that what happened to you must have been deeply upsetting and traumatic," he said sympathetically.

"You're beginning to scare me. You told me there was more I could do to help, then you invite me to meet in an empty building with an antiterrorism specialist. I've had about as much trauma as I can handle for one week. So, with the greatest respect, Mr Masterson, what the fuck is going on?" I asked, not pulling any punches. Lieutenant Harper smiled at my frankness, though his associate looked awkward at being called out.

"If I may?" Lieutenant Harper said, looking towards Mr Masterson, who nodded his permission.

"At any one time, we monitor a high number of suspected terrorists within the UK. We could deport them of course, but that doesn't remove the threat. It just relocates it to a place that's more difficult for us to scrutinise. We watch these people with as many resources as we can for as long as we can, in the hope that we can gather enough intel to stop terrorist attacks, both here and in allied countries, before they can happen," Lieutenant Harper explained.

"What does that have to do with me?" I questioned nervously. "I've already told you everything I know. What more can I do?"

"You can honour the deal between Agheenco and your father," he replied.

"Excuse me? I can't have any part in knowingly transporting weapons or drugs, or worse still, human beings. I can't do it. I won't do it." My reply was emphatic. A testament to how strongly I abhorred his suggestion

In response, Lieutenant Harper leaned forward in his seat and rested his forearms on his thighs. "I get it. I do." His

33

voice was gentle. "But if Tatem Shipping closes tomorrow, they'll just use another firm to do the same thing, and we'll have lost our window for tracking the source of these weapons. More importantly, we lose the only chance we have of tracing the clients that want the weapons in the first place."

I wanted to throw up all over again. Even if the thought of being a part of so many heinous crimes didn't trigger my upchuck reflex, the idea of knowingly putting myself in Vasili's presence again terrified me.

"He'll kill me," I whispered. It was to myself, but they both heard it.

"I can assure you that won't happen, Sarah. We'll be monitoring your every move and theirs. Lieutenant Harper here will be your liaison, and his team will always be close by. From what I understand, your board are keen to push you as the next generation figurehead of your company, spearing them into the future of international shipping. Pretty soon, you'll be a high-profile public person. Believe me, you're of more use to them alive than you are dead," Mr Masterson said.

"That's very reassuring. Thank you. Please remind me of that when I'm wearing concrete shoes at the bottom of the Thames," I replied.

"That's the mafia you're thinking of. Russians are more likely to go with a double tap to the head," Lieutenant Harper chipped in.

"Ah, well, there's that at least. I never did like the water,"

I replied, strangely appreciating his black humour.

"Ironic, considering you own a shipping firm," Lieutenant Harper observed.

"It is, isn't it?" I said, with a small grin.

Mr Masterson looked back and forth at us as though we were both a little unbalanced. Unexpectedly though, it helped me calm down and focus instead of freaking out.

"So, will you do it?" Mr Masterson asked me.

"In the last four weeks, I've lost my father and my brother, not in a terrible accident, but by the hand of a Russian gang. I've left a flat I love to live in a cold, soulless monstrosity and a job I adored to work for a business I hate in order to save the jobs of people, most of whom I will probably never meet. I've learned that my family's legacy is a lie based on the pain and suffering of others, and I've been threatened and abused by a terrifying criminal that you want me to invite permanently into my life. Don't you think I've had about as much as I can take?"

"No," Lieutenant Harper replied.

"Pardon me?" I asked, sure I'd misheard.

"No. I don't think you've had as much as you can take. Yes, you've lost people. Yes, you've had a tough time, and yes, we're asking you to put yourself in danger. But it's not forever. It will take us two months at most to get what we need. That's eight weeks where you'll probably have very little to do with Vasili Agheenco. Eight weeks to act like a society princess and live in the lap of luxury. When we're done, your job and your flat will still be there and you can go back to normality, able to sleep at night because what you did saved lives. And that's exactly what you'll be doing. Saving lives." He must have seen something in my face that made him realise he'd gone too far, and softened his tone.

"Look, we wouldn't be asking if we had any other choice. But we believe the clients buying the Russian arms are terrorists operating out of the UK. If you don't help, you're telling me you can watch the television the next time another suicide bomb goes off killing innocent people and not feel anything.".

"You can't put that on me," I answered, tears filling my eyes because I knew he was right.

"We can, Sarah, because we have to," Mr Masterson responded. "We no longer live in a world that can afford to turn its back and hope for the best."

I wiped away the self-pitying tear from the corner of my eye and swallowed as I nodded in reply. They were right. There was no other choice.

"Thank you, Sarah," Mr Masterson said, seeming pleased that I had come to a decision. Despite his persuasion, Lieutenant Harper looked anything but happy. I could only hope he really was joking about the double tap to the head.

CHAPTER THREE

Tom

"Why here?" Eli asked me.

"It's upscale, newly refurbished, and in central London. If she's being watched, it's a perfect cover story to claim that she's scouting for new office space. The current headquarters are located in an older building, so it's believable that she'd want a new start as head of the company. We gave her the number to set up a meeting with a bogus letting agent. If her phones are tapped, they'll think it's legit," I explained.

"Shit. Can you imagine waking up to find you're a millionaire or some shit?" Crash chipped in. "I wonder how much she's worth."

"I'm sure it was a barrel full of fucking laughs, having to bury the last of her immediate family and then giving up her life to save the livelihood of hundreds of people, only to discover her family's legacy is funded by Russian gun money," I threw back at him.

"Sorry, sir. I didn't realise it was a touchy subject. I just figured she was nothing more than intel," he protested.

"You're being a dick," Eli pointed out. "You know how much it winds him up when you act like a dick."

"I thought it was me being immature that wound him up?" Crash asked, in all seriousness.

"When you're being immature, you act like a dick, so in a sense, it's a double whammy that makes him want to nut punch you," Eli explained to him.

I wasn't sure if it was just because Crash was the youngest, but I hoped that a little more operational experience would season him. He was a fucking good soldier and an asset to my team, but he had all the subtlety and compassion of a sledgehammer. I couldn't give a shit about the compassion, but the subtlety would come in handy at times.

Contrary to appearances, formalities of rank existed between us, same as any other military unit, at least when it came to taking orders. When I talked, they listened. End of story. Anyone who didn't do what they were told, when they were told, could fuck off. Outside of that, the boys were far more relaxed in the way they addressed me than their ranks would ever normally allow. It was a camaraderie unique to our regiment, and one permitted amongst us at my discretion. I ran the most lethal counterterrorist team in the Special Air Service, and I did it my way.

"What's the score, Tom. Why are we even here?" Will

asked me. Although not the most senior-ranked member of my unit, he held more combat experience than the rest of the team and was definitely the most steadfastly reliable man I knew. His deep voice and thick northern accent had an almost calming effect, even in the most hostile situations. Hearing his question, the rest of the guys tuned in, waiting for my response.

"Things are changing for the regiment, lads, and I'm not sure it's for the better. The prime minister's getting nailed by the press for her soft stance on terrorism. She needs a blunt instrument as a show of strength, and we're it. The word from MI5 is that something big is going down. Things are escalating, and the government wants something done before suicide bombers are knocking at the gates of Buckingham Palace," I explained.

The last three months had seen attacks on British soil, the likes of which were unprecedented. The latest assaults were as horrific as they were effective. Recently petrol cans rigged with explosives had been thrown simultaneously into all the entrances and exits of a central London school. The building was old and several stories high, but with no way out, the kids climbed to the upper floors to escape the fire while they waited for the emergency services to arrive. When they did, a powerful explosive device was triggered, collapsing a stairwell. Firefighters regrouped, but by then the inferno had breached the already damaged fire doors. The devastation had been catastrophic, and when the smoke cleared, five firefighters, two teachers, and twenty-three children were dead. In the weeks prior, the same practice had resulted in fatalities at a nightclub and a department store. But it was those iconic images, the burnt corpses of innocent British children being stretchered from the rubble, that had the prime minister making the call. London would burn no more.

"The brass says the PM wants the SAS to send a message. We work in conjunction with MI5. They provide the intel, we provide the muscle and protect the asset as far as we can without jeopardising the operation. If it works, it will model a new era of interagency and military cooperation for domestic terrorist threats. They line 'em up, we take 'em down. Given the pressure from up high, I wouldn't mind betting the regiment's budget hinges on our success," I replied.

"Makes sense when you think about it. We do well, she gets to reassert her strength and make a statement about how the country will respond to attacks on home soil. What about Special Branch?" Will asked, astutely referring to the branch of the police force integral to investigating domestic terrorism.

"Someone's obviously pissed her off there, because they're out of the picture completely on this one. They'll be kept in the loop, but ultimately this is a military operation," I told him. The room went quiet as the weight of expectation settled on everyone's shoulders. "We just have to make sure not to fuck it up now," I replied.

"How does the girl fit in? Any guidance on when we need to pull her from the set up?" Will asked.

"Her name's been splashed around the papers a fair bit lately, and given that she's about to become pretty high profile at our request, the cabinet would prefer to avoid the bad publicity that would come from her death. But ultimately, if it means our success, she's expendable. They can make her out to be a martyr, so long as they get to say we're winning," I admitted, nonchalantly feigning my indifference.

"This is new ground for us. I mean, we're not secret agents for fuck's sake. How's this supposed to work?" Eli asked with a frown.

The radio at my side cracked.

"She's on her way," the voice said over the line.

"Look lively, lads. You'll get a rundown when she's briefed," I said. The elevator along the hallway pinged, and then I could hear it. The soft, gentle swish of silk fabric brushing against her thighs as she walked. Man, those fucking legs of hers would be the end of me. Long, toned, and downright sinful, they were the sexiest pair I'd ever seen. Handmade to wrap around my waist. Not that it could or would happen, but that didn't stop me and my hand from dreaming about it.

Rounding the corner, she stopped suddenly as my team and the guys from MI5 came into view. She knew they were going to be there, but I imagined at first glance they made quite an imposing sight. These guys were hand-picked and individually trained to be the most elite special forces operatives in the world. They weren't just highly skilled soldiers; they were trained killers. Fortunately for her, they were all in her corner.

"Hi," she squeaked, giving everyone an awkward wave. On the other side of the room, the group of MI5 operatives that had been huddled together and talking quietly in the corner, broke apart at Sarah's arrival. It was almost comical how similar they all looked with their soft hands, neatly trimmed hair, and suits so uniform, I was beginning to think they were standard government issue. Same as before, the dickless wonder that was Simon Masterson emerged from the pack to swallow Sarah's hand between his bony paws, like he was embracing an old friend. For absolutely no reason I could fathom, I had the sudden urge to find out exactly how much pressure it would take to break one of his fingers.

Just one.

Preferably the index finger on his left hand that he was surreptitiously using to stroke the soft skin on the back of hers.

Dropping her hand, he turned to place a palm on the small of her back and guided her towards his group where he was making introductions, effectively excluding my guys from the proceedings. If I had any doubts about whether our two teams could work cohesively together, I had my answer. Sarah turned to look for me over her shoulder, and when her eyes met mine, she released the tension in her body and relaxed. Sensing that she was looking for me to rescue her, and given how the dickless wonder was pissing me off, I was only too happy to oblige.

Sauntering over to them, I stood on the periphery, crossed my arms across my broad chest, and waited. At six foot four, my imposing figure sent a silent message. There was an air of smug entitlement surrounding all of these pen-pushers, who'd likely grown up wanting to be James Bond and were living with the disappointing reality of being tied to an intelligence desk with a mediocre salary. A chance to flex their figurative muscles in front of a beautiful woman against the likes of us was obviously too good for them to pass up. I didn't care to measure dicks with any of them. If they had a problem with us, they could fucking live with it, but neglecting to introduce her to both teams was just bad manners. And bad manners pissed me off.

"Lieutenant Harper," Masterson said, acknowledging me with a nod of his head when he'd finished speaking.

"Shall we get on with the briefing then?" he suggested, holding out a chair for Sarah.

Ignoring him, I turned my body to face her. "Would you like to meet the rest of the team?" I asked.

Masterson's jaw stiffened at the snub, but setting boundaries from the outset was a good thing. He needed to know early on that the muscle wouldn't be a pushover in this relationship.

"Thanks. I'd love to," she replied without hesitation, and

stepping out of their circle, she moved towards me. The lads looked on with great amusement, uncaring of the unspoken politics.

"I don't know what the mission is, but fuck me I'm in," Crash said, holding his hand out towards her. We were out of earshot of Dickless and the others, so my posture remained stoic, but I longed to cover my eyes and groan. The MI5 guys were giving her resumes and my guys were trying to get some action.

Sarah shook his hand politely, but pulled away quickly, leaving Crash genuinely gobsmacked. As he ran a hand through his dishevelled blond hair, I could practically hear his confusion. He'd delivered a cheeky one-liner, flashed his pearly whites, even smiled extra hard for that dimple to pop. All to no avail. Despite having telekinetic abilities over the knickers of most single women in a half-mile radius, she was completely immune to his charm. And damn if that didn't make her infinitely sexier.

"You've met Corporal Crash McCaffrey. This is Sergeant Eli Spears and Staff Sergeant Will Edwards," I said, familiarising her with the rest of the guys. Most gave her a quick nod of acknowledgement, save for Will who walked over to shake her hand.

"I read about your dad and brother," he said quietly. "I'm sorry for your loss."

His quiet empathy spoke volumes about the man. An army brat himself, he flew through the ranks at a speed that belied his age before ending up with us. Despite the hint of salt and pepper in his closely cropped black hair, it wasn't his appearance that gave Staff Sergeant Will "Badger" Edwards his name. It was his innate sense of moral absolutism. Everything in his world was black and white. I'd never known him to argue or lose his temper. He was stoic. The calmest, most steadfast person in the crew. He was also the most dangerous. When he needed to make the hard calls, there was no indecision, no hesitancy, and when it was done, there was no remorse. He did what he did, and he did it well. The perfect killing machine.

In our own ways, we all were.

"It's nice to meet you all," she said to them. "But I'll be honest, I could have used you guys a few days ago," she said, pulling at her collar with a smile. If I expected her to seem afraid or sheepish about what she'd been through or what lay ahead, I'd have been wrong. The woman before me held her head high and looked into the eyes of every one of my men as she joked about having been thrown around like a rag doll by a Russian gangster.

"Don't worry, miss. When the dust settles, we'll make the fucker pay for what he did to you," Crash reassured her, earning himself one of her smiles. I rolled my eyes as Eli coughed "kiss arse" behind his fist, making her smile wider.

"I have no doubt you can take them all down, but can you keep me alive while you're doing it?" she asked him, honestly.

If he was surprised by her question, he didn't show it.

"I wouldn't be here if I couldn't," he replied, cockily.

"Promise?" she said, grinning.

I knew she was afraid. I could sense it. The slight tremble of her hands and the occasional dart of her eyes around the room full of men gave her away, but she kept it together. She'd walked alone into a room full of hard-arses, her balls bigger than Dickless could ever dream of having, and smiled at the men who could end up holding her life in their hands. I gave my obedience to many and my respect to few, but she didn't ask for respect, she fucking demanded it. It was hot as fuck, and I wasn't the only one who thought so. By the way the MI5 arseholes were eyeing her up and down, I figured Masterson wasn't the only one who needed watching.

"Shall we get started?" Masterson said, and after holding out a chair for her, I sat down myself.

"Thank you again, Sarah, for agreeing to assist us. I mentioned yesterday that Lieutenant Harper would be your liaison. This is in fact a joint operation between MI5 and the SAS, both of whom will be conducting surveillance, though we'll be following through the intelligence leads while the SAS will provide close protection and will ultimately take out the terrorist cell when we're able to track it down."

"Is that usual?" Sarah asked. "I mean, the SAS acting as bodyguards?" She turned to me to ask the question rather than Masterson, which earned her major brownie points.

"We've trained most police and special branch close

protection teams since the attack on Princess Anne in the seventies. You'll be safer with us than you would be with royal family close protection," I replied, aware that I was puffing up my feathers, but unable to stop myself, especially when she looked so impressed. I didn't know what it was about this woman that had me so fucking possessive, but she was pushing buttons I didn't even know I had. Me and my guys were the toughest, strongest, deadliest people she would ever meet, and I wanted her to know it. Not because I wanted her to be scared, but because I wanted her to feel like she never had to be.

"I'm not exactly sure how you're going to get close enough to protect me. No disrespect, but you're not exactly inconspicuous," she said.

The mere mention of my size had her running her eyes over my body. When she reached my face, it took all my self-control not to wink at her. Like she knew what I was thinking, a blush flooded her cheeks. But still, she held my stare. Even if I was imagining all the ways I'd like to get up close and personal with her, it was a line I couldn't cross. My entire career depended on my refusal to indulge in the current fantasy I had of pushing up that prim little skirt and fucking her on the boardroom table. It didn't stop me from thinking it though.

"We've been over a number of scenarios, but as you aren't a trained field operative, we feel the best way to avoid getting called out on a lie is to keep as close to the truth as possible. You'll explain to the Russians that you're extremely cautious after a recent experience with a less-than-savoury character, and you'll introduce Tom as your personal security," Masterson interjected before I could answer her. The fact that he referred to me as Tom, without deference to my rank, didn't go unnoticed either.

"You'll give them his real name, though not his rank of course, and Tom will convince them he's ex-military, now working in the more profitable private sector," he continued.

"What if they see my hiring him as ratting them out?"

"Sarah, believe it or not, they don't want to kill you. They just want to scare you into doing as you're told. Just follow our instructions, and this will all be over before you know it," he said, in the least reassuring way possible. Sarah nodded in agreement, but in reality, there was nothing else she could do, even if she wasn't happy with the arrangement. She'd crossed the Rubicon and there was no going back.

Around the table, other operatives spoke up with questions about the technicality of the operation and expected intelligence yield. Next to me, I could see Sarah disappear into her own head, likely running through the list of everything that would likely happen to her if we were caught. Perhaps it was because she kept her fists hidden that nobody else noticed their violent tremble. In a room full of people, she looked completely alone. So, I did the stupidest thing I'd ever done. Making sure that no one was watching, I reached under the table.

CHAPTER FOUR

Sarah

I'd been standing in front of my wardrobe for at least ten minutes, looking over the same pitiful selection of suitable office attire, while contemplating what outfit I'd want to be in when I died. If I had my way, I'd wear one of my favourite brightly coloured dresses, because fuck the Russians. If I was going to die, I wanted to do it in colour. Unfortunately, going to the office dressed like that might actually kill off my aunt. Not that anyone, least of all me, would mourn her passing, but I'd had my fill of funerals lately. It wasn't that I lacked the means to buy more business wear either, more that wearing dreary clothes was about as life sucking and soul destroying as the job. A few days before I'd taking the helm of Tatem Shipping, I'd gone out and purchased five suits in various shades of grey, navy, and black, which included the one I'd worn to the funeral. Honestly, they were the bleakest clothes I'd ever owned, and seeing them hanging in my wardrobe depressed the shit out of me. They reeked of despondency and gloom, and I had no desire to see any more of that bleed into my stuff.

My one small act of mutiny was the lingerie beneath the surface that nobody could see. It was only a little rebellion, but still it made me smile when I thought of it. Especially knowing how Aunt Elizabeth would literally shit a brick if she ever found out that I wore Batman underwear to the funeral. Today, I needed every ounce of valour and colour I could get. Today, courage came in the form of my Wonder Woman knickers. They weren't bulletproof, but they made me feel like I was. She was my icon. The woman who needed a hero, so she became one. Some girls got excited over matching sets from Victoria's Secret. I, on the other hand, would literally lose my shit if I could've found matching bras to my secret stash of superhero pants. Somewhere out there in the world, there had to be a man who valued my little quirks and all my sexy bad arsery.

Fifteen minutes later and I realised that I'd dressed with more care than I had in weeks. Layering the boring black skirt and jacket with a fire-engine red top and gold jewellery, I told myself that I was simply channelling my inner superhero. I absolutely was not dressing for Tom Harper. And I definitely wasn't thinking of him when I sprayed on a little extra perfume. The buzz of the intercom at the entrance gate announced his arrival, precisely at the time he'd given. Pushing the button to open up, I took a minute to put on my coat and gloves as he drove to the house. Opening the front door before he had a chance to knock, I closed it behind me and hurried down the steps to meet the stern soldier glaring up at me.

"What's wrong?" I asked, anxious at the look on his face.

"Get in the car," he replied. His curt tone surprised me. Putting my hands on my hips, I readied for a fight. Whatever he was pissed about, I didn't appreciate being ordered about. He held the car door open for me as he surveyed the grounds, seemingly oblivious to my annoyance. When he finally realised I wasn't doing as I was told, he turned that intense stare on me.

"Don't you be giving me those scary eyes. I don't know who pissed on your Cornflakes this morning, but there's no need to speak to me like that," I said, marvelling at my power of bravery, courtesy of the magic pants. When his jaw clenched and a blood vessel started throbbing at his temple, I figured discretion was the better part of valour, and dropped my hands to climb into the car. Expecting him to slam the door, I was surprised when it gently clicked shut.

"Right, I'm in. So, what's with the bad mood?" I asked, once he'd walked around the car and climbed in next to me. He gave me some kind of weird hand signal that I had no idea how to interpret. As I scrunched up my nose in confusion, he rolled his eyes and put his finger sharply to his lips, making the universal sign for "shut the hell up." Folding my arms across my chest, I fumed indignantly for a couple of miles until he deigned to speak to me. Eli, was driving, but as the privacy screen in the gleaming black Jaguar was up and given that he didn't even acknowledge me, I didn't try and speak to him either.

"Jesus Christ, woman, do you have any sense of self-preservation at all?" Tom protested suddenly, breaking the chilling silence between us.

"Oh, so you're finally speaking to me, you nut job," I replied. "I literally just let you in and walked down to meet you. How could that possibly have pissed you off?"

"Did you listen to anything I said after the briefing yesterday? You never, ever let anyone into the main gate without checking the video feed first and confirming the password so you know they're not acting under duress," he admonished.

"Don't you think that's a little overkill considering that you told me you'd be here dead on seven thirty," I said.

"And what if it wasn't me? What if it was the Russians? You're throwing away the precious seconds you might need to get you to the panic room. You have to think, Sar, you're smarter than this," he argued. It didn't occur to me to mind his abbreviation of my name. It sounded so natural it was like he'd always done it.

"Why would they come for me at Dad's place?" I asked. "You told me I'd be safe. As long as I did what they were asking me to, I'd be safe. So why would anyone come for me?" My earlier bravado disappearing like the morning mist, I couldn't stop the panic from bleeding into my voice.

"Okay, you have to stop freaking out and try and be smart. Their organisation wants you in charge. But what's to say the guy making the decisions today is the same one making decisions tomorrow? Or that someone doesn't go rogue and think you make a better hostage than you do an ally? You don't stay alive by accepting every situation at face value. You do it by being vigilant and staying smart."

"Don't freak out? Easy for you to say. When was the last time your life was ever threatened by somebody dangerous?" I asked.

He didn't reply, just raised one eyebrow and looked at me like I was a moron.

"Fine, stupid question," I huffed, realising it was ridiculous to expect a special forces operative to understand how I was feeling. In all honesty, I thought I was handling all the crap that had been thrown my way pretty well.

"But you could try being nicer though. It's not like there's a manual on how to go from illustrator to British spy. I'm doing the best I can, and if I mess up with security from time to time, it's because I've never had to think about it before. So do you think you could cut me some frickin slack please? I don't like you when you're being a dick."

"Newsflash, baby, lots of people don't like me," he replied.

"Anyone who's ever met you I imagine," I muttered. When Eli scoffed then laughed to cover it, I figured the privacy glass wasn't so private after all.

"You don't need to like me to listen to me. I'm here to do a job, and that job will save lives. If you start doing what I tell you, when I tell you to do it, one of those lives will be yours. For now, you're relatively safe, but when they don't need you anymore, they'll retire you like they did your old man. The only person who'll stop that from happening is me," he said.

"Gone is the nice guy from yesterday I see. Now that you've got me like a worm on a hook, things are different. You know, I'm beginning to think I've been mis-sold on this whole thing."

"Well, suck it up, buttercup. If you're going to get through this, you're going to need to toughen up. And for your information, I was never the nice guy. I'm the weapon that's going to keep you alive."

I got it. He was all business, and that's how things need to be. He had a job to do, and it was easier all round if he saw me as an asset rather than a person. But it still stung that he was being so cold. I wanted the protective warrior back again. Absently rubbing at my fading bruise, I wondered how he could seem so incensed before and so cold now. I knew what he did for a living, but surely nobody could switch off their emotions like that.

"He won't hurt you like that again," he said, out of the blue. He was watching my hands and must have guessed what I was thinking.

"You don't know that. Haven't you just been reminding

me of how easily he can get to me? I don't know why you care anyway. All you want is the Russians and their buyers. You want my compliance and cooperation, same as Vasili," I said.

"Don't lump me into the same category as that fucker. Ever. And he won't hurt you. To do that, he'll have to get through me. I can't allow another lapse in security, so from now on, we'll be joined at the hip. Where you go, I go."

"What do you mean, where you go, I go?" I asked.

"I mean, that for the foreseeable future, I'll be moving in with you. I'll sleep in the room next to yours and accompany you to the office during the day and any company events in the evening. Two teams can monitor the house in rotation while we sleep."

"You can't just move in!" I protested. "We hardly know each other, and you want complete unfettered access to my personal life. Surely, there's another way you can make sure that I'm secure when we're not together?"

While I'd admit that his attitude was bothering me, I still wanted to jump his bones. Whether I liked it or not, his tough façade and raw sexuality were magnetic, and if anything, arguing with him just amped up the tension between us.

"No problem. I'll give you a Swiss army knife and send you a link to a YouTube self-defence video, and I'm sure you'll be just fine," he grumbled sarcastically, and for the first time ever, I felt a burning desire to know what it felt like to punch someone in the face.

"I'm telling you it won't work. The Russians might buy

the security thing, but my aunt won't."

"Do you trust her?" he asked, and I scoffed.

"About as far as I can throw her."

"Then we spin it. We tell the Russians that I'm your security, but as far as your aunt is concerned, I'm a consultant you brought in to help you navigate your way through the business. On top of that, we've just recently started seeing each other," he explained.

This time it was my turn to look at him like he was a moron. "And you really think she'll buy that?"

"Look, you hardly know each other, and I doubt you'll interact with each other more than is necessary at the office or socially. If you want to make her believe you, you will."

I watched the London streets glide passed the window as I thought about what he said. Undoubtedly, I'd feel safer having him with me. But the idea of living together twenty-four seven, of having him see me without makeup first thing in the morning, or lounging around watching Netflix in my unicorn pyjamas, was less than appealing. That was my vanity talking though. In reality, I might manage to start sleeping at night again with him there. Instead of waking from nightmares in the early hours of the morning, where I could imagine the faces of all those people who had been abused or killed by my family's greed. The fact that I was concerned for my own safety over their justice was shameful. When I thought about it that way, I had no right to act like a brat.

"If you think it will help, then I'll make up the bed in the spare room. It might be easier anyway. If the Russians bring in their own man to work with the company, it's not going to be safe trying to feed information back to MI5. This way, it will be easier giving them what they need out of hours," I said softly.

If he was surprised by my change of mind, he didn't show it. Instead, he simply studied me through narrowed eyes, like he was trying to figure something out.

"I'll have Will pack up my equipment and some clothes and have it waiting in the car when Eli collects us."

"What do we do about their tech? You said I should assume the house was bugged and that they're listening all the time," I pointed out.

"We've already been over the house, and yes, it's bugged. But we leave them where they are. Better to feed them false information than to give them a reason to suspect you. You don't need to give any Oscar-worthy performances. Just act like I'm your security and that you don't know me that well. It's not that far from the truth. You have to assume they're listening outside of the house as well. The car is a safe place to talk, but only when we're moving and a few miles away," he instructed.

I was tensed and already exhausted at the thought of having to live under a microscope, and as time ticked by, I realised that the car journey wasn't helping. Stuck in the circle of hell that was central London congestion, I began to fidget, and I had no idea what to do with my hands. At first, I placed them on either side of me. But then I realised how close Tom's hand was as it rested beside mine. When I started fantasising about how his calloused fingertips would feel, I moved them again. Finally, Tom'd had enough. As he'd done yesterday when he reached beneath the table, he passed me a sweet. Slowly, I peeled open the wrapper and popped the buttery toffee into my mouth. It wasn't the most nutritious breakfast I'd ever had, but it made me smile.

"Why toffee?"

He was staring intently at the slow-moving vista and didn't spare me a glance. "What are you thinking about right now?"

"Honestly? I'm trying not to slurp with a mouth full of toffee and saliva, and I'm fighting the urge to pick it out of my gums before I've even finished eating it," I said, and I swore I saw the smallest hint of a smile.

"Exactly," he replied. "Which is the exact opposite of what was probably racing through that pretty head of yours a minute ago."

I marvelled at how right he was. As I let the deliciously sweet treat roll around my mouth, I realised something else. All the groundwork he put in this morning to put things back on a professional footing, unravelled the minute he handed me the confectionery.

"How come a hard-arsed, tough-as-nails SAS soldier has a pocket full of toffees anyway?" I asked, still holding onto a grin.

"Trade secret," he replied gruffly, and went back to ignoring me.

Fifteen minutes later and we were pulling up in front of the office. This time Eli stepped out of the car and opened my door for me.

"He has a sweet tooth," he whispered to me conspiratorially as Tom let himself out. "If he gets pissy with you again, find him some chocolate. He's like a premenstrual teenager when he doesn't get his fix."

"You know he'd probably demote you for telling me that," I whispered back.

"Nah, kick my arse at best," Eli replied. He flashed me a cheeky grin, and with a quick wink, he was back in the car and on his way.

"You know, there's underground parking spaces for executives here if he doesn't want to drive around." I said.

"He's fine," Tom replied dismissively. Of course, he probably already knew every inch of this place. "Ready?"

"Not in the slightest," I replied.

"Good, then let's go."

We walked through the heavy entrance door to reception, my gut churning with every step.

"Good morning, Alfred," I said to the concierge. "This is Mr Harper. He's new here and will be working alongside me from now on. If I send down his details later, can I trouble you to have an ID pass made up for him please?"

"No problem at all, Miss Tatem. I'll have it waiting for you tomorrow morning," he replied warmly. "Hope your first day goes well," he said, addressing Tom.

"Thanks," Tom replied, and placing his hand on the small of my back, manoeuvred me towards the elevators. He left it there as we waited for the lift to descend. Although it was impossible to feel the warmth of his touch through my thick winter coat, it was reassuring nonetheless. At least until the doors opened.

"What the hell is this?" Aunt Elizabeth asked, thrusting the print out of an emailed memo into my hand. "My office now!" she demanded.

Repressing the urge to give her my middle finger while simultaneously telling her to "fuck off," I sighed and walked into what felt like the elevator of impending doom. My only comfort was the giant of a man behind me who promised to have my back.

CHAPTER FIVE

Sarah

"When I said 'my office now,' I meant her, not you," Aunt Elizabeth said, addressing Tom sternly. He crossed his huge arms over his chest, making him even more intimidating, and actually smirked at her.

"I'd like him to stay, thank you. I think this concerns him as much as us," I replied.

"Why? Does he perhaps own shares in the company I don't know about?" she asked sarcastically.

"I'll be honest. I don't really understand your concern. You wanted me take the helm of Tatem Shipping to keep share prices afloat, and that's exactly what I'm doing," I pointed out.

"What I wanted was for you to show up, smile nicely for pictures, and use your voting options in the best interests of the company."

"And who exactly am I supposed to listen to you when it

comes to the best interests of the company? Because from where I'm sitting, the majority of the board can't seem to agree on anything."

"You certainly don't listen to some little upstart who doesn't know the first thing about this business. I've certainly never heard his name in shipping circles," she said. Her catty tone was scathing, but it didn't seem to bother Tom in the slightest.

"Thank you for your concern, but as you pointed out, Tom doesn't have shares or voting rights and, therefore, no vested interest in the company. The reason that you've never heard of him is that he isn't involved in transport or logistics. He's a shipping lawyer who was recommended to me by a friend of mine. Tom's been working in Oslo for the last five years. He's starting a new contract here in London in three months, and as he has a little time on his hands, he was kind enough to allow me to contract him on a freelance basis, not to make decisions for me, but to interpret what I'm being told into layman's terms."

"Why would you not just ask for my advice? I've been the guiding hand behind this firm for over thirty years. Besides which, we're family," she argued, becoming more and more venomous at my refusal to back down easily.

"With the greatest of respect, it's not advice I need, it's clarity. You want me to act in the best interests of the business. Don't you think I should understand what I'm hearing and reading before I make decisions?" I asked, becoming increasingly exasperated. Sneaking a quick peek at Tom, who'd been completely silent, I expected him to share my look of irritation. If anything, he simply seemed amused.

"I want you to do as you're told and stop worrying about things that don't concern you. You don't get to waltz into an empire I've spent my life building and poke and prod around things you know nothing about. Is it too much to ask that, for once in your life, you show some gratitude for a life of privilege that my hard work has given you and do as you're asked?" She was practically screaming at me. I was so shocked from the tidal wave of malice, that I took a step back. It would be wrong to say that I was hurt. I'd have to have some semblance of feeling towards her for that. Stunned would be more appropriate. Stunned that Tom's presence was enough for her to drop any veil of civility between us, especially with Tom himself as witness.

I was still speechless when she seemed to collect herself as she patted down her flawless silver bobbed hair.

"Regardless of my personal feelings on the subject, the company doesn't sanction hirings that don't have board approval. So, I think it's in everyone's best interest if you thank Mr Harper for his time and show him out." She had the audacity to smile as she said it, as though that creepy expression could completely erase the last thirty seconds. After an awkward pause, my reply was barely more than a whisper.

"Tom isn't an employee of Tatem Shipping. He's

contracted to me. I will take care of his fee personally, so the board's approval is no longer an issue. And if you expected me to be a society puppet for the next two years, I'm afraid you don't know me at all. What you always called wilful and disobedient, I call independent and strong-minded. I'm grateful for everything you do, and I hope we can find some middle ground together, but I won't be railroaded. Ever. I didn't bend for my father, and I won't bend for you," I replied coolly and calmly. Her expression told me I may have won the battle, but I hadn't won the war.

"Very well. If that's your final word on the subject, let's see if we can find this middle ground that you speak of. After two years, when market shares are stable, if we find that we cannot work cohesively together, I'll make you an offer for your shares. Does that seem reasonable?" she asked. It did, surprisingly, as nothing that ever came from her mouth had sounded reasonable before.

"Sounds good to me."

Tom held open the door to Aunt Elizabeth's office and waited for me to walk through it before shutting it gently behind him. He followed me to my office, and only when I collapsed at my desk with my head buried in my arms did he speak.

"A lawyer?"

"I had a brain fart," I replied. "It was literally the only explanation I could think of. We should have worked out more details for our backstory before we came in."

"You did great. You were quick thinking and calm. Totally believable if it weren't for the fact that I look nothing like a lawyer."

"And what exactly are lawyers supposed to look like?" I asked with amusement.

"I don't know, but not like me. Maybe I should get some glasses," he suggested.

I lifted my head and took a moment to appreciate his fine form in a suit, and damn it was fine. The suit wasn't bespoke, but that didn't make a blind bit of difference. The charcoal jacket and crisp white shirt stretched snuggly over broad shoulders that tapered down into a flat, washboard stomach. His military-looking watch, the one that looked like it could do everything from tell the time to remote land a jet plane, had been replaced with a neat steel strapped timepiece. I didn't get much further than that when I glanced up at his face and realised I was totally busted. He'd clocked me blatantly checking him out, and feeling my cheeks flood with colour, I buried my head once again to cover my embarrassment. My morning was clearly going from bad to worse. All I needed was another encounter with Vasili, and the day from hell would be complete.

"Why didn't you say anything in there?" I asked, as the use of my brain cells came back to me one by one.

"Have you even met a soldier before? I'm pretty sure, as soon as I open my mouth, she's going to realise I'm not a lawyer."

"You act like you've spent your entire career in the trenches. You're an officer, surely you've spent time at mess dinners and all that stuff, talking shit with your superiors."

"I don't bullshit with anyone, Buttercup. The SAS isn't like any other regiment. I have a degree, which is why I joined the army as an officer, but I was promoted because of how I perform in combat. If you want me to bullshit your aunt into thinking I'm something I'm not, you're out of luck. You want her silenced and incapacitated with a single throat punch, I'm your man," he told me, matter-of-factly.

The thought of him being my man in any capacity made parts of me come to life that I didn't even know worked anymore. Even testy, sarcastic, and outright grumpy, my attraction to him was almost indescribable.

Electric.

Explosive.

Addictive.

My reaction to his presence was abnormal. Fear should override everything else, but it didn't. If anything, it heightened the magnetism. His strength made me feel protected. In his presence, I could almost believe I was safe. It was a delusion of course. Ultimately, I was aware that I was expendable. If it came down to a choice, his mission, his country would always be first. The knowledge did nothing to lessen the chemistry between us. It only served to make him more honourable.

"This is never going to work you know," I told him softly.

"Of course it is. Your aunt will believe what you tell her to believe, and who cares if she doesn't? The Russians will think it's a cover story to explain away your security. Stop borrowing worry. You did great with her today. Confrontations with the old bitch probably happen all the time. No point stressing over the next one," he replied, making everything sound so easy.

"I don't get how she found out about it so fast. She was waving an email bearing my name that didn't come from me."

"Best guess would be MI5. You can't back out if you're already committed."

"Shit! You think they deliberately threw me under the bus with her without giving me a chance to introduce you myself, without consulting me first?" I asked, feeling pretty pissed off, not only that they were making decisions like that without my permission, but also that they apparently had unfettered access to my email.

"Like I said, best guess. But it's done now, so let's get on with it. I want to go over every shipping manifest for the past three months and for the next three months, but I want to do it discretely. We're looking for any entries regarding shipments that may have come from Russia or countries close to it. Once we have those we need to look at the cargo manifests and compare them with dock records for anomalies. The Russians gave you one Company name, but they could be running this operation through any number of shell corporations. If we can locate any of the dirty shipments and track them, we'll find what we're looking for," he said, bringing everything back to business.

"I have access to all of that, but we're talking hundreds of entries. The direct shipments are easy, but few of them are ever direct. They stop at as many ports as possible to pick up and drop off cargo. You're looking for things like containers weighing more as they arrive in dock than they're listed as weighing on the manifest. It's going to take us weeks," I explained.

"Well, let's get started before the Russians install their own man and things get a lot more complicated," he replied.

"I'm assuming it's okay for us to talk freely in this office?" I said.

"Bit fucking late now, wouldn't you say?" he replied. I could only imagine the look of horror on my face, because he actually smirked.

"Like I would have let you keep yapping if there was a chance this room was bugged." Amusement coloured his tone.

"Crash thoroughly swept the place first thing this morning, posing as one of the cleaning staff. It was clean, and it'll be checked daily. MI5 installed a micro camera into your desk lamp. As and when you're asked to sign anything, place the papers directly under the lamp and try and go through each page slowly so the tech guys have got a couple of seconds of frame on each page. That should be enough for them to work through the stuff later. They've also installed a blocker in here to stop signals being transmitted from the room, so your phone will pretty much be useless while you're here," he explained.

"Great, so not even YouTube and Facebook can save me. If the Russians don't kill me, boredom might," I deadpanned.

"You know what I'm going to say, don't you?"

"If it goes along the lines of 'suck it up, buttercup,' I swear to God I'll be the one doing the throat punching," I replied, and he actually laughed.

"It's a miracle! You do smile after all!" I exclaimed, make him instantly scowl.

"When they train you guys, do they teach you that bad-arse glare and how to repress a smile? I have visions of you being tickled by your instructors while you try and hold a straight face," I teased.

"Of course," he replied. "And after a hard day of blowing shit up and shooting people in the head, we toddle on back to the barracks for tea and biscuits."

"I totally thought so." I nodded. "You should try a cucumber face mask with the tea. It's very refreshing."

"You are different from how I thought you'd be, you know? I literally have no idea what's going to come out of your mouth from one minute to the next."

By different, I, of course, interpreted that to mean he thought I was wonderfully novel, creative, and bohemian. I was nothing if not delusional.

"Don't worry. My dad and brother reminded me often of

how strange I am. But what you call different, I call unique. I don't mind being different. It sure as shit beats being the same as everyone else. Five generations of Tatems have been grey elephants. I guess I'm the Elmer."

"The what?" he asked.

"Elmer! You know, like the children's book. He's a multi-coloured patchwork elephant, but all his family are grey. He paints his body like everyone else to blend in, but he hates being the same and learns to love his colours. I'm Elmer." I beamed as I explained it to him, totally amazed with myself for having come up with such a brilliant analogy.

He bent his head forward and pinched the bridge of his nose like he had a headache coming on.

"This is going to be a long couple of months," he muttered under his breath, but I was already wondering where I could shop for a stuffed elephant.

———

By the end of the fourth day of doing much of the same thing, I arrived home exhausted. Accessing individual shipping manifests and cross referencing them against dock records involved a lot more than I thought. I understood the need for security. Dad had explained before that piracy being what it was, there were always people out there willing to buy information on shipping lanes, cargo manifests, and trade routes. Closely guarding this information, in addition to the number of other measures, made some small contribution to minimising the threat. But still, it took me half an hour of arguing with the tech guy, who insisted that I needed approval of a second board member to access those records. When Tom simply cracked his knuckles in front of him like he was gearing up for a fight, the tech manager, Terry, caved. After that, we'd started at the most recent records and worked backwards. The fact that we were completely unfamiliar with the documents slowed us down considerably, and having to save everything to a flash drive for the MI5 guys to take a look, didn't help. When my stomach started to sound like a creature from *Aliens*, Tom had called time and phoned for Eli.

My mood hadn't improved at being delivered back to Dad's place either. Tom insisted we stay there because of the high level of security Dad had installed together with a panic room. He also didn't want the Russians to clue into the fact that we knew about the bugs. He assured me they were only audio, but knowing that everything I did, every move I made, was being listened to, literally made my skin crawl. Every day I'd come home, throw together a meal for us both and go straight to bed after, but that couldn't continue. Sensing my fatigue, Tom requested that Eli go back out to grab us some food after dropping us off, and I agreed happily.

After the quickest shower in history, I found myself sitting on Dad's designer black sofa, in my favourite brushed cotton, unicorn pyjamas. I was squirming all over the place when Tom walked in carrying, what I assumed from the smell was, Chinese food. My jaw literally dropped open at the sight of him in loose sweat pants. A black T-shirt stretched across his torso. I was salivating over him and the takeout. Both were equally edible.

"What the fuck are you doing?" he asked, tilting his head to one side. "And what the fuck are you wearing?" he added as an afterthought.

"What? You don't like unicorns?" I asked, aware of the hurt in my tone.

"Is that what they are? They look like rhinos. And why are you breakdancing?"

"I'm trying to get comfortable. Aunt Elizabeth brought some stupid designer in to do up this place for Dad. Apparently, the sofa is for decorative purposes only," I said, reaching for my phone.

"What are you doing now?"

"Ordering a beanbag. I'm not wasting money on a sofa when I have a perfectly comfortable one at home," I said, wondering if I could find an Elmer themed beanbag just to fuck up the living room décor.

"Will you order one for me?" Tom asked, squirming on the instrument of torture as he sat down next to me. Eventually, we compromised by pulling off some of the cushions and eating at the coffee table. Finally, with a full belly and some stupid comedy playing on the TV, I began to relax. I must have drifted off for a little while, because I woke to find my head lying on Tom's shoulder. His body was as stiff as a board. Instantly, I jumped away from him, and we looked at one another. The space between us was tense and thick with the intensity of some force I couldn't even begin to describe.

Electric.

Magnetic.

Addictive.

It compelled us both. Millimetre by millimetre, we edged slowly closer, as we both fought against the unthinkable. When I was close enough to smell the subtle scent of his shaving soap, I closed my eyes, just in time to hear his phone buzz.

CHAPTER

SIX

Tom

The alert notified me someone was at the gate and moments later the buzzer sounded. Activating the camera feed to my phone, I clocked a guy wearing the uniform of a well-known parcel delivery firm. Dialling Will's number, I waited for it to connect but didn't speak. I didn't have to. They knew the place was bugged.

"Plates are clean and registered to the company. Thermal imaging doesn't show anyone else in the van. No sign of weapons, 'course we'd need a pat-down for sure. No bulky coat or easy place to hide one though. You wearing Kevlar?" he asked. I scoffed then coughed straight after to cover.

"I'll take that as a no," he replied. "Your call, boss." I disconnected the call, then pressed the intercom to talk to the driver.

"Yes?" I barked

"Parcel for Miss Tatem," he replied in a friendly manner.

"Give me a couple of minutes to put some shoes on. I'll meet you at the gate."

"No problem."

I checked the video feed to see if he went back into the van, giving him an opportunity to reach for a gun. When he simply pulled out his phone and relaxed against the pillar, I went to my bag in the hall and pulled on some training shoes.

"You expecting any deliveries?" I asked Sarah, as she followed behind me.

"No. Nothing," she replied, her arms folded tightly across her chest in a movement that told me how nervous she was. I handed her my phone that was still streaming the camera feeds.

"Anything happens, anything at all, you take this into the panic room and you don't open it up until my boys get here, okay?" I instructed.

Her hand trembled, but she took it regardless. "If there is trouble, just remember to combat roll into the daffodils. We're not due rain for a couple of days, and I don't want to have to wash blood off the driveway. I hear it stains if you don't get it out quick," she said.

And it happened. I gave her the smile she'd been trying so hard to pry out of me. At every turn, when I expected fear, I found steel. She surprised me, and I was a man not easily surprised.

"You have a lot of metal for someone so small," I told

her. It was probably the only compliment I'd ever given a woman.

"You need to stop judging people's strength by their size. When the storm comes, sometimes the fragile flower will still be standing, long after the sturdy tree has fallen."

"You read that on a cushion somewhere," I accused.

"Illustrated it in a children's book actually. I'll get you a copy."

As always, I couldn't tell whether she was yanking my chain or she meant it.

"I'm not big on reading."

"Don't worry, it has lots of colourful pictures, and you'll never learn the big words if you don't practise," she said, being a smartarse.

"You do remember I have a degree, don't you?" I reminded her.

"Well I don't, and it isn't nice to show off, so go and get my parcel for me before the man who may or may not shoot you gets cold," she ordered, and I smiled again. We had our own bugs in here too, so no doubt MI5 and my guys were pissing themselves over this. Reaching once more into my bag, I pulled out my 9mm Browning HP, tucked it into the back of my sweat pants, and made for the door.

"Panic room," I reminded her, and went to leave as she grabbed my bicep.

"Be careful," she whispered, showing me her concern behind the bravado.

"Piece of cake," I replied and left, shutting the door tight behind me. For a second, I allowed myself the thought that Nan had been the only person to ever utter those words to me. After that, I was all business. As I strode down the driveway, my mind worked overtime, noting detail after detail that might prove useful later. Seeing me coming, the driver straightened and reached for his parcel. It was long and thin and would fit easily through the bars.

"Do I need to sign anything?" I asked, gesturing towards the box.

"Who are you?" he asked, his tone a little cautious.

"Security," I replied, watching his movements closely.

"Sorry, my instructions are only to deliver this directly to Miss Tatem. She needs to sign for it," he said.

"Miss Tatem's in bed. Either you give it to me or you take it back with you."

"Shit," he said on a sigh. "Look I don't want to have to come back tomorrow, but I'll get in serious trouble without this signature."

"I'll sign her name, and nobody will be any the wiser," I replied.

Reluctantly, he handed me the pen and clipboard. I scrawled something that probably bore no resemblance to her autograph, and we swapped items through the bars. He'd been gone for a few minutes when a black Range Rover pulled up sharply in front of the gates. Crash left the engine running while he hopped out, gave me a quick nod, then jumped back in the car with the package and drove off. With one last look around, I jogged back up to the house.

"Oh good. You're alive. How's the driveway looking?" Sarah asked me as I entered.

"Still spotless."

She gave me a confused look as she noticed my empty hands, but I put my finger to my lips, warning her to be quiet.

"Want to find out who your parcel's from?" I asked, waving my arms and shaking my head in an emphatic no. The frown disappeared when she realised what I wanted her to do.

"Ah, no, that's fine. Leave it on the hallway table and I'll open it later. Shall we finish the end of the movie?"

"Sounds good," I replied casually. "Coffee first?"

"Tea please. I don't like coffee."

"Who doesn't like coffee?"

"Err... me."

"Weirdo," I called out as she went back to the living room, making her giggle. Usually women giggling pissed me off. It was a noise reserved for kids, not grown fucking women. Especially not women trying to work their way into my bed. When Sarah did it though, all bets were off. It was a sound that bypassed my brain and went straight to my cock. I'd only known her a couple of weeks, and already I knew I was in serious trouble. My reluctance to form any kind of meaningful relationship wasn't just based on the job, though that was definitely a part of it. Truth was, I honestly didn't think I was capable of it. My entire life I'd had the capacity to simply switch off certain aspects of my psyche. Empathy. Fear. Regret. I could storm a room, take out every one of my targets as I looked them in the eyes, and still sleep like a baby at night. To some, that would make me a monster. To the British Army, it made me the perfect soldier.

On the rare occasion a casual hookup had turned into a regular repeat, the woman always seemed to want to spoon or cuddle or some shit I didn't do. Despite assurances that they were fine with nothing more than sex, what they really wanted was emotion. Attachment. A human connection. I got it. I totally did. I just wasn't capable of it. Things usually ended in tears, because I wasn't good at the "letting them down easy" shit either. The difference with Sarah? For the first time in as long as I could ever remember, I had no control over how I felt for her. This thing between us was like a vine. I didn't remember planting a seed, but the more time we spent together, the more it grew. Now I had to chop it down before we were so totally bound together that I couldn't let her go. Because one day I would have to.

In an effort to convince myself that she was no different to every other girl I'd ever met, I tried to pinpoint what it was about her I was so attracted to. For a start, she was fucking beautiful. And I wasn't talking the fake tan, Botox-induced, silicone-filled kind. Her long mahogany hair curled at the ends, just like her thick, silky eyelashes that framed the prettiest big, blue eyes. Her skin was pale like porcelain, and her body was curvy in every place mine was hard. So much so

I knew our fit together, if we ever had sex, would be perfect. Just picturing her tonight in those fuck ugly pyjamas made me hard as a stone. Her beauty was natural—ethereal almost, because it came, not just from her looks, but from the fire inside her. The humour, the spunk, the strength that constantly challenged me. My plan was an epic fail. She wasn't like anyone I'd ever met, but that didn't matter. And when Will texted me to confirm that the parcel was on the doorstep, I was reminded why.

Putting her tea down on the table in front of her, I handed her the delivery I'd retrieved.

"As your security, I'd prefer you to open this in front of me," I told her, for the benefit of everyone listening in. She nodded, then peeled the red silk ribbon from the long, golden box. Inside was a single stemmed red rose and a neatly printed card.

"What does it say?" I asked.

She swallowed hard before replying. "It says, 'Be ready for me tomorrow, Sarah. I've missed you, and I'm very much looking forward to meeting your new boyfriend. Love Always, your favourite Russian'"

She let go of the card and leaned back against the sofa, absently rubbing her almost completely faded bruise without even realising it. After staring into space for a moment, she turned to me and whispered, "You won't leave me alone tomorrow, will you?"

"Not even for a second," I promised. Instinct had

warned that the parcel was bad news and to bin the fucking thing before she ever saw it, but that wasn't how this was supposed to work. She needed to look afraid. She needed to feel afraid for the Russians to really believe that she was in it all the way with this deal. I couldn't shield her from all the shit that she had no business seeing, but I wouldn't leave her.

In fact, it would take a great deal of composure to stop myself from gutting that fucker as soon as he walked in the door tomorrow. Guys like that never stopped at assaulting a woman once. He was a weak man who needed to hurt someone to feel stronger. I didn't want to knock him around like he'd done to Sarah. I wanted to cut out his liver with my hunting knife. Only the knowledge that I might get a sanctioned chance to put a bullet between his eyes held me back.

"Listen to me. I know you're starting to freak out now. I can see it in your eyes. But you need to keep dealing with shit the same way you have been doing and keep it together," I said.

"I don't know how to do that. When something bad happens, I'm going to freak out. Who can control stuff like that?" she asked, panic bleeding into her voice

"The girl who was talking about stuffed elephants in the same office where she'd gotten a beat down. Same girl who giggles at being called a weirdo while living in a house she hates that belonged to her dead father. You compartmentalise fear. Put shit in boxes. Whitty banter, dark humour, use whatever you've got and get the job done."

"I can do that," she whispered, resolutely. Then, without saying another word, she threw her unicorn-clad arms around my body and hugged me. Shocked again, I didn't have a chance to hold her back before she was gone and heading upstairs. Stuck in the same spot, I watched her go, absolutely certain those unicorns were actually rhinos.

———

The next day, I expected things to be tense and edgy, but Sarah came downstairs all business. Quiet but calm, she remained the same all the way to the office. As we rode the lift, I could feel the tension coming off her in waves, but she didn't break at the thought of seeing Vasili again. She didn't even falter. When the lift doors opened, she put one sexy, black stiletto in front of the other and sashayed her arse all the way to the end of the corridor. Only when we reached her office did she pause for a moment at the doorway, before going all the way in. As I followed behind her and shut the door, I saw the reason for her hesitation. Leant against Sarah's desk with her arms crossed aggressively was the evil aunt herself.

"It's like you're the harbinger of doom," Sarah wearily said to her aunt, as she took off her coat and scarf and folded them over the back of a chair next to the one I'd taken. Walking over to the kettle, she boiled water for my coffee and her tea, which had become part of the working day routine.

"Charming, Sarah. What a lovely way to greet your

closest relative, and what on earth are you doing with a kettle in here? This is completely undignified," her aunt replied, reaching over the desk to press the intercom button. "Victoria, could you come in here please," Elizabeth snapped.

Seconds later, Victoria appeared, having most likely broken some kind of record to arrive that fast. The fear of Elizabeth's wrath must have been a great motivator.

"Have you seen this?" Elizabeth said, waving disdainfully towards Sarah's tea station.

"Cup of tea, Victoria?" Sarah asked casually, for once not letting the old crone get to her.

"Err, no thank you, Miss Tatem," Victoria replied. "And yes, Ms Tatem, I've noticed Miss Tatum's hot beverage making facilities. I have assured her many times that I'm quite prepared to make her a hot drink, however frequently she wishes, but Miss Tatum prefers to see to herself."

"I'm thirty years old and perfectly capable of sorting myself out with a cuppa. Besides, with the amount of tea I drink, you'd never get any work done, Victoria. Now, you're welcome to stay for this car crash, but feel free to go back to doing whatever you were doing before we so rudely interrupted you," Sarah reassured her as she handed me a coffee in the black mug she'd bought me that read, "Always be you, unless you can be a unicorn. Then, always be a unicorn." Without asking, she handed the bitter old trout tea in a plain white mug, and I couldn't help feeling a little disappointed by it.

"Honestly, it's like you were raised by wolves. Tea should only ever be loose leaf and served in a bone china mug with a saucer," Elizabeth reprimanded, while Victoria slipped away quietly.

"Well, this is made from tea bags in the only spare mug I have, so do me a favour and drink it. Middle ground, remember?" Sarah replied. I smirked that some of her gumption, which seemed missing this morning, was back.

"Very well," Elizabeth said. "Now I want to talk with you about Saturday night."

"What's happening Saturday?" Sarah asked, sipping tea that was way too hot from a mug that read, "I can be bright or early. Pick one."

"Really, Sarah? What's the point of you having a secretary if you don't have her check your diary? The Tallingers are hosting their annual charity fundraiser and the board is invited. Your friend, however, is not," she said, then drank her tea while regarding me contemptuously over the top of her mug.

"I'm heartbroken," I muttered. They were the first words I'd wasted on the bitch, knowing I had to keep my mouth shut to continue the façade. But if I ever had the chance to treat her the way she treated Sarah, I was taking it.

"If Tom doesn't go, then I don't go. It's that simple," Sarah said, and I wondered if she'd put lemon in Elizabeth's tea to make her look that bitter.

"You are so wilfully obstinate," Elizabeth scoffed. "This

will be one of London's most prestigious parties, and photographed for society pages. If you're pictured together, how exactly am I supposed to introduce him?"

"As her boyfriend," I replied, watching her cheeks flare with temper from corpse white to flaming red as the news sank in.

"Well, that didn't take you long, you grubby little parasite. Only took a sniff of money to get you interested. Enjoy it while you can, because you won't see a penny of this family's fortune," she said. Her tone was nothing short of venomous and she stood when something in the bottom of the mug caught her eye. "I do not find a single thing about this meeting amusing, Sarah, including this vulgar mug. Tatum Shipping has a reputation to uphold, and I will not have you tarnish that reputation. So, if you insist on bringing the freeloader as your plus one to the Tallingers', then at least tidy him up a bit," she said, planting the empty mug firmly on the desk, and stormed out.

I rubbed at my five o'clock shadow that had been so offensive, not in the least bit perturbed by the battle-ax's temper. The truth was that most of us let a short beard grow in when we were on a mission. It made us harder to recognise and more approachable.

"What was written in the bottom of the mug?" I asked.

"It said 'You've been poisoned,' "she replied with a small smile.

"Boom!" I offered Sarah my knuckles to bump hers

against, before she dropped the metaphorical mike.

"Ready at the gate," Crash's voice said in my ear. The blocker stopped the signal to my phone, but I wore a discrete earpiece and cuff microphone, curtesy of the tech boys at MI5. It was smaller and more advanced than anything I'd used before. It wasn't hard to guess who had the bigger budget.

"Shall we get started?" I asked, wanting her back behind her desk.

Nodding her agreement, she sat down in her chair. If she wondered why I was standing sentry and flanking her from behind, she didn't have time to ask before the devil himself walked in through the door.

CHAPTER SEVEN

Sarah

I trembled when I saw him. Like a knee-jerk reaction, I couldn't help myself. The gleam in his eye as he ran his gaze over my body told me just how much he enjoyed seeing me lay in pain at his feet. It was a promise that he'd have me there again before long. Taking a shaky, if not fortifying breath, I reminded myself of the giant at my back, watching over me. Like he knew how much I needed him in that moment, he rested his hand on my shoulder.

"In a world of ordinary mortals, I am Wonder Woman," I whispered to the room, so quietly it was barely audible even to me.

"Mr Agheenco. I would say that it's a pleasure to see you again, but I think we both know I'd be lying. I will say though that I didn't expect you to wait so long before you returned for my decision," I said, proud that my voice sounded strong and powerful. As far as I was concerned, having him see me at my lowest point didn't mean I was weak. It only meant that he could see how far I could rise. I was fucking Wonder Woman. He might knock me down, but as long as I could stand back up, I could fight. And even if he killed me, I had an army behind me, listening and waiting to bring hellfire down on his arse.

Behind me, Tom squeezed my shoulder before letting me go, and I could almost imagine that he was proud of me. Vasili smiled, in that ever so slightly creepy way of his as he sat down opposite me, his eyes moving slowly from Tom to me.

"No 'Vasili,' Sarah? I thought we'd moved past formalities?"

"Though perhaps not to first-name terms," I replied. "Oddly enough, having my oxygen supply sharply removed tends to make me prickly that way."

"You know, that fiery spirit of yours amuses me. When the time is right, I will enjoy breaking it very much. I would imagine that it is your hired muscle that is making you brave. Tell me, Mr Harper, when was it that you were dishonourably discharged from the British Army? Or more specifically, I should say, the twenty second Special Air Service. I'm interested to know if Miss Tatem realises that she's invested in damaged goods." Vasili looked smug, as though I'd somehow be terrified at the realisation that he'd unearthed information MI5 had every intention of him knowing. God, I hoped Tom put a bullet in this piece of shit when we were done. Preferably, up his arse, I decided when I thought about all the people this guy had likely trafficked and abused in his lifetime.

"I can't recall the exact date of my discharge, though I would imagine you already know. It's irrelevant however. Miss Tatem has an exact picture of my career and credentials," Tom said. Nothing more. Nothing less. Although highly trained in close protection, the SAS weren't well versed in subterfuge, so we'd both been given a kind of crash course by government agents. The first thing we'd been told was not to hang ourselves in a lie. Stick as close to the truth as possible to make things easier to remember and not to give any more details than necessary. Most people give themselves away by talking too fast or over embellishing. Tom wasn't exactly verbose, so I couldn't image it being that difficult for him. I, on the other hand, was much more likely to speed talk at a mile a minute in stressful situations.

"I know a great many things, and I have been watching you, my little mouse. Watching and waiting to see what you would do. It displeases me greatly that you have engaged Mr Harper's services," Vasili said, shaking his head in disappointment.

"It displeases me greatly to be manhandled, but there are some disappointments in life we have to live with, and some we learn from. As you see, Mr Agheenco, I am learning. If you're concerned that his presence affects my decision, I can assure you that his purpose is merely to act as my personal bodyguard, not to influence my decisions and certainly not to involve himself in my business," I challenged.

"You keep using that word 'decision' like you actually have a choice. There is no choice. There is only my will. One of your employees by the name of Mark Devaney, a rather ordinary and overlooked individual in your chartering department, is also one of my employees. From Monday, Mr Devaney will be making significant alterations to a number of cargo manifests over the next two weeks. For every weekday of those two weeks, you will ensure that you are here and you will sign anything that he puts in front of you. After that, you are free to spend your time flittering about as you wish like the irrelevant social butterfly you are, until I need you again. That is what will happen," he informed me.

"You forgot to mention the part where we all get rich," I added, making him smile.

"Perhaps you are more like your father than I gave you credit for."

"Perhaps." My fake smile was becoming more strained with every minute of his presence. "I will do as you ask and will sign every manifest amendment that he puts in front of me, and I will play my part socially so as to maintain the stability of the stock prices, but do not send flowers to my father's house again. This arrangement works because it's mutually beneficially to us both. When I no longer feel safe, there is little benefit to me."

"Whether you feel safe or not, is not really any of my

concern. The reality of the situation is that you are not safe and never will be. I own you. You are my puppet, and you will do what I tell you to do, when I tell you to do it. If your new friend helps you maintain the illusion that I can't get to you whenever and wherever I want, then you may keep him. But if I feel like you're out of line, that you are testing my patience, I will demonstrate on him exactly what happens if you disobey me."

"Very well," I agreed, trying hard to swallow back the bile as I contemplated the extend of the horrors he would rain down on Tom if he realised what we were doing. The fact that I was suddenly being amicable was about the only thing keeping this highly volatile arrangement on an even keel, but even I could see that Vasili was itching to tip the balance of power further and further in his direction. I suspected the only thing that stopped him tipping too far was the knowledge I might fall off the edge. Brutalise and intimidate me too much and I would no longer be able to play the public figure needed to maintain the stability of the company, no doubt pissing off his boss. And everybody had a boss.

I breathed a sigh of relief when he stood, figuring it signalled the end of our meeting. I should have known I wasn't that lucky. Buttoning his jacket closed, he walked quickly around my desk and braced one hand on it. Before I could even register his intention, his other hand reached for the scarf around my neck, most likely so he could see if I still bore the marks of his brutality. His tainted fingers didn't make contact with the silk before Tom grabbed at his wrist and bent it slightly at an angle.

"No," Tom said, practically growling.

"You'll pay for that," Vasili warned.

"Don't touch her again," Tom replied, ignoring Vasili's warning. After a tense stare down Tom let him go, and Vasili stepped back, hate exuding from every pore.

"Your guard dog needs to be brought to heel, Sarah, but no matter. I simply wanted to see what superhero you were wearing today. I'm sure that I will find out for myself soon enough though. Until the next time," Vasili said, still wearing a nasty sneer, and turning on his heel, left as abruptly as he'd arrived.

As soon as the door closed, I stumbled over to the small sofa in the corner of the office and sank down into the seat with my head in my hands. Vasili was right. Tom's presence had allowed me to create the illusion that I was safe when, in reality, I was anything but. My breathing became more and more shallow as my panic worsened, but there was nothing I could do to control it, until I felt Tom's hand grip my chin, forcing my eyes up to meet his.

"In and out. Come on, Sar. Breathe with me. In and out. Nice and slow." His voice was calm. It worked. The longer I stared deep into his big brown eyes, the less I struggled for air. By the time I was breathing normally again, there were tears in my eyes. Moving his hand, he brought my head down to rest against his shoulder.

"Want to tell me what that was all about?" he said, as he rubbed reassuring circles on the back of my neck with his thumb.

"He knows what kind of underwear I'm wearing. It means, either he's been in my bedroom or he has cameras there. If he can get into my bedroom, he can get to me," I said. Even though Vasili hadn't touched me this time, I felt dirty. I was so embroiled in the stench of his corruption, I worried that no amount of water in the world would ever make me clean.

"I promise you there are no cameras in your bedroom and nobody has been in there since you became a part of this operation. My guess is the house was scouted before he ever approached you. He's probably been through all your personal stuff, maybe even stolen a pair or two of your knickers so he can remind you that he can get to you. They're all classic intimidation techniques, and they'll only work if you let them," he reassured me.

"Two weeks, he said. Two weeks of knowing every time I shower or undress, he's listening. Two weeks of signing anything he puts in front of me. How many lives will I be destroying in those two weeks? Every document I sign could be another human life smuggled or another shipment of weapons aimed at women and children. How can I ever close my eyes again knowing that I made that happen? That I okayed it, all for the greater good?"

No matter how often I built up my walls, talked myself

around, and convinced myself that I was acting for the best, Vasili's presence stripped all of that away. In the aftermath of his warning was the realisation, not only that I would never be free of this, but that I was as bad as he was. Running to the government might have seemed like the right thing to do, but my goal had been to end the tragedy, not to partake in more misery. My intentions were good, but the path to hell was still paved with good intentions. The very first time I signed one of those manifesto changes, I was condemning myself and someone else's soul to hell.

"We've downloaded and saved every shipping manifest for the next six months, and MI5 will cross reference that against the changes. They'll be tracking each and every shipment and where it goes. These aren't actions without consequences. This isn't one of those times where you have to sacrifice one life to save hundreds. We're trying to save them all. But if we take down Vasili now, we stop one criminal. We wait a little longer and we get the entire organisation and their clients. Then we're not just talking one life, we're talking thousands," he reasoned.

"Do you think that will make a difference to the person waiting to be saved?"

"I don't know. But I do know that unless we bring this operation down from the very top, this will happen over and over again. Like fucking weeds, we need to dig them out from the root before we kill them, or they'll just grow back. If you really want to save lives, you help me find those shipments and keep it together."

I pulled back to look him square in the face, and he met my gaze unflinchingly. In his eyes, I saw nothing but honesty and determination. He truly believed that what we were doing was for the best, and his conviction gave me hope. Hope that I really was doing the right thing. That I would save lives, even if, ultimately, that life wasn't my own.

"I'm sorry. You're supposed to be my babysitter, and instead you seem to be peeling me off the walls every two minutes. I am strong enough to handle this, I promise. But I'm glad you were here. I lose my nerve completely when he's around," I admitted.

"Appear weak when you are strong and strong when you are weak."

"Now who's been reading cushions?" The corner of my mouth lifted in a small, grateful smile.

"Sun Tzu. *The Art of War*." His answer impressed me.

"What did you say your degree was in again?"

"I didn't. Now get your arse up, buttercup. We've got a job to do."

We worked diligently for the next eight hours, gathering as much information as we could before Vasili's contact began changing everything. It angered me to realise he'd had a permanent spy here all along. How many times had Tom and I walked past him without realising it? We scanned hundreds of documents and saved thousands more to flash drives. Not only manifests but memorandums, dock reports, faxes, anything that would clue us in to the shipments that were being altered and the buyers collecting those shipments at the other end. If we could locate any legitimate evidence of tampered containers, MI5 might get lucky in tracing the buyer at the other end. Most docks these days had pretty intensive surveillance for insurance purposes. I was practically falling asleep on a report, when Tom hauled me to my feet and reached for my coat.

"We don't have to go yet. I'm fine to keep going for a while," I protested.

"No. You're not. You're exhausted, and between the pacing and the tossing and turning I hear from your bedroom each night, I know you're not sleeping much. You need to get some rest before you burn out and slip up somehow."

"Just a little longer?" I begged.

"I get that you don't want to go home, but you know you can't stay here."

"Dad's place is about as far from home as you can get."

"Well, stop getting your knickers in a knot and put your coat on. We're not going there. Not tonight. We're going somewhere you can feel safe and get some sleep." I had no idea where he meant, but I was already sold.

"What about the fundraiser?" I asked, sleepily. My first corporate party was in less than twenty-four hours, and honestly, pulling teeth was more preferable than going.

"Don't worry, we'll be back in time for the party."

"And MI5? Are they okay with us going off the reservation?" I asked, putting on my coat and gloves.

"You worry too much," he replied, without ever really answering my question.

Eli pulled up in the car, and within minutes, we were on the road. It took forever to get through traffic, and by the time we hit the motorway, I was drifting off. The comfort of not being under the microscope, combined with the dull hum of traffic, was all it took. Jostling around on the seat, I struggled to find a comfortable position to rest, until a strong arm wrapped around me. Resting my head on Tom's shoulder, I found the peace I was looking for, and the last thing I remembered for the next hundred miles was the addictive scent of soap and aftershave that belonged to the only man who'd ever made me feel safe.

CHAPTER EIGHT

Sarah

"Fuck me, she sleeps like the dead. Want me to carry her in?" Eli said. On the periphery between awake and asleep, my eyelids felt lead-lined, they were so heavy, so I kept them closed.

"I've got her," Tom replied quietly. A quick release of the catch and the seatbelt slithered away, leaving Tom room to slide his arms beneath me and haul me effortlessly into the warm cocoon of his chest.

"I'm awake," I protested, without feeling.

"Go back to sleep, buttercup. I've got this." His deep, calm voice in the darkness felt like a soft fleece blanket on a cold winter's night. Warm and reassuring, the sound wrapped itself around me, seeping into my bones. Fatigue had lowered my resistance, and though I sensed I would regret my decision when the sun rose, I succumbed to the comfort of his strong arms and relaxed against him.

"What's the ETA for the rest of the guys?" Tom asked.

"They'll be here in a little over an hour. Crash went in straight after we left. He wanted to install more surveillance in Sar's office. MI5 are in there too, loading up that Devaney guy's computer full of shit. Five minutes after his name was mentioned, they were probably tearing his life apart," Eli replied.

"They'll be half starved when they arrive, and we need to debrief after today. Can you order some food? Takeaway menu's on the fridge. We eat first, then I want to go through Agheenco's meeting transcripts, make sure I didn't miss anything. After that, I want to look at the target shortlists. I'd be surprised if the final takedown is anything other than a forcible entry before the cargo is unloaded, so I want that simulated until we have it nailed. That means we need to know what kind of container ships we're looking at. Entry points and exits, blind spots, the lot," Tom said. He rarely raised his voice, but it was so commanding, he didn't need to.

"You got it. What do we do with her while we're running the sims?"

"She comes with us," Tom replied.

"Seriously?" Eli exclaimed in disbelief.

"Can you think of any place safer?" Tom asked, making Eli chuckle.

"Fair point, but the brass are gonna have a field day over this one."

"They won't have a problem with it as long as she's

under SAS close protection," Tom reassured him.

I guessed the conversation was over when car doors slammed and Tom started walking. At around five foot five, I had curves in all the places women were meant to. Although I hated gyms with the fiery passion of a thousand suns, running regularly allowed me to continue an avid adiction to chocolate dipped doughnuts. My obsession with the sugary devil would last a lifetime. They might not be the best substitute for a healthy relationship, or even a healthy diet, but God help the man who parted us. Of course, when I embarked on this love affair, I never contemplated that I'd be carried princess style by a giant of a man with washboard abs and zero body fat. The urge to hold my breath, as though I could somehow forcibly suck into my body every excess pound, was strong.

I shouldn't want him to be attracted to me, but I did. I wanted him to crave my touch in every way that I craved his, so I wouldn't be alone in suffering this constant ache. The way that he cradled me, like I was delicate and precious and light as a feather, made me feel all of those things. The delicious scent of his skin called to me, inviting me to nuzzle my nose against his neck, but even in my sleepy state I resisted. Our "almost kiss" had us perilously close to crossing a line we couldn't come back from. Already that line was becoming blurry and faded. If we weren't careful, someday soon we would forget it ever existed at all.

He laid me down on the softest of beds, and I dared to

open one eye. Light spilled into the darkened room from the hallway, but I couldn't really see past him. With very little assistance from me, he peeled away my coat as I toed off my shoes and collapsed back against the luxurious feather pillows.

"You hungry?" he asked.

I shook my head, too exhausted to contemplate eating.

"Get some sleep then, buttercup. I'll bring your bag up later so you have something to change into tomorrow."

"Thanks, Tom," I whispered on a yawn, so drowsy I was a hair's breadth from slumber. The room was completely silent for a few moments, and I could only imagine he was watching over me, before strong, gentle fingers tucked a lock of hair behind my ear. His touch was barely a whisper across my cheek, but it was so intimately personal that I carried it with me to my dreams, and I was asleep before he reached the door.

When I woke, sunlight streamed in through the gap in the curtains, bathing me in its warmth. I'd slept more deeply and restfully than I had since before the accident. Like my system had undergone a much needed reboot, I felt invigorated. Walking over to the window, I found myself looking over a huge garden, dusted with an early winter's frost that looked so unearthly I yearned to sketch it. The past few weeks were the longest I'd ever gone without a pencil or charcoal in my hand. It was such a huge part of my life, but the weight of grief and responsibility had plunged me into a monochromatic darkness. Now I wanted colour and light. I wanted to claim back the parts of myself that would remain when Vasili was long gone.

As promised, my bag was by the side of my bed next to a stack of neatly folded bedding that had me wondering whether Tom had spent the night on the floor next to me. It would explain why I'd slept so soundly, realising subconsciously that I hadn't been alone in the dark. Everything about my room was designed for comfort, from the thick, luxurious carpet that tastefully complimented the pale cream walls, to the beautifully appointed oak doors and windows enhanced with bespoke ironmongery. The wrought iron bed fit the moderately sized room well, and along with an oak wardrobe and matching bedside tables, it made up the only furniture in what was a modern take on a traditional cottage bedroom. Add in a few brightly coloured cushions and throws, and it would be exactly the sort of place I could see myself living in. A quick bit of investigating led me to a tiny bathroom, just big enough for me to wash up and dress. I was just about to go and look for everyone when Crash knocked and poked his head around the door.

"You decent?" he asked.

"You should probably ask a girl that before you walk into her room," I replied, smiling.

"Honey, the sort of girls that have me in their bedrooms are never decent."

I rolled my eyes in reply, because there really was no answering that one. "Where is everyone?"

"Battle planning," he replied. "We heard you up and about, so the boss wanted you to know we'll be about fifteen more minutes, then Eli's drawn the short straw for cooking a fried breakfast if you're interested."

"Why don't I start breakfast so it's ready when you finish? I'd rather be useful than sit here twiddling my thumbs," I offered.

"I'll probably get lynched for letting you do anything other than sleep, but fuck it. Eli can't cook for shit, and I'm bloody starving. So if you're half decent in the kitchen, have at it."

"By the way, where's the kitchen and where exactly are we?"

"Turn right at the bottom of the stairs and follow the corridor to the end. And we're at the boss's place," he replied, before disappearing back the way he came, as though that useless little titbit told me anything.

"Would you mind telling me who you are, and just what exactly you're doing in my house?" The stocky, fearsome woman addressing me was more than a little intimidating. I'd guess her age to be late sixties, but honestly it could be ten years either way. Her thick hair, of a beautiful colour that rested somewhere between bleach blonde and white, was scraped back in an elegant chignon. A perfectly made up face, the primary reason her age was indistinguishable, made it glaringly obviously that this was someone with both time to spare and money. She was a couple of inches shorter than me, but what she lacked in size she made up for in stature, carrying her figure with a powerful confidence. One arm rested on the other in a pose reminiscent of Tom, while her free hand puffed away on a cigarette, completely uncaring of the fact that we were indoors.

"It was my house last time I looked," Tom replied, taking in my bemused expression, "and no smoking in the house."

"Good luck with that," she replied, but moved over to the French doors so she could flick her ash into the garden.

"I gave you this house, and the least you could do is keep an ashtray or two in here for me. God knows I've bought enough of them over the years," she replied.

"I throw them out when you're gone to discourage you," he answered. "Smoking will kill you."

"Like you're one to lecture me on what'll get you killed," she retorted, and was answered with the death stare I was fast becoming accustomed to.

"Chuck out the next ashtray I buy, and I'm disinheriting you!" she threatened.

He rolled his eyes and smiled, and without knowing a thing about their relationship, I knew he'd keep doing it.

"Hey, Nan, how's my favourite girl?" Crash asked her, striding across the kitchen to grab both of her cheeks between his hands and plant a noisy kiss on her lips.

"Keep your lips to yourself please, Benjamin McCaffrey. Lord only knows where they've been" she admonished, making Crash chuckle.

"Don't be like that Nan. You don't know what you're missing."

"I'll do my best to live with the loss," she replied, sarcastically. "You know it isn't compulsory for you to hit on a woman just because she's sharing oxygen with you. Try saving up all that charm for a girl you really like."

"Fuck, I think my mojo must be broken," he admitted. "The only person I've hit on lately is Sarah here, and she isn't interested in getting any action. Now, you don't even want my kisses."

"How about you show some fucking respect please?" Tom's amusement at Crash's smart mouth had finally run out.

The scary lady looked from Tom to me, then back again. "Interesting," she said, raising one eyebrow smugly, as though there were secrets of the world that only she was privy to. Eventually, she seemed to come to some sort of a decision and turned her attention towards me.

"As I was saying, would you mind telling me who are you and what you're doing in my kitchen?" she asked me.

"My kitchen," Tom corrected.

"Fine, if you're going to be difficult," she conceded. "Who are you and what are you doing in the kitchen I gave him?"

"This is Sarah, our new housekeeper," he said. I guessed he hadn't expected to have to explain away my presence, and from the death stare he was giving me, I figured keeping my mouth shut was probably the most sensible option. Unfortunately for Tom, I never was much good at keeping quiet.

"Can't she speak for herself then? And why may I ask do you need a housekeeper anyway? Or is housekeeper some code you kids have these days?" she asked, eyeing me up as though I was some bacon frying prostitute.

"I speak just fine thank you, and as a housekeeper, I do exactly what my title suggests, I keep the house, cook, and clean, and despite what you seem to be suggesting, I manage to do all that with my knickers on," I replied.

By the end of my angry retort, my hands were on my hips and I was staring at her just as hard as she was staring at me.

"You're a proper little bitch, aren't you?" she said, finally. Her heated glare morphed into a smirk. "I like that."

"On the contrary, I'm very nice normally. Or I try to be," I added. I hadn't been very nice when I was running my mouth off, but I hated the idea of her thinking that I'd slept my way into my imaginary employment. Perhaps I wouldn't have felt so self-righteous if I'd stopped to think about how many times I'd thought about a naked Tom in the last twenty-four hours alone. Only then did it occur to me that this was someone he probably knew well and that I might have pissed him off with my runaway mouth, though a quick glance his way assured me that wasn't the case. In fact, he looked more amused than I'd ever seen him.

"Well it's nice to meet you Sarah. Now tell me, do you play poker at all?" she asked.

"I wouldn't go anywhere near that woman with a deck of cards if I were you," Eli chipped in. "She's a shark."

"How about you mind your own business Elijah Spears! And now I think of it, you and Benjamin owe me twenty-five pounds from poker last Friday, now ante up," Nan said, throwing the last of her cigarette outside before filling up the kettle and putting it on to boil.

"The fuck I do!" Eli replied, and they launched into a full-scale argument, which she won. He was counting notes out of his wallet and mumbling about senile old people when she placed a hot cup of tea down next to me with a wink. It's a good thing I didn't take sugar, because she didn't ask.

"How come you don't call Crash by his nickname?" I asked her, noticing that Crash hadn't blinked when she'd called him Benjamin.

"I'm not using bloody ridiculous code names, like they're some twelve-year-old Boy Scouts, and if you had an ounce of sense, you wouldn't encourage them either. Thank goodness you've got a normal name. If you were a 'Destiny' or a 'Chardonnay,' I'd insist that Tom fire you on principle," she replied. Slightly bemused by the strength of her conviction, it was the first time I could ever say I was pleased to have a relatively normal sounding name.

"Not liking someone's name is not a reason to fire them," Tom argued.

"Of course it is. It means they have stupid parents, and who wants to employ someone who's genetically predestined to be stupid," she replied.

"This is Nan by the way," Crash told me.

"Took you long enough to introduce me," she scolded him.

"Like I could get a word in," he replied.

"Are you Tom's grandmother?" I asked, having guessed that must be why he called her Nan.

"Do I really look old enough to be a grandmother?" she asked, clearly horrified by my presumption. "My name's Nancy, which they all shorten to Nan, and I'm his mother," she explained, before I had a chance to apologise.

"Adopted mother!" Tom chimed in.

"Like you're good looking enough to have been birthed from these loins," she scoffed, making him grin.

"Now tell me dear, are you single?"

"She only arrived yesterday, and you're going to scare her away," Tom warned.

"Not at all. Sarah and I are going to get on swimmingly. I can tell," she said, leaving me more than a little scared.

CHAPTER

NINE

Sarah

"Your housekeeper?" I said, an eyebrow raised in disbelief.

"I panicked," Tom admitted.

"You're in the SAS. Isn't panic pretty much bred out of you in the selection process?"

"Yeah, well, selection would be a lot tighter if they had Nan running interrogation-resistance training. I'd take waterboarding over half an hour under the spotlight with that woman any day of the week," he replied, giving me a fake shiver.

"What's waterboarding?" I asked, envisaging how something that sounded so much like surfing could be considered torture.

"Ugh, forget I said anything, buttercup. You don't want that in your head."

"It's already in my head. And you know I'm just going to

google it, so if you think what I'll find on the net is worse than your explanation, you're obliged to give it to me."

He sighed deeply, like I was being a royal pain in the arse. "Fine. It's a kind of water torture that simulates drowning. You tie someone down, cover their nose and mouth and pour water intermittently over the cloth." It astounded me the way he described it so matter-of-factly. The fact that this form of torture existed, and was used often enough to necessitate it being named, upset me profoundly. Truthfully, it was the idea of Tom suffering that fate that upset me the most.

"Why would someone do that?" I asked, making him shrug.

"It's simple and effective. Best way to extract information from someone quickly," he said, bumping my arm to hurry me along with the dishes. Shaking myself out of my stupor, I handed him a wet plate for drying. It seemed so surreal to be doing dishes while casually discussing effective torture techniques. After a moment or two of silence, I asked him a question I dreaded hearing the answer to.

"Have you ever been waterboarded?" He nodded, but didn't explain, so I asked, "Does it bother you to talk about it?"

"No. I couldn't give a shit about that. It bothers me for you to hear it. You look like you're about to burst into tears."

"Well, wouldn't you be upset at the idea of me being tortured?" I asked, making him frown.

"That's never going to happen. Anyway, it's not like it was in a combat situation. I volunteered."

"Why the fuck would you volunteer for something like that?" I asked, shoving a plate at him angrily.

"Most people fear what they don't understand. They don't know how much it will hurt and how they'll survive it, so they fear it. Now I know what it's like and how my body and my mind reacts against questioning under torture. I don't fear it," he explained. "Anyway, it's pretty good incentive never to get captured. I'm not in any hurry to repeat the experience."

"You must've had some shitty career advisors at university to make your job sound appealing." My reply made him chuckle.

"What about you?" he asked, changing the subject. "How'd you end up as an illustrator?"

"It was all a bit of an accident really. Much to Dad's disappointment, I was always kind of flaky and unfocused in school. I wasn't a troublemaker or anything. I mean, I never really made waves or acted out, but there was always somewhere I'd rather be than where I was. Art class was pretty much the only time I took an interest. Anyway, Dad let me keep going with the art on the condition I joined the family business after college, but while I was there, a friend of mine told me she was writing a children's book. She was strapped for cash and asked if I would illustrate it in exchange for co-credit and a share in the royalties. That went on to be an international bestseller, and I had a way out."

"A way out?" he asked, and it was my turn to shrug.

"I didn't want to be part of Tatem Shipping, but Dad insisted. I think he hoped to give me some nice little admin job where he could keep an eye on me until he could marry me off."

"So you walked away from it completely?"

"Not from Dad and my brother, John, just the business. I never wanted to be estranged, but I guess we were halfway there before it happened anyway. There's ten years between John and me, so once he went off to university, I barely saw him. After Mum died, Dad wasn't the same either. It's like a light went out in his heart when she left us, and he never figured out how to turn it back on again. I think, especially in the beginning, it hurt him to see me because I look so much like Mum. But in the end, Aunt Elizabeth had driven a wedge so big between us, neither of us knew how to close it. Maybe his wanting me to work for him was his way of bringing us back together, but I guess we'll never know now."

"Do you miss them?"

"At the moment, all I can think of are the wasted years between us. I was a kid when I lost Mum, and I needed them. Desperately. And they weren't there. So, I felt like all my family had died. When I think of them now, I want to be able to remember how they were before. I'm just not there yet."

"You will be," he replied with conviction. "Life's like any other story. It's inevitable that what you remember most is the last chapter you read. But one chapter doesn't define the whole book."

"Is that your way of saying time heals all wounds?"

"No. I'm saying that time lets you find a way to live with them."

"I hope so." I ducked my head as I wiped down the sink. It seemed so strange to be sharing such a personal moment of grief with a near stranger. But he spoke with such conviction and authority, it was hard not to believe him.

"Are you going to get into trouble for bringing me here?" I asked, looking around the kitchen. The house was much newer than I'd realised last night and was decorated in a way that had me swooning over every room. It was probably half the size of Dad's monstrosity, but it felt cosy and lived-in. Little details everywhere, from the framed photos of Nan with Tom as a teenager to the cushions coordinated with bedding, screamed of a woman's touch.

"Probably, but I'm hoping the fact that they've given me command will give me some leeway. Tomorrow, I'll have to submit my log of your whereabouts through the night and of my operational conduct. Once MI5 has seen it, we'll know how badly the shit has hit the fan." He didn't seem too bothered, and his lack of concern helped me relax.

"I needed this. So badly," I admitted, biting my lip nervously. "I'm not sure how much more I could've taken of being monitored and observed all day every day. It's bad enough knowing that someone is constantly listening and watching, but hearing that lowlife has been through my underwear drawer was just a step too far."

"I'll probably get a bollocking from my boss for not taking you to a hotel or something, but you needed to feel safe. You're not trained for this, and if you slip up with Vasili because you're tired and stressed, this whole operation will all be for nothing anyway."

Folding the tea towel, I draped it over the handle of the oven, then crossed my arms and turned to lean against it. To say that I was disappointed was a colossal understatement. Of course, this was all about the mission. Tom was one of the most determined and focused people I'd ever met. Bringing an end to the trafficking and locating the buyers was his top priority. It should have been mine, but somewhere along the way my focus had shifted. We both shared the same goal, but I wanted to share more. I wanted to know that he made this incredibly reckless decision because he cared about me. I'd romanticised things between us, and it needed to stop. There was a fairly good chance that I wouldn't be walking away from this situation at all. I knew that the minute I made the phone call to the government. But on the slim chance that one day my life would be my own again, I owed it to myself to try and keep this battered heart intact. Mum, Dad, John. They were all gone, and the minute this was over, Tom would be too.

"What's going on in that head of yours?" he asked. Standing in front of me, he consumed my space until you could barely slip a piece of paper between us.

"I know you want to make sure I won't break and mess up the operation, but this rest was just what I needed. If it would help, I can make a statement for your superiors stating that I threatened to pull from the operation if I didn't get some space, so you brought me here. I don't want you getting into trouble over this. Over me...."

He used his knuckle to raise my head until I was looking deep into those big brown eyes.

"The truth is, there are a million places I could've taken you to feel safe, but I wanted you here. Sleeping in my bed, cooking in my kitchen, and making yourself at home. I might not get the chance again. So stop worrying so much. Some people are worth a little trouble. I'll get a rap over the knuckles at most, and I'd take that any day of the week for the chance to have you here."

"You mean that?" I asked softly. My whole body relaxed in relief as he said the words I'd so longed to hear. Succumbing to the intimacy of the moment, I placed my hands on his chest as he rested his on the stove behind me, trapping me in the security of his arms. The unique scent of his soap and aftershave drugged my senses like nothing else, and I closed my eyes as I tried to memorise it. There were so many consequences to what we were about to do, a price that we would both have to pay. But in that moment, I didn't care. All I could think about, all I could feel, all I could see, was him. His nose rubbed gently along mine as his warm breath danced across my lips. My whole body ached with the need to feel his weight pressed against me, and the small groan he let slip through his lips told me he felt the same way.

"What are you doing to me?" he whispered.

"Same thing you're doing to me," I whispered back.

I opened my eyes long enough to see the expression of pure torture on his face before it turned to resolve. As his head dipped towards me, my breath hitched, knowing, finally, he was going to kiss me.

"Hey, boss. What time were you thinking of making a move back to...whoa." Will's voice trailed off as he came around the corner and caught us. This time, Tom didn't jump or pull away. He placed a protective hand on the small of my back, cementing our closeness before turning slightly to face Will.

"What do you need?" Tom asked him.

"Urgh, just wondering what time you wanted to go up to Hereford? The lads are a little restless and want to get some training in before we need to head back to London," he replied.

"Give it twenty minutes. Nan's going soon, and I want to make sure she's safely home before we leave," Tom said.

"No problem," Will responded. "And sorry to disturb you. I'll keep the lads out of your hair until we leave." He gave Tom an indecipherable look, then nodded to me before leaving the room.

Emboldened by his confession, I rested my forehead against his chest, and he wrapped his strong arms around my body, binding us together as one. In the other room, I could hear Nan laughing and joking with the guys, and I knew we'd missed our moment.

"One day, buttercup," Tom said.

"One day," I agreed.

We stayed there, holding onto each other for as long as we could, until we heard Nan and Will arguing.

"I think they'd appreciate some privacy," Will said.

"Then they can go to a hotel. Now get out of my way, William. I don't want to hurt you, but if you don't remove yourself from the doorway, I will take away your mother's chance of ever having grandchildren," Nan replied before barrelling into the room.

"Housekeeper? Really? You always were a terrible liar," she said, pointing an accusatory finger at Tom. I had no idea how she could hold it up for so long with the weight of the heavy looking gold and jewelled rings she wore. Tom gave a long-suffering sigh before kissing me gently on the forehead and turning to face her.

"What is it you think you know then, you nosy old crone?" he asked. It was shocking to hear the way they spoke to one another, but their witty banter back and forth seemed to be based on genuine affection. Tom wasn't a man who smiled often, but he smiled for Nan.

"She owns a shipping company worth bloody millions, so why is she in my house pretending to be a maid?"

"Housekeeper, actually," I muttered, put out that my

imaginary position had just been demoted.

"It's my house, and maybe I'm marrying her for her money so I don't have to hear you bitch about cutting me out of your will all the time," he said, baiting Nan, which only seemed to wind her up further.

"It'll be your house when I'm dead, and is it too much to hope for a straight answer?"

"It's my name on the deed, and how could you possibly know who she is anyway?" Tom replied.

"I took her picture on my phone and did a reverse image search. I got a couple of hits, and then I found her. What I want to know is what she's doing here."

"Jesus Christ, Nan. The CIA and MI5 combined have nothing on you," Tom protested. "Look, trust me when I say you're better off not knowing. Sarah only came for one night, and I had no idea you'd be stopping by. I'm grateful to you for keeping up the place when I'm gone, but it's safer all around if you pretend we weren't here."

"Oh, cut the crap, Thomas. Either you tell me what's going on or I'll work it out for myself." Tom rolled his eyes at the use of his full name, but the look of resignation on his face told me that Nan would get her way.

"Just tell her, Tom. What harm can it do now that we've eloped," I said. His eyes met mine, and the conspiratorial look we shared told me he'd caught on to what I was doing.

"I guess it was only a matter of time before she found out about the baby anyway," he replied, adding to the farce.

"I do hope it's twins, darling. A boy and a girl. One of each would be wonderful, wouldn't it?" I gushed. At this point, Nan's eyes were bulging out of their sockets.

"We'll call the girl Nan so her name will remind us to visit you when we finally get your wrinkly arse into a care home," he said, and she finally cottoned onto the fact that we were winding her up.

"You're a terrible son, you know that? It would serve you right if I did disinherit you!"

"Like I give a shit about your money," he said, planting a huge, wet kiss on her cheek.

"And you, young lady, shouldn't encourage him," she said, pointing her finger at me. "If it weren't for the fact that I've seen my boy smile more this morning than he has in years, I'd say you were a bad influence. Now, enough fooling around. Spill it," she ordered as she walked around the kitchen to put the kettle on.

"We'll have a cuppa if there's one on the go," Will shouted from the other room as the water began to boil.

"Does this look like a bloody café?" she shouted back, and was met with laughter, but she lined up enough mugs for everyone regardless.

"I took over the running of my father's company about a month ago and discovered that the underlying core of the business is in trafficking for a Russian gang operating out of London," I explained, not wanting to put Tom in the position of having to be insubordinate again. I was warned not to tell anyone, but I wasn't military. Nobody could order me to do anything. "MI5 are tracing the shipments in the hope of tracking the buyers, and Tom is watching over me in case they decide they'd prefer a change of management."

She levelled a glare at me, likely trying to access whether we were yanking her chain again. When she saw the truth of it in my face, she turned towards Tom again.

"Was it too much to hope you'd find a nice school teacher or something, leave the army, and pop out a couple of grandkids?" she said, sighing.

"We don't get to choose," he replied cryptically.

"No, we don't, son," she agreed.

One by one, the guys filtered in, until Will, Eli, and Crash were lined up beside us.

"What's the plan then? I mean, I'm assuming you've got a plan for when the government cuts her loose and this all goes pear-shaped," Nan said.

Will looked towards Tom, and I could see then that this was something they'd already contemplated.

"Are you saying the government is going to throw me to the wolves when this is over?" I asked Tom.

"If they are, we've not been told of it. But I'll be honest. The minute I was told about this operation, it occurred to me they'd consider you expendable," he admitted. The confession was enough to make my blood run cold. Without these guys protecting me, I had no chance.

"Am I expendable?" I asked him quietly.

The intensity of emotion in his beautiful brown eyes, had a shiver running down my spine. "Not to me."

CHAPTER TEN

Tom

"Do you have any idea how much trouble you're in, soldier?" Lieutenant Colonel Timothy Davies said to me. In basic training as a new recruit, I'd been screamed at more times than I could count. Falling back on the same techniques I'd used throughout my childhood, I processed the command and blocked out the barracking as simply white noise. It was a skill that had developed into adulthood, giving me the ability to tune out crowds and screams to focus completely on a target. But Davies wasn't a man to raise his voice often. If he did, you knew you were in deep shit.

"Yes, sir," I admitted.

"Well, do you have anything to say that justifies your actions? I've heard from Staff Sergeant Edwards that you were concerned for Miss Tatem's state of mind and that you felt that your home was a secure, defensible environment in which you could get her back on track. Is that correct?"

"To a degree, sir. It's true that the constant monitoring and aggressive meetings with the Russians, from which Miss Tatem felt she had no reprieve, was causing some fear and stress. I felt as though a good night's sleep in an unmonitored environment, where she was nevertheless protected, would help eliminate that anxiety. But I should have saught approval before taking that decision into my hands, and I should have taken her to an independent location that was secure." What I failed to say was that, if I had the choice all over again, I still would have done the same thing. The minute I carried Sarah over the threshold of the only home I'd ever known, I knew she belonged there. She belonged with me. Something between us had shifted in those few precious hours. I'd let go of the illusion that she was just another mission. Just one of a hundred civilians I'd saved in my career.

"What am I going to do with you, Tom?" he asked, his tone becoming exasperated. "This operation is extremely high profile. Success will make your career, and failure will likely end it. You were chosen for this operation because you're one of my best, which is why I'll give you a little leeway this time, but once MI5 analyse the logs, they'll be all over this. We can't afford any fuck-ups, and you cannot afford to become attached to this woman. She's an asset. Nothing more. I'm going to justify your actions by pointing out that this is the first time the SAS have worked with civilian assets at this level and that you made a judgement call to rectify her fragile state of mind and get her back in the game quickly. By doing so, I'm having to admit a weakness in the regiment, which goes against everything we're trying to achieve here. Going cap in hand to explain myself to a bunch of uptight, condescending suits makes me look stupid, Lieutenant, and I do not like looking stupid. Am I clear?"

"Yes, sir," I replied.

"You will accompany Miss Tatem to the benefit dinner tonight as planned, and you will remain with her for the rest of the week. In order to give her the reprieve she needs, next Friday, Alpha Team B will take her to a secure location and you and your team will chopper out to the North Sea where you'll simulate a cargo ship assault. You will return to guarding her for the final week, following which we will be meeting with MI5 where they'll appraise us of their findings."

He wasn't removing my command of the operation, but it was clear that he was doing what was necessary to put some distance between Sarah and me. Little did he know that I was already past the point of no return.

"May I make a request, sir?" I asked.

"What is it, Lieutenant?"

"Have Alpha Team B take her back to my house next weekend. It's familiar territory where she'll feel comfortable. It's remote and fairly isolated, so easy for the team to see an assault coming, and the security is integrated. If the Russians are tracking her in any way, it won't be suspicious that she's staying in my house given that I'm supposed to be her primary security. If you take her to a different location and they tie that to the regiment, the whole operation is blown."

I fucking hated the idea of her being separated from me and my guys, and I sure as hell didn't want her anywhere near those dick swingers in Team B. But if it was going to happen, the Neanderthal in me wanted to know she was safe and comfortable in my bed. Seeing her sleep, her long mahogany hair shot through with streaks of copper spread out over my pillow, had given me a moment of absolute peace in a lifetime of war. Besides which, I had a secure link to my phone from camera feeds across the property. I might be hanging over the side of a helicopter and freezing my arse off on the Baring Sea, but that would be a hell of a lot easier knowing she was safe.

"Very well," Davies agreed. "The damage is done, so we'll just have to make the best of it. But I don't want you going anywhere near that place as long as she's there."

"Yes, sir," I replied robotically. I respected Davies and appreciated the opportunities he'd given me. If I had to guess, I'd say he was most likely responsible for my selection for this command. But agreeing to follow an order you knew was made for the right reasons was its own kind of torture when every fibre of your being told you it was wrong. Regardless of how safe she might be with another team, walking away from her went against every gut instinct that I had. Defying Davies though would have me shipped out instantly without even a chance to say goodbye, so either way I was fucked. A quick salute and I was dismissed. Leaving his office, I stalked angrily back to the Range Rover where Will was waiting.

"What's the verdict then?" he asked as he turned around and drove towards the base exit.

"He gave me the bollocking I expected, but nothing official. He's covering for me with MI5, but if the mission goes to shit, it's my head on the chopping block. Command is still mine, but he wants some distance between me and Sarah."

"That might not be a bad thing, Tom. You're getting too close to this girl. I mean, I'm the last one to pull you up on shit like this, but you're in so deep you can't see how fucked up it is to be messing with this chick. I get that you're with her night and day, but shit, can a pretty piece of arse really be worth fucking your career over?"

My jaw clicked, and my fist tightened as I fought to rein in my temper. Taking a deep breath, I turned slowly to face Will. "You and I have been friends for a long time, but you call her a piece of arse again, and you and I are going to have some serious fucking problems," I warned him.

"Well, shit. You've fallen for her, haven't you? Do you have any idea how royally fucked you are? Even if by some miracle we get through this operation and she gets to go back to her normal life, what then? Happy ever afters don't work for guys like us. You think she'll settle for a few weeks a year where you're not training or in combat? Maybe pop out a couple of kids who turn out to be strangers because you never get to see them grow up? And even if she goes along with that, where do you fit into her world? You're a fucking orphan, and she's a millionaire."

"Jesus Christ! Enough!" I protested. "I've never even kissed the girl, and you've got me married with kids and divorced already. Don't you think I've thought about all of that? I've been fighting this since the day I fucking met her, and even if I could find a way to make it work, she's too fucking good for the likes of me. But her life is mine to protect. Mine to watch over. I was made for war, and it's what I'll wage to bring her peace. If I need to walk away after that, I will, but until then, I'll be fucked if I'm handing her over to someone who cares more about promotion than her life."

"Beautiful speech. Very moving," Will replied, grinning.

"Laugh it up, fucker. Let's see how fucking funny you find it when you fall for someone you can't have."

"Stop. Honestly, there's tears in my eyes. I feel like we should write some of this shit down. Then when some fucking terrorist shoots you in the head because you were too busy with your head up your arse mooning over this chick to pay attention, we can retell the whole thing as a modern take on Romeo and Juliet. Maybe even get a movie deal out of it." He was practically pissing himself with laughter, as he wiped away the fake tears.

Not bothering to reply, I gave him both middle fingers, which made him laugh even harder. Everything he said made sense, and it was nothing I hadn't told myself a million times before. But this thing between us was stronger than logic or reason or even common sense. The truth was, when there were a hundred reasons to let go, she was the only reason I needed to hold on.

Having fiddled with my black bow tie until it was damn near perfect, I reached for my tux jacket. It wasn't like I'd never dressed up before. Despite my best efforts, I couldn't avoid every university function and mess dinner, but it wasn't a skin that fitted me well. I was more at ease in the shadows, waiting and watching from the darkness. For Sarah, I would walk in the light. I knew that she was dreading tonight, but just like always, she squared her shoulders, put her chin up, and got on with it. With the monkey suit on, I slid the wires through for my cuff mike and fitted a discrete little earpiece. Just as I closed my own bedroom door, Sarah's opened.

"Wow," I said, and instantly she blushed. If I ever had the chance, I'd catalogue every which way there was of making those cheeks turn pink. I tried to think of any adjective to describe the way she looked, but I had nothing. Stunned into silence, I could do little more than gawk. Man, she was fucking gorgeous. The gown was wine red, with capped sleeves and a simple round neckline. It fitted to every curve of her body before flaring out at the skirt. The front was covered with tiny red crystals so that every time moved, she caught the light. She was absolutely breath-taking.

And then she twirled for me. The dress was completely backless, stopping just above the curve of her arse. Never in my life had I considered a woman's back to be the sexiest part of her body. I was wrong on every level. The lightly sun-kissed skin, the arch of her back, even the contour of her shoulder blades had me hard as a rock. I knew then, with absolute certainty, that I was going to kiss every inch of it one day.

Soon.

"You look amazing," she said to me.

"You look fucking incredible."

Her breath hitched as she caught the intensity of my gaze. The invisible, impenetrable thread that had formed between us the moment we met was now a rope that pulled us closer together every day. We'd played tug of war with it for long enough. Stalking towards her, I felt an overwhelmingly animalistic need to claim her as my own, to let every man out there, who even thought about speaking to her, know that she was mine.

Intimidated by the ferocity of my pursuit, she took a step backwards just as I reached her. The craving to lift her into my arms and carry her to bed was overpowering, but I fought against it. She needed tender and gentle from a man that was anything but. Bracing one hand on the doorframe above her, I gripped it so hard I thought it might crack, as I eliminated the space between us and let my other hand sweep its way along the dips and curve of her spine. She was perfection, and her reaction only added fuel to the fire. Like she was born for my touch and my touch alone, wherever my hand was, that part of her body arched towards me. Closing her eyes, she gripped the lapels of my tux and sighed against me. That breathy moan would be my undoing. Bending my head, I ran my nose lightly along the side of her neck. Her scent was sexy and subtle, and I filled my lungs as I tried to memorise it, knowing instinctively it would smell differently from the bottle. As with everything else, she took it and made it her own. Cupping the globe of her perfect arse, I pressed her harder against my body, letting her feel every inch of her effect on me. We had yet to kiss, but it was still the single most erotic thing I had ever experienced. Because the moment wasn't just about sex. It was about so much more. It was a promise of the passion and pleasure and everything I had yet to experience with someone I cared about. It destroyed the notion that meaningless encounters with faceless women would ever be satisfying again, because I couldn't imagine anything comparing to this.

"Do you think anyone would mind if I marked you just here?" I whispered, touching my lips to the peach-soft skin of her neck.

"I wouldn't," she replied breathlessly.

"Ready at the gate," came the crackle followed by the voice in my earpiece.

"Motherfucker," I muttered. Touching my forehead against hers, I tried desperately to regain my composure.

"Soon," she said.

"Soon," I agreed.

Since I'd moved in, the team had complete access to the main gate and keys to all the doors. When Sarah was home, only Eli, posing as her chauffer and additional security, ever came to the door. He knocked to respect her privacy, but no longer bothered with the formality of buzzing at the main gate. The downside to this was that he was at the entrance long before I was ready to leave.

"Come on. Let's get this over with," she said, threading her fingers though mine, squeezing them ever so slightly. I led her downstairs and opened the door for her as she grabbed her clutch bag from the side table.

"Hi!" she greeted Eli.

He let out a long wolf whistle as he took in her dress, and she curtseyed as she giggled. My first instinct was to slap him upside the head for looking at her that way, but the smile on her face took my breath away. For the first time since I'd met her, she looked happy. I locked the door as Eli helped her into the car. She knew the protocol and said nothing for the first few miles, but neither of us could stop the little touches that no one could see. Usually there was at least a foot between us, but tonight our legs were pressed up against each other. Her hands, hidden behind Eli's seat, rested in her lap. Reaching over, I turned up her palm and slid my fingers between hers. Back and forth we caressed each other, finding erogenous zones in the most unlikely of places. This prolonged foreplay between us was the most intensive kind of sexual torture. I'd only ever indulged in sex that was hard and fast and completely forgettable. How naive I was not to realise that it was these hidden touches and secret caresses that would burn their way into my soul forever.

Will's voice in my ear broke the spell and brought me back down to reality with a crash.

"You're not going to like this, boss, but you're about to make a stop," he said, and a feeling of foreboding came over me.

"Talk to me, Will," I said, into my cuff.

"You're picking up Masterson. He's Sarah's date for the evening," he replied.

"You're fucking kidding me!" I felt my anger building uncontrollably at the thought of that dickless wonder anywhere near her. I'd seen the way he looked at her at the briefings and knew that this was no coincidence. The slimy fucker had engineered this somehow. "Why wasn't I informed?"

"Why do you think? MI5 submitted the request shortly after we left, and Davies signed off on it. Sarah's going to be photographed from the minute she gets out of the car. Masterson's an analyst, not a field agent, so it doesn't matter if he's pictured with her, but you don't have that luxury. So for tonight, you slip in unnoticed and act as her close protection whilst being as inconspicuous as possible. Davies gets a man in the field, some distance between you and Sarah, and keeps MI5 happy. It's a done deal, my friend," Will explained.

"Fuck," I muttered, furious that the evening had gone completely to shit.

"You got this handled?" he asked. "Because you have less than two minutes before the car stops. He's going to be pushing your buttons all night, so you need to make sure you have this locked down."

"Yeah. Yeah, I'm good," I told him, before dropping my hand.

"Tom?" Sarah asked quietly, her happy expression now replaced with one of apprehension.

"Trust me?" I asked, and without hesitation, she nodded her reply.

CHAPTER ELEVEN

Sarah

"What's going on?" I asked him.

"Simon Masterson's about to join us. MI5 put in a request for him to escort you to the function. My job depends on protecting my identity, so they don't want me to be photographed."

"I understand that, but why not just let me go alone? Why make someone I've never been seen with before be my date?"

"I guess they think you being seen with someone else takes the focus off me. Believe me, I'm not any happier about this than you are," he replied.

I looked down at our hands and tried to focus. I'd been so caught up in the chemistry between us, I hadn't stopped to think about what it would be like without Tom by my side.

"Hey, I'm still going to be there you know. Guarding over you and making sure you're safe. Only now I get to focus all my attention on you tonight rather than making you laugh with my pathetic attempts at small talk," he teased. Tom wasn't the sort of man to tease. Minutes ago, I could practically feel the violence vibrating from him in waves. He was putting on a front, and he was doing it for me. Tonight was all part of the job, and whether we stood side by side or a few steps behind the other, we were in this together.

"You're right," I agreed. "Let's get this done and out of the way. But first I need to do something. Can I please speak to Will?"

He looked at me with some amusement, but held out his cuff for me to talk into.

"Will, can you hear me?" I asked, feeling a little foolish at talking to a hand. Tom nodded at me as Will spoke to him in his earpiece.

"Can you please inform your superior officer that whilst Tom may be part of the British Army, I am not. My cooperation here is completely voluntary. I don't take orders and I don't appreciate having dates or companions scheduled for me without my consent, especially if you're expecting me to smile like an idiot and pose for photographs. If you wouldn't mind passing on the message, I'd be very grateful," I said, before huffing quietly and wishing that Tom's senior officer were actually here so that I could yell at him in person.

Tom smiled at whatever Will said back to him, and if nothing else, I knew I'd taken a little of the wind out of his sails.

"Don't ever change, buttercup," he said to me as the car rolled gently to a stop.

Tom climbed out and moved into the passenger seat. We were still in the same car and already I missed him. Holding the door open, Eli waited patiently for Simon to settle himself in the back. I thought it rude the way he completely ignored them both, but neither of them seemed bothered. In fact, Eli seemed downright amused by Simon's presence.

"How wonderful to see you again," Simon gushed. "And I must say, you look absolutely ravishing."

The weather was far too cold for a simple shawl, so I'd opted for a thick black coat. There wasn't a great deal visible for him to find "ravishing," but I appreciated the compliment.

"Thank you, Simon. That's kind of you to say."

"Not kind at all, I assure you. I mean every word. I must say, I was rather pleased to have the opportunity to be able to spend some time with you socially. I'm afraid that our previous meetings have, out of necessity, been a little serious," he said.

I must have misheard. I was tied up with Russian gangsters who were using me to transport arms to terrorists, and he was dismissing the reason for our association like it was nothing at all.

"I believe this evening is just as serious as our other meetings have been. Being photographed, watched, and recorded everywhere I go is not my idea of fun I'm afraid."

"No, I would imagine not, Sarah. But let's do our best to

forget all that tonight, shall we? A few drinks and a little dancing should help."

I was quite sure my jaw literally dropped open. I had no idea what Tom and Eli were thinking, because I couldn't stop staring at Simon. When Tom told me he'd be joining us, I considered that this could be MI5's response to my going home with Tom. That perhaps this was their way of helping me to stay on point and maintain my cover story, the fiction of the part I was supposed to play. It never occurred to me that Simon might actually consider this to be some warped version of a date.

I was still trying to think of an appropriate way to respond when we pulled up at the beautiful turn-of-the-century hotel that was to be the venue for this event. As Aunt Elizabeth promised, a gaggle of photographers was in attendance, though in deference to the cold, the red carpet and backdrop for photographs had been laid out inside. Eli helped me out of the car, and within seconds, Tom was standing a discrete distance behind me. Walking alongside Simon up the steps to the hotel, I turned back just in time to see Eli drive away.

"He'll be back when we need him," Tom assured me. The glass turnstile was a wonderful window into the majesty of the historic building that had recently been renovated, bringing it back to its former glory.

"Wow," I exclaimed, looking up at the dome ceiling and gilded mouldings.

"Pretty fancy, huh?" Tom replied, sharing my appreciation of the amazing view. It disappointed me to see so many people walking around, and not a single one taking a moment to appreciate the magnificence and grandeur of this amazing sight. I wondered if that might have been my fate if I hadn't walked away from the family money and everything it represented, to make my own way in the world. Would I have become so conditioned to wealth and opulence that I missed the beauty in the everyday?

"Can we get a picture, Miss Tatem?" one of the photographers asked.

"Of course," I said, smiling tightly, hating that I had to put on a show.

"Why don't I take care of your coat and you can make them all fall in love with you," Tom whispered so that only I could hear.

"I've been dreading this part all day. I'm so rubbish at smiling for pictures. Somehow I always look like I'm in pain," I admitted.

"Try picturing Dickless over there posing naked in front of the mirror. That should keep you laughing long enough for them to get their shot," he suggested as he nodded towards our companion. Following his gaze, I watched Simon alternate between checking out the red carpet line and perfecting his hair and tie in his glass reflection. It occurred to me then that his appearance tonight had absolutely nothing to do with me. It was about the parts of me that were completely meaningless. The money. The society connections. The company. Not one of those things defined who I was in any way. As far as I was concerned, they stopped me from being who I was meant to me. It was an anathema to me that anyone would covet them. While he was distracted by his own vanity, I gave Tom a cheeky wink and sauntered to the spot the photographer indicated. Twisting and posing, I let them snap shot after shot of me smiling naturally as I took Tom's advice. After that, I gave a few of them soundbites about how much I relished taking over my father's work and guiding the company towards a bright future. When I was done, Simon's face was practically puce.

"I was hoping to accompany you on the red carpet," he commented. "I know how much you detest being in the limelight, and I wanted to be there for you to lean on."

"Don't worry, Simon. Having you here was actually really helpful," I replied, a glimmer of mischief in my smile as I caught Tom's eye. Somewhat mollified, his face returned to a normal colour, and he offered me his arm as guests began to file into the main function room.

Accepting a glass of champagne from a passing waiter for Dutch courage, I imagined that it was a stronger arm that I was holding on to, one that cared more for me than my money. My circuit around the hall wasn't nearly as painful as I imagined. I conversed with the people I recognised from the funeral first and discovered that they were actually an eclectic group of people. The weight of the chip on my shoulder about

Dad's ethics and the corruption of wealth had me making sweeping generalisations about a crowd of people I assumed were all the same. It was slightly shaming to converse with couples who genuinely wished me well, knowing that I had completely misjudged so many of them under the umbrella of my father's character.

Tom seemed to slip effortlessly into the crowd, but I always felt him close by, his presence giving me the confidence to keep going. By the time we were seated for dinner, I'd even begun to relax slightly—until Simon realised that my dress was backless. He was seated alongside my Aunt Elizabeth at dinner, and spent a great deal of time engaging with her and playing to her vanities in a way that he had tried to do with me. At first I presumed he was trying to redirect her ceaseless ire away from me. Quickly, it became apparent that he was trying to win her over for his own cause. Even then I was unfazed, until his efforts to include me in the conversation seemed to involve him touching my lower back frequently, something that was making me extremely uncomfortable.

After dinner and a few more glasses of vintage champagne, Aunt Elizabeth excused herself to visit the restroom, and Simon took the opportunity to coax and cajole me onto the dance floor. I could smell the alcohol on his breath as he pulled me closer than necessary, but I didn't know how to extricate myself without making a scene. Over his shoulder, I could see Tom in the crowd staring daggers at

Simon. The set of his jaw told me how hard he was working to leash his temper, but when Simon placed his hand low on the small of my back and dipped his finger slightly under the fabric, I'd had enough.

"Mr Masterson, would you please move your hand? I feel very uncomfortable, and this is inappropriate from someone who is essentially a professional colleague." I was quiet but firm in my rebuke, yet he seemed completely unfazed.

"Professional colleagues. I like that," he replied, smiling. "But you know, we could be so much more than that. I appreciate my timing isn't great, but I'm a firm believer in making the most of opportunities where you find them."

The thing of it was, he didn't sound sleazy or aggressive. It was as though he'd woken one morning having had this great dream of all we could be and accomplish together and he couldn't wait to share it with me. In his world, I supposed marriages were often based on great ideas that were planned and executed with military precision. Perhaps in his mind, he saw us as two people from compatible backgrounds who could simply make a successful partnership. There was no doubt that he could conduct himself confidently in social settings, mingling with London's finest as though he was born to it.

His mistake though was in believing I was the woman I portrayed myself to be. Given the choice, the real me would be in worn jeans and a soft cotton shirt, with pencils stuck in my messy bun and not a lick of makeup in sight, while I sat by the fire sketching and singing off-key to some cheesy pop song. He was blind to the dichotomy of how we viewed relationships. To me, anything that truly involved the heart would never be neat and tidy. Love wasn't colour by numbers and always inside the lines. It was crazy and messy and chaotic, but always full of warmth and passion, and like all great art, it didn't matter what worth others attributed to it. What mattered was how it made you feel.

"Mr Masterson—"

"Please call me, Simon," he interjected.

"Simon, I don't want to be thought of as an opportunity. Your proposal seems so business like and logical, but that's not the sort of relationship I want. On paper I would imagine that we'd make a perfect match, but there's just no chemistry between us."

"But there could be. Let me take you on a date where we can get to know each other better. Where you can open yourself up to the idea of us."

"Chemistry is the most amazing, unpredictable, crazy thing. But the one thing I do know is that there's no opening yourself up to it. It's either there or it isn't. But even if regard alone was a substantial enough basis for a relationship, this wouldn't be a good idea. I want my old life back. A life that you wouldn't want to share. After all this is over, I plan on saying goodbye to London permanently."

"You know," he said, smiling, "even when you're letting

me down, you're beautiful. I handled tonight in completely the wrong way. Despite the fact that I've probably made an arse of myself, I really did want to impress you. Perhaps if I were a secret agent I'd know the tricks of the trade. But I'm an analyst. A computer geek really. I thought a drink or two would bolster my confidence, but all I've done is make an absolute hash of things."

"I don't know," I teased, "I think my Aunt Elizabeth was actually quite taken with you."

"Ah, well, at least that's one Tatem I've won over."

"You know, you're a lot more fun to be around when you forget about trying to impress people and actually act like yourself."

"Hang on now. I wouldn't go that far. There are aspects to my personality that I'm planning on concealing until after I'm married, and there's nothing my wife can do about it," he joked.

"Such as?"

"My OCD need to keep every one of my *Star Trek* Blu-rays in alphabetical order, my complete aversion to letting my foods touch on the plate, and my obsession with *The Big Bang Theory*," he admitted.

"You're fine with *The Big Bang Theory*, but yeah, I'd keep the other two to yourself," I agreed.

"It's the alcohol." He sighed. "I had two martinis early on, then champagne at dinner. You missed my bout of hiccups earlier. That was particularly sexy," he said, and I laughed.

"Wow. You really are drunk. Come on, Mr Masterson. I've smiled for a thousand pictures, but my feet hurt and my pyjamas are calling, so if you want a lift home with me, now's your chance."

"Are you propositioning me, Miss Tatem?" He slung his arm around my shoulders as I guided him off the dance floor and instinctively towards Tom.

"That would be an absolute, categorical, resounding no," I replied.

"I'll wear you down, you know," he warned. "I may lack the brawn of your Neanderthal guard dogs, but I make up for it in brain cells. And now I know you're quite partial to my sweet, sensitive side, there'll be no stopping me."

"You're incorrigible, and you were doing so well! But then you resorted to insulting people who would give their lives to protect mine, and that doesn't sit right with me. So, in addition to working on your sensitivity, can I suggest laying off the alcohol and exercising a little quality control by thinking about what you say before you actually say it?"

"Stick with me. I'm a work in progress," he replied, but he didn't look all that contrite.

"Why do you dislike them so much?" I asked him, looking directly at Tom.

"Because, whether they mean to or not, they're going to fuck everything up," he replied ominously.

CHAPTER TWELVE

Sarah

The atmosphere was as frosty as the weather. I still hadn't gotten to the bottom of why Simon disliked the SAS so much, but he seemed to go out of his way to deliberately piss them off. For the most part, Eli just ignored him, acting the part of the dutiful chauffeur and paying him little attention. But Tom was another matter. By the time he held the car door open for me, he looked as though he was one stray hand away from knocking Simon out cold. No doubt it was exactly the reaction Simon was hoping for. It would mean an end to Tom's involvement in this operation, and I guessed there was always the possibility of MI5 taking over completely. So I did the only thing I could think of to ground him. As Simon walked around the car, I climbed in through the door Tom held open and reached for his hand. Stroking my fingers gently from his wrist to the tips of his fingers, the touch was fleeting and lasted barely a second or two. But it was enough.

Enough to ignite the spark from earlier that never really went out.

As soon as he sat in the passenger seat, I felt the intensity between us as though it was a physical, tangible thing. Simon chatted, making polite conversation as we drove, and I hoped I nodded and smiled in all the right places, because the truth was I had no idea what he said. I was oblivious, locked in a world that belonged solely to the both of us. We couldn't touch or speak to one another, but it didn't stop us from communicating. Every now and then, he would give me a heated look that spoke of everything he was going to do to me when we were finally alone. I wasn't skilled enough in the games that some women played to bat my eyelashes and look coy. I met that look with a huge smile that stayed with me for the whole journey. I could tell he was affected by my good mood, as though happiness was infectious. Even when he turned away from me to face the road, his profile still showed the ghost of his smile. From a man who was always so serious, it felt like a monumental achievement. The only one who didn't share my excitement was Simon. As if realising that he wasn't the one responsible for my good mood, he soon abandoned the chatter in favour of sulking.

As the car slid smoothly to a halt, he took one more opportunity to take a jab at Tom. Sliding next to me, he leaned forward to kiss my cheek goodbye.

"God, you smell divine," he murmured, quietly enough

to seem intimate but loud enough to be heard. "Thank you for a wonderful evening, Sarah. I thoroughly enjoyed our dance, and I'll do my very best to ensure that we repeat the experience again soon."

I rolled my eyes at Tom's scowling face, completely bemused by the way he allowed Simon to rattle him, given the truth of the way things were between us. His lips had never touched mine, but I was already his, and we both knew it.

"Goodnight, Simon. I look forward to seeing you at *work*," I replied, emphasising the word work to make my point.

"We'll see!" he said cheerfully, his spirits buoyed by having successfully pissed off Tom. When he climbed out Tom and Eli followed, shutting the doors behind them and effectively blocking me from eavesdropping on their conversation. Eventually, the door opened again and Tom climbed in to sit next to me, immediately reaching for my hand.

"Better?" I asked him as he let out a sigh. Eli was back in the driver's seat, and we glided along once more through the brightly lit London roads.

"If I had five minutes alone time with the dickless wonder, I would be, but this definitely helps. That fucker's got more hands than an octopus." He gently squeezed my hand.

Not wanting my next words to be overheard, I leant my head back to whisper in his ear. "How about if I let you put your hands everywhere that he did, so that yours is the last touch I'll feel?"

In answer, he reached inside the split in my coat to wrap a hand around my hip. I had no idea how Eli felt about us, but if Tom wasn't stressing his reaction, then neither was I. Tom's head tilted towards me like he was going to whisper back to me. Instead, he grasped the lobe of my ear, being careful of my earring, and teased it with his teeth. My quiet groan was instinctive. Grabbing hold of his strong bicep to anchor me, I arched my body involuntarily towards him. Like an instrument, he played me, making me want things here in the car that nice girls shouldn't even be thinking about. When I'd twisted enough that his hand reached the small of my back, I moaned again. The feather-like strokes from Tom's calloused fingers fired arrows of pleasure straight through my body, making me achy for relief that only he could deliver.

Eli coughed discretely, and reason wormed its way between us enough for me to realise that I didn't want an audience to something I wasn't willing to share.

"Please tell me the evening doesn't have to end with you and I in separate bedrooms because the world and his wife are listening to every word we say," I said, knowing full well he couldn't do anything about the reality of our situation, but complaining anyway.

"You know the bathrooms don't have any microphones, and that shower of yours is pretty roomy," he replied, quietly enough for just my ears. "I wouldn't want that for our first night together, but there are still things I can do to take the edge off."

I closed my eyes against the onslaught of images, the most powerful of which had Tom on his knees between my legs, bringing me to the edge of oblivion. So lost was I in the spell of lust, that I barely registered the explosion before the brakes of the car screamed in protest and my head whipped to the side sharply enough to crack against the window. At first there was nothing, just a loud buzz in my ear that was killing my head. But as that sound faded away and my normal hearing returned, I could hear screams and the pounding feet of people running. Something very bad was happening, and we were in the middle of it.

"Sar, are you okay?" Tom asked. He grasped my head firmly between his hands and stared deeply into each eye, obviously looking to see if my pupils were dilated.

"I think so. What's going on?"

"We think there's been some kind of explosion up ahead. There's been a pile up and the car behind slammed us into the car in front. You sure you're okay?"

I swallowed hard as I tried to find my voice. "I'm fine," I croaked, and I was. My whole body hurt like I'd been thrown from a moving bus, but it could have been so much worse. We were all in one piece, and the car was still upright. Unsurprisingly, Tom and Eli reacted instantly. Eli issuing rapid-fire updates to Will through his communication unit, while Tom freed me from my seat belt and carried on checking me over.

"Are we in danger?" I asked. Panic crept into my voice, despite my best intentions to remain calm.

"Baby, we're going to be just fine. I'm going to get us out of here, okay?"

I nodded my head in reply, and he gave me a tight smile as he rubbed his thumb reassuringly across my cheek. Letting me go, he moved over to speak to Eli. They spoke quietly, but I could still hear them.

"We need to move," Tom said.

"I don't have any intel on the ground yet. No word on whether the area is secure," Eli replied.

"I don't care," Tom exclaimed. "I need to get her out now, Brit. She's not looking good, and I'm pretty sure we're leaking fuel. Blue Thunder will be here in under five minutes, so we take our chances."

"Yes, sir," Eli replied. "Emergency extraction needed on Tower Bridge now. Cover vehicle unsafe. ETA for pick up required," he barked at Will before pulling out a handgun from a holster inside his jacket and climbing out of the car.

Tom tried both our doors, but they were stuck. He was so fast and fluid, while I felt like I was swimming through treacle. Lying back, almost across me, he kicked hard at the door, which flew open, flooding the vehicle with the sound of panic and fear. Somewhere in the distance a siren wailed, but there was no time to register where it came from. Dragged from my seat, we ran hard and fast. When we found the cover of the vehicle they were aiming for, I was pushed to the ground and flanked by the guys. With their weapons raised, and on bended knee, they looked like sentries guarding over me. The acrid stench of petrol and burnt rubber filled my lungs and I raised my head slightly to witness the panorama of lights that illuminated this beautiful landmark at night, punctured with ominous and terrifying plumes of black smoke. It was the only evidence I could see of the explosion. The wretched piles of twisted steel that had once been cars bled with the cries of those trapped inside, and injured victims that could, scrambled to find any sort of safety. The look of abject terror on their faces was one that would haunt me forever.

The first wave of frightened bystanders had fled, but unbelievably, I could see at least two people remained, their mobile phones held out in front of them like talismans to ward off impending doom. It took me a moment to process that they were actually documenting the carnage. I could understand if they were immobilised with fear, but taking out a phone and pressing record took rational thought. In a fight-or-flight situation, the conscious decision to do neither baffled me. I guess most choices in this situation were instinctive, and the minute I heard a scream of pain, mine was too. Pumped full of adrenaline, I lifted myself off the road and tried to run towards the sound, before a strong hand pushed me back down.

"They need help!" I screamed.

"If you get shot, you'll be another casualty in the way of

them getting the treatment they need. Now stay down," Tom ordered. There was no affection or any other emotion in his voice. No panic or fear. He was all soldier, and his orders left no room for negotiation. I wanted to argue against him. Promise him that I wouldn't come to any harm if he only let me help, but as my vision started to blur, I was blindsided by a wave of dizziness. Above me the whir of helicopter blades drowned out any other sound, its search light illuminating us all just as everything went black.

———

I woke to a room full of tired, angry-looking hard-arses. Nobody had realised that I was awake, so I took a moment to orientate myself and make sure everything still worked. The whole team was there. Eli, his open mouth emitting a soft snore, napped on a chair, while Will, Tom, and Crash were in a heated discussion, their voices low and almost whispered. Having been in combat situations where stealth and discretion were necessities, I imagined the skill to communicate silently was one they'd perfected. It was clear we were in a hospital room of some sort, but I had absolutely no idea how we got there. Intrigued to hear what they were talking about, I pushed myself to sit higher in the bed, but the jarring movement brought on the mother of all pains to the side of my head.

"Fuck," I muttered, pressing my hand to the gauze pad taped there.

"Take it easy, buttercup," Tom said, rushing to my side.

He was still dressed in that deliciously fitted tux that made him look ridiculously handsome, even if it did look as though it had been through a meat grinder.

"You know, when I thought about you getting me into bed, this wasn't what I had in mind," I said, making him laugh.

"Only you could make jokes about being blown up."

"So it was definitely a bomb then" I asked, completely stunned.

"It went off on the far end of Tower Bridge. We're still trying to get to the bottom of what went down, but we don't think the bridge was the intended target."

"Why not? It's a big landmark."

"Not enough casualties," Will said, matter-of-factly. I was horrified that this was their reasoning, but nobody argued against him.

"This doesn't leave the room," Tom told me, "but MI5 have already started their initial investigation on the scene. The explosives used in the blast are the same ones the terrorist cell responsible for the recent attacks has been using in their firebombs, and it went off at a time of night where traffic was fairly minimal."

"Assuming the bridge was the target, our best guess is that the explosives were being planted, ready to go off at rush hour. There's a passenger ferry that passes under the bridge several times a day. If they followed their usual M.O. and firebombed that while exploding the bridge, it would be a massacre," Will added.

"What went wrong?" I asked.

"The explosives might not have been packed properly, making them unstable, or the trigger could have been dodgy. It could be anything," Eli said. "Because it detonated out in the open though, it only damaged the bridge. It wasn't enough to collapse it."

"How many people died?" I whispered, scared to know the answer as I recalled the haunting sound of the screaming casualty.

"Only the bomber. Nobody else. Not this time," Tom reassured me. "The explosion caused a multi-car pileup, and the woman you heard screaming was trapped in a car. She was airlifted to hospital, and she's fine now. There were multiple casualties, but no fatalities."

I breathed a huge sigh of relief as I leant back against the pillows. For one brief moment in time, we had escaped. We were safe.

"Do you think we were the targets?" I was horrified at the idea that, simply by being on that bridge, we'd put so many people in danger.

"For now, Vasili needs you alive. Besides, it wouldn't be his style to take you out like this. I'm afraid it was just a case of being in the wrong place at the wrong time," Tom reassured me, leaning forward to tuck a strand of my hair behind my ear. I closed my eyes as I savoured the brush of his fingers against my cheek.

"Thank you. For being there. For taking care of me," I whispered.

"You suffered a concussion while I walked away injury free. I don't feel much like being thanked," he replied, making me smile.

"If you'd have been hurt, who would've been there to save me?"

"Buttercup, I have no doubt at all that you'd save yourself, and me most likely."

"You're absolutely right. If the SAS started recruitting women, this would never have happened," I replied, making all the guys chuckle. I tried keeping up with their background chatter, but it was getting difficult to keep my eyes open. Reaching up to finger the lapels of his tux, I mourned the fact that it was ruined.

"You should shower and change, go and get yourself something to eat," I suggested.

"I'm not leaving here without you."

"Come on, boss, you've been up all night," Will reasoned. "Your girl talks more sense than you do. We brought in some clothes for you and Brit. You can grab a quick shower and something to eat on the concourse, and I swear to you, the lads and I will watch over her till you get back." I liked the "your girl" bit, and it was comforting to think that Will, at least, was on board with the idea.

"I'm only going to sleep. You won't miss anything," I added, unable to contain a yawn from escaping.

"Fine. I'll check in with the nurses' station. They won't let you sleep too long with a concussion, so I'll be back before they wake you up." He starred at me like he was trying to memorise my face, and I had no doubt that, if we'd been alone, he would have kissed me.

"One day," I whispered.

"One day," he replied.

Grabbing his stuff from Will, he gave me one last lingering look, before giving a quick nod to Will and leaving us alone.

"I thought he'd never leave," Will said, settling into the battered old chair next to me. Across the room, Crash went back to messing on his phones, pausing only to laugh at Eli, who snorted every now and then between snores.

"Why do you call him Brit?" I asked, curiously. When Tom was speaking to me, he always referred to him as Eli, but when he was chatting with his men, he reverted to using the nickname as well.

"Do you remember what his full name is?" Will asked me.

"Lance Corporal Eli Spears, isn't it? Oh, I get it. But really, you named him after Britney Spears?"

"Very fucking unoriginal, I know. With the number of people who sing that shit to him, even I get sick of the fucking nickname," Will admitted.

"Do you remember that time we were in a bar in Paderborn?" Crash said, looking up from his phone. "This fat bastard thought it would be funny to block him from going to the can so he could serenade him with one her songs, thinking it would embarrass Eli or some shit."

"What did he do?" I asked, feeling bad for the guy after hearing how much grief he got for his name.

"Punched him in the face and knocked out two of his teeth. What did he expect, singing 'Hit me baby one more time'?" Crash replied. "I think he reined it in pretty well, until the guy started rubbing his nipples as he sang. That shit's just wrong."

I tried to imagine Eli knocking some guy out, but I couldn't. He just seemed too laid back to me.

"The stupid bastard had no idea Brit was SAS. When we work with other soldiers, we don't exactly advertise it. He took one look at his size and thought he'd have a bit of fun. He's fucking lucky Brit didn't ram those missing teeth up his arse," Will explained, reading my mind.

"How about you, Crash. How did you get your name?" I asked him.

"Stupid fucker crashed a tank into a tree," Will explained.

"Don't they fire you for that?" I asked, shocked at the thought that he could have been involved in such a tragic accident.

"Nah, you'd be amazed how much it happens," Crash said. "It's not fair that no one lets me drive anymore though. It was at night, and nobody can see shit at night."

"You crashed that tank because you were pissing about. You're lucky they let you drive again at all," Will told him. Crash replied by flipping him the bird with a grin.

"Does Tom have a nickname?" I asked. If he did I wanted to hear the story behind it, but fatigue was weighing heavy on me.

"It's Reaper and how he got it is pretty self-explanatory," Will told me, pulling my blanket up higher. It was an uncharacteristically gentle move from a man that was nothing but steel and bone.

"Get some sleep, little Tatem," he suggested, leaning back in his chair and covering his face with his cap so he could nap as well.

"The boss is going to love that I dropped that bombshell," he muttered, and they were the last words I heard before drifting off into a deep, dreamless sleep.

CHAPTER THIRTEEN

Tom

"Wake up, buttercup. We're home," I whispered. She looked small and fragile, curled up on the seat. Her face was so pale that the ugly bruise around her eye was already starting to show. My gut knotted up inside when I thought of how close she'd come to being seriously hurt. I'd been in too many dangerous situations to count, and while I had a healthy sense of self-preservation, I never looked back after to consider the "what ifs." If my men and I made it back from a mission unharmed, it was on to the next one. If there were any near misses, an immediate debrief uncovered the problem and we fixed it before the next operation. This was different. Never had I been in a combat situation with someone I cared about. As a general rule, I didn't fucking care. About anyone. Perhaps that wasn't true about my unit, but if they were injured, I would still be clear and level-headed enough to get the job done. Outside of that, Nan was possibly the only person on the planet I actually gave a shit about.

Until now.

It was fair to say that I wasn't handling the fact well either. Was I freaked out about the idea of being in a relationship? Fuck no. It was still as true as it ever was that I didn't deserve her, but I couldn't think of a single person who did. Every moment we spent together was a fucking gift, and I'd give my last breath to make sure she was safe. She was mine, and the thought of her with another man, even a better one, had me wanting to tear apart the world with my bare hands. What I wasn't doing so well with was my tendency to be a tad overprotective. After last night, that protective streak was a mile fucking wide. Sarah had been hurt. On my watch. She was two feet away from me, and I couldn't stop it. The fact that there was nothing I could've done about it made absolutely no difference at all. It actually made it worse. Because I was keeping her in danger, when every fibre of my being told me to take her and run. A strange sense of foreboding hovered over us all the time, and no matter how much I planned or prepared or trained, we were headed towards the unknown. And I didn't like it. Not one little bit.

"This isn't home. It's Dad's place," she mumbled sleepily, peeling open one eye. Sliding my arms beneath her back and legs, I hoisted her into the air, then settled her in my arms. "I can walk," she offered. It was a half-hearted protest at best, given how quickly she burrowed into the warmth of my chest. It was the only place I wanted her to be.

Walking through the house with her in my arms made me wonder why she hated it so much. I'd never given much thought to what made a home before. Until I was fifteen, I moved from foster home to foster home before I finally landed at Nan's. My eyes nearly fell out my head when I saw the place. Everything was new and soft and a million miles away from some of the shitholes I'd stayed in. But it never felt like mine. Even with Nan cleaning and filling it with photos and stuff, it was still just a fancy place to rest my head. Like a luxury hotel room in between jobs. It wasn't a huge stretch to see why Nan gifted the place to me. She wanted me to lay down roots. She wanted to anchor me to a place that would always bring me back to her. She had no idea that she was that anchor.

As I laid Sarah down on the bed, a modern art monstrosity with a velvet headboard so big it made the whole fucking room look like a padded cell, it hit me. The reason why my place was a home wasn't anything to do with where it was or how it was decorated. It was the memories I had there. It was Nan kicking my arse to finish my homework at the kitchen table, her teaching me to play poker so I could fleece the kids at school, and it was seeing the look of complete and utter peace on Sarah's face as she lay comfortably in my bed. When I watched her and Nan going toe to toe in my kitchen, Sar cooking up breakfast like she lived there, something in me shifted. I wanted to be there. I wanted to be in the place that gave me all those memories. And I wanted to be there with her.

"You know, I didn't know your dad, but his decorating preferences left a lot to be desired. I hope bad taste doesn't run in the family."

"Of course it does or I wouldn't be attracted to you," she mumbled.

"If we were at my place, I'd be smacking your arse for that," I whispered in her ear. My words were barely audible, knowing that any louder and MI5 and the Russians would both be jacking off to thoughts of her being spanked. In the beginning, it hadn't bothered me, living in a goldfish bowl. Pretty much my entire career had been monitored and recorded. Before that, it was social workers and teachers. Now, things were different. I was possessive, even over her words. The idea of them listening to her, even hearing her breathing while she slept had me wanting to fucking shoot something.

So far I'd shown her the parts of myself I knew she could live with. But if she could see inside my head, if she even glimpsed at the empty, soulless, remorseless killer that watched over her, I would become her nightmare, not her saviour. Everything about my personality type should have her running for the fucking hills. Domineering, controlling, overprotective, suspicious. What made for the perfect warrior, also made for the imperfect man. My job was to change her ideal. I might not make great boyfriend material, but no fucking normal boyfriend would protect her like I could. Besides, anyone else wanting to take a shot at the job, they had to come through me for the interview.

"Promises, promises," she replied, making me smile.

"How are you feeling?" I was still worried over that head wound. I'd had more than a few concussions myself, but none of them had bothered me like this one did.

"Like shit," she replied, "but a good rest today and I'll be right as rain for work tomorrow."

"Sorry, Sar, there's no way you're going back to the office tomorrow. In case you missed it, you were in a car accident yesterday and you're still concust," I told her, stunned that she'd even think about going back. If I had my way, she'd be wrapped in cotton wool for a month. And tied to my bed as well, come to think of it. The look on my face was one that usually had rookie squaddies pissing in their pants, so I hoped it conveyed the fact that there was no room for fucking argument. She gave me that hard, determined look that was pretty fucking adorable, and sat up, gripping my face firmly in her gentle hands.

"I'm alive. But if I'm not back in the office by tomorrow morning, I might not be for much longer."

My blood boiled at her words, but when I breathed through the rage and found the reason, I knew she was right. Her safety wasn't supposed to come before the operation, but it did, and we both knew it.

"You have a choice, you know," I replied. "Despite what

anyone else makes you think, you always have a choice."

"I know." She stroked my cheek gently. "This is me making it."

It was in the nature of us all to shelter and protect what we cared about. So maybe then it was understandable that I wanted to sweep in and take over, order her to follow my command. But these were her decisions to make, and I needed to step back and let her make them. My job wasn't to stop her from jumping, it was to catch her if she fell.

"Look, if you're going back in tomorrow, why don't you rest up for a bit. Maybe watch a few movies and pig-out on some junk food. Take care of yourself today. Tomorrow will come soon enough."

"That sounds perfect." All of a sudden, she looked a little sheepish, like she wanted to ask me something and didn't know how.

"Come on, spit it out," I told her.

"I was wondering if you'd stay with me? You don't have to. I mean, you must have a ton of stuff to do—"

"Sounds good to me," I replied, not even giving her a chance to finish.

She grinned so big, she looked like an excited little kid. It was a strange feeling, knowing that somebody could be that happy just at the thought of spending time with you.

"Well, there's no fucking way I'm sitting through a movie on that instrument of torture your dad called a sofa, so you down for watching them in here?" I asked, nodding my head towards the big-arsed television on the wall across from the bed.

"Works for me," she said, shrugging and then wincing as the movement hurt.

"Right, you find the movie, and I'll order us a pizza. What do you fancy?"

"A medium margarita please," she replied. She was already searching through Netflix, so it took her a moment to realise I was staring.

"What?" she asked, her face a picture of confusion.

"What the fuck, buttercup? Who orders cheese and tomato pizza? You might as well eat the box!"

"I got food poisoning when I was a kid from eating a dodgy chicken pizza, and now I can't get past the whole idea that it'll make me sick if I eat it again. And let me guess, you order the stereotypical meat feast, covered with a sampling of pretty much every animal on the farm." She rolled her eyes at me.

"Jesus, you're not a vegetarian, are you?" I asked in horror.

"We've been together for weeks, and you've watched me eat chicken how many times?"

"What? Vegetarians eat chicken!" I protested.

"In the immortal words of Inigo Montoya, 'I do not think it means what you think it means,'" she replied.

"Who's Inigo Montoya?" I asked.

"Seriously! *The Princess Bride*," she said, like that was

some magical clue that would tell me what the fuck she was talking about. Apparently, my vacant stare clued her in.

"It's a classic cult film from the 80s. I can't believe you haven't seen it! Let's watch it now."

"Yeah, there's no way I'm watching a chick film. Keep searching, Sar."

"Come on, give it a go. I bet you like it. And it's not a total chick flick, I promise. There's adventure and revenge, a fire swamp, and rodents of unusual size," she explained, trying to sell this thing. I wouldn't admit it, but if sitting through a shitty movie was all it took to put that look on her face, I'd sit through them all day.

"If you want it that bad, I'll do you a deal. I'll watch your fairy tale shit if you eat meat on a pizza," I said, offering a compromise I immediately wanted to take back when she started looking a bit green.

"I can't eat chicken. Not on a pizza." Her voice allowed no room for negotiation.

"Okay. Baby steps. How about pulled pork with barbeque sauce?" I offered, figuring that was a girl's pizza. With the amount of time she took to contemplate her answer, her gaze flitting between me and the television, you'd think this was a life-and-death decision.

"Face your fears," I cajoled.

"Fine. It's a deal," she said, eventually. "But if I'm eating that crap, can you order me the melt-in-the-middle chocolate cookies too. My taste buds need to know they're getting a treat after having to eat all your man meat."

I raised an eyebrow, smiling, as she realised what she'd said.

"Yeah, that sounded different in my head," she mumbled, waving circles around her brain, as if to explain its inner workings.

"Don't ever change, buttercup."

———————

Two hours, two pizzas, and four melt-in-the-middle chocolate cookies later, I figured I'd be living in the gym for a month after this to get myself operational ready again. We were both slouched against the pillows in a food coma by the time the movie ended.

"What did you think?" I asked her about the pizza.

"It was all right. Not as vomit-inducing as I feared, but nowhere near as nice as a good margarita."

"Inconceivable!" I replied, quoting the film and knowing I'd make her giggle.

"So? Was it as horrible as you thought it would be?"

"Unlike your awesome pizza, there were a few vomit-inducing moments, but it wasn't the total crock of shit I thought it'd be."

By the look of sheer horror she gave me, you'd think I'd kicked a puppy.

"Cool your heels, I was kidding," I said, before she blew a gasket.

"Very funny," she grumbled. "What do you think? Shall

we watch something else?"

I looked at my watch, finding it was still early.

"How about a TV show?" I suggested, taking in her relaxed, sleepy expression. "I don't think you'd make it through another movie."

"Good idea," she replied, as I carted the takeaway boxes to the kitchen.

"What about this one?" she asked when I returned. "It's about a kid who goes missing in the 1980s. His friends set out to find him and uncover secret government experiments and supernatural forces along the way."

"Are there any princesses or other members of the royal family in it?"

"Doubtful." She snorted.

"Then I'm game."

We were hooked. It turned out that the show wasn't just good, it was fucking compulsive viewing. One episode turned into four, and while I was trained to handle serious sleep deprivation, Sar was out cold. Her little body curled into my warmth until her pillow wasn't doing it for her, and then she half climbed my chest in any effort to get comfortable. My arm had gone dead around half an hour ago, but I didn't care. Watching her sleep brought me peace, but having her in my arms was a special kind of torture. At some point during episode three, she'd thrown a leg over my thigh, and her knee was now pressed firmly against my cock. When she breathed, she moved up and down slightly, rubbing against me. Now I was as hard as a tent peg. But I had willpower like you'd never seen. Willpower, tenacity, and a single-minded determination to play the long game.

Aside from the fact that we were being overheard, I wouldn't have wanted our first time together to be there. There were too many ghosts for Sarah. She needed new memories. Happy ones. And I wanted to be the man to deliver them to her. Flicking off the television with the remote, I reached across for a fleece throw blanket and tucked it in around us both, cocooning us in its warmth. Never had I shared a bed with a woman I wasn't having sex with. In fact, I'd go as far as to say I'd never actually slept with a woman. For me, there was sex and there was sleeping. The fact that both activities occupied the same real estate made no difference as far as I was concerned. For me, it was one or the other but not both together.

Until now.

Because, as I lay in the darkness, the scent of Sarah's perfume filling my lungs and her tiny hand resting over my heart, I knew that there was no other way I'd want to fall asleep again.

CHAPTER FOURTEEN

Sarah

Mark Devaney was completely ordinary in every way. His sandy brown hair was parted to the side and just long enough that it looked like he needed a good trim. He wore plain, oversized, black-framed glasses and carried a battered leather briefcase that would look just as at home on the desk of some antiquated literary professor. His suit was appropriate office wear, but off the peg and ever so slightly dishevelled. New accountants were conspicuous in their neatness. Pressed suits, smartly trimmed hair, and shiny shoes. They strode in and out of the building with a palpable aura of eagerness and ambition. Mark fell into the mid-level category. Those men and women often struggling to balance young families with a demanding career, and with enough experience to know that they were probably years away from the major promotion that would take them into the next income bracket. All in all, he was a man you would say hello to as you walked past, maybe share a word or two with as you were riding the lift, but the minute those doors closed, he would be instantly forgettable.

At five minutes past nine on that Monday morning, he followed Victoria into my office. He strode confidently, as though he knew exactly where he was going but was in no hurry to get there.

"Good morning, Miss Tatem," he said. "Thank you for seeing me today." I looked at Tom in confusion before turning back. For the white-collar puppet of an international criminal, he was exceedingly polite.

"Um, no problem," I replied, unsure of the right way to go about all of this. After all, his boss was rather partial to strangulation when presented with a similar situation.

"Was there something you needed me to sign?" I asked, taking out Dad's marbled green Waterman Patrician fountain pen. It was a beautiful old piece of stationery, probably suited more to Dad's style of writing rather than my own. But I treasured it. Not for its monetary value, but because of its value to me. It had been a Christmas gift from Mum the year she died, and I'd never seen him without it.

Never.

Today I would begin to sign my name. Not once, but over and over again, knowing that each stroke, each brush of ink could send someone to their death. I wasn't a religious person, but I prayed. To God. To the fates. To anybody. I prayed that I'd made the right decision. That my actions would save lives. And I prayed for forgiveness. Because deep down inside, where the voice of conscience and reason that we so often ignore resides, I knew that I lacked the luxury of naivety. Despite the man-hours and the hard work of every government employee who would be scouring these manifests, somebody would slip the net. Maybe it would be a child, shot with a weapon my company had shipped, or a woman trafficked to a place of slavery. I might never know, but the possibility was real. Whatever my reasons, however I justified my decision and however many lives I saved, it was a stain that would forever mark my soul.

"Of course," he said, shuffling through his briefcase. "All of these amendments will need to be implemented in a very short timeframe. But making them all on one day will arouse too much suspicion. We've decided therefore to spread them over a two-week period. Adverse weather conditions along with various other reasons will go some way towards explaining the changes," he explained, pulling out a number of neatly printed sheets. "You'll need to sign the bottom of each page where I have indicated," he said, handing them over.

I nodded, the lump in my throat making me completely incapable of formulating a reply. Remembering everything we'd practised, I took the first sheet and placed it directly under the lamp, moving my hand slightly to the right as unobtrusively as I could so MI5 could get a clear shot. If anything went wrong, if they didn't get a copy of the sheet, they'd have to go through thousands of manifests and try and compare it to the ones we'd downloaded. If the date on the document in front of me was anything to go by, they'd never do it in time. One of the ships listed was due to depart dock in two days.

"Everything all right?" Mark asked, his voice layered with a hint of suspicion. When Tom laid a gentle hand on my shoulder, I jumped. Only then did I realise how badly I was shaking. Taking a deep breath, I imagined my mum standing next to Tom behind me.

"I'm proud of you, baby girl. You are so strong. Stronger than I'll ever be. Things are going to be pretty dark for a while, but it won't be forever. You can do this, I promise. And when you feel like you can't, I want you to close your eyes and imagine that I'm there with you, because I always will be, you know. Always." They were the last words she'd spoken to me before I'd been ushered away to let her sleep. A slumber she never woke from.

Gripping her pen a little tighter, I believed her. She was there with me, and I was strong enough for this. Strong enough to do what was necessary. With a sure and steady hand, I scanned and signed page after page until it was done.

"Thank you, Miss Tatum," Mark said. "You've been most cooperative. You won't be needed again today, but I'd be grateful if you could ensure that you're here at the same time tomorrow."

"Of course," I replied. He packed the papers into his

case.

"One more thing," he said, pulling a shiny golden box tied with a red ribbon from his briefcase, and setting it down on my desk.

"A gift from Mr Agheenco" he explained, and was gone.

Before Tom could protest, I grabbed the box and ripped off the ribbon, determined to find out what it was and get rid of it as quickly as I could. Out fell a square box filled with handmade, heart shaped chocolates. On top was another note, in the same handwriting as the one that had accompanied the rose.

"What does it say?" Tom asked.

"Just because I'm not there, doesn't mean I can't see you. I see everything. I look forward to our next meeting with great anticipation. Love D."

"Son of a Bitch!" Tom muttered.

Standing on shaky legs, I turned and threw myself into his arms. He held me so tightly, his hand cradling the back of my head, that it felt okay to let go.

"Please, please say I've done the right thing," I said.

"I don't need to. You know you have, or you wouldn't have done it," he replied. "All those weeks ago, you knew you had the power to stop it all, and you used it, regardless of the personal cost to yourself. Don't lose that faith."

I didn't have time to respond before Aunt Elizabeth barged into my office like she owned the place, a harried-looking Victoria following closely on her heels.

"In the office? Really, Sarah, if you insist on fraternising with your little money grabber, at least do it in your own time. The building is fully glazed and anyone at all with a mind to can see you," she said.

I took a deep breath, knowing I'd need it to deal with the next trial of the day. I expected Tom to move away from me now that we had an audience, but he simply sat against the ledge of my desk, turned me around so that my back was to him, and pulled me back into his arms. My aunt rolled her eyes dramatically at us and took a seat.

"What is it I can do for you today?" I asked her sweetly.

She narrowed her eyes and launched a newspaper at me. "I actually came to congratulate you for doing your job. I also came to berate you for trying to play me like a fool."

"You're going to have to explain that one to me," I replied, having absolutely no idea what she was talking about.

"Page seven," she said enigmatically.

I thumbed through the paper until two grainy, smiling photos of myself stared back at me, and I realised what she was talking about. The caption to the story read, "Britain's Athina Onassis Escapes Near Fatal Accident."

"What a crock of shit," I muttered, skimming through the article. "They're directly comparing my life to Athina's. Talking about how we lost our parents and how it seemed like my inheritance was cursed, until I walked away from the accident last night."

It was on the tip of my tongue to ask why they were

referring to this as an accident at all when it was clear that a bomb exploded, but the fact that Tom didn't look at all surprised told me that he was expecting this. It was a conversation that would wait until we were alone.

"Comparing Tatem Shipping to the Onassis Shipping empire is publicity we just can't buy. Company stock has already gone up two points since the paper was released," Aunt Elizabeth said.

"I had nothing to do with this. I answered a few questions from a reporter, but I assumed he was a society photographer. I had no idea that he worked for a national newspaper," I admitted.

"He doesn't. He's a free-lance journalist who saw an opportunity to spin a story that would glamorise your involvement in the company, and he took it. It's what I hoped for when I encouraged you to come into the fold. You did your job as you were supposed to, and Tatum Shipping thrived. Well done," she said.

I assumed that by "encouraged," she meant badgered, cajoled, and emotionally blackmailed me into joining the business. Nevertheless, it was, quite possibly, the highest compliment that she'd ever given me.

"I can't believe they're reporting on the accident already," I mused.

"It was probably the angle that turned it from a society page photograph to a national news story. Rather fortuitous timing if you ask me," she mumbled, and I looked up in horror.

"I can see you're concerned, given that Sarah was hospitalised less than twenty-four hours ago, but don't worry, she's doing much better," Tom added pointedly.

In return, Aunt Elizabeth simply crossed her legs and raised a disapproving eyebrow. "There was hardly a cause for concern. If Sarah had been seriously injured, I assume I'd have been notified by her personal security," Aunt Elizabeth said.

"The penny's dropped I take it?" Tom replied.

"Quite," she replied. "Did it amuse you to concoct an over embellished fantasy to disguise someone who is essentially little more than a security guard? Or did you honestly believe that purporting him to be more than he actually is would make him seem like more of an acceptable catch?" she asked me. Her tone was filled with more than a hint of malice. It fuelled me with indignation far more than the words.

"It didn't amuse me in the slightest to deceive you. Letting people believe Tom was a lawyer explained his appearance far more easily than the truth would have done. It afforded him a mundane, anonymous persona that allows him to do his job. It was never about deceiving you, it was about protecting me. And as far as I'm concerned, whether he's lead council to the most affluent shipping company in the world or a security guard is completely immaterial. I'm glad he's on my side," I informed her. The hand touching my waist squeezed in a gesture of solidarity and support.

"You will drag this family's name through the mud before you're done here. How could you? He's a leech! A sycophant! An uneducated opportunist, no doubt trying to get to the family money through your knickers if he hasn't done already." She was scathing. The hatred and contempt in her voice a palpable thing, as though she really did loathe him for not being privileged and rich.

I took a deep breath before replying. The embarrassment of sharing a bloodline with this woman was acute. "I don't understand where this is coming from. Having Tom with me saved my life last night. Without him, I wouldn't be standing here now. We're not engaged, and he is not after my inheritance. I don't know what more I can do to prove to you that I have this company's best interests at heart."

"You're a fool, Sarah," she said, standing. "I've seen the way he looks at you. Believe what you want about him, but I've known men like him my whole life. He wants your body and your money. Thinking otherwise is simply delusional."

"Look, I can see this is a lost cause. Tom will remain here at my request. He will attend public appearances with me, but I will do my best to avoid drawing attention to him or allow us to be photographed together. In the unlikely event that I'm asked, I will explain that we're work colleagues. I very much doubt that one newspaper article will propel me into the media spotlight, and after two years, I'll be gone in any event."

"A lot of damage can be done in two years, Sarah. Just remember that. And don't lie to me again. I don't like to be made a fool of," she warned menacingly.

"How did you find out who he was?" I asked, as she headed for the door.

"Despite what you obviously thought, I'm not stupid. He's about as far from a lawyer as you can get. His behaviour at the party confirmed it. A private investigator confirmed his military background, so it was a logical jump to assume you'd hire him as security. Though I must say that hiring your own private security does suggest an overinflated sense of self-importance. I mean, we're hardly the Getty's, Sarah," she remarked dismissively and left.

Turning around in Tom's arms, I allowed my forehead to rest on his shoulder in defeat. Instead of wrapping his arms around me like I hoped, he stood.

"Come on. Let's blow this joint," he suggested, grabbing our jackets.

"And go where? Please don't say home, unless you mean your place," I replied, making him chuckle.

"Eager to get back into my bed again, huh?" he said. "Don't worry, you'll be back there by Saturday."

"Not with you," I complained sulkily. After my last visit, I knew if we went back there again together, I wouldn't be able to resist the urge to jump him the minute the door was closed. Even now, the thought of what I wanted to do had me squirming.

"Get your mind out of the gutter," he said, holding out my soft, woollen coat, and as I put my arms through and fastened it around me, his warm, soft lips pressed gently to the back of my neck in the lightest of kisses. My Pavlovian reaction to his touch turned my legs to jelly.

"Like you weren't thinking the same thing," I replied with a shiver.

"I'm always thinking that when it comes to you."

I watched him fasten his buttons and put on his gloves, and I wondered how one man could hold such power over me. I was tired and hurting, and ten minutes ago, I was in despair. One kiss was all it took to make me realise that my heart was his. He didn't steal me away or hide me from the ugly truth of what it was we had to do. He simply made me feel like I was no longer alone. That in the dark, he was there with me.

"So where are we going?" I asked, grabbing hold of the hand he held out for me.

"You'll see," he answered with a cheeky wink.

———

An hour and a half later, I was freezing my arse off in the grounds of Kew Gardens, but I couldn't remember the last time I'd felt more relaxed. We'd collected drive-through coffee on the way, and I'd opted for a hot chocolate that I'd clutched gratefully on our walk, thankful for the warmth against my icy-cold hands. The humidity in the Palm House had been pretty tolerable, but sat on an open bench as we were, I began to feel the cold seeping into my bones. Still, the weather could be Arctic and I wouldn't want to leave.

"Why here?" I asked.

"Can you think of anywhere more peaceful in London?"

"But how did you even know this place existed?"

"Nan brought me here once, not long after the adoption," he explained, and I answered with a ghost of a smile.

"What?" Tom asked as he caught sight of the look on my face.

"I'm just having a hard time picturing it, that's all. I can't imagine that, as a teenager, you were any less of a hard-arse. So how'd Nan manage to get you to come to a place like this?"

"Have you met Nan?" he replied sarcastically. "In the beginning, she knew as much about being a parent as I did about being part of a family. I had a homework assignment to write about a family day trip, so she made a list of the top ten places to visit in London and dragged Reg and me around to every one of them."

"Reg?"

"Reginald Arthur Shaw the second," he replied. "Heir to his father's fortune from inventing some kind of reflective glass on road signs and husband number three."

"Wow. How many times has she been married?"

"Just three. Reg was the last. I only knew him for about a year before he died of a massive heart attack. Nan refused to marry again. After outliving three husbands, she's come to the conclusion that she's a bit of a jinx as far as men are concerned."

"Poor woman. That must be awful to have to lose three men that you've loved," I replied, making him scoff.

"Poor woman my arse. A few years with her and they were probably banging on the pearly gates begging to come in," he joked and laughed as my jaw dropped open in horror.

"You can't say that! That's just awful!"

"Nan tells me frequently that I'm the worst son she's ever had," he replied with a fond smile that told me how close they actually were. Their bizarre banter was just part of their odd relationship.

"And of all the places she took you, this is the one you remembered most?" I asked, looking across the bench from where we were sitting to the old, fairy tale cottage in front of us.

"I grew up in care homes, which were always pretty loud and chaotic. We came first thing in the morning on a spring day when the grounds were full of bluebells. Reg went off to find a coffee, and Nan and I sat where we are now, just listening to the quiet. That trip was the first time I remember experiencing anything close to peace." Him sharing the memory felt like a deeply personal confession.

"Being here has me itching to pick up a pen. I didn't draw or paint for a year after Mum died, and with everything that's happened, I haven't done it since Dad," I told him.

"So, do it now," he suggested, and I smiled at his foolishness.

"With what?"

Reaching into his coat pocket, he pulled out a couple of napkins from the coffee shop and a pen. I craved a proper sketchbook and my watercolours, but the urge to draw overrode the craziness of his suggestion.

"And while I'm sat here, what will you be doing?" I asked.

"What I do best, buttercup. Watching over you," he replied, smiling.

The second my pen touched the paper, I felt the peace that he'd been talking about. In the time that followed, I realised that the meaningful silence between us was more precious to me than all the meaningless words I'd ever wasted on anyone else.

CHAPTER FIFTEEN

Sarah

Throwing my dirty laundry into the hamper, I reached for my blue silk robe while I waited for the shower water to warm. It was a habit left over from living in my old flat, where the water would have to run for at least ten minutes before you could avoid the risk of frostbit. At Dad's place it was hot almost instantly, though I hardly noticed. My mind was elsewhere, focused on thoughts only of Tom. The last few days had been like nothing I'd ever known. Every day was a gauntlet of emotion, from fear, guilt, and self-loathing to affection, lust, and even respect. I authorised manifest change after manifest change, all with no word as to whether MI5 had tracked any of the shipments or traced any of the buyers. All with no hope that success might be in sight. So much of my time over the last few weeks had been spent copying records that I was now hopelessly behind with everything else. Every visit from Mark Devaney was followed by endless hours of work that made little sense to me. The days were filled with despair, but the nights, the nights were filled with hope. Watched constantly as we were, there was little opportunity for intimacy. But I didn't need his hands on me to feel his touch. It was in every glance that lingered and every shallow breath. I felt his kiss long before his lips ever touched mine.

It was Thursday before I knew it. Tom would stay long enough for Mark Devaney's visit tomorrow, and then he and the whole team would be gone. The usual government four by four vehicles with blacked-out windows would transport the guys to a helipad where they'd go to a military base and then onto a training exercise in the North Sea. Tonight would be our last night together before I was officially handed over to Alpha Team B. My only comfort was the fact that I would be spending the days apart in Tom's home. A place worlds apart from Dad's mausoleum.

A warm flush swept across my body as I imagined slipping between his sheets. Lying in his bed, protected in his walls from the outside world. Wiping away the sheen of condensation that covered the mirror, I looked at the face staring back at me. The heat of the bath had curled my dark hair into waves that fell down my back, and the constant biting of my bottom lip while I bathed had left it plump and reddened. The bathroom was the only room in the house not under surveillance, and I dreaded leaving it.

I needed more time. More time to compose myself. To

feign indifference for the microphones like Tom could. To perfect my mask like the one he gave the world. By unspoken agreement, every night since I'd been discharged from hospital had been spent either in Tom's bed or mine. No one would believe me if I admitted that he'd done nothing more than hold me. But something had changed. It was palpable. The feeling of anticipation, almost desperation to act on this attraction. He was leaving tomorrow, my bruises from the accident had faded and as the days went on, we knew the expiration date for our time together was drawing nearer. I wasn't sure I was ready to lose him, or that I ever would be. Sighing deeply, I wrestled to control the fire in my blood, when I heard a gentle, almost inaudible knock.

As I opened it, Tom pushed his way past me and closed the door to press me up against it. I'd barely drawn breath when his lips were on mine. Every minute that had passed from the first time we met had been an interminable seduction that culminated in this kiss. Beneath his huge frame, I felt so small, but not fragile. His touch wasn't delicate. I wasn't made from glass. I was steel. Made from metal every bit as strong as his. Our hands were everywhere. All over each other in frenzied desperation. He turned his head as he ducked towards me, finding that perfect angle. I speared my fingers into his hair, gripping tightly as we eliminated any last vestige of oxygen between us. My hand slid under his T-shirt as his tongue slipped into my mouth.

The skin beneath my fingertips was hot and smooth, but

it was an illusion. Nothing about his body was soft. Scars that mark healed wounds peppered his torso. The seemingly imperfect blemishes doing nothing to detract from the beauty of a body built for combat. They were part of who he was.

My angel of war.

The man who would sacrifice his life to save mine.

I tried to memorise every inch, and suddenly, even the thin cotton between us was too much. Like he could read my thoughts, he reached behind him and pulled it over his head, dropping it carelessly to the floor. As he did, his abdominals contracted, drawing my hungry eyes to the corded muscles that made me ache to touch. I closed my eyes as his scent, a mixture of shaving soap and something uniquely him, filled my lungs and drugged my senses. Strong hands threaded in my hair as he buried his nose in my neck and inhaled deeply. A shudder ran through me as he groaned. The sound reverberated through my body, answered unconsciously with a whimper as his calloused thumb brushed across my beaded nipple. Painfully slowly, his lips traced a path up my neck. I opened my mouth to beg for more when he kissed me. My ability to make a conscious decision evaporated. Every action now was born of thousands of years of instinct.

To mate. To worship. To claim.

I wanted him so badly I could taste it, and my hunger was only matched by his own. It wasn't a gentle, tentative kiss. He devoured me in the best, most delicious way possible. His lips pushed mine to open wider, and I gave him what he wanted. It was his to take. The wet heat of his mouth enveloped me as his tongue led mine.

Craving more, I pressed closer. We were restless, feverish, out of control. I wanted him inside me more than my next breath, and then I wanted him all over again. I knew, with absolute certainty, that once would never be enough. We'd both waited so long, and that waiting meant something.

Time. That interminable void so difficult to endure, now seemed like a gift. It was an abyss filled with friendship, respect, affection, and memories. This was no clumsy fumble in the dark. Without realising, the wait had elevated this beyond anything I'd ever experienced. Calloused fingertips skimmed the hem of my robe as he lifted my thigh to wrap a leg around him. Our breathing escalated as he hit home. His rock-hard cock hit exactly the right spot, and my back arched, bringing us closer still. His pelvis rocked, leaving me powerless to do anything other than grip the counter behind me and ride out the storm. His kisses slowed, and I let go to grasp at his bicep, silently begging him not to stop.

"You are so fucking beautiful," he whispered, almost reverently as he stared deep into my eyes. Nobody had ever made me feel this special. This cherished. This loved. His hips ground against mine, and I was so caught up in this tide of ecstasy, I barely registered that he'd loosened the knot of my robe until the silk slid over my shoulders. His strong, tanned hands coiled around my waist, and I was airborne, lifted onto the marble counter as though I weighed nothing at all. The room echoed with the sounds of our kisses, our tongues colliding wildly as we gasped for air. The desire to breathe second only to the need to finish what we'd started.

I cried out as he rubbed his thumb gently across my nipple, then cupped my breast, lifting it to worship with his mouth. The pleasure was acute. Even more so when he repeated the action with the other one. I was a slave to his touch. My body his to control. His hands slid to the tops of my thighs, and they opened wider in answer to his silent command. When he dropped to his knees, I was lost. His tongue slid against me, and I was on fire, burning in the most exquisitely torturous way. I gripped the counter so hard that my knuckles turned white. I wanted to scream at him to stop, then beg him not to. It was too powerful, too intense, and the most unbelievably intimate thing that I've ever experienced. I was so close to that sweet oblivion that would end the torture, when his fingers slid inside me, moving seamlessly to the rhythm of his tongue. Throwing my head back, my spine bowed as blinding light flashed across my eyelids. I convulsed as my body exploded with pleasure, my orgasm riding over me in wave after wave.

Reality was cruel and unforgiving, but there was no room for reality in the moments that followed. As I drifted languidly back to earth, his urgent kisses became tender, his touch almost reverent. Lifting me once more, he carried me into the shower and rained hot water down on us, cocooning us in its warmth. We were a million miles away from the troubles that haunted us. Hands that were trained to fight, trained to kill, were nothing but tender as he cared for me in a way that brought tears to my eyes. My giant of a man shampooed and rinsed my hair, in between kissing my shoulders and the back of my neck. When he was done, I smiled before dropping to my knees, wanting to worship him like he'd done for me.

"Fuck," he groaned, as I caressed him with my tongue, drawing out his pleasure as long as I could. Running my hands up his thickly muscled legs, I used his perfect arse to deepen my touch. Like he'd been struck by lightning, tension ran throughout his body, and he came with a horse cry of pleasure. When he lifted me to my feet, he was still hard.

"Again?" I asked, melting into his arms.

"With you? Always. But I'm greedy. I want a bed and enough food to ensure we don't have to leave it for a week," he replied, gently tracing his fingers along my spine and making me shiver.

"One day," I whispered.

"One day," he answered, laying a gentle kiss on my shoulder. We procrastinated for as long as we could, feasting on and caressing one another long after our skin pruned. When we could hold back the world no longer, he turned off the water and wrapped me in an oversized fluffy towel before reaching for one himself.

"I wish you didn't have to leave tomorrow," I admitted.

"Not as much as I do," he replied. "Freezing my arse off

in the North Sea is not my idea of fun. But we need the training, and if I have to leave you, I'd rather do it knowing you'll be safe at my place."

"And this Alpha Team B, are they as good as you guys are?"

"Baby, no one is as good as we are, but they're the only ones I'd trust your safety to. That being said, I don't want you getting too friendly with any of them. They're led by a guy called Hunter Jackson who lives to give me shit. I have no doubt that he'll do his best to charm you just to piss me the fuck off."

"And not because he actually likes me?" I teased.

"You'll have them all on their knees begging within five minutes of meeting you. But I've never had anyone who was mine before. Turns out I'm pretty fucking possessive when it comes to you. The thought of that arsehole making you smile when I'm hanging out of a helicopter off the coast of Scotland is like a kick in the balls in sub-zero temperatures."

"Aah, and they are such nice balls," I replied, nudging him playfully.

"So can I count on you to give him the cold shoulder and tell me every one of his cheesy pickup lines, so I can make him bleed that little bit more when we have combat training together?"

"For you," I replied, sliding my arms around his neck, "I'll be positively arctic."

Apparently, it was the answer he needed to hear.

Smiling triumphantly, he bent his head to kiss me again, and it was a very long time before we left that bathroom.

Droplets of rain blanketed the window as we sped through the lanes to Tom's home.

"We should be arriving in the next fifteen minutes, ma'am," Hunter informed me. Honestly, it looked like it was taking a serious amount of willpower for him not to wink at me. I imagined what Tom's face would look like if he sat here with us, and I had to hold back a grin. As the weather worsened, I couldn't help but wonder what he was having to endure, and my smile faded. The melancholy clung to me the rest of the way to the cottage, and when we arrived, I headed straight for my room. Hunter had informed me that food would be arriving in the hour, but until then, I needed some time alone.

Dropping my bag, I switched on the light and threw myself down on the bed, nearly crushing something in the process. Sitting straight back up, it took me a moment to register what I was looking at. I had no idea how he'd done it, but wrapped in a big yellow ribbon, topped off with an enormous bow, was an A3 artist's sketch book, Windsor & Newton painter's journal, a set of charcoal, and a watercolour block set. The man was my hero. It was a gift that spoke to the heart of who I was. It told me that he paid attention, that he listened and that he knew me better than any man I'd ever met.

Shrugging off my coat, I grabbed the supplies, flicked off the light, and raced back downstairs. For the next hour, I sat by the fire and lost myself in my art. The charcoal flew across the page as I poured my heart onto the paper, stopping only when Hunter thrust a plate of Chinese food in front of me. For the most part, the guys gave me a wide berth, and I suspected one or two threats of violence had been passed on ahead of the handover between the teams. Hunter tried to make conversation a few times, but rolled his eyes at my brief, uncommunicative responses. There came a point where, if he kept me from drawing much longer, I resolved to reply only in grunts. I'd seen the guys do it enough times that I figured it was a perfectly acceptable form of communication in the military. Finally giving up, he left me to it.

By two o'clock in the morning, I had inky black fingers and a beautiful likeness of Tom in charcoal. Too tired to do much else, I trudged upstairs for a quick shower before stinking myself into the decadent bed. Feeling profoundly grateful for such a beautiful gift, I slept soundly, until strained threats of violence and aggression filtered through to my room.

"Young man, I realise that a body like that isn't a gift from God. I imagine you've worked very hard to look like something most women would like to climb. So you can imagine how much regret and remorse I'll be filled with when I'm forced to rip off your nipples and feed them to you, which is exactly what I'll do if you don't move that fine arse and get out of my way!"

As I opened the wardrobe and pulled out a hoodie of Tom's that almost reached my knees, I wondered if the poor soul, who was clearly the object of Nan's ire, realised that she probably meant every word.

CHAPTER SIXTEEN

Sarah

"So, a flush is five cards of the same suit, but a straight flush is five cards of the same suit in any order, right?" I asked, looking to Nan.

"Right. The straight flush is the higher hand, but both are beaten by the royal flush," she replied, tapping her cigarette into the glass ashtray before bringing it back to her lips. I was pretty sure Tom would have a coronary at seeing her smoking in the dining room, but even if it bothered anyone, there wasn't a single person in this house full of trained killers who would have the guts to complain about it.

"And there's an Ace high straight flush, right? All the same suit going in numerical order from Ace to ten?" I said.

"Exactly. Now, am I going to have to go over this shit again or are you actually going to try a hand this time?" she asked.

Outside, the storm continued to rage. The occasional

crack of thunder against the backdrop of the smoke-filled room lent the place an atmosphere that was more than a little intimidating. The dining table had been covered with worn baize that was obviously well used. Around it sat stone-faced men, well-practised in interrogation resistance. Whether they were as clueless as I was at playing poker didn't matter. I was a tiny little mouse at a table full of predators. When it no longer amused them to watch me scurry about, I'd be squashed and eaten.

"Okay," I agreed, taking a deep breath. "I'll give it a go. What are the stakes again?"

"It's a £5 buy in, 50p a blind. There's no re-buy. When your chips are gone, you're out of the game. Red chips are 50p.Blue chips are £5," she replied, shuffling the cards like a professional croupier.

"You know, I'm happy to sit this one out," Hunter volunteered. "I can help you with your hands until you get the hang of it."

"Her hands don't need the sort of help you're offering, so I suggest you keep your arse where it is," Nan replied curtly, giving him a death stare that would've had me crying under the table.

Her admonishment was met with a few chuckles, and Hunter scowled in reply as he picked up the hand she'd dealt. It took me all of an hour to lose my chips. I had half hoped that I'd be allowed to win at least one hand in deference to the fact that I was a beginner, but this was a game without mercy, and the players took no prisoners. The battle played out for over three hours, and in the end, only Nan and Hunter were left. I filled the time keeping everyone fed with snacks and watching over Nan's shoulder as I learnt more about the game than I ever could from a book. Only once did I make the mistake of showing my excitement to the others when she had a good hand, but after she threatened to cut me if I did it again, I perfected my poker face pretty quickly. Once I had a chance to just watch, it became easier to read everyone's tells. Although Hunter was amazingly good, I could tell by the tapping of his little finger he thought he had this game in the bag. Nan, on the other hand, looked as sour faced as ever.

"Call," Hunter said, smugly pushing an inordinately big pile of chips towards us.

Painfully slowly, Nan withdrew her cigarette and blew a perfect ring of smoke towards him. Putting it back in her mouth, she reached for her cards. Each finger bore either a solid gold or jewel-encrusted ring, and she wore them like badges of honour. I imagined them as medals from a lifetime of poker victories. She turned over her cards, her unflinching stare never leaving Hunter's. A slow whistle pierced the silence, and his self-satisfied grin fell.

"Royal flush," Nan said.

"Fuck," was Hunter's reply.

She scooped up the chips and, with my help, began packing them back into the wooden box they came from. Despondently, the team filed out one by one, until only the three of us were left.

"Had enough, Mr Jackson?" she asked, lighting up another cigarette.

"I'll win it back," he replied confidently. "I'm lucky like that. Your son, however, is not so lucky. If he doesn't end this soon, he's going to throw away his entire career."

"You know, you're right. Thomas isn't lucky. He's good. In fact, I'd go as far as to say he's the best there is. Isn't that why he's in Alpha Team A and you're in Alpha Team B," she replied.

"And how do you know what he does at all? The fact that you know about Alpha Team A and B is a serious breach of security," he pointed out.

"Then it's probably best that you advise your men not to argue about how the teams were allocated or the operational experience of the men in each team within earshot of civilians. Walls have ears, Mr Jackson," she replied. Hunter narrowed his eyes at her, looking seriously irritated. It was clear as day that Nan knew all about Tom and the team, same as I did. But if his men had been talking inappropriately, there was no way Hunter could prove it.

"I'm not stupid, Mrs Harper. I don't need to see Lieutenant Harper and Sarah together to know that there's something going on between them. You don't bring an asset to your family home or move in with them without rumours flying. I have no doubt that his actions go beyond his brief. He's one of the most highly decorated officers of his rank in the unit, but if he's not careful, he's going to throw it all away," he said, and I caught my breath. I wasn't an idiot. I realised that Tom having a relationship with me would be frowned upon, but I had no idea it could destroy his career.

"On the contrary, Lieutenant Jackson, I think you may well be one of the stupidest people I've ever met. You believed my son to be in a relationship with *Miss Tatem*," she said, emphasising the fact that he'd referred to me by my first name, "and yet you've done nothing but flirt with her since you arrived. Do you have any idea what he's capable of? Although I'm sure he, like your superiors, will appreciate you sharing your concerns with his mother of all people, perhaps you'd be better placed saving your advice until you can give it to my son in person."

"Very well," he agreed curtly. "I'm sorry if I offended you, or upset you. It wasn't my intention." I imagined that Nan's response was unexpected, especially when she made reference to his senior officers.

"Good. And for your information, this is my house, not Tom's, and Sarah is here by my invitation and with the consent of Lieutenant Colonel Timothy Davies. Now," she added, and with a curt nod of acknowledgement, he left looking pissed.

"Could being with me really end his career?" I asked, getting straight to the heart of what was bothering me.

"I certainly hope so, darling," she replied.

"Why would you want that? He's married to this job."

"Don't get me wrong, as far as I'm concerned, the army saved his life. But there isn't a day that goes by that I don't wait for a knock at my door."

"A knock at your door?" I repeated in confusion.

"When a soldier is killed in action, the army don't call. They send an officer to tell you in person."

"But, he's the best at what he does. You said it yourself?" I argued.

"Sarah, I like you. I really do. But you really can't afford to be this naive. He's not immortal. He has one of the most dangerous jobs in the world, and he knowingly puts himself in situations that could get him killed on a daily basis. I want him out, and preferably before he's killed, or so institutionalised that he can't function outside the regiment. I'm not stupid enough to think that he'll leave on my advice. He needs some incentive, and as far as I'm concerned, you're it."

"No offense, Nan, but I'm not the one being naive. He's known me barely a few months. Even if he does have feelings for me, he's not going to throw away his career over the possibility of what might be between us." I hated to burst her bubble, but if I couldn't afford to lie to myself, then neither could she.

"Have you ever heard of something called inhibited reactive attachment disorder?" she asked me, and I shook my head. "When I adopted Tom, I was warned by the social worker that he'd been treated for it. What he went through before that is his story to tell, but when he first came here, his behaviour was just...strange. He was quiet and polite, but he didn't react to anything. It was like living with a robot that hadn't been programmed with any emotional responses. Nothing seemed to scare him or make him angry, but he never smiled or laughed at anything either. No matter how hard I or anyone else pushed or pulled, he was an immoveable closed door. After about six months, I was beginning to think that we'd made a mistake. It wasn't that we didn't want him. More like he didn't seem to want or need us."

"So what changed?" I asked, unable to connect the picture of the boy she'd painted with the man I knew.

"My husband went away on business, and while he was gone, I popped down to the corner shop for some cigarettes. It was getting a little late, but it was less than half a mile away, so I didn't think anything of it. On the way home, I was mugged by a couple of teenagers. My pride was hurt more than anything else. As you know, I have a bit of a mouth on me, but it didn't seem to deter the little sods. They knocked me to the ground and stole my purse and cigarettes. I made it back home and called the police. When I told Tom what had happened, he seemed completely unaffected. He asked if I was okay and if I needed anything, and I told him I was fine, so he left. By the time the police arrived, he'd gone after the kids who attacked me."

"What happened?" I prompted, desperate to learn more.

"He took them both on together and hospitalised the pair of them. One with a broken nose, the other with a broken arm. Came home and handed me back my purse and cigarettes, then calmly went off for a shower like nothing had ever happened. Of course, the police arrested him and wanted to charge him with assault, but I knew the parents of the little thugs who'd attacked me. I agreed to drop the charges if they did. The police weren't happy, but without testimony from anyone, there wasn't much they could do. When the police asked him why he'd done it, he simply answered, 'They hurt my family.' You see, it wasn't that he didn't have an emotional response, or that he was incapable of forming any attachment, it was that he lacked the ability to show it. We tried making him see psychologists, but in the end, it was my big mouth that had him answering back and opening up. I kept up the sessions, even when he refused to go anymore. I mean, what did I know about being a mother? I talked to him most of the time like a friend rather than a parent, and I needed to know I wasn't messing him up anymore."

"And what did they say?" I asked.

"They told me I was give him stability. Someone of permanence in his life that he could form an attachment to. As long as he was communicating, they were happy. When he left school, he told me he was joining the army. Didn't ask my opinion or my permission, just told me. It wasn't surprising really. The house is close to a military base, so you'd often see soldiers in the village. And I think in them he saw another family. Something disciplined and dependable that he could rely on and a profession that embraced emotional detachment rather than shunned it."

"If he was so adamant about what he wanted, why are you so convinced anything is different now?"

"I knew the minute I saw you together," she replied, lighting up another cigarette. "You've known him a couple of months. He's possessive, caring, protective. For crying out loud, he even teases you. It took years for me to get even a sarcastic response from him. You may not see it, but I do. Whether the Army or the British Government like it or not, my boy's claimed you, and if anyone messes with you or tries to take you away from him, I have a feeling he's going to do a lot more than break a few bones," she answered with a throaty chuckle.

Any other woman might've been scared away by Nan's words. I was empowered by them. I mourned for his childhood, but I wanted him for who and what he was. For the man he had become. Nan was brash, sarcastic, and in your face, but she was strong. She stood by the damaged boy who became a great man, and if he chose me, if he wanted me, then I would do the same. I would show him the same love and loyalty that Nan had.

"How will I know if I'm enough? If he had me, could he live without the army?" I asked. My only worry was that, despite his wanting me, that the army would make him choose between me and his career. I wanted him to have it all on his terms, but if we stayed together, that choice would be beyond my control.

"You don't have a very high opinion of yourself, do you?" she said, laughing. "Tom knows what his options are. It's his decision to make, and if you ask me, he's made it. Indecision has never been his problem. But I would say this. Be very sure of yours before you walk down this path with him. Hurt my boy, and I will hurt you in ways you will feel for a very long time."

"Holy shit! You're absolutely terrifying!"

"I know," she replied, "it's a gift. Tom might possibly be the only person I know completely immune to my bullshit. Eventually, he'll rub off on you and you'll be immune too. Until that happens, try not to let my big mouth scare you away. Tom chooses you, you're part of this crazy family, and I can be pretty protective of my family."

"I'll do my best," I agreed, smiling. "What did you mean when you said the house was yours? Tom seemed pretty adamant that it's his."

"Oh, so that's how it is. Want to know about his assets before you throw in your chips, do you?" she teased.

"Do you have any idea how much my shares in Tatem Shipping are worth?" I replied, arching my eyebrow as I did.

"No idea. How much?" she asked, making me chuckle. It was so like her to call me on it. There was no such thing as conversational etiquette with Nan. If she wanted to know something, she'd just come out and ask.

"Actually, I have no idea, but you add the value of the shares and properties I inherited from my Dad and brother, both here and abroad, I'm probably worth a couple hundred million," I replied as I concentrated on sorting the chips into the right colours.

After a beat, I realised she hadn't replied. Looking up, I saw her mouth agog, her cigarette hanging precariously from her lower lip.

"Holy shit," she said, eventually.

"Well, don't get too excited. When all's said and done, I don't plan on keeping the majority of it."

"Why the hell not?"

"I can't tell you much, but let's just say the money is tainted. As far as I'm concerned, it's brought my family nothing but pain and misery."

She stared at me through narrowed eyes before stubbing the cigarette out in the ashtray. "Fair enough. I'd advise that you don't leave yourself financially crippled. Anyone who says money doesn't make you happy, probably hasn't had to endure what it feels like not having two pennies to scratch their arse with. But if you want to get rid of the rest for a worthy cause, that's your choice. I think you're crazy, but it's your choice. I sort of enjoy being the richest one in the family anyway."

"Well, now that I have your permission to do what I want with my fortune, cup of tea?" I asked sarcastically.

"Cheeky bitch! Thought you'd never ask!" she replied. As rude and completely offensive as she was, I couldn't wait for the day I got to introduce her to Aunt Elizabeth.

———

Having spent most of the afternoon chatting with Nan, I found myself at the stove.

"Are you staying for dinner?" I asked her.

"With Mr 'Hunt His Way Into Your Knickers' loitering about, I'm staying for the weekend," she said. Hunter leant against the kitchen counter with his arms folded menacingly. He didn't respond to Nan's taunt, but his eyes were shooting her daggers. In return she gave him her death stare back and I chuckled at the both of them for acting like children.

"I'm so sick of takeaway," I chipped in, hunting through the cupboards for real food, finding only some frozen vegetables in the freezer and gravy granules and baked beans in the pantry.

"I brought bread, milk, and a chicken with me, but I've got no idea how to cook it," she said.

"Roast chicken it is then," I said, pulling out everything I'd need. When it was done, I didn't have to call everyone to the table. As soon as the chicken smell started to drift through the house, they all hovered about the kitchen like flies around honey. The minute the meal hit the table, they devoured it like locusts, but before they could escape, Nan had put them to work cleaning the kitchen and doing the dishes.

"Doesn't Tom have a dishwasher?" I asked curiously.

"Of course he does," she replied, "but have you looked at the view?" We both poked our noses around the door to see three of the team stood at the sink. They all wore the black combat trousers that fitted snugly across the arse, and the one washing the dishes had opted to take off his T-shirt rather than risk getting it wet. I sighed appreciatively, though my perverted mind couldn't help but imagine a shirtless Tom drying dishes at the sink.

"I'm getting rid of the dishwasher the minute I get back," I muttered, and Nan snorted with laughter.

When we sat down later, she turned on an action movie, much to the guys' appreciation, and I went back to my sketching. Not being able to communicate with Tom in any way was killing me, but the more time I spent here, the more relaxed I felt. That was until Hunter walked in, stern faced and gripping his mobile phone.

"What's happened?" I whispered, my heart sinking as I waited for his news.

"There's been another attack," he replied gravely. "It's bad."

CHAPTER SEVENTEEN

Vasili

"Send in Alek and Mikhail," I said, pressing the button to end the call. Seconds later they knocked at the door, then entered the room.

"Take her away," I said to Alek, indicating towards the little bitch in the corner. Curled up naked, she barely whimpered when Alek dragged her roughly out of my office, having learned only too well what happened if she cried out. I liked to test out any of the new merchandise that caught my eye.

It was relaxing, seeing if their spirit broke before their bodies. But I was far from relaxed. From the back, the bitch looked remarkably like someone else, but she was no substitute. No matter how brutally I fucked her, she wasn't the little spitfire I really wanted. Venting my frustration out on that pale, little body helped somewhat, but once I was done I no longer wanted her stinking up the place. Everything about her, and all the other cargo, pissed me off. Their fear. Their hopelessness. Even their fucking poverty. They were all reminders of my own pitiful start. A place I'd literally crawled out of to make something of myself.

Looking around the opulence of my office, I reminded myself that I deserved more. A woman of class and breeding. A wildcat with a fiery spirit. I couldn't keep her of course. Plans for her future had already been secured long before I laid eyes on the bitch. But after our first encounter, I knew I'd be renegotiating the arrangement. I wanted her under me. Wanted to feel my hand around her pale, soft throat as I choked her. Wanted to fuck her raw as the life drained from her eyes, only to let her breathe before she passed out. I could do that for hours. Test her limits before I broke her for good. And when she was no longer of any use. When I'd fucked her enough to rid myself of the obsession, I'd throw her back to the wolves. My cock was rock hard just thinking of it.

"I want the transcripts for the bugs on the Tatem woman for the last twenty-four hours," I barked at Mikhail.

"We don't have them," he answered. I narrowed my eyes as I contemplated how to punish whoever had fucked up.

"What do you mean you don't have them?"

"She has not returned home. Our man says that the bodyguard has left her and that she has a new detail."

"Has she replaced him?" I asked.

"It is unlikely. She is with the security team at his home," he explained. I stared at him hard but said nothing. To show any kind of emotion to my men, including anger, was beneath me.

"I want to be informed the minute she leaves," I said, and nodded towards the door, indicating that he was dismissed. He left quietly, and I sat down as I picked up the phoned and dialled.

"Hello?" the voice answered.

"Is everything in place?" I asked.

"Yes. The call's been made."

"Very well. There is one more thing. I'll deal with the handover of the Tatem girl," I said.

"Why? We need to check the buyers are ok with this?"

"I wasn't asking permission; I was telling you what is going to happen. She and I have some unfinished business. After that the buyers can have her. It won't matter what state she's in by the time they're done," I replied. After a brief pause to contemplate my order, the voice at the other end of the line answered.

"Very well. It's your decision." I disconnected the call and threw my phone down on the desk. A man as powerful as I was didn't wait for what he wanted, he fucking took it. I wanted the bodyguard dead and the Tatem girl under me, begging to join him. All I had to do was make it happen.

CHAPTER EIGHTEEN

Tom

The chopper hovered high above the freezing waters, the rotors a blur but for a reflection of the moonlight. The precisely designed blades curved specifically to reduce radar splash and noise. Normally, I lived for moments like that. The adrenaline pumping through my veins, the spray of cold water on my face reminding me of how alive I was, how ready for the moment I'd be given the go sign to repel into the darkness. The stealthy whir from the Black Hawk was so different from the sound of the unmarked Blue Thunder or the growl of the supporting armed Apache Gunship we'd been using for training in recent months. Maybe that's what it was. The unfamiliarity, the departure from the norm that was making my gut twist.

We'd repeated this fucking drill more than ten times since we'd arrived, and I still wasn't happy. It was taking too long for the team to repel and clear the deck. We only had two days to nail this, and I was determined we'd get it right, even if that did make me the most unpopular guy on the bird. Finally, the green light to descend lit. Pulling on the rope to double-check the anchor connection, I was about to give the command to drop rope, when the radios blew up and all hell broke loose.

––––––––––

"Jesus H. Christ, tell me I'm not seeing this," Will said to me. We all gathered round in silence to watch the carnage. High-definition cameras, telescopic lenses, mobile phones. Every convenience of the modern age all combined to bring death to your doorstep. The media, so hungry to be the first to deliver the ground-breaking news with the most graphic footage, rarely stopped to consider whether they should. There were some things once seen, couldn't be unseen. I'd been witness to so much shit in my life, I was desensitised to most of it. But the images of young children, their little bodies limp and lifeless, most blackened with soot and some burned, as they were carried from the wreckage was something that would live with me forever.

"Same fuckers?" Eli asked.

"They haven't claimed responsibility yet, but it's the same M.O.," Crash replied.

The room was silent. There was no bravado. No grandstanding, testosterone-fuel rants about what we were going to do to these fuckers when we caught them. There was only horror and the pain of watching innocence die. A generation of children would never be the same. The ones who died, the ones who survived, and the ones who watched it all live and uncensored around the world were forever altered.

"Any word on why they've called us back if we're not on the ground?" Will asked.

"Davies is in with the brass from the military and MI5. The meeting was called before the attack happened. As far as I can tell, MI5 have some major intel. My best guess after today, is that they'll want to act on it quick. I reckon an operation is in the pipeline," I replied.

After all these years, I'd learned to rely on my gut. Maybe it was an awareness born of discipline and training. Perhaps it was just intuition. Whatever it was, it filled me with a sense of foreboding. Our objective was to end this siege of terror. My priority was keeping Sarah safe. I didn't know when one became more important to me than the other, but that was the way it was. If luck was on my side, I'd never have to choose between them.

The room was filled with both SAS and MI5 teams that made up the task force. As usual, we stuck to one side and they kept to the other. Most talked amongst themselves until Lieutenant Colonel Davies walked in with his staff and addressed everyone.

"Gentlemen, you've all watched today I'm sure, the horrific and senseless act of violence that took place in our capital. We understand that the entrances and exits to the school were barricaded from the outside and firebombs thrown through many of the windows. Although it has become mandatory following recent events for all schools to be fitted with sprinkler systems, this institution is located in a deprived area with funding problems, and the installation hadn't yet been completed. Whether this is the reason it was targeted is uncertain, but there is no doubt that this deliberate and inhumane act was intended to cause maximum possible loss of life. Despite the certain risk to emergency service personnel, I'm told that over thirty of the first on scene firefighters battled courageously to save as many children as possible. Eight of those firefighters were killed by the explosive device that detonated during the rescue, which also collapsed part of the building. In total, more than a hundred people are confirmed dead, mostly children, with many more unaccounted for.

"This represents the most catastrophic terrorist event to have taken place on British soil in the last thirty years. I have no words to describe the sort of people who would choose to target the weak and the vulnerable, but it's clear that when humanity dies, all that's left is evil. Albert Einstein once said that the world will not be destroyed by those who do evil, but by those who watch them without doing anything. Well, gentlemen, we will watch no longer. As of this morning, we believe that we have pinpointed the location and time of the next delivery of firearms and explosives to the terrorist cell responsible for these attacks. In a coordinated night assault,

Alpha Team A will follow the buyers after the exchange and take out the cell, while Alpha Team B will target the Russian delivery agents. We believe that within this cache of weapons will be enough explosives to take out half of London's financial district. The operation, which is to be known as Operation Sceptre, will take place seven days from today. I don't need to tell you that an attack like that would cripple this country's economy and lead to a devastating loss of life.

"After today's events, the prime minister wants to send a clear message to any terrorist operating on British soil. There will be no arrests here. No mercy. The SAS do not take prisoners. Your orders are to wipe out this terrorist cell entirely. We want a quick, clean operation with zero casualties to our personnel. When it's done, the PM will address the nation, and if we are successful, this joint task force between our two departments will become permanent with SAS personnel operating on a rotational basis as per standard protocol. I can't tell you how important this operation is to the security of our nation. Defending this country is our only priority. Do your job well, gentlemen, so that none of us ever have to see the bodies of our burning children again. May God be with you all." With that, he stepped back, and headed towards the briefing room.

"Sir, may I speak with you a moment?" I asked, rushing over to catch him.

"If you must," he said with a deep sigh, "but I have a feeling I know what you're going to say." He gave a nod to his staff team, who stepped away to give us some privacy.

"What's going to happen with Miss Tatem's security?" I asked.

"So as not to arouse any suspicion before the operation takes place, Alpha Team A will continue to offer the young lady our close protection services until Mr Devaney's last visit on Friday. Thereafter, all security will be withdrawn. After all, the Russian gang will have been eliminated and any remaining personnel on the Russian payroll will be rounded up when we seize the cargo of incoming shipments as they hit port," he replied wearily.

"With all due respect, sir, that leaves Miss Tatem completely vulnerable. She's put herself at great risk to give us the intelligence we need to make this operation a success. There's no way we can hit a Russian unit of that size and not expect any retaliation from the families, and the first person they're going to come after for retribution is Sarah," I protested.

"Miss Tatem," he corrected.

"What?" I said, in confusion.

"You said Sarah. Her name, as far as this regiment is concerned, is Miss Tatem. I've warned you before about getting too close to this asset. We're very grateful to her for her patriotism, but the SAS are not a witness protection service, son. If she feels that our withdrawal after the operation leaves her in a vulnerable position, she can apply to MI5 or the Metropolitan Police for close protection services. If that isn't sufficient, I'm sure they'll offer her witness protection. Regardless, that's not for you to worry about. You have five more days of close protection to say your goodbyes and get your head on straight. After that, I want to know that you've severed all connections and that you're back in the game. Tom, you're one of my most experienced and trusted officers, well on the way to promotion if this goes down right. But I need to know I can depend on you. I'd hate to have to replace you, but I will in a heartbeat if I think for one minute that you're compromised," he said. The implication was abundantly clear. Follow orders and stay on the job, oppose him and I'd be packing my bags.

"Yes, sir," I replied, through narrowed eyes and gritted teeth. Seemingly appeased, he smiled and gave me a condescending tap on the arm before skulking back to his staff flunkies. I walked over to the window and sliding my phone out of my pocket, I scrolled through the camera feeds at the house one more time. Rubbing my thumb across the grainy image of Sarah's face and reassuring myself that she was safe. Reluctantly putting it back into my pocket, I folded my arms defensively as I stared out into the distance and considered my options.

"What was that all about?" Will asked, having followed me with the rest of the guys. I looked at them all gravely and wondered how many of them would share my concerns.

"Brass is pulling Sarah's security. We have until Friday with her, then we're back at Hereford for tactical training and operational prep. After that, she's on her own as far as they're concerned," I replied.

"Fuck!" Eli said. Will knew best what Sarah meant to me, but of all the team, Eli had become closest to her.

"The Russians will kill her. Even if we cut the head off the snake, as soon as those shipments start getting seized, they'll know she snitched. After that, it'll be open season on her. It's how they teach people not to fuck with them.

"It's not going to happen," I vowed. "No fucking way am I hanging her out to dry on their nod. If they won't protect her, I will."

"What's the plan?" Crash asked.

"I'm not letting them take me off point. If I'm not involved, I don't know what's happening. Without intel and resources, I can protect her even less. While Sceptre goes down, I guess I'll set her up at my place. Nan will keep an eye on her until we get back, but I don't know where we'll go from there," I replied.

"Listen, you need help keeping her safe while you figure things out, I'm there," Eli offered.

"Same here," said Crash.

"I hate to be the bearing of bad tidings, but I don't think there's going to be an opportunity for that. Davies knows you're attached to this girl. Once this is over, my guess is we're all getting shipped somewhere else for a posting or training, so he can put some distance between you both. He's going to make her even more of a sitting duck than she already is,"

Will added as the voice of reason.

"You're right," Eli agreed. "The press would have a field day with this story, and God knows how they'll spin it. If we pull off this op, the SAS is going to come out of this looking squeaky clean, and Davies isn't going to let anyone mess with that."

"I'm actually surprised he hasn't separated you both already," Will added.

"He's given me a week to break it off with her and get my head on straight, which is bullshit. He just doesn't want to tip his hand to the Russians. If I get her away from here, somewhere remote, I can protect her, but I can't do that here. Even if I could, I've got a couple of years left on my ticket before I can punch out," I replied, referring to the length of time I had on my contract before I could leave the army.

"You'd do that?" Will asked in surprise. "You'd leave the regiment for her?"

"To keep her alive, I'd leave the fucking army," I replied without hesitation. It was easy enough to say the words, but deep inside I knew I meant them. This girl was special. Like no one I'd ever met before. I didn't know if you could ever really pinpoint the exact moment when you knew you'd fallen, and I wasn't the sort of person to over-analyse that sort of stuff. What I did know was that she was mine. Mine to protect. Mine to hold. And nobody, not Lieutenant Colonel Davies, not the British Army, not even the fucking Russian mafia, was going to take her away from me.

"That's fucking huge!" Crash exclaimed, looking shocked.

"When you know, you know," I answered. "Look, leaving you guys wouldn't be my first choice. Truth be told, I'm not entirely sure you boys could last a week without me there saving your arses. But I've found something worth fighting for. And Davies isn't asking her to stay at home while I go off to war. He's asking me to turn my back and run, when the only thing that's right is to stay and fight."

"Well, they can't fire us all, can they?" Eli said resignedly.

"I'm pretty sure that if we fuck this up, they'll fire the whole fucking regiment," Will replied. "But fuck it, Reaper. I'm in anyway. Who needs a pension?"

I didn't have much faith in people. Besides Nan and my brief and fleeting relationship with my step-father before he died, I'd never had much reason to. But time after time, each one of the team had given me their loyalty as easily as they put their life in my hands.

"Thanks, man. That means a lot. But I can't ask you to do this. You guys all have long careers ahead of you. Eli, I know you send money home to help your sister out with her kids," I said.

"All the more reason to do it. If we can't protect our family, what the fuck are we fighting for?" he asked.

"Fuck it," Crash answered. "If it all goes pear-shaped, I might give stripping a go. I've got the body for it, and Nan's always asking me to shake my arse for her."

"Have at it," I replied, without missing a beat. "Two weeks as Nan's bitch boy and you'll be begging to come back."

"Worried she'll marry me and that I'll end up with your inheritance?" he asked jokingly.

"Nah, I'm more concerned that your battered, broken body won't be able to handle it as her sex slave. Ever wondered how the last three husbands died?" I asked, chuckling at the horrified expression on his face.

"What about you, Brit?" Crash asked him.

"I'm pretty sure I've got the better body for stripping, but I'll pass on being Nan's bitch boy thanks. The real money's in the private sector. Four special forces guys with our combined experience would make a fortune in security. It's where half the regiment go before retirement anyway," Eli replied.

"Or I could write a book," Crash suggested, looking pensive as he contemplated his retirement options.

"About what?" Eli asked.

"If Sceptre goes down like it's supposed it, I'll write about that. Throw in a British heiress and a bit of romance. Bound to be a bestseller," he replied.

"You so much as think her name, and me and you will have problems," I told him.

"Relax, Reaper. Jeez, I'll make her a Lexi or something. Write her in as an heiress whose yacht was used by the Russians. I'll save the day and we'll live happily ever after.

Course, I'm you in this bit of fiction," he said, nodding his head to indicate it was me he was talking about.

"You realise that a publisher will want some big words in this masterpiece of yours. You can't just use all the little ones," Eli said.

"And if it's fiction, there's no pictures either," Will added.

"You guys are fucking buzzkills, you know that?" he replied moodily, as though we'd just stripped him of his New York Times bestseller.

"Private security it is then," Eli said happily, as though our future careers had all been settled on. It didn't occur to anyone that we might not make it out of this operation alive. That wasn't how the SAS worked. As far as we were concerned, we were infallible. We were the bogeyman. Ghosts in the night who despatched evil men to hell before we evaporated in the shadows. We didn't fear death. We were death.

"I appreciate the support, and I really hope it doesn't come to that. Let's just see what happens this weekend. If everything goes well, I'll have a sit-down with Davies. Maybe getting another medal or two for our hard work will help loosen the stick up his arse," I said, eliciting a few chuckles.

"Sounds sensible, which is completely unlike you," Will retorted, and I gave him the finger, which was just the moment that Dickless Masterson approached me. He coughed awkwardly to get my attention.

"Might I have a word?" he asked. I nodded towards the guys, and they left us to go and pack up their kit. The sooner I was on my way back to Sarah, the better as far as I was concerned.

"How can I help you, Mr Masterson?" I asked, my tone loitering somewhere between frosty and arctic.

"I'm aware that we don't have the best working relationship, but we both care for the same woman. So for her sake, I think you're going to want to hear what I have to say," he replied cryptically. And for Sarah's sake, I nodded in agreement.

CHAPTER NINETEEN

Sarah

Nan chain-smoked a pack of cigarettes as we all, the SAS squad included, watched in horror at the harrowing scene before us. Finally, when I could take it no more, I disappeared to the bathroom and broke down. As silently as I could, I wept for those poor children and prayed to God that their death wasn't on my hands. The possibility that the explosives could have been transported through Tatem Shipping had bile rising in my throat. I had no right to feel sorry for myself. Tom was right. I'd made my decision, and for the greater good I was living with it.

"Take one more foot closer to that bedroom, and I'll ram my foot right up your arse," I heard Nan shout.

Knowing that my five minutes of self-pity were over, I blew my nose and washed my face.

"What's your problem, Mrs Harper? Sarah's clearly upset. I was just checking to see that she's all right!" Hunter protested.

"I was welling up a bit too. Didn't see you using those grabby hands to make me feel better, did I?" she replied.

"What grabby hands? I'm starting to get a bit pissed off with you suggesting shit. It's your son's grabby hands you want to be worrying about," he said.

After a moment of silence, I heard, "I thought for the sake of your own career we'd agreed to leave my son out of this, and I doubt you swearing at me and making unwanted visits to my bedroom will go down well either," she replied.

"It's not your bedroom I was heading towards; it was Sarah's," he protested.

"It's Miss Tatem to you, and they're all my bedrooms," she answered. "Now why don't you go back downstairs and put the kettle on? There's a good lad. A nice cuppa would do wonders for the both of us, wouldn't it, Sarah?" she shouted the last part to me from the stairs. Coming out of the bathroom, I flattened out my necklace, a nervous habit to compose myself, and pasted on a smile.

"I can do it," I offered.

"No, it's okay, Miss Tatem. I'll get you some tea," Hunter replied.

"Please, call me Sarah. Everyone else does," I offered. I realised this would piss Nan off, but I wasn't going to encourage her. He really hadn't been anything but kind to me.

"Thanks, Sarah," he said, giving Nan a smug smile.

"Oh, sod off," she said to him, making him scowl again.

"You really shouldn't encourage him," she admonished me when he was out of earshot.

"And you should try being a bit nicer. Tom has to work with him when all this is over," I said.

"Tom would be doing more than that if he could see the way he looks at you," she scoffed.

"He doesn't look at me any way. And even if he did, it wouldn't matter. I'm Tom's. Now let's go and have that tea before it gets cold."

"Are you okay now?" she asked. It was the most compassionate thing I'd ever heard her say.

"I'm all right. Just a little tired and overemotional. Nothing a cup of tea and a good night's sleep won't fix."

"Good. Because if I'm left alone with these testosterone-fuelled dick swingers any longer, I might actually maim one of them," she complained, barrelling back down the stairs.

———

Despite the comfort of Tom's soft bed, my sleep was fitful. I finally drifted off around four in the morning, only to be woken again two hours later when a warm, hard body moulded itself around mine.

"How come you're home? I didn't think I'd get to see you until tomorrow?" I asked, knowing immediately who it was.

"They called us back early after what happened in London," he replied, peeling the thin strap of my tank down my shoulder and gently kissing the skin beneath.

"Are the boys with you?" I asked, bending my head to

the side to give him more access.

"Yeah. They're shooting the shit with the B team downstairs. Nan's up too, giving Hunter crap no doubt."

"That poor man. She's been giving him grief all night," I replied, on a sigh.

"Poor man my arse. We might be on the same side, but the two of us don't play well together. He's getting his shit together now. They'll be gone in half an hour."

"We should get up then too, baby. They're all going to know you're in here with me," I said, barely containing a moan as his calloused hand slipped beneath the silk to cup my breast, his thumb lazily strumming my painfully hard nipple.

"Say that again," he growled.

"Baby?" I said. He growled as he kissed his way down my spine. I pressed my legs tightly together, trying to contain the throbbing as my back reactively arched at his touch. His hand disappeared, and I was bereft, until, painfully slowly, he slid my top up my body and over my head, throwing it carelessly on the floor behind him. Strong arms reached for me, anchoring us together, his chest flush with my naked back. Reaching back, I speared my fingers into his hair, clenching frantically as he ground against me. I was out of control. Mindless to the spell he had over my body. I should have been worried about the guys downstairs, but the second he touched me, reason fled. I didn't care, knowing that he was as blinded by desire as I was.

His lips skimmed the shell of my ear before he sucked the lobe between his teeth and bit gently. One hand continued to tease my nipple, while the other slid slowly past the band of my sleep shorts.

"Tom!" I cried out as his finger slid inside me. I was so wet, so ready for him, so desperate to give us both what we wanted.

"Take off your clothes," I pleaded.

"With those fuckers downstairs? No way! When I fuck you for the first time, there isn't going to be a second of it that isn't all mine and mine alone. I'm fucking selfish like that. I want every moan, every breath, every whimper, and when I'm done, I want you screaming so loud, even the angels will hear you," he replied, sliding in a second finger.

"Please?" I begged. "We won't go that far. But I want to touch you too." I felt his hesitation, but I knew I'd won when he pushed himself up on his knees. Although barefoot and shirtless, he still wore his black combat trousers. I was mesmerised at the sight of him, sliding open his belt as he watched me back, his eyes filled with pure, unadulterated hunger. No longer content to be a bystander, I joined him on my knees and ran my fingers down the path of perfect abdominals. His oblique muscles curved under his waistband, but I didn't stop there, letting my touched trail gently along the length of his granite-hard cock and making him shiver.

"You'll be the death of me, woman," he protested, and

with lightning-quick reflexes, he lifted me into his arms. In a heartbeat, my legs were wrapped around his waist. His lips slammed into mine, our tongues duelling as a fierce hunger rushed through me. The pounding, throbbing, almost primitive need to have him inside me was almost painful. When his hard length rocked against that perfect spot, I cried out. His kisses became more urgent, our tongues twisting together as we ignored the need to breathe. Nothing, not even oxygen, could be more vital than this. Lowering me back down, he nestled between my legs and used his free hand to push away the rest of his clothes.

His fingers slipped back inside of me, sliding in and out as my hands memorised every muscle by touch. I climbed ever closer to the impossible abyss when he swirled his tongue around my breast. He blew gently across my nipple before suckling it into his mouth, the pace of his fingers relentless. Deeper and deeper they went, and higher and higher I climbed. His eyes darkened as mine grew wider. My pleasure fuelled him, but I needed more. I needed to know that he was with me as I fell. I reached for his length. Impossibly thick and hard, I couldn't possible fathom how it would fit inside me, but damn. In that moment, I would have given anything to try. Instead, I slid my fingers gently up and down him. Stroking him as reverently as he had me, until we were both as lost as the other. When I exploded, he swallowed my groan into his mouth. I pumped him wildly as I rode the crest of the wave as he thrust against me. Braced above me, his eyes never left mine as he showed me the naked need behind them. The moment was perfection. A slither of time where we could see and touch a part of one another that would be forever hidden from the world. A secret garden of desire, open only to us. His free hand fell urgently to my hip and his body became stone as he joined me in falling into the abyss. I brushed my thumb gently across his tip, making him tremble before he collapsed against me, his body as spent as mine.

Breathlessly, we held onto each other while our racing heartbeats slowed.

"Forget waterboarding," I said eventually. "Do that again, and I'll tell you anything you want to know."

He chuckled, as I escaped to the bathroom to clean up. When I returned, he caught my hand and dragged me back into bed, pulling me close to his chest, his lips nuzzling the curve of my neck. "I want to know if you missed me as much as I missed you," he admitted, his hand sliding lazily along the curve between my hip and my breast.

"No. I missed you more," I replied, feeling his cock behind me growing hard between my legs.

"Not possible," he whispered, as the nuzzling turned to kisses and he began to rock his hips slowly against me.

"Already?" I asked, unable to believe that he was ready so soon. He'd trained relentlessly in sub-zero temperatures and probably hadn't slept for over twenty-four hours, but still he found the energy to leave me breathless.

"Baby, this is all that's kept me going this weekend. All I've thought about. Having you here in my bed, being able to smell your perfume with every breath. I better be an old fucking man before I don't have the energy to appreciate that while I can have it."

"You know you can have it forever. If you want it?" I whispered, then held my breath. It was the first time we'd talked about any kind of future together. For all I knew, this was it for him. The weekend had been eye opening in so many ways. Choosing a future with me could mean the end of his career. He could be risking everything on the promise of what might be. But I wouldn't be the one to end this. I would understand if this moment wasn't enough for him to take that risk, but I wasn't strong enough to be the one to walk away. Not when every part of me knew, with absolutely certainty, that this was it. That there would never be another man who could ever make me feel like this.

"Promise?" He spoke so quietly, I barely heard him. It wasn't the warrior with the world at his feet who was asking. It was the little boy who'd once been alone in the dark.

"If you'll still want me. No inheritance, no legacy. Just me," I said, needing to know that he was getting me, with all the money and privilege stripped away. Just me.

"If you'll still want me," he replied. "No uniform, no career. Just me."

"I do," I whispered back.

"Me too," he replied.

It was funny how two little words could change the course of your life forever. I believed in the sanctity of marriage and the many other ways there were to tie two people together. But none were more important to me than those words spoken aloud, because commitment wasn't a piece of paper. It was a solemn vow to bind your life to that person's and forever keep them in your heart.

I closed my eyes as he leaned forward to brush a kiss against my throat. The memory of my last orgasm echoed through my body. I was trembling even before he reached down, tracing patterns across my stomach in gentle teasing strokes, painfully close to where his touch could end this torture. Twisting around in his arms, I turned to face him. His playful grin broke my heart. He was violent, possessive, intimidating. A trained killer. But for me, and only me, he was everything. Tender, loving, a man who would give his last breath to keep me safe and happy.

He was mine.

And the way he looked at me, like I was some impossible dream he never imagined he could have, it made me whole like nothing else ever could.

"You're in my head, you know that?" he said to me. "All the time, you're in my

head."

I frowned back at him. "That's bad right? When you're on a mission, aren't you supposed to forget everything. Be emotionally detached?" I couldn't be the reason for him to fuck up. The one person to get him killed in the job he was so perfect for.

"It's never bad. It doesn't stop me from doing what needs to be done. Just reminds me that I'm not alone when I'm doing it. That I have you to come back to. Always there. Safe and warm. Waiting for me."

"Always," I promised. There were no words after that. His tongue flicked out to taste me before he pulled my lip between his teeth to nip at it. I was mindless to the craving as his pelvis ground against mine. I wrapped my leg around his and arched my back, every inch of my body ready to be claimed.

Loud voices filtered into the room from below before a door slammed loudly. To Tom, it was like a starter pistol going off.

"We have to stop," I warned him, as he kissed and nipped his way down my body.

"Buttercup, we're not going anywhere until you've come at least once more. This one's for me. So the next time I'm hanging out of a helicopter over the North Sea, freezing my arse off, I remember every second of this. The smell of your skin," he said, kissing my stomach. "The sound of your breath as it hitches when you orgasm," he added, moving down a little further to place a kiss on the inside of my thigh. "The way you taste," he finished, taking me in the most vulnerable way possible. Letting me hide from nothing as he fractured my body into so many pieces, I knew I would never be whole again unless he was with me. Because every single time he took a piece with him.

My eyes fluttered closed, my body completely weightless, like falling asleep in water. He collapsed next to me, his cock still painfully hard against my thigh. I reached out to touch him, and instantly I was airborne, lifted to nestle into his side, my hand captured in his as I rested on his chest.

"I'm going to need that hand back," I said sleepily, determined to tease and taste and undo him as completely as he had undone me.

"No way. I don't trust you not to attack me, and I'm saving myself," he replied, making me laugh aloud. "Fuck, that might just be my favourite sound in the whole world."

"Saving yourself for what?"

"For when I can make you scream," he replied, his hand drifting up and down my thigh like he was afraid I'd disappear if he stopped touching me.

"Oh God! I got so carried away! Do you think they heard us?" I asked, suddenly mortified at the idea that the whole team knew what we were doing.

"Don't worry about it. You're mine, and I'm not hiding that fact."

"I'm not hiding it either, but I'd rather advertise it some other way than by letting your men and Nan know what I sound like when I orgasm."

"Like I'd let that happen," he replied with a chuckle. We were both exhausted, but restless, kissing and whispering together in the early morning light. Knowing, if not acknowledging that the sand in the hourglass of our time together was running out. He asked me question after question, hungry for any scrap of information I would give him. I was the same way. Hoarding knowledge of him in the secret library of my heart. Eventually I got to asking about something I'd been wondering for a while.

"Why do they call you Reaper?" I asked. Given his profession, the answer seemed fairly obvious, but I asked anyway. Never for one minute expecting that it would turn his body to stone.

CHAPTER TWENTY

Sarah

"What's wrong?" I asked. I knew what he did for a living. I knew that he had killed people. I couldn't understand what more there could possibly be to make him hesitate before answering.

"It's just...," he said, hesitating again. "I've never talked about this out loud before. Not since it happened. I can't say I'm ashamed of my past, because I'm not. I just don't want you looking at me differently after you know."

"I know the man you are, Tom. I can't imagine that there's anything you could say that would do that." I rubbed reassuringly over his heart.

He folded one arm beneath his head and stared up at the ceiling. I stayed quiet, watching and waiting as he found the right words.

"Remember I said I was in care before I went to live with Nan?" he asked, and I nodded.

"Nan said you were about fifteen when she and her husband adopted you," I replied. His brow furrowed at the memory.

"I don't remember the first time I was beaten, and I don't remember why. The shrinks Nan used to make me see told me that lots of kids block out the traumatic stuff. I just think that it all blends into one after a while. I never met my real parents, but then I was left in a box outside the public library when I was a few days old, so I can't imagine they were anything worth shouting about.

"The group home wasn't so bad, but when I was six, a social work came to tell me that I was being adopted by Clive and Martha Bowen. There's more money in fostering than adopting, but that isn't why they did it. Clive was firing blanks; you see? It was a source of constant disappointment to his dad that he couldn't give him any grandkids, so he got me. I imagine the fucker was a disappointment to his dad for a lot of reasons actually. Nothing that waste of fucking space did was ever going to be good enough for his cranky old man, so I guess I became the whipping boy. The more his dad complained, the more beatings I took." His tone was so cold, so dispassionate, it was almost like he was telling the story about someone else. Like he was completed unaffected by it.

"He started beating you when you were six? But why didn't the social workers do anything? Why didn't your adoptive mother?" I asked in horror.

"It started off as the odd clip around the ear. You know,

cuffing me with his elbow as he walked by. Things didn't start getting really bad until after the social worker visits ended. Even then I'm not sure I would have said anything. I'd never had parents before. Who's to say shit like that wasn't normal for kids," he replied.

"And his wife? Martha?"

"She was twelve years younger than him. I imagine he seemed like quite a good catch when they met. He had a nice house and a good job, and she was pretty but poor with little family and no real prospects. She was a trophy wife. But when she didn't give him any kids, he started taking out his old man's resentment on her too. She didn't get it as bad as I did. Clive liked showing her off to his friends, and a pretty wife isn't so pretty with a black eye and a split lip. The only one who ever really had any spunk about her was Martha's mother, Sally. I'd never met anyone like her until Nan. She talked to Clive like shit, and he hated her for it. She never wanted Martha to marry him, but there wasn't really much she could do about it. Eventually Clive banned her from visiting when he was home, so she used to stop by for an hour after I left school. She'd bring cookies or chocolate, and she'd sit with me while I did my homework. I'd take a beating every day for an hour with her."

"What happened to her?" I asked, a horrible, knowing feeling settling in the pit of my stomach.

"She'd bought some books from a charity shop she thought I might like to read. I was a big reader when I was a kid, but after that, picking up a book just reminded me of her," he explained. "Anyway, she'd forgotten to give them to me on that Friday, so she figured it would be okay to drop them off over the weekend. Clive usually played golf with his father on Saturday mornings. Only his Dad was pissed that he'd dropped a couple of shots the week before, so he told him that one of his employees was going instead. Clive's presence wasn't required, and he took it pretty bad. When Sally stopped by, Clive was explaining with his belt how I'd fucked up his golf game. She rushed him, and he shoved her, hard. It wouldn't have taken much to knock her down. She was frail and unsteady on her feet. If I'd seen her coming, I'd have stepped in. But when he got like that, I learned to curl in a ball and go somewhere else in my head until it stopped. I'd pretend I was in Narnia or some other place I read about. I was fourteen at the time and already pretty big. I probably could have defended myself, but I just got used to shutting down I guess. By the time I realised what happened, it was too late. She hit her head on the newel post of the staircase and died instantly. I knew she was gone the minute she hit the ground. You can just tell with some people when life has left them," he said flatly.

"What did you do?" I asked, knowing there was more to the story. There was no way Tom would be as tense as he was if it ended there. He took a deep breath, and it was the first time in his whole retelling of the story that he seemed nervous.

"Clive was freaking out. Pacing up and down the hallway, grabbing at his hair and moaning and fucking whining about how his dad was going to kill him. Not giving a shit that he'd ended Sally's life, just worried about his dad's reaction. But not me. I stepped over Sally's body, went to the kitchen, and grabbed a sharp knife from the dish drainer, walked back and stabbed it straight through his heart."

My heart bled for him. This lost little boy who accepted evil until it was done unto others.

"I know you think it was wrong, but I don't regret it. Men like Clive will never change. They're weak and scared, and the only thing that gives them power is fear. He didn't give a shit about the value of life until I took his away. Martha called the police, but she didn't do anything to help him. I watched his life slip away as I sat on the stairs and held Sally's hand, and I didn't do anything to help him either. I don't know why I held her hand. She wouldn't care. The dead don't know any different. I guess in those final moments, I wanted him to know that she had me, while he had no one. He died on the hallway floor in fucking stupid plaid golfing trousers, and the last thing he saw in this world was me.

"I didn't say anything when they questioned me, and eventually they deemed it self-defence. After all, I was the quiet kid who liked to read. No prior history of trouble or violence, and he'd just killed an elderly lady. Martha didn't say anything. Too busy justifying why she was hiding upstairs while I was taking a beating I guess. She sold the house and ran with what was left of Clive's estate. Came to see me once before she left to try and justify what happened. To share her grief over losing the one person that bound us. I didn't care to be honest. She wasn't my mother. She was little more than a stranger, and she had no loyalty to me. I have no idea where she is now. I went back to the group home until I met Nan, but by then I already knew. I had a high tolerance for pain and a talent for killing without remorse. They call me Reaper, because that's what I am. The fucking Grim Reaper." He let out a deep breath that was almost cathartic. He was done. I knew everything and how I reacted to that was in my hands now.

"But that's not how the story ends," I said.

"What do you mean?" He looked down at me in confusion.

"Well, you make it sound as though you're some sort of sociopath. You didn't grow up to be some kind of serial killer, and you don't torture or kill people for fun. There are plenty of professions, like psychologists and police officers, where you have to learn to turn off emotion and judge a situation dispassionately. Having the ability to distance yourself emotionally from something doesn't make you a bad person. It's what you do with that ability that matters. You chose to use those skills in a profession that you felt was morally defensible. You kill people, yes. But evil people who threaten the safety and security of others. You take lives only when you have to and to preserve the freedom of innocents. Isn't that the moral code of every soldier? Nobody loves the warrior until the enemy is at the gate. There are many people who live safe, easy lives. Who will never be touched by evil. You do what you do so that these people can keep sleeping peacefully in their beds at night. And maybe there are people who would judge you, but I'm not one of them."

He didn't reply, but the look he gave me was one that would be burned into my memory for as long as I lived. If he killed for Sally, he would burn down the whole world for me. Because I didn't judge him. Didn't want to change him. I just loved him, for the man he was and for what he stood for.

"I don't deserve you," he told me. "I have more blood on my hands than you'll ever know. I'm not good at the romance stuff or talking about how I feel. Shit, there's going to be times you'll scream at me in frustration because I don't know how to do shit like normal people. But I'm never letting you go, buttercup. And until the day comes when they put me in a box in the ground, I'm yours."

I moved in his arms until I leant on his chest, my chin resting on my fist as I looked him square in the eye.

"Just make sure they don't put you in that box anytime soon, okay? I've been waiting for you a long time, so I deserve at least fifty years with you, right?"

"Yes, ma'am," he replied with a grin, pulling the sheet over our heads as he rolled me under him.

———

By the afternoon, Nan had declared that she'd had

enough of listening to us fornicate and that we were all going shopping. This elicited more than a few grumbles from the guys, but their protests had been half-hearted at best. While Tom and I had made good use of our time, they were restless and antsy. Whether he was supposed to or not, Tom told me about Operation Sceptre. My feelings about it were mixed. On the one hand, I was relieved. Being subject to constant surveillance and having the threat of the Russians hanging over me was wearing, and I was soul sick of being party to it all. I understood that they needed to be sure, but the longer MI5 took, the higher the risk that innocent people would get hurt. On the other hand, I knew that in order have a life with Tom on our terms, a life that was normal and safe, he had to go back into the fray. It was the unknown that scared me most of all. Would he be okay? Would he be able to send word to me when he was safe? When would I see him again once all this was over? They were all questions I didn't have an answer to, but I guess that didn't make me any different to most other military wives and girlfriends. I believed in Tom. He would find his way back to me, or die trying.

As much as I loved his home in Breinton, there weren't exactly a wide range of shops to choose from, which was why, at three o'clock on a Sunday afternoon, we found ourselves drinking coffee on Hereford High Street. I'd opted for a hot chocolate with an extra helping of mini marshmallows, much to Tom's amusement. I could see by the way he watched everything that he was soaking up information like a sponge, always wanting to know what I was reading, what food I enjoyed most. By the predatory look in his eyes every time I brought that sweet, decadent drink to my lips, I knew he was replaying back our time together. When he started brushing his thumb back and forth across his lip, I knew I'd never look at hot chocolate in the same was again.

High Street was an eclectic mix of quaint buildings interspersed with well-known retailers, but the Tudor fronts and quirky buildings gave the place an old-world charm that I'd been missing in London. As I closed my eyes against the low winter sun, I tried to block out all thoughts of going back. If I had my way, I never would.

"Right, you've had a sit-down. We've only an hour before the shops shut, so let's get moving," Nan ordered.

"What's the rush?" Crash asked. "Unless you're off to the pub, in which case I'd be happy to join you." Will coughed in reply and gave him the infamous Dwayne Johnson eyebrow. "I wasn't gonna drink on duty," Crash protested. "But drink or no drink, I'd rather be shooting pool in the pub than shopping."

"Well, you're out of luck, son. My incontinence pads aren't going to buy themselves, but if you're a good boy after we've finished, I'll take you for a bag of peanuts in the pub," she replied, and he rolled his eyes as we all laughed. Standing up, we all got ready to leave when Tom tugged gently on my sleeve.

"Are you okay to go with Nan? I'll catch up with you in a

bit. I just have something I need to pick up first?" he asked.

"Sure," I replied. I stood instinctively on my tiptoes, but dropped back down when something occurred to me. Tugging him towards me by the lapel of his overcoat, which reminded me of the one Daniel Craig wore looking out over a London rooftop in Skyfall, I inhaled the subtle scent of his aftershave before whispering in his ear.

"Is it okay to kiss you goodbye? You know, with people around us?" I asked.

He gave me a half smile, like he was amused by the question, and then turned slightly to grasp the lapels of my coat.

"Not only is it allowed," he replied, grinning, "I'm pretty sure it's mandatory whenever you leave me." With that, he tipped his head and kissed me so thoroughly, my knees nearly buckled. The guys all catcalled, making us smile, and with a last quick peck, he let me go.

"Will?" he asked, looking over towards his friend.

"You go, I've got this," he replied. And with a wink to me, Tom was gone.

"Good Lord," Nan said, threading her arm through mine. "I feel pregnant just watching you two. I think you'd better follow me to the chemist, dear. Wouldn't hurt you to stock up on condoms while I get my pads. A woman as damn fine and exuberant as I'm far too young to be a grandmother."

I was far too used to her shocking one-liners to be horrified or offended. Instead, I embraced the mantra, "If you can't beat them, join them."

"Don't worry, Nan, we're far too busy working out how we want to christen all the rooms in your house to think about children yet," I replied.

"Shameless hussy!" she scolded, as she tried to hide her smile.

We walked together down High Street until a store caught my eye.

"Do you mind if we stop here quickly?" I asked her.

"Lead the way," she replied.

Will pushed open the heavy black door, and we all piled inside. It took me ten minutes to find what I was looking for before grabbing some tape and wrapping paper at the till. I looked over my gift as I stood waiting to pay, not knowing if he'd like it, but absolutely certain that some things should not be forgotten.

CHAPTER TWENTY ONE

Sarah

The drive back to London was surprisingly upbeat. With our relationship pretty much out in the open, we were a lot more tactile in the back of the car than we'd allowed ourselves to be before. That wasn't to say that I spent the journey straddling him and kissing until we were both breathless like I wanted to, but sometimes the smallest of touches were the sweetest seduction. His calloused fingers would trace over mine before he'd turn my palm upwards and repeat the dance. A ribbon of desire unfurled inside me with every stroke. It was like having every sensitive nerve ending linked to his touch by invisible threads.

I twisted and turned restlessly in my seat, clamping my thighs together tightly and trying in vain to control the rush of need rippling through my body. I could tell by his sexy smile that the bastard knew exactly what he was doing. His military training gave him absolute control over everything from his breathing to his heart beat, and he was a master at hiding his reaction. The rock-hard bulge in his suit trousers gave him away though, reassuring me that I wasn't the only one suffering. When he brushed his thumb of his free hand along his plump bottom lip in a way he knew drove me crazy, I shivered and promptly poked my tongue out at him. His laugh was rich and full of happiness, making Eli turn around sharply in his seat. After all, it was a sound none of us heard very often. Lifting our joined hands in his warm grip, he brushed a kiss over the back of my knuckles, his deep brown eyes filled with playful affection.

It was early evening by the time we arrived at Dad's place. Will and the rest of the team disappeared to wherever it was they went when they weren't with us. At some point during the journey, I'd become so fed up with looking out of the black windows, that I scooted over to press up against Tom, resting my head wearily against his shoulder. It was in that position, the comforting scent of his shaving soap and aftershave surrounding me, that I woke to find myself at the one place guaranteed to deflate my euphoria.

"It's like coming back to a prison," I whispered, almost to myself. I should have known he would hear me. He heard everything. Squeezing my hand reassuringly, he pulled me into the house. Wearing a sulk like a petulant kid, I followed him reluctantly inside.

"Do you want anything to eat?" he asked.

"I'm not hungry for a big meal, but I could snack," I

admitted.

"Netflix and pizza?" he suggested, cocking his head to the side, and I knew he was remembering the last time we did that. I smiled affectionately, loving that he knew exactly what I needed to make me feel better.

"Perfect," I replied.

"Why don't you grab a shower and load up that series we watched before. I'll order the pizza and bring it up when it gets here."

"Sounds great." I brushed my fingers across his, wishing desperately that there weren't people listening to every word we said, and headed upstairs. Ten minutes later, the shower was running, and having stripped off my jeans, I stood in front of the mirror removing my makeup, clad only in a sweater and my underwear, when Tom burst in. Closing the door as quickly as he'd opened it, he spun me round to press me up against it and spearing his big hand into my hair as he kissed me senseless. The instant his lips touched mine, I was lost. Hours of secret touches and pent-up desire boiled to the surface, and I groaned as I opened wider, giving him everything he demanded. He slid his hand up my thigh, pulling my leg to wrap around him, and lining his hard length against that one spot that set my body on fire.

A moan escaped me as his tongue tangled with mine, his huge frame making me feel so small and fragile and protected. He rocked slightly so I could feel the full force of his erection, and I grabbed the back of his head in desperation, frantically needing to anchor myself against the tidal wave of longing rushing over us both. Reluctantly breaking our kiss, he leant his forehead against mine and closed his eyes as he slowed his breathing.

"What was that for?" I asked softly, aware of the microphones in the next room. His eyes were still closed as I nipped slightly at that bottom lip that would be the death of me.

"That was for me. Because I can't fall asleep next to you tonight without taking a taste of you with me," he replied. Keeping me in the cage of his arms, we spent the next few minutes sharing gentle kisses and nuzzling one another as steam from the shower filled the room. Cupping my face one last time, he stroked my cheek gently with his thumb when his phone buzzed to announce that someone was at the gate, dragging us back to reality. I moved to let him by, and with one final kiss, he was gone, leaving me, a complete boneless mess alone in the shower, contemplating how it was that I had fallen so absolutely and completely in love with this man.

For the next five days, we fell into a strange sort of routine. Mark Delaney continued to visit, and I diligently scanned each of the manifest changes before signing them. Tom felt that it would arouse too much suspicion with Vasili if I didn't look as if I was playing an active role in the business, and so I continued my usual duties after Mark left, though I found myself caring less and less about the company when I realised that my presence was essentially immaterial. The board made any important decisions and no one member, myself included, had enough of a majority to overrule the rest, and few of those decisions made while I was there were ground-breaking. The company had been running for over two hundred years without me, and my existence there felt almost like a blip on the radar. With not even a door plaque to my name, I could simply pick up my handbag and my mother's pen and walk out, and it would be as though I'd never been there at all. Minute by minute, the idea seemed to become more and more appealing.

Tom, on the other hand, took it all in his stride. He'd found a way to access the images of the scanned manifests though a secure link, given to him by MI5, so he spent his time trawling through the paperwork, determined that not one shipment would be missed, no matter what it contained. I'd decided to give him his gift Friday, but by Wednesday I couldn't wait any longer. When I saw his face as he opened it, I ached for my charcoals. I wanted to encapsulate that moment by my own hand forever. He peeled the paper off in a careful way that spoke of how few presents he received before running his hand reverently across the gold-embossed cover.

"*The Chronicles of Narnia: The Lion, The Witch and the Wardrobe*," he read, swallowing hard as he finished.

"I know it's silly," I replied, beginning to second-guess myself now that it was actually in his hands. "But you said it was your safe place. Something you shared with Sally. No matter what that man did to you both, it would be such a travesty if you allowed him to take away from you something you both loved so much. Sally is a part of you, like Nan and me. And there are some things that should never be forgotten."

"Thank you," he choked, his eyes filled with sincerity and his voice bleeding with emotion.

"You're welcome." I pushed up on my tiptoes to plant a gentle kiss on his lips.

He sat down on the sofa and stared at it for a good five minutes, running his hands over the cover and flicking through the pages. It was a special edition print with gold-edged pages, interspersed with beautiful glossy illustrations that were preserved with tissue paper. A keepsake book to be passed down through the generations.

Eventually, he placed the book down on the edge of the table and went back to work, but his eyes kept wandering back to it. I could feel his inner turmoil as if it were my own. Opening such an innocent, innocuous children's book meant opening the door to a barrage of memories that might come flooding out, some of them good and some of them bad. But if he dealt with those memories, he'd reclaim a love of reading, and books were always a safe harbour in the darkest of storms.

Things didn't seem quite so bleak after that. At the end of each and every day, Tom always arranged for us to do something that would perpetuate the illusion that we were a normal couple, even for a little while. We'd been out for dinner and been to the theatre, but my favourite had been cuddling up together in the back row of the cinema, eating popcorn and laughing with everyone else at some comedy, like we didn't have a care in the world.

And still, he gave me more. When I came out of the shower one night to see him sat in the bedroom window seat, his tie missing, shirt sleeves rolled up to his elbows, and hair mused as he read. I kissed the top of his head affectionately, and he reached back to squeeze my fingers, but he was gone, lost through the invisible portal of magic to that paper world so far away from here. He always came back to me though. With a half-smile belonging to the child who'd found the key to a treasure thought lost forever. As I watched him read, something occurred to me. That there might be no sight sexier than that of a man completely engrossed in a book. While he read, I sketched him, and little by little, pieces of our souls drifted back to us both.

An air of inevitability surrounded us as we prepared for the cocktail party that would be my last social event for Tatem Shipping. Tomorrow Mark Delany's visits would be done and by Saturday he'd be gone. Who knew what would happen to the company after that. But I did know my days as a marionette were over. The event seemed like such a waste of our time together, and I was even more certain that I couldn't face going without him. Even if he couldn't stand by my side, he'd become my rock. The one I depended on to make me strong when all I felt was tired and weak.

"Hello, Sarah," Aunt Elizabeth said, after I posed wearily for society photographs along the short, pretentious red carpet.

"I'm glad to see that you came on behalf of the company, but I dare say you could have made a little more effort. Really! You're supposed to be the glittering heiress, the shining beacon with the media at her feet. That's a little hard to do when you have bags the size of craters underneath your eyes," she said, being as snarky as ever.

"Hello, Aunt Elizabeth. I've missed you this last week."

"You have?"

"No, I really haven't," I replied honestly, making her scowl. "For at least one night, can you remove the stick up your arse and at least act like my next of kin."

I was done.

I'd had it with her snarky retorts and hurtful comments. When I was grief-stricken over the loss of my mother, she'd ripped me apart from the only family I had left and corrupted my father until all trace of the man my mother had loved was gone. Even then, after his death, I would have buried the hatchet for a chance at a real relationship with the only other person left that I knew who bore the Tatem name.

It hadn't mattered what I wanted though. Before me stood a bitter, twisted old spinster who used any situation she could to her own advantage. Asking me to come back was never about getting close to me. It was about power and money and keeping my shares in the family. But even after my epiphany, I wasn't hateful. I felt little more than pity for her. She would never allow herself to experience what I had with Tom and with Nan. Money made her poor; they made me wealthy. Until she could see that, she'd never be happy. What I was looking for from our relationship wasn't there. I'd found it somewhere else. What was left was a hollow, empty connection between two people with nothing in common. I could tell that she wanted to challenge me about the way I'd spoken to her, to scream and rage in my face, but I was stronger than that now. Too strong to take any more shit from anyone who probably knew next to nothing about who I really was.

The look on her face was ugly. It was a torrent of malice and rage so aggressive that I had to take a step back. When a board member from one of our largest client companies approached to say hello, it disappeared, hidden once more behind a perfect mask of civility. The client was deep in conversation when she excused herself to go to the bathroom, and I didn't see her for the rest of the evening. Perhaps I should have mourned the death of our affiliation, but Lord knew I'd mourned enough over the years.

By ten thirty, the evening was far from over, but I'd had my fill of only being able to glance at Tom without speaking to him or drawing attention to us. As far as I was concerned, he should be by my side and not two feet behind me. Add to that my aching feet and uncomfortable dress, and I was ready to ditch it all for a cup of tea in my pyjamas, cuddled up next to the hardest man in the room.

"May I have this dance?" came a voice from behind me.

"Simon!" I replied in shock. "What are you doing here?"

"I actually came to speak with Lieutenant Harper, but I see no reason not to mess with him now that I'm here," he replied cheekily. "May I?" He took my hand and led me towards the small dance floor that was surprisingly well occupied.

"Mess with him how?" I asked suspiciously.

"You'd have to be blind and deaf not to realise that the relationship between you both has far exceeded the boundaries of professionalism," he replied. "Aside from the risk that poses to your lives, and of course Lieutenant Harper's career, I can't help but warn you that you have absolutely atrocious taste in men. As far as I'm concerned, the man is a troglodyte from a bygone era whose usefulness died with the creation of drones. Still, not everyone at Whitehall feels the same way, which is why he still has a job, but I sincerely hope you both know what you're doing."

"Simon, I can safely say with absolute certainty, that neither of us has the first clue what we're doing. But that's the exact reason why you and I would never have worked. When you meet the right person, you jump. Even knowing there's no safety net. You jump anyway," I explained, and he sighed.

"You know, that makes no sense at all. I'm sure he's

drugged you with some kind of pheromones. You seemed like such a sensible woman when we first met," he said, making me laugh.

"I don't know why! I can't think of a single sensible decision I've made since I met you to give you that impression, but as a rule, when it comes to making decisions, I always follow my heart rather than my head."

"The more you talk, the more I do believe I've had rather a narrow escape," he joked, as he waltzed me around the floor.

"Please don't shatter my illusions about a future filled with an alphabetised Blu-ray collection or colour-coded meals," I teased back.

"Ugh, you've been spending too much time in the company of that man. He's made you mean," he complained, making me laugh. "Until the next time, Sarah," he said as the dance finished, and kissed the back of my hand in such an old-fashioned way before leaving me on the dance floor to speak with Tom.

He looked every inch the bodyguard that he was for the night as he watched us both like hawks. Never taking his eyes off me, even when Masterson engaged him in conversation. Whatever it was they were discussing, both looked grave and serious. Eventually, they finished their conversation, and with a quick nod and a wave to me, Simon left. I wouldn't probe Tom about the meeting. I knew there was very little about his job that I'd ever be privy to, but whatever had passed between them, I had a feeling it wasn't good.

———————

Mark Delaney's final visit was anticlimactic at best. After I'd scrawled my signature for the final time, he simply took possession of the papers, popped them into his brief case, and clicked it shut. Pushing his glasses back up his nose with one finger, he took his leave.

"Thank you, Miss Tatem. You've been most amiable. I don't anticipate that I will be returning for several weeks, though of course you'll see me around the office. If circumstances should change, I'm sure Mr Agheenco will be in touch. In the meantime, he has asked me to leave you with this." Placing another gold box down on my desk he left, closing the door behind him with a quiet click. Before I had chance, Tom had ripped off the paper and opened the box. He handed it to me as he read the card. Inside was a beautiful steel and diamond Patek Philippe watch.

"What does the card say?" I asked. He looked pained as though he'd do anything to spare me from knowing. Reluctantly he handed it over. It read 'Tick Tock. Tick Tock. Looking forward to our time together with great anticipation. Love V."

"We're done," Tom reassured me. "He can't get to you anymore and I promise you'll never have to see him again."

"Can we get out of here? I just want to get as far away from this place as possible," I said, throwing myself into Tom's arms. He held me close and rubbed my back reassuringly as he kissed the top of my head.

"Let's go," he answered. As we left, I threw the watch and card into the waste paper basket and took one last look around Dad's office. I'd hoped to find there some sense of attachment for the man that had once been the centre of my universe. But there was nothing. The walls of Tatem Shipping were lined with lies and misery. The only thing to be found there was unhappiness.

"Bye, Dad. Bye, John," I whispered, and picking up my mother's pen, the physical manifestation of the only good thing to connect me to this foreign world of greed and commerce, wealth and power, I left. Ready to dive into the abyss of a better life than the one I was leaving behind.

My weekend bag had already been packed and placed in the boot of the car that Eli had driven us to the office in that morning. After picking us up, he made a quick, scheduled stop to Dad's solicitors so that I could sign some papers, before driving twenty minutes until we reached Tom's black four by four. The windows were tinted for privacy.

"It's like they buy these things for you guys in bulk." I chuckled, having seen most of the guys driving nothing else. He shrugged in that way of his, but I was still smiling. Come what may, it was like a noose had slipped from my neck. I'd been oblivious to just how much it had tightened in my months with the firm, until I was free of it. I was a little upset not to have said a proper goodbye to Victoria, but on the off chance that Vasili turned up before the operation went down,

I couldn't allow her reactions to raise any kind of suspicion. I vowed to get in touch with her though when things were safe, and I'd made arrangements through my solicitor to have a substantial sum of money from Dad's estate gifted to her. It was the very least I could offer for all her years of service and it would ensure that she never had to work again if she didn't want to.

As we piled out of Eli's car, I could see Will and Crash lined up and ready to go. After so many weeks of seeing them all in black, or in Tom and Eli's case dressed in suits, it seemed strange to see them now in civilian clothes.

"I'm going to miss you guys," I admitted, throwing my arms around Eli. Who knew when I'd see them again after this, if at all.

"Don't you be getting all nostalgic. We'll be seeing you again soon. I've lost too much money from Nan to not try and win some of it back," he replied.

"Well, don't you let her talk shit about me when I'm gone," Crash said, pulling me into his arms for a hug. "Fuck knows I could do without her spreading any more rumours about me and venereal diseases."

Finally, I was saying goodbye to Will. "Stay safe?" I whispered, willing him to make me a promise I knew he couldn't keep. "And bring him back alive for me."

"Darlin', he's the one that's going to be bringing us back alive. You haven't seen him in action, but your boy doesn't know how to die. So stop worrying about us and start worrying about how you're going to survive a weekend alone with Nan," he replied, squeezing me in his big arms.

"She'll be a full-on fucking card shark by the time we get back," Crash grumbled.

"Great. Then she can fleece all your arses to pay for my retirement. Now, if you don't mind, can I have my girl back please?" Tom said. He was joking, but I knew the possessive side of him hated seeing me in another man's arms, even if those arms belonged to his best friend.

Will kissed the top of my head, just to piss Tom off, and he promptly answered with his middle finger as he opened the passenger door for me.

"Get some rest tonight, lads, and I want everyone back at base for twelve tomorrow," he said.

"Right you are, boss" Eli replied.

"Pub anyone?" Crash suggested, just as Tom climbed into the driver's side.

"Cheeky fucker," he muttered with an amused look on his face.

They waved goodbye as they picked up their kitbags, and each headed to their own vehicles. But as they pulled away from the curb, I couldn't control the overwhelming sense of foreboding, that something terrible was on the horizon.

CHAPTER TWENTY TWO

Sarah

"Nervous?" he asked, grinning like a little kid.

"About a night alone with you?" I squeaked in reply. "No bodyguards, no surveillance, just you me and that bed. I can't wait!"

We laughed and teased one another the whole drive down, and with nobody to tell me I couldn't, I spent most of the journey staring at that gorgeous face. In SAS mode, he was terrifying. A man that, for all the world, you knew was capable of incredible violence. But like this, relaxed, happy, and unobserved, he was breath-taking. The further away from London we travelled, the more relaxed we became. By the time we arrived, I was giddy with excitement.

The front door shut behind him, and his eyes turned predatory. The instinct to take a step back was overwhelming, but I held my ground. This predator was mine, and I would own him just as thoroughly as he owned me. I registered the surprise in his eyes as I rushed to meet him, crushing my mouth against his. This wasn't a gentle, tentative kiss. It was hungry and possessive and not nearly enough to quell the fire that had been building in us both.

As though I were completely weightless, he lifted me to his hips, my legs automatically wrapping themselves around him. Grabbing a handful of his hair, I tilted back his head, my lips starved for a taste of him. Wrenching his mouth away from mine, he buried his face in the crook of my neck and inhaled deeply as he tried to catch his breath.

"Fuck," he muttered. "If we don't move, I'm going to fuck you right here on the stairs."

"So? Fuck me on the stairs."

He groaned at my easy acceptance and slammed his mouth into mine, our tongues duelling as he tightened his hold and lowered us both down onto the steps. His pelvis nestled in between my legs and rocked hard against that sweet spot that had me climbing him with need. A deep groan rumbled through his chest as the craving raged out of control. Hands fumbled clumsily as we fought to strip off our clothes. I only managed to shed my coat and sweater before he lost control. Ripping down the strap of my tank to expose my breast, he allowed himself a moment to feast on the sight of my rose-coloured nipple, beading as it caressed the cool air before his rough hands lifted it to his mouth. His tongue swirled around teasingly before he suckled hard and darts of pleasure shot straight through me.

"Tom!" I cried out, arching my back to deepen his touch. I was drugged with pleasure, mindless to anything but the instrument of my body and the way he was playing it. There was no way to describe what he did to me. There was no awkwardness or embarrassment. No searching to discover what gave me pleasure. Everything he did to me wound me impossibly tighter until I was completely powerless to do anything other than let go and allow my body to explode. There wasn't a breath of air between us as he held me while I rode out the waves of my orgasm.

"We need to go upstairs," he muttered. "Now."

"Why?" The hunger to taste him clawed at me once more.

"Because I'm about thirty seconds from blowing my load in my jeans like some fucking teenager. The next time you come like that, I want to be inside you, and our first time together is not going to be on a fucking staircase."

"How about the second time?"

"Baby, by the time I've finished, we'll have christened every room in this house, including the stairs."

Standing up, he threw me over his shoulder, and I squealed with laughter as he slapped my rear. Reaching down, I decided to make the most of having his arse at my fingertips. Years of rigorous training and exercise had left it rock solid. Impossibly toned, tanned muscle tapered enticingly into the back of his jeans. Lifting the edge of his T-shirt, I allowed myself to thoroughly explore until he shivered.

"Having fun down there?" he asked, his voice coloured with amusement.

"Absolutely." I sighed in the self-satisfied tone of a woman who was about to get extremely intimate with the rest of his muscle groups. He chuckled as he lowered me gently to the bed, but the amusement stopped when he reached for the zipper of my skirt. Stripping it off with my tank, he threw them both aside, his stare never breaking mine. And then his eyes were everywhere, feasting in the sight of me, clad only in my underwear. His burst of laughter was unexpected until I remembered what he was looking at.

"Wonder Woman? Really? No lacy black lingerie for my girl then?" he asked affectionately.

"Wonder Woman's the sexiest woman alive, buddy. And screw you for thinking otherwise. Besides, if there was ever a day I needed my bravery pants on, it's today."

"Firstly, I beg to differ. Wonder Woman is not the sexiest woman alive. You are." He hooked his thumbs into my knickers and peeled them down my legs, so incredibly slowly that he literally made me squirm. Reaching behind him, he pulled the back of his white T-shirt over his head before dropping it next to my clothes.

The sun streaming through the windows highlighted his impossibly sculpted torso, and I salivated as my eyes caressed his broad shoulders, rigid abdominals, and deep obliques that slid into the waistband of his low-slung jeans. Undoing my bra, I added it carelessly to the pile until I was laid completely bare before him. Never had I been completely naked before another man, and certainly not in full sunlight. I'd somehow managed to perfect the art of undressing beneath the sheets. But there was no room for self-consciousness. Not between us. Not when he looked down on me like I was the sun and the moon and every fucking Christmas present he ever had or wanted all rolled into one. His thick, inky eyelashes fluttered closed as he braced himself on the bed to lay a kiss on my thighs.

All I could think about was how fucking beautiful he was. I ached to draw him like this, but there were other aches, and as his kisses moved higher up my leg, mine only intensified.

"Secondly," he added, "why do you need brave girl pants?" I'd forgotten what we were taking about, in fact I'd pretty much forgotten how to do anything, including speak. "Buttercup?" he prompted.

"Tom, if you want me to formulate actual sentences, you have to stop doing that," I replied breathlessly.

"What, this?" he asked, feigning innocence as he kissed me again, millimetres away from the promised land. "Come on," he cajoled. "Why do you need them?"

"Because I'm losing you tomorrow. Because you've made me fall in love with you, because you've made me so addicted to your touch that I have to cross my legs every time you enter the room, and tomorrow you'll be gone." I'd thoughtlessly blurted out the truth, so drugged by lust that I hadn't stopped to consider what I was saying until I said it. He froze. His body turning to stone as every muscle seized.

"Do you mean that?" he asked warily.

"Yes, I mean that. I love you," I repeated, gently cupping his face.

"No matter what?"

"No matter what," I vowed.

His eyes fluttered closed, and I waited for that moment. The one where he told me he didn't love me back. That it was all too quick. Too intense. But that moment never came. Doubt began to creep in, but the second he opened his eyes, it disappeared. He curled a hand around my hip and leaned forward to stare deep into my eyes, and that look told me everything I needed to know.

"Nobody's ever said that to me before. Nobody," he told me in his deep, guttural voice. "You have no fucking clue how much I love you, or what I'll do if anyone ever tries to take you away from me. Living mission by mission, it's not enough anymore. I've had a glimpse of what my life is like with you in it, and I want it so fucking badly, I'm fucking starving for it. I want holidays and Christmas trees and all that other shit that normal guys complain about. And I want to see this body," he said, rocking backwards to lay a kiss on my stomach, "swollen with my baby."

"You want kids?" I asked, my heart in my mouth because I yearned for the big family I never had.

"Only with you. Black-haired kids with hazel eyes as pretty as their mother's."

"We'll have Nan teach them how to swear and play poker," I added.

"Can you not mention my mother seconds before I'm about to make you scream my name?" he said, groaning.

"Promises, promises...," I replied, never finishing my sentence because he took my breath away.

Literally.

Burying his head between my legs, he licked deep and slow, and I couldn't stop the shudder that ran through my body as he thrusted and rubbed his tongue in pure, torturous agony.

"Please...," I cried out, clutching at the sheets with a death grip, unsure of what I was crying for.

"So fucking beautiful," he murmured, and the vibrations of his voice sent waves of desire through me. Raising himself up, he undid his jeans and pushed them and his boxers down his thick, strong thighs. Just the sight of him, jutting stiff and proud had me desperate for more. I wanted him in my mouth. I wanted to taste him. To tear his soul from his body as absolutely as he'd done to mine. Like he could sense my thoughts, his hand clasped my leg and he shook his head playfully, his eyes determined and predatory.

"Please, I want to taste you too," I begged.

"Sorry, baby. I won't last five minutes with your mouth around my cock," he replied, and before I could protest, his lips were on mine, teasing and tasting as he drove me crazy. Our fingers threaded together, and he raised our joined hands above my head. Trapping my wrists with one hand, he ran his free one down my side, lifting my leg slightly and widening my hips as he thrust all the way into me, filling me so completely that I screamed out his name.

My orgasm was so close, I was throbbing with pleasure, even before he was inside me. He was tormenting me, making me a slave to the deep, lazy rhythm he set as he withdrew slowly before sliding back. Impaling himself deeper and deeper each time until I forgot where he ended and I began. His eyes were primal and wild as he watched me. I shuddered as he hit that perfect spot every time, winding my body tighter and tighter like a coiled spring about to snap. That was what it felt like. As though I'd snap if he didn't let me go soon. Let me fall in the abyss that my body craved.

But still he held back. Every moan, every tremble, every ounce of my pleasure belonged to him, and he was greedy for it. It drove him higher and higher to see me writhe, to see me so desperate for what only he could provide.

"Harder!" I demanded, and like he'd reached the limit of his own endurance, he slammed himself into me. His mouth swallowed every groan, and my body was liquid against him. I could feel his impossibly hard cock swelling and growing, and I gripped him even tighter, clawing at his bicep for more. I'd experienced him gentle and loving and tender, but that wasn't what I needed from him just then. I wanted raw and animalistic. I wanted him as out of control as I was, and that was exactly what I got.

With a roar, he rammed deeper, pistoning inside me at a relentless pace. I pushed back, meeting him thrust for thrust as he drove us both. Surging back, he watched me come undone. Watched my face as he fucked me fiercely. When his thumb reached down to brush against my clit, I snapped, crying out as I convulsed around him. Milking him mindlessly until he too came, every muscle in his body taut and hard as granite as he spilled himself inside me. Still he didn't stop. He pumped in and out slowly, lazily, as the tremors subsided before collapsing bonelessly against me.

He reached for me as I escaped under his arm, squealing "bathroom," to his chuckles. Minutes later, I emerged and threw myself back into bed, practically bouncing into his arms. We were silent for a moment, as he twisted and rubbed my fingers through his like he liked to do. Sometimes it felt like he was trying to memorise my touch.

"I've got a present for you," he said, out of the blue. His head twisted slightly to gauge my reaction, but I was all smiles. Not for the present that he was going to give me, but for the gift he already had. His hair was dishevelled and longer than his standard military buzz cut. He'd complained recently that he needed it buzzed again, so I ran my hands through the dark strands, determined to make the most of it before it was gone. He closed his eyes at my gentle touch, looking so peaceful and happy that I couldn't help reaching up to drop a little kiss on his lips.

"What was that for?" he asked, looking lovingly at me.

"For my present," I replied, smiling. "I enjoyed it very much. It really is the gift that keeps on giving."

Knowing I was talking about his cock, he rolled his eyes. "You really are a dork," he said, reaching over to his bedside table.

"But you love me anyway?"

"I love you because you're a dork, baby. Because you care more about bringing that elephant thing than you did about makeup. Because you could buy yourself Harry Winston diamonds and instead you only buy shit to make people happy."

I knew he was talking about the book and the Hawkins High AV Club T-shirt I bought him that reminded us both of our latest Netflix obsession. When I saw him wearing it while he read, my ovaries pretty much exploded. I was always careful though only to spend the money from my illustration jobs. The rest of it didn't feel like mine to spend.

"I can't take any credit for that. I think I've had just as much fun from those things as you have."

"And I love you because you could have any man you wanted. And you chose me. So while I can't buy you Harry Winston diamonds, I do want you to have something from me."

Turning to face me, he bent his elbow to rest his head on his fist and placed the long, black, velvet box down on the bed between us. I would love to say that I was gracious and sophisticated enough to have pressed my hand against my chest sighing, "my, how wonderful!" Instead, I peeked into the box and screamed like a little girl, snapping it shut before launching myself on top of him. Inside was the most beautiful necklace I'd ever seen. Hanging from a beautiful white gold chain was an egg-shaped pendant, covered in multi-coloured stones. He laughed as he caught me, and I kissed his face all over.

"You like it then?" he asked, excitedly.

"I love it! It's so beautiful. So unusual," I gushed. "Can you put it on me?"

He took it carefully out of the box, his big thumbs struggling with the tiny, delicate clasp. When he had it, I swept my hair up in my hand and exposed my neck for him to secure it. The weight, that sat just slightly above my breasts, was already warming against my skin. The dazzling stones glittering in the light.

"What are they?" I asked, looking down at the unusual colours.

"Sapphires, tanzanite, aquamarine, and diamonds," he replied.

"This must have cost you a fortune," I scolded. "I've never seen anything like it before."

"It's Elmer, like you," he said, and I looked up into the eyes of this man who understood me so completely. "My beautiful splash of colour in a sea of grey."

I didn't have the words to explain how he looked at me. It was more than just love. It was the look of a man who had been handed life. A life he never expected to live. He looked at me as though he'd spent his entire life seeing only shades of grey, and now, for the first time, he was learning what it meant to live in colour. To look towards the horizon over a sea of endless possibilities and know they were all meant for you.

"I wish I had something to give you that was as precious," I said, making him laugh.

"Baby, you've already given me the world. Although, there is one more thing I want," he admitted, looking unusually nervous.

"Anything," I agreed, knowing absolutely that I meant it.

He reached back to the bedside table and grabbed something, grasping it tightly in his fist. "Hold out your hand," he said, and as I did, a set of keys attached to an Elmer the Elephant keyring fell into it. It took me a moment to realise they were Tom's house keys.

"You want me to water your plants when you go away?" I asked.

He rolled his eyes again and leant forward to press a kiss against my lips. "I know you probably think it's too soon, that we've only known each other for a few months, but when I think of you going back to London, or worse, back to your flat in Yorkshire, my guts twist up inside. I can't always promise

I'll be here. Unless they kick me out, the army will send me all over the world at a moment's notice until I can finish out my contract, but this place isn't home unless you're in it. You're home to me, and I want to know that wherever I am, whatever shithole that I end up in, whatever I'm suffering, I'm coming home to you," he said, arguing his case.

"Okay."

"And I know you want to go back to your normal job, but you can illustrate books from anywhere. I can even convert one of the reception rooms or the conservatory into a studio. And we could sell your flat or rent it out if you want to keep it, because I know how much you love it," he rambled on.

"Okay."

"Plus, you'll have Nan close by, although I'm not sure I should be adding that to the incentives, and this place is huge, so your friends can come down and stay whenever they like. Wait... what?" he said in confusion as he finally registered my answer.

"I said yes. I'll move in. This place already feels more like home than Yorkshire did. I understand that you have to go away, but when you do, the only place I want to be is where I feel closest to you. Although, now you've offered, I'm definitely taking you up on the idea of a studio."

"Buttercup, you can have the whole fucking house," he said. I screamed with laughter as he pulled me under him, tickling me in the process. In that moment, I realised what I'd truly been missing in all the years since Mum died. A home full of laughter and love.

CHAPTER TWENTY THREE

Tom

I was groggy. Struggling to orientate myself and wondering why. Then I realised the answer.

I'd slept.

For as many years back as I could remember, I hadn't been able to nap for more than a few hours at a time without reorientating myself before going back to sleep. Maybe it was a skill, to be able to regularly wake to check the safety of your surroundings. Or perhaps it was the legacy of a shitty childhood. Whatever the fuck it was, last night, in the comfort of my own bed with Sarah in my arms, I'd slept like the dead. It was fair to say that we'd pretty much worn each other out. There was a brief intermission where we gorged on Chinese food, but within hours, any carbs we'd scored from the food had long since been burned off. I made it my mission to christen every room as promised, but by the time we made it to the stairs, I'd pretty much fucked her unconscious. Still, I knew there'd be plenty of time to christen our place all over again when I got back.

Fuck, it felt good to call it our place. Maybe there were guys who ran away from commitment faster than their legs would carry them. It never occurred to me to be bothered by it, because I'd never met a woman I was attracted to before that was any more than a passing fuck. Sarah, though, had my whole fucking world in the palm of her hand. I lived to make her happy. She was crazy and chaotic and colourful, and she lit up the room like a fucking lightbulb. She was a beacon of hope for a guy like me.

I was well aware that I was romanticised in her eyes though. In fact, I encouraged it. If she could see the shit in my head, if she could see what I'd seen or had an inkling of what I was actually capable of, she'd run away screaming. My job now was to protect her, even from my dark side. Divorce rates in the regiment were higher than any other division in the army. Not being able to make plans, or having to cancel them at the drop of a hat, and never being able to say where you were going or how long you'd be gone, took its toll on the strongest relationships. These weren't the only challenges we were up against. It was almost impossible to describe how difficult it was transitioning between life-or-death situations in war zones to civilian life, something that had to become bread and butter to us. PTSD as well had affected so many bloody good soldiers over the years, and there were also those boys who were essentially adrenaline junkies, craving that high in civilian life that you could only get from extreme combat.

To say that the life of a military partner was hard was an understatement of epic fucking proportions. They were mothers and fathers, supporters and friends. The silent ranks with no uniforms or stripes. They weren't saluted or promoted or lauded or praised. They were the quiet strength. The lighthouses in the darkest of storms, guiding their soldiers home.

Despite all that, I knew Sarah had the metal to make it in my world. She'd faced so many hardships and challenges, torrents that would have swept away weaker characters. But she'd planted her feet and raged against the rising flood. Stood up for what was right, even when it would have been easier to let the current carry her away. There wasn't a single part of me that doubted whether she had the strength for this life. But it wasn't a life that I wanted for her, for us both. The SAS was in my blood. I was proud to say that I'd defended my country, and I was honoured to have worked alongside some of the finest military personnel in the world. But Sarah had become the most important person in my life, and I wanted for her all the things she'd never had. A home, children, and a husband who stood an above average chance of making it home alive after work every day.

Yes, you heard right. I said husband. Because only a fucking idiot would find a woman as amazing as she was and not marry her before she wised up and realised she could do so much better. I was aware that I wasn't like most men. In place of a quick temper, I had steely control and patience. I planned, I strategized, and I executed. But Sarah wasn't a military operation. She was the love of my fucking life. She needed things from me I'd never learned to give to her. Communication. Emotion. Trust. But for her, I would learn. For her I would be the most studied student the world had ever fucking seen. Because she was mine and I was hers, and if it took every day for the rest of my life, I'd do everything in my power to make sure she never regretted that.

The smell of sausage and bacon hit me, along with the sound of Sarah's off-key singing, and I grinned to myself, thinking that I would happily wake up this way for the rest of my life. After a quick shower, I shrugged on some jeans, but given that the heating was cranked to the max, left off my T-shirt. I ambled down the stairs to see my girl loading everything onto plates and setting them on a table already laden with coffee, juices, and fruit. I paused and took a moment to look my fill before she noticed me. Her feet were encased in big, thick slouch socks, probably in deference to the cold flagstones on the kitchen floor, and she wore one of my old army hoodies. It swamped her, ending mid-thigh, and I hoped to fuck she wasn't wearing anything underneath it. Forget women dressed up in this Victoria's Secret shit. Seeing my girl wearing my clothes did something to me. The idea of bending her over that kitchen table and fucking her hard was looking pretty appealing.

"I can always tell when you're thinking about sex," she said, finally noticing me ogling her.

"Baby, anytime I'm looking at you, I'm thinking about sex," I replied, wandering over to wrap my hands around her from behind.

"Well, I'd like some sausage before anything else," she replied, chuckling.

"Pretty sure, I can help you out there, buttercup." I sat and pulled her into my lap so I could check out whether my lack of underwear theory was correct. Sadly, it wasn't. She rolled her eyes but fed me a piece of bacon anyway. When she would've pulled away, I grabbed her wrist and sucked the salty goodness from each of her fingers, until she shivered. Leaning forward, she kissed me gently.

"Love you," she whispered softly.

"I love you too. More than you'll ever know."

Happy with my answer, she smiled and dug heartily into her breakfast. With her hair tied back, the curve of her neck was exposed, and I nuzzled my nose against it, inhaling her scent deep into my lungs. I wanted to breathe it in so deep it became a part of me. I wanted to bottle the moment and hide it away, so if and when the worst ever happened, I could open it in the secret vault of my mind, the part of me that every special ops soldier relied on when they were blocking out pain. When they needed that one memory, that one reason to endure what couldn't be endured. With a squeeze to her hip to make sure she wasn't going anywhere, I used my hand to attack my own breakfast, devouring it in huge bites and revelling in the fact that Sar was an amazing cook.

After a lazy coffee, I helped her clean up and then helped her back to bed, but all too soon it was time to say goodbye. This was the shit I'd never had to deal with. Where I could, I always made a point of stopping by Nan's the night before an op, but her idea of a goodbye was "Don't die or I'm donating all your shit to the cat's home charity shop on High Street." She said it with a great deal of affection mind you.

In my black fatigues and combat boots, I felt the comfort of familiarity. With Sarah, I was trying my best not to fuck anything up, but I was essentially charting new ground. In this job though, my confidence knew no bounds. I knew exactly what I was doing, and I was fucking good at it. The best team in the world was by my side, and I had a score to settle. Each one of the arseholes I'd be facing tomorrow had some hand in putting my girl's life in danger. For that, they would all die by mine. I'd make it as quick and clean as possible, but that was the only concession. This house gave the illusion of protection, but it was only a matter of time before the terrorist group or the Russians tracked her down, and after that, what they'd do to her would be the stuff of nightmares. But as long as there was breath in my body, that wasn't happening.

"You look more like armed police than SAS," she said to me, doing her best to put on a brave face.

"And how many SAS guys have you met before me?" I

asked, raising my eyebrow questioningly.

"Oh, a few," she lied playfully. "But none of them had any real endurance, so they never really lasted."

"That right?" I replied, picking her up and wrapping her around me like a monkey. "Any complaints about my endurance, because we've got ten minutes? I'm pretty sure that's all it would take to christen the stairs."

"Ten minutes isn't nearly enough time for what I want to do to you. Now get going before I don't let you go at all," she replied. She wriggled until I put her down then wrapped her arms around her torso like she was trying desperately to hold herself together.

I wanted to reassure her that it was only for a few days. That I'd be back home, safe and sound and fucking her seven ways from Sunday, before she had her Monday morning toast and coffee. But I wouldn't. I couldn't. Because we both knew that wasn't a promise I could keep.

"I'm not saying goodbye," I warned her.

"Neither am I," she replied. "I am going to kiss you though. And then I'm going to make myself a cup of tea, work out the best place in the house to set up my studio, order a load of art stuff online that I don't really need because we're bringing a ton of it back from Yorkshire, and do my very best not to worry myself sick when you're gone."

"Good plan," I agreed, wrapping my arms around her tiny body. "Just remember what I said though. Keep a low profile until I know it's safe. That means no calls, no emails, no texting friends. I know it's going to be hard, but until I'm back, the fewer people who know you're here, the better. Nan'll stop by tomorrow. I've asked her to knock, but we'll need to change the locks to keep her from using her key."

"Promise me a runny boiled egg sandwich next week?" she asked, looking up at me with watery eyes.

"Sorry, babe. But what the fuck?" I asked in confusion.

"I'm not going to tell you to be safe or ask you to come back alive and unharmed. But a runny boiled egg sandwich is the most random thing in the world, and nobody else knows how much I love them. So, if you promise me that, I know everything's going to be fine," she said earnestly.

I held her close with one hand and used the other to tuck a rogue strand of hair behind her ear.

"You're a nut job, but you're my nut job, and I promise that come hell or high water, next week you will have a runny boiled egg sandwich. Now will you promise me something?" I asked, rubbing my thumb across her cheek.

"Anything," she replied.

"Promise me you'll sleep in my T-shirts when I'm gone. I need something good to dream about while I'm away."

She didn't promise, but she smiled like I knew she would. I didn't have the vocabulary to give her the words she deserved, so I did the only thing I could. Cupping her jaw with my hand, I kissed her. One kiss was all I had to show her that she was the fire in my blood, the light in my dark soul.

My redemption.

I kissed her, and then I did the hardest thing I've ever had to do. I let her go, so that I could set her free. So that I could save her. I brushed my thumb over her cheek one last time, picked up my kitbag, and left without looking back. I'd carved my soul from my body and left it in her hands. I wouldn't need it where I was going.

———————

The Ministry of Defence officer at the gates of the Royal Air Force base at Credenhill waved me through, and I could see the loaded chopper already on the tarmac. I was the first to arrive, but by the time the rest of the team rolled in, I was ready. All thoughts of Sarah were hidden away, locked deep inside where they'd be safe until this thing was done. If we succeeded, I'd never have to stand there and watch while another child died at the hands of these fucking terrorists. Never before had our motivation been greater. Guys from both alpha teams were assembled and looking sharp. They'd all seen the horrific images of innocent burning bodies, and it'd hit hard. Especially to some of these boys who had kids or were expecting. Hunter was suspiciously absent, so I addressed them all.

"Right, lads, no fucking about today. I want this thing done by the book. MI5 have eyes on Agheenco and his major players. You do not move until you have them all in your sights. Team A, we need kill shots for every one of the terrorist cell before we call it. Lieutenant Jackson and I will be coordinating both operations with one another, but it's essential that they take place simultaneously. If one of the targets has a chance to tip off the other, this thing will be over before it starts. These terrorists will disappear into the wind, and who knows how many people will die before we get another crack at this, so nobody fucks this up. They cannot be allowed to inform someone that their meeting has been compromised. Authorisation for this op comes straight from the prime minister, so you can be damn sure that anyone who cocks up is gonna lose at least a stripe.

"I don't need to tell you how much is at stake here, boys. For those of you who haven't heard through the grape vine, the Russians are after my girl. These bastards are trafficking weapons, women, and kids, and I'm told the shipment we're intercepting today contains enough explosives to take down half of London. Well, that's not happening on my watch. I'm not letting them put one more innocent kid in a body bag because my team fucked up. Each one of you has been hand-picked because you are the best of the fucking best at what you do, so get the job done and show people what the SAS are fucking made of. Do you understand me?"

"Yes, sir," they shouted back.

"Good. Now gear up. We have a full briefing in fifteen minutes. Then I want Team A in the armoury," I replied, giving them their marching orders.

"Where the fuck do you get off addressing my team?" Hunter shouted, running over to me from his car. Most of the guys had disappeared to get their shit together, but even without them in earshot, I didn't appreciate being barked at like some junkyard dog. He was a bloody good SAS operative, but although we were the same rank, he never could quite get over losing out on the command of Team A to me.

"We were scheduled to assemble twenty minutes ago. Both teams have shit to get done, so next time, if want to address your team separately, try showing up on time," I answered calmly. He was a hothead, and I knew my aloofness drove him nuts.

"All right, Harper, have it your way, but let's see if you're this high and mighty when the operation is over," he said.

"What's that supposed to mean?" I asked. If he had something to say to me, I'd rather he just spit it out.

"It means, enjoy your command while you can. You fucked an asset! I hope for your sake she was a good lay, because the minute this operation's over, you'll be kissing your career goodbye," he yelled.

I replied by punching him square in the face.

"Don't ever talk shit about her again, Jackson. Just do your job properly and leave my career to me," I said, and walked off to find my men. He wouldn't risk losing face by reporting me, though I didn't much care if he did. If he thought he could insult my girl and get away with it, he thought wrong. If he didn't want to end up on his arse again, he'd remember that.

CHAPTER TWENTY FOUR

Sarah

Waiting for Tom to come home was nothing short of torture. I couldn't go out, couldn't phone any of my friends, or check in on social media, or do any of the other things you might think of to pass the time while you waited to see if your man made it home alive. I couldn't imagine what it would be like if he was deployed overseas. Sporadic letters and phone calls with only a vague notion of when he might return. But if that was what his life was, I was all in. He was it for me, and whenever he could make it home, I'd be there.

The first few hours weren't so bad. I sketched and watched movies, read a book for five minutes, then slammed it shut because I couldn't concentrate. I even vacuumed and dusted the house from top to bottom and finally stripped and remade the bed. I drew the line at changing the pillowcases though. Aside from a hoodie and T-shirt that he left hanging over the back of a chair in the bedroom, they held his scent.

That faint smell of shaving soap and aftershave. He'd washed all of those scents off before he'd gone, explaining when I questioned that, although the terrorists would probably appreciate him making the effort, it didn't much help when you were trying to be stealthy. Smothering my nose with the pillow was torture I knew, but there were some things you just couldn't help. Like turning on a tap, it triggered a waterfall of uncontrollable tears. He might be the best of the best, but he was going up against an unknown number of fanatical terrorists. Men who valued their cause above that of any life. Cowards who volunteered the last vestiges of their humanity when they sacrificed innocent children.

It wasn't a case of being weak. Sometimes tears were all we needed to wash away the fear so that we could see clearly again. It was cathartic. They were tears of worry, perhaps tears of frustration, but in the end, I felt better for having shed them. Of course, I didn't look so hot after. My red nose and puffy eyes tell-tale signs that I'd been crying like a baby. So when Nan walked through the door a day early and said, "Good Lord, am I ever glad I brought some chocolate; something tells me we're going to need it," I launched myself into her arms and started crying all over again. This time they were tears of happiness that she was there. With a cigarette in her mouth and hands laden with shopping bags, she could do little to fend me off.

"Less than twelve hours and you're this desperate for human contact?" she asked. "I can go three days at home without seeing anyone and still be pissed off when the postman knocks at the door."

"Well, that's because you hate people, and I'm actually glad to see you," I said, unburdening her of her load.

"I don't think anyone's ever said that to me before and actually meant it," she admitted. Not that it was said with any degree of self-pity. More that it was further evidence weighted to the fact that I was clearly strange for enjoying, rather than enduring, her company.

"Give it a few months, I'm sure it'll wear off," I said audaciously.

"Cheeky bitch," she grumbled affectionately as she opened the door to flick away her cigarette ash.

"You know Tom's going to freak if he catches you smoking in here."

"He's got to catch me first. Why, are you going to grass me up?" She narrowed her eyes as if to gauge whether I actually had the balls.

"Depends on whether you've got any wine in here," I replied, narrowing my eyes right back.

"Wine is for when you're eating out silly girl. In this house, we drink spirits. Now I've got vodka or gin?" She held up a rather hefty bottle of each.

"Bit of both?"

"Darling, welcome to the family," she replied.

———

By eight o'clock, Nan had confiscated the booze and cut

me off. By nine o'clock, she was making me coffee, and by ten o'clock, I learned the reason why.

"The first night he goes is always the worst. I've learned that now and refined my routine somewhat. A few shots of a good hard spirit takes the edge off, but you can't let yourself get drunk. Because always, no matter how many times you promise yourself you're not going to, you always end up watching the ten o'clock news. Drunk you'll get over emotional and melancholy, and you're no use to anyone. With the edge off, you can watch the news, rationally appreciate that in no segment of the news was he or the regiment pictured or mentioned, but still have enough alcohol in your system to sleep," she explained.

"Does it ever get any easier?"

"Never," she replied, telling me exactly what I didn't want to hear. "But you learn to live with it. You know this time, where he's gone, don't you?"

"Yes. But I can't tell you or anyone else."

"Does it have something to do with you?"

This time I nodded my head. "I'm not being difficult, but I really can't tell you anything. It's the reason he probably asked you not to talk about me. I can say though, that if he's successful, I'll be able to stay."

"Like that boy knows how to fail," she scoffed with a wry smile, and I couldn't help but share her optimism. As Nan promised, there was no mention of the SAS in the news, so an hour later when it ended, she shut off the television and announced it was bedtime.

Most women ease into the role of military girlfriend. I'd dived in head first without so much as a helmet. Seeing how badly I was floundering, Nan took over. She couldn't cook, refused to smoke outside the house or stop cursing, and she barked at people more than she spoke to them. But she was strong and stoic, and more importantly, experienced in loving a man who walked head first into danger on a regular basis. So I allowed her to boss and cajole me. Tell me when to go to bed and when to wake up, what to cook for us both and when we would eat. For all intents and purposes, I was a zombie. Sleepwalking through life, waiting for any news that Tom was safe and that the danger was over.

Sunday was the worst day. It dragged interminably. Even Nan was climbing the walls by the afternoon. She'd only expected to visit for a few hours and ended up staying the whole weekend. My nerves only served to exacerbate hers. She'd chain-smoked and shuffled cards before forcing me to endure enough hands of poker that I didn't think I'd ever want to play again.

What I knew that Nan didn't, was that the operation was scheduled to take place later that evening. By tomorrow morning, it would all be over. After that, it was anyone's guess how long it would take Tom to make it back, but I'd be fine once I knew he was safe. Sunday night followed pretty much the same routine as the evening before, although long into the early hours of the morning I found myself in bed, staring into the dark. I managed to catch a few hours of sleep, and when the sun rose above the horizon, I knew it was done. I'd made it through the night. The mission would be over, and Tom would get a message to us at some point today to let us know how it went.

While Nan was making a cup of tea in the kitchen, I wandered into the living room with my toast and turned on the television.

"Nan!" I screamed, not being able to comprehend more than the "breaking news" banner and the bold black headline that began "SAS."

"Why in the hell are you screaming at me like a banshee...dear God," she said, as she saw too, her hand coming up to cover her mouth in horror. I scrabbled about, uncovering sofa cushions until I'd located the remote control and cranked up the volume.

"You are watching a BBC news special, where reports are coming in that several members of a terrorist cell thought to be responsible for the many attacks on schools, hospitals, and care homes in the city of London over the last six months have been shot dead by the Army's Special Air Services Regiment, the SAS. The assault, said to be as a result of months of intelligence work, was intended, not only to eliminate the continuing terrorist threat to our national security but also to intercept weapons and explosives thought to be intended to mount the most serious terrorist attack in the country's history. In all, sixteen men are known to have died, including one SAS officer whose name has not yet been released to us. We are joined now by our correspondent Katherine Aldlington, who is live from Downing Street where a statement is expected from the prime minster later this morning."

For twenty minutes, we listened in silence as the BBC dragged out and laid bare the few facts they were able to confirm. The cell was thought to be a small radical splinter group of a much larger and well-known terrorist organisation, several of whom were understood to have been on the government's watch list. The haul of weapons and semtex that were intercepted as part of the operation was thought to have been the biggest ever single seizure of illegal firearms and explosives in the UK. They dragged out every political analyst, every politician they could find, none of whom could confirm the one thing I needed to know. The name of the soldier killed.

"How could they possibly know?" Nan asked finally.

"What do you mean?" I asked, my voice sounding rusty and dry.

"It's the BBC," she said, lighting up a cigarette despite her shaking hands. "I mean, Facebook reports the news quicker than they do. If this thing was supposed to have gone down in the early hours of this morning like they said, how could they possibly know what happened already. It takes weeks for this stuff to come out. They're already talking about how much has been seized. I mean, there's no way the police would release that kind of information yet. And we'd have been told if it was Tom; we'd have been told long before the news was released to the media," she ranted. Ash hung precariously from the end of her cigarette as she continued to shake, but I had nothing to say. I tuned back into the news report, starving for any detail I could get, desperate for that one scrap of information that would give me hope.

"Katherine, I'm sorry to interrupt, but I'm afraid I'm going to have to cut you off for a moment," the news anchor said. "We have just received exclusive footage, thought to have been taken by one of the SAS operatives during the operation, which documents the events as they unfolded. These scenes may be harrowing to some viewers."

Some reporter continued to talk intermittently over the top of the footage, narrating a play-by-play of events. It was grainy and filmed in night vision, but you could clearly make out long bursts of lights from night scopes darting through the air and hear the unmistakable popping sounds of rapid gunfire. I was practically kneeling in front of the screen as I tried to understand what I was seeing. Men were shouting at one another, though their words were indecipherable.

The person filming darted out from behind a shipping container to take more shots. Everything was happening so fast, the camera moving wildly with the person it was attached to. Finally, I realised it was a body cam by the way it was flailing and jerking all over the place. I had no idea what shipyard they were in, but it made sense that the assault would be there rather than a boat. They would have wanted to take the terrorists after the handover happened, just to be sure.

A soldier came into shot across the way, crouched behind another container, and I guessed he was one of ours. Covered from head to toe, it was impossible to know who it was, but I held my breath anyway. The camera at last became steady as the gunfire slowly ebbed, though focused now on the last of the targets. In the periphery of the screen, the kneeling soldier leant further forward to take a shot when he was yanked sharply backwards in a move that literally saved his life. As the last shot rang out, sounding a death knell to the terrorists who'd been responsible for taking so many innocent civilian lives, the rest of the team seemed to realise what I already knew. The rescuer, the guardian angel who'd ripped his teammate away from the path of certain death, had exposed himself to make the ultimate sacrifice, saving his friend's life at the expense of his own. Soldiers darted in front of the camera again, and a few more indistinguishable voices called out before the silence. The excruciating, insufferable, tormenting silence, broken only by the clear voice that cut through the darkness like a scythe, ripping a hole through my heart as it did.

"Man down."

"It can't be him," Nan protested.

I looked down my palms. Clear as day, I could picture how his big hands engulfed mine. How the callouses felt as he traced his large digits over my own, entwining our fingers together before slipping away and twisting them around to do it all again. They were so warm, his hands. Always so warm. I'd have given anything for just thirty seconds more, even if I had to close my eyes. I'd sacrifice his voice in my ear and the sight of his face, the smell of his skin that made me feel so safe and warm. I'd trade it all for just one more moment of his hand in mine, or the feel of his big arms around me as he held me close. I'd taken so many embraces for granted, throwing them away like hellos and goodbyes. Like confetti into the wind. And now there would never be another.

I worried, but I never truly believed anything would happen to him, my iron man that everyone convinced me was infallible. I never believed he would die. If I had, I would've hugged him even harder. I might never have let him go. Because the tragedy of it all was that you never really knew which hug would be your last.

I clenched my palms tightly, ignoring the fact that they were icy cold. The ghosted memory of Tom's last touch hidden away in my heart as I steeled myself for what was to come. My grief would have its time. But it had no place at his mother's feet.

"It's not him! I'm telling you, it's not him! Someone would have come to see us by now. Someone from Hereford would be here. You'll see! He'll call later today, telling us to put the kettle on," she protested.

I'd heard that shock and denial were the first stages of

grief. If Nan was in denial, perhaps I was still in shock. I thought it was more likely that my heart had taken as much sorrow as it could for one lifetime and was hardening like cement, drying in the sun. When the cheerful chime of the doorbell rang brightly through the house, she sobbed. This anchor, this monolith, this sassy tower of unending strength, cried as though her heart was broken. The painful, brutal sob of a mother faced with the inescapable realisation that she'd just lost her child.

I stood on shaky legs and stopped to grasp her shoulder. Her face buried in her tissue, her smouldering cigarette languishing in the ashtray, she reached up to squeeze my hand before releasing me to do what needed to be done. I opened the door to two officers, resplendent in their full dress greens, their chests so covered with medals I was sure they blinded people in full sun.

"Miss Tatem, my name is Lieutenant Colonel Timothy Davies, and this is my colleague, Major Robert Munroe. May we come in please?"

I nodded in reply, and led them to Nan, my voice croaky as I introduced them to her.

"Mrs Harper, I regret that we didn't meet under better circumstances, and I am deeply sorry to be the bearer of such bad tidings. But I must unfortunately confirm that at approximately 4.20a.m. this morning, your son was shot twice, and despite our best efforts, we were unable to save him. He was a hero who gave his life in service of his country, and his sacrifice will not be forgotten."

CHAPTER TWENTY FIVE

Sarah

"What happened?" Nan asked, tears still streaming from her eyes as she discreetly wiped them with a tissue.

"As I explained, Mrs Harper, he was shot—" Lieutenant Colonel Davies said.

"I heard that bit. But what happened with the SAS operation? We've seen the news report, but I want the truth about exactly what happened. I'm owed that at least," she said.

Davies and his cohort shuffled around uncomfortably, looking painfully uncomfortable as he answered.

"I'm sorry, Mrs Harper, but Lieutenant Harper was not part of the twenty-second Special Air Service Regiment. He served with the 1st Battalion Parachute Regiment and was killed in a live-fire training exercise last night," he said, looking pointedly at me, daring me to argue with him. We both knew full well that I'd signed a confidentiality agreement with the Ministry of Defence. I'd be surprised if Tom hadn't as well, so technically Nan shouldn't know anything other than the fact that he was in the army. Preserving an illusion was one thing, but to lie to her now, so brazenly, seemed like such a slap in the face. An insult to her intelligence and Tom's memory.

"Get out!" she said venomously.

"Excuse me?" he said, seeming a little taken aback.

"I said, get out of my house! I'm not interested in your army bullshit. If you can't honour my son's memory by giving me the truth, get out of my house," she shouted. She was absolutely distraught, but seeing her backbone shocked me out of my stupor.

"I think you should leave now," I said, my croaky voice a quiet authority.

"Very well. If you think that's best," he replied stiffly. "I really am very sorry."

Either Nan didn't hear him or she didn't care for his false platitudes. I showed both men to the door before confronting them.

"Would it really hurt to have told her the truth?"

"Miss Tatem, while you may be privy to certain matters of national security, you'd do well to remember that the success of our regiment depends entirely on discretion and secrecy. How many families of our soldiers would be endangered if what they did became public knowledge? It's for their safety and the safety of their loved ones that we conceal the identities of those who work for us," he explained.

"But what possible difference could it make now that he's dead?" I pleaded.

"And what of the lives of his friends and colleagues? Do you really feel that Mrs Harper or any parent could lie about something like that when they're about to put their child in the ground? Do you think it's fair of us to even ask? And whether you agree with my reasons or not, I don't think I need to remind you of the consequences of divulging certain truths in breach of the secrecy agreement that you signed of your own free will," he replied. Stern and unrelenting, he only softened when he saw the tears welling up in my eyes.

"He'll be buried then?" I asked, the image of my beautiful man lying in the cold, hard ground was burned into my brain.

"As his next of kin, that's up to his mother. A visiting officer will attend in due course to discuss matters further, but for now, if there's anything we can do, just have her call me," he said, passing me a card. I nodded as I took it, but held the door open in a silent invitation for him to leave.

"Look, Lieutenant Harper admitted to me that you were in a relationship of sorts, so I understand just how difficult this is. But the best advice I can give you is to move on. You're young with your whole life ahead of you. Don't live it shackled to the memory of a man you hardly knew. Now, I'm informed that Mr Masterson of MI5 will be contacting you soon. I would ask that you listen to what he has to say with an open mind. Losing Tom was a terrible tragedy, but he knew the risks and his mission was a success. The public will never know, but both of you have saved countless lives. Now I implore you to move on with yours. We both know it's what he would have wanted." With that, he left.

Walking back in the living room, I turned off the television and perched on the footstool next to Nan.

"What a stupid old fool you must think I am," she said, drying her face. Giving Lieutenant Colonel Davies a bollocking seemed to have calmed her a little.

"Ask me anything you want to know, and I'll tell you," I said calmly. I was about to commit treason. I was breaching the Official Secrets Act. I could go to prison for the rest of my life, but I didn't care. That bullshit blanket rule of Davies's might have a solid foundation, but I knew that Nan would take my secrets to the grave. If it wasn't for me, Tom wouldn't have been anywhere near that operation. I wasn't delusional enough to convince myself that I was the reason he was dead, but I did know that I owed Nan a debt I couldn't hope to repay. If the truth was her price, I'd gladly give it.

"How did you meet him?" she asked. And so I told her. The long, unbelievable story of how a children's book illustrator of modest means became a millionaire embroiled with international terrorists and Russian gangsters. When I got to the end, I thought I'd actually shocked the speech out of her.

"I'll get you some tea," I said, leaving her to digest

everything. When I put a cup down in front of us both, she warmed her hands before bringing it to her lips and chuckling.

"What's funny?" I asked.

She pointed to my mug which read, "A woman is like a tea bag. You never know how strong she's going to be until you put her in hot water."

"I can't cry," I admitted to her shamefully. "It's like being submerged in water, completely in limbo. I can't scream, and I can't cry. I'm just numb. What does that say about me? That the man I love is dead and I can't shed a single tear?"

"I've loved and lost enough men in my life to know that you will. Your heart can only take so much grief before it shuts down. And then, when you're least expecting it, you'll be doing something mundane, like the dishes or filling the car up with petrol, and out of nowhere, like a tsunami, it will hit you. A wave of grief so powerful it will bend you in half. And everyone will stare at the crazy lady crying in the supermarket car park and wonder what happened to make you lose the plot. Maybe some of them will even come over and offer to help, but that will just make the pain so much worse, because you realise they can't help. The man you love is gone, and he is never, ever coming back."

The future she spoke of was a living hell, and she was right. I couldn't cope with it, so I shut down. A future without him was more than I could comprehend. We'd both done the right thing, we were supposed to get our happy ever after. Surely we'd earned it? There were no answers to the questions rattling around in my head, and so I stopped looking for them. All I wanted was to curl into a ball and pretend. Pretend that they were wrong. That the news had been intended for someone else. That if I closed my eyes tight enough, I'd be able to feel his arms around me as I slept.

We sipped our tea in morbid silence, neither of us knowing what to do with ourselves. The fight seemed to have left Nan with Davies's departure. His loss was like a constant pain in my hollowed-out chest. It was so bad it hurt even to breathe.

"Do you know, all I can think about is the day I first heard him laugh," she said wistfully as her mind took her back to the memory. "Not long after my husband died, I wasn't in a great place. Tom hadn't been with me all that long when it happened, and I felt guilty that I should have been focused on what he needed, but in reality, I was consumed with my own grief. When I think back now, I honestly don't know how I'd have got through that time without him. But anyway, I'd grown sick of just staring at the four walls at home, so I dragged him out with me to grab some dinner. It wasn't anywhere fancy, but it was pretty busy when we got there.

"We started chatting about how school and sports were going, and we got so caught up that I hadn't remembered to take the onions off my burger. Well, onions are a big no-no for me. They repeat on me something terrible, and we were waiting for the cheque to arrive when I just had an overwhelming urge to burp. I knew the waitress was going to be back soon, and remember this is back in the day when you needed a signature to pay by card, so I couldn't leave Tom to deal with the bill while I nipped to the bathroom. Anyway, the restaurant was full of kids, so it was pretty loud, and I figured a little burp would probably go unnoticed. So I let it build, and just at the moment it was about to come out, the music goes off and the waitress walks out with a birthday cake for the table of kids."

By this stage in her story, I was already giggling because I had a pretty good idea where this was going.

"Just as they were about to start singing, this burp came out, and it was pretty tame, but without any idea what else was building, I let out the loudest fart in the history of mankind. I mean, this thing was so loud I'm sure even the table shook. Everyone, and I mean everyone, turned to look at me. The entire place was silent, and I was just sitting there, dying, wishing the ground could swallow me whole. And Tom looked at me and just laughed. He wasn't the slightest bit embarrassed, but he was laughing so hard he was almost doubled over, which got me going and, of course, the more I laughed, the more I farted. Pretty soon the both of us were in a flood of tears."

She was laughing so hard as she retold the story, and I got carried away too. But then of course there was that moment, when we both remembered why we were there, and the laughter died as the happy tears became sad once more.

"You know what? That was the last time I ever held it in around him. And I don't just mean the farting. I said what I thought and I gave him shit, but I was real. And in return, I got a son," she said.

"He got you too, you know? I mean, you both gave each other shit, but it was plain as day how much he loved you," I said, reaching out to cover her hand with mine.

"We got each other, and what a screwed-up pair we were. Same as you two. Neither of you made a lick of sense, but you worked."

"And now he's gone," I whispered.

Neither of us had much to say after that. Nan went to have a lie down, and I found a spot as far across the house as I could, slid down the wall and, burying my face in a pillow, sobbed until I was almost sick. The more I cried, the worse I felt, until there was quite simply nothing left. The rest of the day came and went, and it was nearly three in the morning before we found ourselves together again, sharing another cup of tea, the stereotypical response of any British woman in a crisis.

"I know it's early," Nan said to me, "but I want you to think about moving in here."

"Tom asked me the same thing Friday. We were going to go up to Yorkshire in a couple of weeks to empty out my flat. But now, I don't think I can. This place belongs to you, and if it doesn't, it will soon. Besides, I'm not sure it will feel like home without him," I replied, looking around wistfully.

"Of course it will. You can't outrun grief, you know. It's like a shadow that follows you everywhere you go. If you want to learn to heal, you've got to find a place you love, one that makes you feel safe, and you need to face your grief head-on. Three dead husbands taught me that. Besides, the house isn't in either of our names," she said. "The house belongs to a trust I created with the proceeds of his step-father's life insurance policy. Tom was the sole beneficiary. And I'm pretty sure he'd want you to have the place now."

"Nan," I protested, "I can't. It's an incredibly generous offer, but I've inherited more than anyone should in their lifetime. This was your home. You keep it. I'll just be glad to come visit once in a while."

"We can argue about that later," she replied. "But stay for now? At least for a little while." It wasn't in her nature to ask for things, but she was literally the only person in the world who'd loved Tom as much as I did.

"Of course," I replied.

"I'm keeping my key though. I need to know I'm not getting locked out every time I piss you off," she said, and we shared a sad smile.

"What do you think will happen now? With the army I mean?" The idea of arranging his funeral made me want to vomit, but it just wasn't fair to leave things all to her.

"It'll be weeks before we'll be given the body. They'll

want to do a post mortem and investigation, but I won't be party to any of it. The bloody army will keep every scrap of evidence about it to themselves. I may never be given official recognition of who he actually was by those bastards, but I will never forgive them for letting me learn of his death from the news. It grates on me every time I see those images over and over in my head. I still don't understand how the media got hold of the video footage. I mean, this isn't the kind of thing that happens in the SAS. Not one of those boys would leak a tape or sell the story. It just doesn't make sense," she said, reaching for her pack of cigarettes. I walked over to get an ashtray from the windowsill.

"I think it was leaked. Just not by the SAS," I told her.

"What d'you mean?"

"This whole thing started, not just as a response to what the terrorists were doing, but because the prime minister wanted to send a message. Wanted to assert the fact that she wasn't losing control of the country. To send a strong warning to terrorists that the UK would respond to extreme terrorism with extreme action. This whole operation, the joint task force between MI5 and the SAS, was sanctioned directly by the prime minister and the cabinet committee. It was the exact same motivation Margaret Thatcher had when she ordered the SAS to storm the Iranian Embassy. What better way to communicate the message she wants to send than by showing live footage of some of the most highly trained, elite special forces operatives in the world wiping out an entire terrorist cell?"

"But why leave the footage of Tom being shot in there. Surely it looks weak that we sustained a loss too?" she asked.

"Because it doesn't show weakness; it shows strength. The power of the terrorist is that they were willing to lose men, suicide bombers, for their cause. Now she's made it clear that if it means destroying every one of them, we're prepared to make that sacrifice as well."

"Son of a bitch," she responded, and just like that, grief became anger.

CHAPTER TWENTY SIX

Tom

"Jesus Fucking Christ. I feel like I've been hit by a truck. You sure Crash hasn't been at the wheel again?" I complained, swearing a fucking blue streak at the pain of being separated from my Kevlar vest.

"It's good to see your ugly face, you bastard. I thought we'd lost you," Will said, grabbing the back of my neck and leaning in for a hug of sorts.

"Sorry, mate. You're gonna have to shelve those *Brokeback Mountain* fantasies of yours. I've got a girl now, or haven't you heard?" I said, grinning despite the pain.

"Yeah well, your girl was this close to getting you back in a box," he replied, using the distance between his thumb and finger to remind me how close I'd come to death.

"What happened out there? This thing was an ambush. We were prepared, we had good cover, the high ground. Nothing should have gone wrong. This whole thing should have been a fucking cakewalk," Crash asked.

"Let medical give him the once-over before we debrief. The brass will be dissecting this shit for months, so we need to get everything down before someone forgets something," Will replied, ushering the guys out.

"You're going to be pretty bruised and banged up, but the Kevlar's done its job. I don't think you have any permanent damage, but I'd like to get you in for some X-rays, just to be sure," the medic said.

"Okay if I do it after the debrief? Unless you're sure something's broken, I'll be expected to be there," I explained, but I didn't need to. The regiment had its own medics made up of some of the best combat doctors and nurses in the army. I guess they'd have to be to put together what we broke. We often came in beaten, bruised, and bloodied, but they always got us back on our feet.

"Fine," he agreed, "but no more than a few hours tops. I'm going to strap you up, which should help keep you supported, but if you feel any sharp pains or shortness of breath, you need to come in right away. As for the pain, I can only give you a couple of paracetamol I'm afraid. I'm not happy to give you anything else until we get you in for testing and X-rays."

"Paracetamol sounds great, but even that will have to wait until later. I can't have the reports saying that my testimony was affected by painkillers. I'm not feeling any discomfort I can't handle. If it gets worse, I'll come by and you can do your thing."

"Get it done as soon as you can. I won't sign you off as operational fit until you do," he warned.

"Fair enough," I agreed, and with a fair bit of wincing, lifted my arms for him to wrap me. When he was finished, I struggled with my T-shirt then hopped off the bench.

"Ready?" Will asked as I rolled the kinks out of my shoulders.

"Let's get this done," I replied. "Sarah will be climbing the walls by now. I need to let her know I'm okay."

"About that.... There's something you should know. While Doc was doing his thing, we found out that feed from someone's body cam was released to the media. They don't have any names, but they're reporting it that one of the team was wiped out during the op."

"Fuck! We need to call Sarah and Nan. They must be going out of their mind," I said.

"I'm sure one of the brass called them. With it being all over the tv and the net, there's no way they would have left them hanging," he reassured me.

"I'll check with Davies as soon as I see him," I replied.

"Davies has been a busy boy in the last hour. He's already released a statement on behalf of the Regiment and he's been lapping up the attention."

"But who the fuck leaked the footage?"

"None of us have access to those feeds. The footage is streamed live to operations. Maybe MI5 if they were given access. But there's something weird about it. None of us have been questioned. Nobody's kicking off. Maybe they're waiting for the debrief, but it's fucking weird if you ask me. A leak in an operation this size, and I'd expect brass to be all over us like flies on fucking honey."

"They leaked it. They fucking leaked it. That's why nobody's up our arse about it," I replied.

"Who did?"

"I'm betting that orders to release it came straight from the top, and the regiment wouldn't fight it. With all the publicity, we just secured their budget for the next ten years." I pushed open the door to the briefing room. The guys were sat around the table, looking tired but happy.

"Looking pretty good for a ghost, Reaper," Eli said, chuckling nervously.

"You too, Brit," I replied, reminding him that it was very nearly him not me who'd been shot. There's no Kevlar in the world that stops two shots to the head. I could tell by the way he was squirming that he wanted to say something, but he wouldn't until we were alone. Davies chose just that moment to stroll into the room, looking like the cat who got the proverbial cream.

"Gentlemen, after a lengthy operation, I'm sure you're all keen for some downtime, so I'll keep this as brief as possible. The powers that be were extremely happy with last night's results. It will be some time before we get the full report, but early intel from MI5 and SO19 suggest that we hit every mark identified as belonging to the cell. It is possible that not every one of the cell was present at the handover, but we believe that it will take anyone remaining some time to regroup, and with the resources and intel we have on those already dead, it won't take us long to track down the rest. Now, that having been said, the fact that Lieutenant Harper was shot twice means that something went wrong. So, let's start from the beginning, until we're all on the same page," he said.

Giving me the nod, I explained my version of events. "The op started out well. Early recon identified the best positions for line of sight, so we dug in and waited for nightfall. The handover happened exactly when MI5 said it was supposed to. Two Russians turned up to check the shipment. About an hour later, two large transit vans arrived with four marks in each van. One of the marks was carrying a briefcase. He approached the two Russians, opened the briefcase, and the second Russian examined the contents. They were there for around fifteen minutes because the Russian wanted to check every stone, and I assumed payment was being made in rough, uncut conflict diamonds. After he was done, the Russians opened up every crate and the lead mark checked each crate off a manifest. When he was satisfied, he gave the Russians a nod and they took off. The marks loaded the crates into the vans, and as agreed, we waited until the loading was done to reduce the threat of triggering any of the explosives. I checked the team had eyes on all the marks before I shouted, 'SAS, put your weapons down." As expected, they immediately pulled weapons and began shooting towards the sound of my voice. We returned fire, and the ensuing assault took maybe sixty seconds. We were down to the last one or two when they started calling out, scouting who was left. I was in an elevated position, but didn't have eyes on the final marks, so I climbed down from the top of the container to move into a better position. I came up behind Spears just as I saw the Russian in my peripheral vision. He had his weapon raised, and I didn't think I had time to shoot before he discharged his weapon, so I grabbed Spears by the back of his vest and hauled him out of the kill zone. As I did, I took two hits to the chest and went down. I'm pretty sure I was knocked out, but only for a matter of seconds. When I came to, I heard the all clear over my earpiece."

It all seemed so clinical now, but that firefight was anything but pretty. I knew Eli was feeling pretty shit about how things went down, but that was the great thing about debriefs. We went over the operation while it was still fresh, analysed our mistakes, and learned from them. Sure, we might have a word or two between us, but everything after that was forgotten and tomorrow would be a new mission.

"Okay, thanks, Tom. Staff Sergeant Edwards?" Davies said, indicating it was Will's turn. Two hours later, after Davies and his flunkies had made a shit ton of notes, I was more than ready to have a shower and get back to my girl.

"How did Team B make out?" I asked when we were all done.

"Almost as well as you," Davies informed me, sounding quite happy for a change. I wasn't surprised. There would most likely be a medal in this for him. "MI5 identified sixteen members of the gang that were all part of the key players rather than hired muscle. Of the sixteen, only one escaped," he said.

"Who?" I asked. Despite the fact that it was Team B's responsibility to take them out, I'd studied all the available intel and knew the Russians marks as well as I knew the terrorists.

"Vasili Agheenco," he said, and the entire room stopped. Every one of these guys knew what that meant for my girl, and this fucker had pulled her security. After this, Agheenco would know she was involved. We knew too much intel for him to think otherwise.

"And I'm just finding this out now?" I said, my voice a menacing calm. "You gave us the all clear. That wasn't supposed to happen unless B had eyes on everyone."

"Watch your tone, Lieutenant Harper. Need I remind you that I run things around here? For your information, B Team thought they had eyes on everyone, but the driver was a lookalike for Vasili. They didn't realise they didn't have him until seconds before. I made the call, and we completed two successful operations and a significant threat to our national security has been eliminated. Agheenco is now a high-priority target and likely on the run. MI5 is actively searching for him, and they'll pick him up as soon as they find him. You all did a good job today and a letter of commendation will be issued to everyone involved. Now enjoy your downtime while you can, gentlemen. Dismissed," he ordered, but by his glare, I took it that he wasn't done with me yet. Good. I wasn't done with him either. He waited until the last of the boys had left the room before addressing me.

"We need to discuss the consequences of what's taken place over the last twenty-four hours, but before we do, I want to remind you that you're on thin ice here. I'm giving you some leeway for saving Eli's life, but not much. You compromised yourself and your team and broke pretty much every rule in the book by involving yourself with Miss Tatem. Now the operation was a success, so you need to think long and hard about salvaging what's left of your career," he said, looking pissed. I wasn't surprised. Insubordination to a senior officer in any area of the army was bad, but to be insubordinate in front of the entire team meant waving goodbye to your career as it flew out the window.

"With the greatest respect, sir, I did my job and I'd do it again. But if you think I'm remotely bothered about the status of my career after hearing that Vasili Agheenco is still alive and probably gunning for my girl, you don't know me at all."

"Let's not be melodramatic, shall we? Miss Tatem is currently staying at your family home. A house that isn't registered in your name and is, to all intents and purposes, untraceable. The chances of him locating her there, even if he was looking for her, are so remote they're laughable. The reality is that he's probably long gone. Underground until the heat dies down and then on a slow boat back to Russia. There's nowhere he can go in London now. Not with MI5 watching. Besides, I have it on good authority that his face will be leaked to the press. If we don't get him, the Russian mob will. He was in charge of this deal, and how much do you think he's lost them?"

"And if you're wrong? I'm not risking Sarah's life on the hope that he's run away with his tail between his legs. Either reinstate her security or let me get out of here so I can take her some place I know she'll be protected until MI5 cleans up this mess."

"That sounded dangerously close to you giving me an ultimatum," he warned.

I didn't respond, but I was getting sick of his bullshit. If I didn't think he'd have me arrested at the guardhouse just to prove a point, I'd have said, "Fuck this shit" and just walked.

"Every minute I waste here is another minute she's alone and unprotected," I argued.

"I concede that there is a slight risk to her safety, but I believe there is a way to ensure that she will be permanently secure. One that will also allow you to continue on with the SAS," he offered.

Sarah and I had discussed this, and we both knew my time in combat was done, but I wanted to know what plan he had for keeping her protected.

"Earlier today I visited your mother and Miss Tatem and informed them that you were shot and killed last night on a training exercise," he said, as casually as if he'd told me the football scores.

"What the fuck did you just say?" I asked quietly.

Discomfort bled into his smug face, and a brief expression of panic flashed across it. I leant forward menacingly, staring at him with the full intensity of what I was.

A trained killer.

With a single look, I showed myself Unveiling the true face of death behind the mask of civility. And then he knew. If I could kill without remorse for my country, imagine what I'd do for the woman I loved?

"Now, hear me out. MI5 intend to offer Miss Tatem entry into the witness protection. She'll have complete anonymity for the rest of her life. It may not perhaps be at the level of wealth she's used to, but I'm assured that she'll be extremely comfortable. An offer curtesy of Her Majesty's government in thanks to Miss Tatem for playing her part in all of this. But there was no way she would take the offer as long as you were still in the picture."

"That's her choice to make. Not yours."

"There is no choice. We both know that, as long as you're alive, she will choose you over herself every time. Let her go, Tom. Let her live her life in safety and security and find someone to grow old with who doesn't have blood on their hands. You were built for war, son. This idea you have of riding off into the sunset with this girl is a fantasy. This is an opportunity for a clean break, and I urge you to think carefully before you act here. Leading this mission will make your career, and I wouldn't be surprised if there isn't a medal in this for at least you, if not the whole team. You have a career with the regiment and a job still left to do. Let this girl go and move on with your life. For her sake if not yours."

"I'm not your son, sir. I'm an officer in her Majesty's Armed Forces and an elite SAS operative. I will defend my country and my family, and you can be sure as fuck that I'm going to defend my girl's right to live free and happy. After the shit she's been through, she deserves her life back, and I'm going to give it to her. I've seen you plastered all over the news, taking credit for a fight you won without ever having risked your own life or picked up a weapon. At the moment, you're the man of the hour. The Russians get to Sarah, you'll be the man who killed the society princess who gave up everything for her country. The media will crucify you, and that's before I get my turn. Putting Sarah in witness protection is in your best interest, not hers. So, if it's all the same with you, fuck you and the horse you rode in on," I said, calmly pushing back my chair.

"You're blowing this out of all proportion. My call was the right one. Nobody died and the terrorist threat is gone. I did the right thing. We're fighting a war against terror, and the freedom of one woman against the lives of countless others is an acceptable casualty. People will understand that, even if you don't," he reasoned.

"There's no such thing as an acceptable casualty, sir. When the life and freedom of any innocent becomes expendable, you've already lost the war."

"You're making a mistake, Tom, and I'm afraid I can't allow this. MI5 should be on their way to her now. They'll explain that Agheenco is at large, and if she agrees to witness protection, they'll have her moved within the hour."

"And what about my mother? Or are you planning on putting her in witness protection as well?" I asked sarcastically.

"Once Sarah leaves, I'll pay her a visit and inform her that you were wrongly identified on scene and that misinformation was communicated to me. I'll apologise for the misunderstanding and will explain that you're fine and on your way home," he said. "And you will do or say nothing to the contrary, or I'll have you brought up on charges of treason for breaching the Official Secrets Act. I'm holding you for twenty-four hours. After that, as long as I have your assurances that you will say nothing, you may leave."

"Do it. Have me arrested and thrown in the glass house! Let's see how long it takes my mother to go to the national press and every media outlet under the sun, shouting from the rooftops about what you've done. I'm sure she'll paint a fairly graphic picture of how she grieved and how badly her heart was affected from the stress, all because you misidentified a dead soldier. She loves the spotlight. Craves it really. I won't need to say a word. The minute you leave, she'll be tweeting Oprah. I hear that clip of me getting shot's already gone viral. A national hero, isn't that what they're calling me?" I replied.

Vanity was his sin, and it worked in my favour. A trial by media was his worst nightmare, and it was a weapon I'd gladly wield at his table if it got me out of here and back with the only two women I'd ever loved. He thought for a moment. The squeaky-wheeled cogs of his mind moving behind his eyes, as I imagined him running through his options. He wasn't a soldier. He was a politian. A chess player. Moving us all around the board as he played his own game.

"Go," he replied. "Give her the choice about whether to take witness protection when they come calling. But if she dies, that's on you, and if I'm implicated in any way, I will fucking bury you," he warned. But I had no time for his hollow, childish threats. I had phone calls to make and speed limits to break. If I had to move Heaven and Earth, there was no fucking way MI5 was taking my girl.

CHAPTER TWENTY SEVEN

Sarah

For hours the house had been battered as a storm raged outside. The reflection staring back at me through the darkened glass was hollowed out. A shadow of her former self, now that part of her soul was missing. I barely recognised the girl looking back at me. In a matter of hours, grief had stripped away all semblance of joy and hope. What was left was merely a physical manifestation of misery and despair. I'd gone through the motions of showering and drying my hair. Had dragged on some clean jeans and a sweater so that I could face the visiting officer if they turned up today. But that small act, that tiny semblance of normality left me exhausted, and all I wanted to do was change into my pyjamas, crawl back into bed, and wallow in a pool of my own desolation.

The sharp knock at the door made me jump. Barely a second or two passed before it sounded again, and I imagined that the doorbell to the right of the entrance wasn't nearly loud enough to convey the exasperation of person next to it. My steps grew heavy the closer I walked, knowing how real everything would become as soon as we started talking about funeral arrangements. The knocker sounded again, spiking my temper. The visiting officer was definitely going to get a piece of my mind about their distinct lack of patience and sensitivity. But the subject of my ire was not who I thought it would be.

"Hello, Aunt Elizabeth," I said. The sour-faced old boot looked like she'd been sucking lemons the whole way down, but I supposed that a foray into the countryside and away from her usual cosmopolitan scene in London was probably her idea of hell. "What are you doing here?" It didn't occur to me to ask how she was, or how she knew where to find me.

"Your presence is needed in London. There's a problem with the company, and whilst packing your bag and disappearing to the countryside with absolute no notice to anyone as to where you've gone might have seemed like a great idea in that moronic little brain of yours, some of us actually care about this business."

"I care. I just...," I muttered, unable to explain what had happened, as though talking about it aloud would give Tom's death a finality I couldn't take back.

"All you were asked to do is show up and have your picture taken, but even that seems to be above you. Now get your coat please. We have a crisis to sort out, and I've already wasted far too much time driving down here. Something I wouldn't need to do I might add, if you turned on your phone once in a while," she complained.

"I'm afraid I can't go with you. I'm sorry if I haven't performed as well in the role of social butterfly as you wanted me to, but I did the best I could, and despite what you think, I don't want to see the company fail, but somebody I care about needs me right now and I won't abandon her, even for the company."

She wore that same look of rage she'd favoured when I was a child who'd made any kind of suggestion that wasn't aligned with her agenda.

"I'm not asking you, I'm telling you. Get your coat and get in the car now," she demanded. The lingering tendrils of guilt that followed me over the way I'd left, floated away on the wind as she ordered me to do her bidding.

"I'm sure that tone of voice worked when I was a little girl, but I'm not seven any more, Aunt Elizabeth. If something has happened with the company, you're welcome to come in and talk to me about it, and I'll do what I can from here. But leaving at the moment is just out of the question. What you decide to do with that is up to you, but that's my final word," I said, wearily but firmly.

If she continued glaring at me with that scowl and hateful look in her eyes, I was going to slam the door in her face, even if the company was falling apart. The livelihood of the people who worked for us was the only thing keeping me civil.

"You always were an insolent little bitch. When I said I wasn't asking, I meant it," she said and, reaching into her pocket, pulled out a small gun. It looked real enough, but I had no idea whether it actually was. What I did understand was just how much she wanted to use it. Like she'd given free rein to her true feelings, her hate for me was palpable.

"If you're going to use that thing on me, fine. But I'm not going with you," I replied adamantly. Perhaps if Tom were there, I would've fought a little harder, but the idea of dying didn't seem a daunting a prospect anymore. And it was infinitely preferable to giving an inch to that vindictive bitch.

"Oh, this isn't for you, you stupid cow. There's a bullet in here with the old woman's name on it. Now, you either come quietly or I'll introduce her to it, up close and personal," she warned. She looked so unhinged, that I complied immediately. Pulling my boots on and reaching for my jacket, just as Nan rounded the doorway.

"What's going on?" Nan said in confusion. Looking back, I could see that Elizabeth had stuffed the gun back into her pocket, but we both knew it was there.

"Nan, this is my Aunt Elizabeth. Apparently, there's been a terrible crisis with the company and she needs me back in London to sort it out. Will you be all right if I go? It should only take me a few hours to sort it out," I said.

From Elizabeth's behaviour, there was a distinct possibility that I would never see Nan again, but I told her whatever I thought she needed to hear in order to get Elizabeth away from her. Ensuring Nan's safety was my only priority.

"Couldn't it wait?" Nan pleaded, in a way that was so uncharacteristic for her. "Just a day or two?"

"I'm sorry," I said, "but I really need to do this. If Tom calls while I'm gone, will you let him know that I'm fine, and I'll be home as soon as I can." Nan's eyes widened in surprise as she mulled over my words. I willed her not to say anything, praying that Elizabeth didn't know that Tom was dead and hoping she'd understand that I was giving her an SOS. Throwing my arms around her, I hugged her hard and relished in the fact that she held me as tightly as I did her.

"Are you sure there's nothing I can do?" she pleaded, and I hoped that we were speaking the same code.

"No, there's nothing. Just pass on the message to Tom," I replied.

"It's nice to meet you, but we really do need to go," Elizabeth said curtly. I heard the warning in her tone and let Nan go.

I no longer thought of her as my aunt. Any accident of nature that made us blood relatives was a tragedy best left forgotten as far as I was concerned.

"Take care of yourself," I said as I left.

"You too," she replied, and then, with a small sigh of relief that she was safe, I shut the door behind me.

"Get in the car," Elizabeth ordered. "You're driving." She

indicated to a nice, but fairly innocuous black Audi Saloon. The black paint and tinted windows gave it a touch of the ominous.

"Where are we going?" I asked, sliding behind the driver's seat.

"London."

I started the engine, and she pulled up the address in the sat nav. Once we were far enough away from the house that I could breathe, I focused on a solid plan for getting myself out of this mess and getting back to Nan.

"Whatever stupid plan you're concocting, just forget about it. You don't think I make threats I can't go through with, do you? There's a gun aimed at the house right now. If my guy doesn't hear from me when he's supposed to, if anything happens to me, she'll get a bullet between the eyes. And your bullet won't be far behind. So try and muster up a little maturity and do as you're told for once."

"Why are you doing this?" I cried.

"You really don't get it, do you? You still think I brought you back to save the company. I built that fucking company! Years of weak, clueless men chipped away at my legacy until there was nothing left. I watched my own father make bad decision after bad decision, praying all the while that he didn't destroy it before it was my turn. And then what did he do? In his final act of fucking ignorance and idiocrasy, he left his shares to my brother, and I got five percent. Five measly fucking percent! I'm the one who worked her arse off to get a first class honours degree in business. While other teenagers were having fun at parties, drinking and living it up, I was interning at shipping houses. Studying how things worked, calculating how to make the business better, stronger. And do you know what your dad studied?" she screamed, not pausing to let me answer.

Of course I knew what degree Dad had chosen. It was how my parents had met. They'd fallen in love with each other over a love of art.

"History of Fine Art! All he was interested in was your mother, and when he had you brats, I felt it all slipping through my fingers. Being born a male was the only thing he ever had to do to get those shares. Old money for old men. Keeping it in the male line until there's no more left to give. Of course, your mother wanted nothing to do with any of it. The business, the family, London. The ungrateful bitch even convinced him to move to that god awful hellhole up north. But even then, my brother wouldn't sign over the shares. Wanted you and John to inherit the family business he said. A business that selfish bastard did nothing for, and to add insult to injury, he was breaking the line of male succession for you. For the first time in the history of Tatem Shipping, the company would go to a woman. And not the one who'd worked for it, or earned it, who wanted it so badly she sacrificed any chance at a husband or family of her own! No, it was going to a woman who looked on the empire with the same scorn and derision that her bitch of a mother had. I was never going to let that travesty happen."

"Oh my God. You knew about the Russians, didn't you?" I said, my body shaking as the pieces of the puzzle all started to come together.

"And the penny finally drops," she replied sarcastically. "I didn't just know about the Russians, I invited them through the door. I've been around the shipping elite my entire life. I saw how things were going. A single shipment here, a backhander there. When we joined the European Union, that's when the gangs became more organised, and I knew then we had a huge opportunity to change the tide of the company's fortune. To claw back everything my ancestors had thrown away."

"Then why involve Dad? Why bring him and John back into the family fold? When Mum died, if you'd just left him alone, he would have signed over the shares, I'm sure of it. He was broken up, vulnerable, but left alone he would have raised us," I argued, devastated at the injustice of having to lose both parents for her greed.

"Because I needed him. The Russians were old school. From a different world. A different machine. They were even more misogynistic than my forefathers had been. No matter how attractive the offering from Tatem Shipping, they never would have gone for it with a woman at the helm. Typical that they'd rather a tired, weak-willed man to a strong, powerful woman. But, whether they appreciated my worth inconsequential. All they cared about was the puppet.

Nobody ever looks to see who's pulling the strings. So I gave them what they wanted, and they made the deal," she explained. She was psychotic, her moods swinging wildly from fury to a gleeful sense of pride at the cleverness of her own machinations.

"Then why have Dad and John killed? What did they ever do to you?" I asked. There was no love lost between myself and my brother, but I would always mourn for the little boy he'd been before she got her hooks into him. My big brother.

"Poor John. He's my only regret in all of this. I'd like to think he was the nearest I ever had to having a child of my own. Fair skin, fair hair, all of my genetics and none of your mother's I'm happy to say. That boy thought I hung the moon. After your bitch of a mother died, he followed me around like a puppy. Went to university, then business school, absorbing anything he could about the industry like a sponge. He was my protégé. When I introduced him to the Russian involvement in the business, he didn't bat an eyelid, even worked to keep your father in line. That was, of course, until the day the news aired the story of a shipping container at Dover carrying the bodies of thirty-four women. The container wasn't registered to us, but John had his suspicions. He confronted me, and I confirmed that they were true. He told me that he was appalled at what we were involved in. I called him naive, said he had lacked forward planning and a vision for the future. It was an unhappy revelation that we were both disappointed in each other. Still, we could have lived with it. Buried our differences as it were and carried on regardless. But he couldn't let the container thing go. Said he wouldn't be party to trafficking women and children. I told him, that when you cross the line, you never look back. Because how far you crossed it doesn't matter. Once it's done, there's no going back."

"He disagreed with you, and you killed him for it. You killed them both."

"He signed his own death warrant I'm afraid," she said, almost wistfully. "Your father had no real idea just how deeply the Russian deal was imbedded into our business. He'd convinced himself, probably to appease his own conscience, that we were smuggling cigarettes and alcohol to avoid tax. When John confronted him with irrefutable proof that we were trafficking weapons and women as well, he told Vasili he was pulling out of the deal. By then they were already dead, with or without my nod."

"You gave the nod to have them killed? You let them die?" I asked, struggling to believe that it was true, that she could be so calculating and callous to her brother and the man she thought of as a son.

"I made a choice! To get in the lifeboat instead of going down with the ship! By then Vasili had mellowed. Over time he understood the power I wielded and who was really in control of the company, so he came to see me first. I think, secretly, he admires me. My tenacity, my single-minded focus, my drive to protect the business at all costs. Perhaps I remind him a little of himself," she mused.

"Yeah, you're both insane," I muttered.

She slapped me so hard, that my ear was ringing, and I swerved as I struggled to get control of the car, much to the irritation of the other motorists who beeped loudly to communicate their frustration.

"You could've killed us both!" I screamed when I'd righted the vehicle.

"I should've done that a long time ago. The minute you opened that smart mouth of yours, I should've smacked it. But if I had, I don't think I'd have ever have stopped," she told me.

My knuckles were white from clenching the wheel so hard. Slowly, I focused on relaxing them to get the blood flowing back. I kept quiet as I drove steadily down the motorway. My cheek still stung, but I focused more on containing the urge to elbow that manipulative bitch in the face rather than on my pain. With every toxic, poisonous word that spilled from her mouth, I found my anger building. The knowledge that all of my pain and loss could be traced back to one person filled me with an all-consuming rage. I'd been sure that Agheenco was the worst kind of scum, but if he showed any loyalty to his family, he was a prince compared to the soulless monster that sat next to me. I knew, without a shadow of a doubt, that she'd keep doing it long after I was gone. There was too much money in the suffering of others for her to stop. She'd cram human lives into containers like baked beans in a tin if she could. Label them up and sell them cheap. Only the knowledge that there was a gun to Nan's head stopped me from driving the car into a concrete barrier. I'd kill us both if that was what it took to end the cycle of misery. But to save the lives of countless innocents, I'd have to sacrifice one. Nan's soul against the measure of hundreds, and I couldn't do it. For miles I anguished over the decision, and then eventually it was too late.

"Come off this exit," she told me.

"I thought we were going to London?"

"Just shut the fuck up and get off this exit. There's a service station up ahead. Pull into the car park behind it and park in a space at the very back. I have a surprise for you."

CHAPTER TWENTY EIGHT

Sarah

We'd been waiting for around fifteen minutes. Despite the bitter cold, Elizabeth insisted I turn the engine off. Without heaters, it was like sitting in an icebox.

"I don't understand why you brought me into all this. You knew I never wanted anything to do with the company. I would've sold you those shares in a heartbeat if you'd asked me to."

"You may be beautiful Sarah, but you really are swimming in your mother's end of the gene pool when it comes to brains. Of course you would've sold them to me, but really, after everything I've done for Tatem Shipping, why should I part with a penny? Those shares are mine. Mine by birth right and mine because I've earned them. Far better to inherit the shares as your next of kin," she replied smugly.

"If I'm killed, you'd be the first person they'd look at. You can't inherit that kind of money from someone who's been murdered or killed suspiciously and not expect a few eyebrows to be raised," I said, wondering if she really might have been mad after all.

"Really, Sarah, it's clear you don't have a head for this sort of thing at all. You need to start thinking outside of the box. How do you ensure the finger of blame is never pointed at you? Well, you make sure that someone else kills the person you want dead very loudly and very publicly, and you play the part of the grief-stricken lady of misfortune, deprived of the last member of her family in a way the entire country will sympathise with. By the time my inheritance comes through, I'll be a national treasure. My popularity and media presence will put those shares at an all-time high, and that's when I'll sell them. Of course, nobody would expect me to continue on. It will be a sad day for the board that the last living Tatem is leaving Tatem Shipping, and behind my back people will talk about how I must be regretting not having any children now. Those bitches can think what they like though. I'll be smiling on the inside. Because now the Russian trade deal is dead, eventually it will come to light that the bottom is falling out of the company. It will take months, maybe a year even, but I'll be long gone. Doing the talk-show circuit and selling my tale of woe. I might even write a book about it, before retiring to an island somewhere warm."

"At the risk of getting hit again, I have to tell you that you are absolutely fucking delusional. Why would the public give a shit that I died? And how would that possibly help you get a book deal?"

She lunged towards me again, having gotten a taste for violence, only this time I wasn't driving and caught her wrist.

"Gun on Nan or not, you raise your hand to me again, and I will bitch-slap you into the middle of next week," I warned. I'd had enough of crying, of mourning, of feeling like a fucking victim. Now I was fighting back, and the first time she let her attention drift, I was getting that weapon off her. She snatched her arm away indignantly, and I let her.

"It amuses me to see you so upset over a slap. Believe me, that's going to seem like a gentle caress next to what you're going to endure," she said, smiling as she regained some of her composure. I frowned, as a wave of nausea came over me. It didn't sound as though it was her plan to shoot me quickly.

"You didn't answer me," I repeated. "Why would the public give a shit that I died?"

"It's not your death that they'll care about. It's how you'll die that will make me famous," she said, leaning forward so that she was right in my face, "there's a storm coming, and you'll be in the eye of it. That was my price. I don't need money. I'll get that from the sale of my shares. They offered me a few million, but what good is a couple of extra million when it can be traced back to me? Forensic accounts being what they are these days, it just wasn't worth the risk. I'll get what's coming to me when I cash in our combined share value. No, I wanted something else. So, when Vasili came to me and said that he wanted me to ship a biological weapon from Russia to the United Kingdom, we struck a bargain. You see Vasili wants out of the game also. I suppose it is rather tiring to always be at the whim of someone more powerful than you. Between us, we had a buyer, a need, the cash, and a way out. The only thing I struggled with was a way to engineer it all, until you stepped in and set it all up so beautifully." She cackled with gleeful laughter.

"For Christ's sake! Will you stop talking in riddles and just spit it out please? What did you do and what are you talking about, a biological weapon? Everything was seized by the SAS last night. It's been all over the news all day," I said, omitting the fact that Tom had been killed in the assault. She'd immediately work out that I gave Nan a message, and Nan wouldn't be safe after that.

"You stupid bitch, you still haven't figured it out! You were the one who brought in the SAS. You were the one who set this whole thing up for us. The firebombs that have been all over the city, they were just a prelude. A pre-dinner performance! Have you ever heard of a dirty bomb? It's what you get when you attach a biological agent or nuclear material to an ordinary bomb. It doesn't have the same level of devastation as a nuclear bomb, but it will bring a built-up area like London to its knees," she gloated, as though it were some kind of achievement that should be lauded. "I arranged the delivery, Vasili took the payment, and the terrorist cell your boyfriend's been looking so hard for will get the engine for their bomb. The Russian gang wants their money, of course, but thanks to the SAS, they now believe Vasili to be dead and the money lost along with him. Vasili gets his very comfortable retirement, and I get exactly what I need. A niece who dies strapped to a suicide vest in a death I couldn't possibly be connected to."

"What have you done?" I asked in disbelief. "You'd help facilitate in the killing of thousands of innocent lives. Families. Children. Your own people, for shares I would have gifted to you. They meant nothing to me. They never did. And soon they won't mean anything to you either. At the end of the day, whether you're implicated in my death or not won't matter. I stopped by my solicitor before I left London. Figured it was about time to make a will. In the event of my death, the shares, the money, the property, everything goes into a trust fund. The fund will be managed by an appointed trustee with beneficiaries being those closest to me and the bulk going to a charity that helps the victims of human trafficking."

It was my time to sound smug, and it felt good to wipe that entitled smirk off her face. If I'd known she was going to shoot me, I might have kept my mouth shut. The bang startled me because I wasn't expecting it, but it took seconds for the pain to register. I looked down to see the red stain spreading across my sweater, and only then did I realise that the bullet had pierced my side.

"You're ruining everything!" she screamed, before

pretty much losing it, smacking the dash board over and over again with the butt of the gun like some fucking crazy person. I pressed my hand over the wound and pushed, bile instantly rising in my throat. I knew as much about first aid as I knew about football, which was a grand total of fuck all. In the back of my fuzzy little mind though, something was telling me that keeping pressure on it was a good idea.

After her little outburst, Elizabeth brushed back her now wild hair and made a fruitless attempt to comb it back into place, the gun still clutched in one hand as though she'd forgotten it was there.

"No matter. I'll contest the will. There's enough people who'll testify about the adverse effect that money-grabbing parasite of yours had on your mental well-being to get it overturned," she said, ignoring the fact completely that she'd shot me.

"You're going to lose everything," I said on a groan. "Do you have any idea what happened to the US economy on 9/11? The same thing's going to happen here, and then your precious share prices won't be worth shit."

"Not if I short certain stocks and bet against the market. Then when stock hits rock bottom, I'll do very well. Not enough to raise any red flags on a stock market analysis, but well enough. I've been in this industry for more than thirty years. You don't think I've covered every base? By the time I inherit your shares, the economy will have recovered. The long-term effects of a dirty bomb will spread, meaning that food will need to be imported where it can't be grown. Do you know what that will do to the price of those shipping stocks? It's possible that losing the Russian business won't affect Tatem Shipping at all, but I'll be long gone before I find out." She was so pleased with her own cunning that she was positively glowing.

"And the attack on London Bridge? Was that just coincidence?" I asked, my side really beginning to burn in a way that was making my vision blur.

"Of course not," she replied. "That was supposed to be my payment. The terrorist event that would have blown you into the water. But the stupid bastard went too early and ruined the whole thing. And if he'd done his fucking job, you wouldn't have made a will. Still, no use getting upset about it. You just have to roll with the punches I suppose. They were actually a lot more amenable to the idea than I thought. Apparently, a very wealthy, beautiful, and rich British heiress makes a very fine statement when she's strapped to a biological weapon in the centre of London."

"But the SAS seized your shipment," I protested.

"No. The SAS seized *a* shipment. What better way to shut down their operation than by giving them what they think they've been looking for? Our terrorist friends could see the logic in that, and it wasn't really much of a sacrifice to send in a few of their men who were, of course, clueless as to what was about to transpire. The terror level has already been publicly dropped in response to this ridiculous publicity stunt. They have absolutely no idea what's coming."

"Nan will know you came for me." If I'd been any less delirious, I wouldn't have mentioned her name. I wouldn't have drawn attention to her in any way. But this was another base she'd already covered.

"Nancy Harper won't live to see the morning," she gloated, and using the very last reserves of energy left in the tank, I pulled my arm back and punched her hard in the face before passing out cold.

CHAPTER TWENTY NINE

Tom

"Where are you going?" Will asked as I headed towards my Land Rover.

"Davies told Nan and Sarah that I was shot and killed last night. Told them it was during a training exercise, but with the leaked footage, he knows they'll have bought it. Fucker wanted to hold me for twenty-four hours so MI5 could get Sarah in witness protection before I got back."

"I don't get it. How does Sarah going into witness protection help Davies?"

"Vasili Agheenco wasn't taken out with the rest of the Russians, and Davies made the call to go regardless. At the moment, he's looking at a medal and a hefty promotion. If a rags-to-riches heiress who gave up everything to bring down terrorists is killed publicly because Davies made that call, the press will have a fucking field day."

"Dirty fucker. Nan's gonna remove his balls with a rusty

knife when she finds out," Will predicted.

"That's pretty much what I told him." I unlocked my car and sat down in the driver's seat, my aching ribs still giving me grief. Will climbed into the passenger seat, and I just looked at him.

"What? You didn't think I was going to let you do this by yourself, did you?" he asked.

I didn't argue with him because we both knew I'd do the same for him. Not that I could ever see Will racing out to track down the girl he loved, but stranger things had happened. I would've said the same about myself a year ago. I dug out my phone from the centre console of my car where I'd left it. As soon as it powered up, I checked the link to the security feeds. Nan was pacing up and down with her phone to her ear, looking absolutely furious.

"Fuck. I can't see her," I said. I'd pulled up the feed in every camera I had at the house and she wasn't in one. After an unsuccessful attempt to call Nan, I chucked him my phone then started the engine and gunned it towards the main gates.

"Keep trying Nan for me. Her line's constantly engaged, and Sar's is just going straight to voicemail. I'd prefer Nan to find out I'm alive before I just rock up on the doorstep, and I need to know if MI5 or the Ministry of Defence guys have taken Sarah."

The guards waved us through at the exit, and I broke more than a few speed limits as I sped through the country lanes back to the cottage. If Sarah was still there, I had no doubt that's where they'd be holed up. Sarah loved our place, and Nan wouldn't try and take her away from anywhere that gave her comfort. I fucking loved that it was "our" place now, but my gut burned when I let myself think of what they both must have endured in the last twelve hours, thinking I was dead. It strengthened my resolve to leave active combat duties as soon as I could. A small part of me was a little ashamed at the thought of everything I'd put Nan through over the years. The worry of never knowing whether I'd make it back or not alive. But as fucked up as my childhood had been, I needed that outlet. Needed the discipline of the army until I could figure out who I was, who I wanted to be. Now all I needed was Sarah. Fuck it, I'd be a great stay-at-home Dad if it meant she could do what made her happy. Never in a million years did I ever see myself having kids, but now that I had Sar, the idea was stuck in my head. I wanted to see her belly swell with my baby, wanted to hear their first laugh and change their first nappy. No way was I going to miss out on that because I was squatting in some shithole doing intel on the other side of the world. I would be the perfect dad because I knew exactly the sort of father I didn't want to be.

"Any luck?" I asked him for about the fiftieth time.

"Do you hear me talking to anyone?" he grumbled. I was about to tell him to cut off when I heard a voice on the other end of the line. "Hi, Nan, it's Will Edwards," he said.

"Who?" she screeched.

"Will Edwards, Tom's friend," he replied.

"Who?" she screeched louder.

"It's Badger," he practically shouted down the phone.

"Why didn't you bloody say so then?" she shouted back, and he rolled his eyes, despite the fact she couldn't see him. She was talking so quickly, I couldn't hear her through the phone.

"Listen, Nan," he said, trying to calm her down. "I need you to sit down for a sec. I have something really important to tell you. Yes. Yes. Yes...I know all that. Yes. Listen, woman, will you stop talking for a second and let me get a word in edgeways!" Everything went quiet, and then Nan was speaking in a low voice.

"Yes, Mrs Harper. Sorry, Mrs Harper," he said eventually, seeming a bit embarrassed. I chuckled to myself thinking that only my mother could have the hardest special operative fucker I knew apologising like a contrite schoolboy.

"Well, the thing is, I know that Lieutenant Colonel Davies paid you and Sarah a visit earlier, but he wasn't exactly truthful. Tom was shot during the exercise last night, but his Kevlar vest saved him. Davies wanted you to think he was dead so he could get Sarah to agree to witness protection," he told her.

"Why didn't you bloody well say so," Nan screamed down the line. "You've been on the phone five minutes, and you're only just telling me my boy's alive!" Her rant continued, but I didn't hear any more of it. Will covered the mouthpiece and lowered the phone as she continued to scream.

"You and me go back a long way, mate, so no disrespect intended, but your mother drives me up the fucking wall," he said.

I chuckled because she drove everyone up the wall, but I stopped short as we sped up the lane to the cottage. "We're here," I said, screeching to a stop on the gravel drive. He ended the call, cutting her off mid-rant, and I had a feeling he'd pay for that when she saw him. She already had the front door open by the time we reached it, and I lifted her off her feet into a huge hug. For once in her life, she was speechless.

"You okay?" I asked as I put her down.

She wiped the corners of her eyes surreptitiously and smiled. "Well, I am now. But I don't fancy going through that again anytime soon, and I'm taking a sledgehammer to that fucker Davies's kneecaps when I see him next," she said.

"Don't worry, I don't plan on putting you through that again anytime soon. I have a few years left on my ticket, but I'm getting out of special ops," I told her. I felt a little bad that I hadn't discussed it with Will, but he wouldn't be surprised to hear it after everything that had gone down.

"Oh thank God," she said, putting her hand over her heart. The damn woman had never let on that my profession bothered her, but I could see then what I'd been putting her through all those years.

"Where's my girl?" I asked her, needing to feel her safe in my arms.

"You'd better come in," she said, and walked towards the kitchen. Will and I shared a look, and his face reflected the same concern as mine. This didn't sound good at all.

"Where is she, Nan?" I asked, following her.

She put the kettle on and started making tea, more I think to do something with her hands than anything else. "A few hours after Davies left, her aunt turned up and said that there was some crisis with her company or something and that she needed to go back to London. I heard them talking at the door before I went to see what was going on. Sarah told me she had to leave, but there was something wacky about the whole thing. Her aunt drove all the way down from London to get her but didn't come in, even for a minute, and the sour-faced old bitch didn't speak to me at all. Then when she was leaving, Sar hugged me so hard she could've broken one of my ribs, and she said the strangest thing as she left. She told me to tell you if I saw you that she was fine and she'd be home in a few hours."

I was relieved that she wasn't with the Russians, but something definitely wasn't right. "So you think she'll be back in a few hours? Do you have any idea where in London they were going?"

"No, Tom, you're not getting it. When she gave me that message, she thought you were dead. I think it was her way of telling me that she was in trouble. That she was going with her aunt under duress. Of course, I can't prove it. I've called the guardhouse at Hereford, I've called the Ministry of

348

Defence, I've even called the police. They all say the same thing. She went voluntarily with a member of her own family, she said goodbye, there's no ransom or any other evidence of a kidnapping. They won't even let me report her as a missing person."

"Shit!" I muttered. As far as I knew, the aunt wasn't involved in anything, but the woman was a class A bitch. If there was some way of using Sarah to her own advantage, she'd do it.

"Look, Nan, I'm not happy with you being here. If her aunt knew where to find you, chances are that other people know about this place too. Do you think your friend Sandra would let you stay there for a couple of nights?" I asked.

"She'll be fine. I'll grab my bag," she replied, hurrying off upstairs as she called Sandra on her mobile.

"Jesus. That may be the first time in history that woman hasn't argued with you. What do you want to do about Sarah?" Will said.

"Where's my phone?" I asked in reply. I caught it as he chucked it to me and started loading up an app. "I installed a locater app on her phone. It says she's about fifteen miles from here. We try there first."

Fifteen minutes later, we'd drop Nan off and were headed towards the site. The closer we got, the more my gut roiled. Something fucked up was going down, and if my girl was hurt in any way, I was going to butcher anyone who had a hand in her pain. I'd become the monster in the dark that men didn't even know to fear. Death would be a welcome relief by the time I was done. I'd spent my life roaming through the various circles of Hell, content to live that way because I didn't know any better. But I'd been shown Heaven in the arms of someone good and pure. To have that light stolen away, to live once again in Hell, robbed of my ignorance and forever lost, would drive any man to insanity. Or in my case, to war.

Will pulled into the car park. A few lorries and late-night motorists stopping to rest and refuel were located near the service station entrance, but as we moved towards the signal, the area was relatively empty. When we saw that both front doors of the black Audi had been left open, I knew we were too late. Will had been driving, so I was out before the Land Rover had barely stopped. What I saw inside triggered something. Some dark switch deep inside. Sprawled across the console, as if she'd been trying to escape, was the body of Sarah's aunt, a small, neat bullet hole directly between the eyes and another just above it to the right, as if the second shot was taken milliseconds later.

"Double tap to the head. The Russians?" Will asked me.

"Bitch sold out her own niece. The deal with Tatem Shipping's done, so they're eliminating all the witnesses." My tone was flat. Soulless. Will knew what that meant as much as any man in my unit. The Tom that Sarah loved would be with her, always. I was the Reaper. The bringer of death. Will squeezed my shoulder reassuringly. I picked up her smashed up phone from the footwell and threw it back in again, having seen that it'd been completely destroyed.

"She's alive, mate. If they were just eliminating witnesses, she'd be in here too. They need her for something, which means she's still alive. We just have to find her."

"Let's get back to Hereford. I need to speak to MI5, and Davies is going to help me whether he likes it or not," I replied. Once again, we raced down the motorway and back to base, and I called Masterson. After two rings, he picked up.

"Where are you?" I asked.

"On my way to see Lieutenant Colonel Davies. I'm about ten minutes away, but I need to brief him on some new intel. You too as it goes," he said.

"I'm five minutes behind you," I replied. "Masterson, I need you to ask headquarters to activate that tracker you gave me. The Russians have Sarah."

He was completely silent for a moment as he processed what I said. I may not like him for making moves on my girl, but I did know that he cared about her. Enough to help me out when Davies dropped her like a hot fucking potato.

"I'm on it," he said, and disconnected.

"You and Simon Masterson cooperating with each other? I didn't see that one coming," Will said.

"MI5 don't trust anyone but themselves not to fuck things up. I don't agree with it, but I respect it. I wouldn't trust anyone outside of the SAS not to fuck up either. But the intel that led to Operation Sceptre didn't come from MI5, it came from SO19. That didn't sit right with Masterson's department. After all, SO19 couldn't catch the fucking terrorists in the first place, which is why we were brought on board. After Davies pulled security, Masterson came to see me. The intel matched an entry on the shipping paperwork, which is why it was given the green light, but it actually came from an anonymous tip. At that point, he knew there was a mole in Tatem Shipping. The government authorised the withdrawal of Sarah's security, so there wasn't much he could do, but he did warn me and passed on a high-tech, long-range tracking device. I didn't want to scare Sarah, so I had it put into a necklace for her. I'm just crossing my fingers they don't take it off her before we track it."

"Something big's going down, Reap. And I have a shitty feeling it's bigger than the Russians," he replied.

"Team B wiped out half the Russian gang in London. There's no way they could've brought in reinforcements that quick, so either Agheenco's working alone with his own agenda, or there are more terrorists in play," I responded.

We were both silent after that. There wasn't much to say. It didn't matter who had her. Wherever she was, she was scared and alone. My brave little warrior who defied them all because her conscience told her to. Would she still fight to stay alive, thinking I was dead? I wasn't a religious man, had never seen anything that gave me any kind of faith until I met Sarah, but I offered up a silent prayer to anyone who'd listen for the safety of a single life. The one soul, above all others, who deserved saving.

The guards at the base waved us through, and after throwing the car into a space, we barged into Davies's office, to find Masterson already waiting.

"Come on in, gentlemen. Don't worry at all about knocking, just make yourselves at home," Davies said sarcastically.

Ignored him, I shook Masterson's hand when he stood up to offer it to me.

"Any news on the trace?" I asked, urgently.

"We should have it any minute. It's been activated; they're just trying to pinpoint the coordinates so we can get an accurate location, but we know she's in central London," he said, pulling a file out of his briefcase and handing me a print out of a shipping manifest with only one entry highlighted.

"SO19 doesn't have the resources to work the data, but we do. We traced every single one of the cargo changes that Agheenco made in the two weeks his lackey was at your office. Once Operation Sceptre began, we had the green light to intercept the shipments. We got them all. Every weapon, explosive, animal, and human being trafficked or sold through Tatem Shipping was located, all except one. In most cases, MI5 passed the information onto the police or the Border Agency, and we let them do the takedown. The one we didn't get arrived in Liverpool two days ago. The manifest lists the crate that came in as "medical." It was collected an hour before the police got there. Contact details on the shipping documentation was a total bust, so I sent one of our guys down there. He's not SAS and looks pretty harmless, but he scares the shit out of people. Highly trained in interrogation and counter-intelligence. After a day of questioning employees, he gets a confession from one of the dock workers. He was paid to keep quiet, and he couldn't give us much to go on, but his description of the person who collected the package, specifically referring to an unusual birthmark, matches a suspect on the Interpol terrorist watch list. He also said he saw a couple of symbols on the container. He drew them out, and our guy sent back pictures a couple of hours ago. The first was the symbol for biohazard material. The second was harder to interpret, but we eventually traced it to a laboratory in Russia," he explained.

"Jesus," Will muttered, already anticipating what he was going to say.

"In the late 80s, the Soviet Union developed the Chimera Project, which studied the feasibility of combining smallpox and Ebola into one super virus. I don't think it's a coincidence this came from the same lab," he said.

"You think Agheenco is doing this?" I asked him.

"No. I think he found a way to get a bioweapon into the UK and he's sold it to the cell everyone's so pleased at having supposedly wiped out. I think they're going to use it to make a dirty bomb," he said.

"You're fucking kidding me! Does your section chief

know?" Davies roared at Masterson.

"He does. The prime minister is being briefed as we speak," he said.

Davies swore again then picked up the phone, dialling frantically. "You need to get me a trace location. I need to mobilise a team and get in there," I told him.

"I'm on it," Masterson replied, and walked out of the office to make a call.

"You're not going anywhere," Davies warned me. "I'm calling in Jackson and the backup team. Your team is on leave, and you've not even been cleared by medical. I'm not breaching protocol over this."

"My team is on standby, sir, and with respect, fuck protocol. We get one chance at this. You need the very best, and that's me and my guys. My girl is with them, and I'll be fucked if I'm leaving her rescue to anyone else," I said.

"That's exactly my point, Harper. This is not a fucking rescue mission! My objective, my only objective, is the elimination of the terrorist threat and the deactivation of that bomb. Somehow, I don't think your priorities and mine align, do you?"

"Look, sir, if I don't retrieve that bomb, she's dead anyway. We all are. If you're not happy, send my boys in with Jackson's team. We both know you can't justify a fuck up to the prime minister when you're sending in the backup team." I waited for his response. Regardless of his decision, I was going in anyway, but I'd rather have the resources of the regiment behind me.

"Fine, go. But Jackson has operational control," he warned.

I raged internally, but I'd take what I could get if it got me a place on the chopper. The door flew open a moment later, and a ruddy-faced Masterson burst in. "She's at St Martins Le Grand, South of Aldersgate Street."

"Christ, that's next to the stock exchange, isn't it?" Will asked.

"And the Bank of England, Goldman Sachs, Merrill Lynch, and about a dozen other banks," Masterson added. "The bomb will destroy the financial district and the bio agent will take out whatever's left."

"Tom, mobilise your unit. I want a bird in the air in half an hour," Davies said.

Will was already out the door and calling up the team, but I offered Masterson my hand before leaving.

"In case I don't make it back, thanks for everything. I honestly never thought I'd say this, but it was good working with you," I said, meaning it.

"You too," he replied. "Now go get her back."

I nodded and left him as I headed down to the armoury. Twenty minutes later, both teams were prepped, ready, and armed. Five minutes after that, we were airborne. The chopper doors were open and cold air whipped past my face as I stared at the vista of the fast approaching night-lit city. My usual stony calm was gone, and in its place was a twisted ball of ugly rage as I mentally prepared for the carnage I was about to bring down. My only thought of tenderness spared for the girl who had my heart.

"Hold on, baby. Just a little bit longer. I'm coming," I whispered into the wind, hoping like hell she heard me.

CHAPTER THIRTY

Sarah

I regained consciousness in the back of a dirty van to see Vasili on his knees, undoing his trousers. My sweater was pushed up high and one breast was out of my bra. Thankfully, my jeans were still on and buttoned, but it was clear what was about to go down. The wound at my side burned like nothing I'd ever experienced. I didn't know how much blood I could lose before it was too late, but I did know I wasn't going out like this. In the back of a van at the dirty hands of a monster.

If he wanted my life that badly, he could fight me for it.

Knowing I probably only had seconds before he realised I was awake, I bit back a cry of pain and raised my knee hard, catching him sharply in the balls. He growled in agony and slumped to the side. Seizing my chance, I grabbed the internal handle of the door and shoved it open hard. Dizzy and disorientated, I crawled out as quickly as I could and stumbled across the tarmac as I tried to put as much distance between myself and that scumbag as I could.

As far as I could make out, we were in some sort of a car park, but nothing about it seemed familiar. Unlike the place I'd been taken from, there were no bright lights or signs of civilisation close by. I couldn't stop to worry about that though. I had no idea how long it took a man to recover from a hit to the groin, but if he caught me, I'd be paying for it in the worst way.

A tall hedge ran along the perimeter and behind it sounded like a road. Skirting my way along the edges, I desperately tried to find a break in the shrubbery, a gap or a hole big enough to squeeze through. It was dark, but street lamps on the other side gave a little illumination. Clenching my side as hard as I could, I stumbled and thrust out a hand against the sharp branches to steady myself. The pain from my bullet wound was agonising, but the rest of my body hurt as well. I was scratched, bruised, and shot but not broken.

Not yet.

Eventually, I found what I was looking for as my hand pushed through a small opening, barely big enough for someone of my size. Without pausing, I ducked towards it, only to be yanked backwards sharply by my hair.

"You fucking bitch. You're not getting away that easily," he taunted, dragging me back towards the van. The closer and closer we came, the sicker I felt. How many women had died in the same way? In the back of a dirty van at the hands of soulless men, stripped of any semblance of dignity. I scrambled against him, fighting to get free, but his grip on my hair was ironclad. Any physical strength I had left was gone. It was all I could do to break my fall as he threw me into the open door and slammed it shut after climbing in behind me. Seconds later, he had my arms pinned to my sides as he straddled my hips. His dick had unfortunately recovered, and the evidence of how hard my struggles were making him was pressed against my pelvis. I was shaking uncontrollably, my body almost going into shock. It was inevitable really, given what I'd already endured and was about to endure again.

"I should have done this the first time I had you on the floor. I bet you would have enjoyed it. Rich bitch like you loves it rough. I would have liked making your father squirm before I killed him. Should have told him how I was going to fuck his little princess seven ways from Sunday until she was so broken, there was no putting her back together again. And then shared how I was going to strap her to a bomb that would change the face of the Western world," he spat, as he released one of my hands to push my sweater back up and pull down my bra, leaving me back in exactly the same position as I started.

"What are you talking about?" I protested, struggling weakly against his weight.

"The ambush was a setup. The real shipment has already been made. A biological bomb that will destroy this city. But after I get what I want, I'll be long gone. You, I'm afraid, will have a ringside seat," he taunted. His pleasure in my pain at the realisation that Tom had died for nothing was evident. He lunged forward, grabbing my breast as he sucked grotesquely on my nipple, grinding himself against me. I tried blocking everything. Tried focusing only on thoughts of Tom. But it didn't work. Everywhere I looked, Vasili was there. My fear didn't ebb, but it wasn't alone. Anger had risen to join it. Anger that Tom's death had been so needless. Anger that animals liked Vasili could take whatever they wanted and get away with it. Even now, my body wasn't enough. He wanted my kiss too. To steal away the memory of the last man to touch my lips. It's the last thing I had of him, and I wasn't letting it go. I'd rather have died than let it go. So, I leant my head back as far as I could and head-butted him in the face.

"Fuck!" He backhanded me so hard that my face was smashed into the side of the van. A pool of liquid settled beneath my cheek, and I belatedly realised that it was coming from the top of my head. I was vaguely aware of Vasili, pawing at my body and muttering something about making me pay, but my mind was already somewhere else. My consciousness drifting to another place where he'd never be able to touch me. A place that was for Tom and Tom alone. A place where we'd both be together again. My vision was blurred and my hearing muffled when a series of hard bangs resonated in the darkness and the door slid open. I saw only the shirt of the man taking in the scene before him. When he realised what he was looking at, he screamed at my attacker. Though I couldn't understand the words spoken between them, the stranger gestured towards me repeatedly.

"Help," was the last word I whispered, a sound lost in both of their raised voices, as I slipped into the dark embrace of blissful oblivion.

———————

Waking up again was hard. Like the morning after a wild night, when you just lay there, willing yourself to go back to sleep, knowing the pain of an outrageous hangover was only minutes away. When the fog of sleep finally receded, I carried out a brief reconnoitre of the mess that was my body. My jeans were still on and buttoned, and to my great relief, I didn't appear to have been raped. My blood-soaked jumper had been replaced by a large, buttoned-down man's shirt, but as I tried to raise it to inspect the bullet wound beneath, I realised that my hands had been cable tied together in front of me. It was clear that one captor had replaced another, and for a moment, it seemed like my circumstances had improved, until I recalled Vasili's words about being strapped to a bomb. After a little wiggling, I managed to push up my top to discover that my wound had been cleaned, dressed and wrapped tightly. The wound to my head hadn't been bandaged, but it did feel as though it had been cleaned, and although battered and bruised, I didn't feel as though I was in so much pain either, so I must have been given painkillers somewhere along the line.

More than half an hour passed by without interruption, so I felt brave enough to walk around. Trying the doors and windows gently on the off chance that they'd been left open, I wasn't surprised to find myself trapped. The glass had been covered with something from the outside, leaving the room lit only by the overhead light. If it wasn't for the clock high up on the wall, I wouldn't have had a clue what time of day it was. After a search for an escape and weapons proved useless, I gently lowered myself to the floor. Eventually someone would come for me. My only hope was that Nan understood my cry for help and had alerted the SAS. But even then, that vein of hope was slim. If I had no idea where I was, I had no clue how anyone else would find me.

My prison was a strange mixture of government utilitarianism, from the bulk buy, scratchy blue carpets and mismatched metal filing cabinets, to the Victorian grand opulence with high ceilings and ornate crown mouldings. My best guess was that I was in one of London's many turn-of-the-century properties that had been refitted for office use.

Hours passed alone. Without anything to sit on, I was starting to ache, and I figured that any painkillers I'd been given were probably starting to wear off. The sound of raised voices made me jump, and when a key turned in the lock, I scurried back into the corner, trying to make myself as small as possible. Four men, all wielding guns, stormed into the room, but it was the fifth man I was most afraid of. His cold, black, soulless eyes looked through me, as though I wasn't even a person but an object, and a distasteful one at that. He gave me a cursory glance up and down, and apparently satisfied at what he saw, issued orders to two of them who advanced towards me menacingly.

"What do you want with me?" I cried.

They ignored me, gesturing with their guns that I should move out of the corner. Each time they crept forward, I kicked out at them with my feet, aiming towards a kneecap. It was a dangerous strategy. I could easily have found myself at the receiving end of a bullet. But I figured if they wanted me dead, they wouldn't have gone to all the effort of patching me up.

When the fifth man grew impatient with my antics, he grabbed a gun from his companion and, swinging it around, jabbed me hard in the chest with the butt. It was enough to wind me. Throwing the strap of the gun over his shoulder, he reached down to seize me by the hair and yank me out off the floor. I swore to God that if I survived the ordeal, the first thing I was doing was cutting all my hair short as a "fuck you" to every man who thought they could use it like reins to control me.

"Stay still," he ordered.

"Or what?" I asked defiantly. "What are you going to do, shoot me?"

He slapped me hard across my face, which still bore the pain of Vasili's punishment. The men holding tight to my arms were the only things still holding me up. Reaching for my chin, his grip bruising, he turned me to face him. His face was unbearably close to mine as he spoke with little more than a whisper.

"No. I will pump you full of drugs then film as my men take it in turns to mock and abuse you over and over again. Then I'm going to do exactly what I want anyway, and you will die knowing that the last images of you anyone will ever see, will be of you on your hands and knees like a stray dog, begging for death."

I let him see the hate and defiance in my eyes as his men forced the vest of explosives over my chest and shoulders, tying it behind me and doing something with the wires. His smug grin was that of a man who knew he had absolute power over my position, and it made my blood boil.

With one final act of insolence, I spat in his face. His smile turned to rage, and quick as a flash, his handgun was pressed firmly to my forehead. Maintaining his stare as he wiped away my saliva, I practically dared him to do it. The hit that I was expecting never came, the explosive vest probably the only thing to save me from more pain. But mentally, it felt like a victory, even if only a minor one. When you've been worn down enough, when you've taken as much abuse as you believe you can handle, sometimes a tiny act of rebellion is enough to remind you that you're still alive. And where there's life, there's fight. He uttered more harshly spoken words that I didn't understand before he left, his men following behind him. The turning of the key in the lock echoed ominously in the silence.

Alone once more, I retreated to my corner, and on shaky legs slumped to the floor. My bindings had been cut when they forced the vest onto me, but it didn't matter. The thing was wired from behind, and my hands were shaking too badly to do anything of use, even if I knew how. As time passed, the pain grew worse, and it was hard to ignore with little else to focus on. Slipping my hand underneath the vest, I touched the edges of the bandages, only then realising as I pulled my hand away, my fingers wet with fresh blood, that time was running out, in more ways than one.

CHAPTER THIRTY ONE

Tom

Only once we were airborne did we learn that the chopper couldn't get anywhere near the target for either an aerial assault or so we could repel in. The height and close proximity of the buildings around put pay to that. It was probably one of the reasons the terrorists chose it. At the eleventh hour, permission came through from the owner of a private helipad across the Holborn Viaduct. Lacking any other options, the first chopper touched down, with the second following barely a minute later. From there we booted it as fast as we could to Aldersgate Street. When we arrived, the place stood out a mile. In a city where most buildings were lit up like Christmas trees, regardless of the hour, the address we'd traced Sarah to was conspicuous in its near darkness.

"Boys, we need intel, and we need it fast. My team will take the front elevation of the building. Harper's team take the back. Police are setting up a half-mile perimeter roadblock around this place, and they're quietly evacuating buildings. Use them to gather intel if you need to. That gives us half an hour tops before this thing's all over the fucking news and the terrorists are tipped off, if they haven't been already. Use the mics to communicate, secure comms channel 2 only. No chatter. I want heat signatures from every angle of that place. We have ten minutes to figure out exactly how many bad guys we're looking at. Harper and I will coordinate the entry plan, and we go in fifteen minutes after that. Right now, we have the element of surprise. They have no idea they've been made, and they aren't expecting us. I know this is going to be messy, and we'd all like a fuck load more prep time, but we just don't have it. This operation is not getting fucked because they're seeing pictures of us hanging off the building in a special news bulletin. Understand?" Hunter said, addressing both teams. I was reluctantly impressed at his leadership skills. If he hadn't fucked up the last op and lost sight of Vasili Agheenco, I might have even thrown out a compliment.

"We're coming up with an entry plan together, are we?" I asked as the guys ran off.

"Look, it's no secret that I don't like you. You're an arrogant prick who's never given me or my team a fair crack of the whip. But I was wrong to talk shit about Sarah the other day. She's a nice kid, and I feel shitty for fucking up and letting the Russian go. You have more experience with forced-entry operations than I do, so let's get past our bullshit and get this done so we can go back to hating each other."

"Deal," I agreed, and with a grudging nod of respect, went to prep for the most important mission of my life.

————————

A little over twenty minute later, we had a plan. It wasn't the best plan in the world, drafted on the fly and with hardly any intel, but we had little choice. In a world where the media could smell a fart even before it left your arse cheeks, there was no such thing as discretion, even when discretion was the better part of valour. If we didn't go now, at least one news station would report on the police cordon, and Sarah was as good as dead.

The heat signatures put the target count at fourteen. Fourteen terrorists against two, four-man special forces teams. The unknown was the bioweapon. If a rogue shot hit the bioweapon or the explosives they intended to set off with it, we were all dead. Worry about what we couldn't control was pointless. We just had to count on the element of surprise and hope that in the seconds it took us to hit our targets, none of them reached a trigger for the bomb. Three minutes before go ahead, MI5 bought us a Hail Mary. They'd hacked the feed to the internal security cameras, and Hunter had a stream of intel straight to his comms unit.

"Suspect biohazard package is on the fifth floor. Second door to the left after the elevators. There are two marks in the same room and another five in the room adjacent. Sarah is alive. The cameras show Sarah on the floor in a room across the corridor from the bio package. She's not moving, but I'd say she's alive," Hunter reported.

I closed my eyes and concentrated on my breathing, inhaling and exhaling as I calmed the beating of my heart and focused on tuning out everything but the mission ahead. We'd had less than ten minutes to learn the layout of our entry floors, but mine was burned into my brain. I was ready, detached emotionally from everything I was about to do. There would be no hesitation. No pause. No mercy. She was my entire world, and they took her from me. Now I would take the entire world from them.

One minute.

Every step, every movement, every action I was about to take was choreographed in my mind, like a dance that would end only in death. For all the pain and suffering they'd brought on innocents, a quick demise seemed too easy. A mercy they'd denied nearly all of their victims. But Sarah didn't believe in an eye for an eye. Her idea of justice and mine were so very different. Even now I doubted she'd be wishing pain and death on her captors. Unfortunately for the fuckers who thought they could hurt and maim and kill without consequence, I wasn't so forgiving.

Ten seconds.

"They're on the move. They have Sarah and they're dragging her to the biohazard room. She appears to be strapped to an explosives vest, and she looks a little banged up, but she's alive. Pick your target carefully. Do not let them get to a trigger for the explosives, and do not hit that vest. Counting down now.

Three.

Two.

One.

Go. Go. Go."

Hunters voice in our ear gave the go ahead, and we were gone. Creeping up the marble steps to the front lobby, I took cover behind one of the Georgian pillars until the guard who had been pacing the ground floor lobby made a path towards me. I waited until he was almost upon me before slipping around the pillar to approach him from behind. Using one hand to cover his mouth and stifle any noise, I brought the other up sharply, slicing open his throat. He was dead before his body hit the floor.

"Ground floor, first floor, and stairwell clear. Proceed to the second floor," Eli said. Acting like a spotter from the building across the road, he was keeping an eye on the movement of heat signatures and feeding the information back to us. Two floors up and things didn't go quite as smoothly. B team had taken out another man, but he'd cried out as he'd gone down. Spooked from the noise, my guy had turned around before I had the drop on him, pulling a knife. We fought, bouncing off walls and wrestling for control of the weapon. Seconds later, I dislocated his shoulder, loosening his hold enough for me to drive the serrated blade straight through his heart. His body slumped forward, then fell to the ground.

"Stairwell and all remaining floors clear. All targets assembled on the fifth floor," Eli told us. As we made it to the right floor, Crash knelt on the ground, taking up his position by the main door. Will and I continued up as stealthily as we could, until we hit the roof. Finding a suitable anchor, we secured our guide ropes, then hooked on our carabiner clips and edged over the roofline.

"Tango. Alpha. One. Ready," I said into my throat mic.

"Tango. Alpha. Two. Ready," Will said next. The rest of the guys called in to confirm their positions.

"Phase one, go," Hunter ordered, and we repelled seamlessly down the front elevation of the building until we reached the windows that would be our point of entry. We weren't worried about being seen. Every window had been covered in some way. But as I reached mine, my heart stopped. The window cover had slipped, leaving gap big enough for me to see through, and there she was. My beautiful girl. The centre of my fucking universe. She looked lost and alone. So very fucking alone. I willed her to see me. To know that I was coming for her. That I was with her.

Like she heard me, her gaze locked with mine until her eyelids fluttered closed and her expression morphed into one of absolute agony. I took a second or two to scrutinise the men who'd been roughhousing her. Whether Vasili had done that damage to her face or these bastards, didn't matter. They were dead the minute they looked at her.

"Charge 1 set," Will whispered.

"Charge 2 set," one of the guys from Hunter's team replied. That was our cue to move. Pushing ourselves off the building, we moved into position on either side of the window, slid down our gas masks, and turned our heads away from the glass.

"Three, two, one," Hunter counted down. On zero the charge detonated and the window exploded. A fraction of a second behind it, the casement opposite on the other side of the building blew. Unpinning our gas canisters, we launched them into the debris. Smoke engulfed the room, and shouting gave way to coughing as the fuckers struggled for air.

"Go!" Hunter yelled into the earpiece.

I kicked off from the wall and swung left until my boots hit the glass strewn windowsill. Unhooking my carabiner, I pulled myself inside and raised my weapon as I swept the room. The crunch of glass under Will's weight told me that he was right behind me. Disorientated and desperate, the terrorists panic fired in our direction, but their aim was high. Dropping to my knees, I took a deep breath and picked off my targets one by one. Bullets ripped through flesh and bone as the first couple fell to the floor.

Thrown into disarray, they screamed instructions at one another, desperately trying to claw back control from the chaos. It was too late. No one was spared. They scrambled for any sort of cover they could, but there was none. Not from us. I was ruthless. Relentless. Meticulous. Not a bullet was wasted as I carved a path of bodies through the carnage. Two shots each was all they had. One to kill and one to be sure. As soon as the bullets left the chamber, I was on to my next target, cutting through them quickly without compunction or remorse.

A cacophony of cries echoed through the smoke as Hunter worked his way towards us, but with every fallen terrorist, the noise abated, until there was only silence. I surveyed the sea of bodies for the only light in this shit storm. The realisation that she was gone was a painful one. Turning to look at Will, I gave him the hand signal to communicate my intention and moved forward, keeping low and focused.

"Boys, stay sharp. I've got two more heat signal between you both, and it looks like one is dragging the other," Eli informed us. The inhale and exhale of my breath through the mask was the only sound to puncture the quiet. Sweeping from left to right, I moved as quickly as I could through the hallway until I found what I was looking for. A few metres in, stood a terrorist. The last of them left alive. The last to realise the hopelessness of their situation. There would be no trial. No public platform upon which they could announce to the world their justification for the death of innocents. No opportunity to divide people in lies and hate. Not a single one of them was leaving the building alive, and now the last man standing knew it.

This was a different breed from the ones I'd killed. There was no anxiety or fear in this man's eyes. Only hate, and the promise that, if he was going to hell, he was bringing some company along for the road trip. He was slumped low to the floor, unable to hold the weight of his load with one arm. When I saw that he was using my girl as a human shield, my blood ran cold. I convinced myself that she was just unconscious, because I couldn't function any other way.

He shouted loudly at me, and I didn't need to translate to realise that he was telling me to stay back. The low calibre handgun pointed at Sarah's back conveyed the message loud and clear. It didn't matter whether his bullet would trigger the explosives in the vest. It would hit Sarah, and that's all that counted.

I raised my hands in surrender and ever so slowly lowered my gun to the floor, all the time taking small strides in his direction. It was something we were all well practiced at. The trick was to do it in such a way that the target was looking at your hands for the gun and the expression of your face so that he could read your intentions, all the while missing how close you were moving towards his position. My hands were empty and held high, but I was so close I could almost touch him. Maintaining eye contact, I didn't spare Sarah a single glance. One look would have told him everything he needed to know, and there was no way I was voluntarily handing over the knowledge of just how important she was to me. I could pinpoint the moment he made me, realisation washing over his face as he screamed and pushed the gun deeper into Sarah's back. Her poor broken body jerked in reaction. I stilled, not wanting to risk setting him off when Hunter appeared in my peripheral vision. He signalled to his team to stay back, and I knew then what he was going to do. Knew that I'd have seconds to steal away one life as he was risking his.

"SAS. Drop your weapon," Hunter called out loudly. If the mark had thought about it, he'd have realised that he was better off staying exactly where he was. With a gun pointed at the vest, nobody could afford to take a pot-shot at him from a distance. But he reacted in the same way most people do when faced with a threat, the way we hoped he would. He raised his gun towards Hunter and fired. In the infinitesimal amount of time it had taken him to do it, I'd pulled my Sig Sauer P226 from the holster behind my back and fired a bullet at close range through his brain. Blood sprayed across the walls, and he flew back, taking my girl with him.

"Clear," Hunter called out, and a chorus of affirmations came from each of the guys. I ripped off my mask and threw it to the floor as my fingers went to Sarah's pulse. My heart stopped until I could feel hers beating.

"We need the bomb squad in here now," Hunter ordered. The vest swamped her torso, but the blood seeping from beneath it was unmistakable. It soaked the lower part of her shirt and the top of her jeans. Seeing her, barely clinging to life, made me want to kill someone all over again.

"She okay?" Will asked.

"Her pulse is weak, but it's there. I need to get her to the hospital," I told him.

"Sorry, man. We can't move her till the bomb guys get here. We've got a rescue chopper that can airlift her from the roof, but Davies won't risk bringing them in until her vest is off," Hunter explained.

"Then get them in here!" I shouted. He looked at me hard, and I willed the fucker to argue with me. Instead, he spoke into his secure sat phone.

"I want that fucking bomb disposal unit in here now. Fuck any more prep time. The biohazard team has secured and removed the package, so I want bomb disposal to take this fucking vest off in the next five minutes or I'm bringing her down with it on and we'll see how quick they all move."

Whoever was on the line was giving him an earful, but Hunter didn't seem fazed.

"I appreciate that, sir, and I also appreciate the dangers of rushing this, but do you really want to have to explain to the world how we let Miss Tatem die in our arms when she was ten minutes away from the hospital? Because I'm looking at a man who's a hair's breadth away from going postal if this woman doesn't get medical attention soon," he argued. He went silent again while he listened to the response.

"Yes, sir," he said finally, and hung up the phone.

"The unit isn't ready, but one of the guys has volunteered to come up ahead of the rest of his team," he told me.

I really didn't want to move her and risk her losing more

blood, but there was no way he could get to the vest with her on the floor. As gently as I could, I lifted her into my arms, pressing her against my chest and leaving her back exposed.

"Hey, buttercup," I whispered, brushing her hair away from her eyes. "I came back from the dead because I promised you a lifetime with my ugly arse. So don't you bail on me now. We'll go home to the cottage and sleep in late, have that runny egg sandwich I promised you, and do all that shit normal people do when they grow old together, and I promise I will never leave you again, but you have to wake up for me now, okay?"

She didn't answer, and I tucked her in close as I tried to keep it together. Her gentle, shallow breaths caressing my skin were the only sign that she was still with me.

"Hold on, baby. Hold on," I begged, and in those moments that felt like an eternity, I prayed to whatever God was listening to leave me the one person in this shitty world I couldn't live without.

"Can we clear the area please? I'd like as many nonessential personnel out of here as possible." I presumed from the padded suit that the muffled voice belonged to the bomb disposal technician.

I could see my team were all reluctant to abandon us, but I gave them the nod to do as he said. As far as I was concerned, this guy could have the world as long as he got me my girl back. He wasted no time in bending down to examine the back of the vest where she was wired in.

"Okay, the good news is that it looks like they strapped her up but didn't have time to connect her up to the remote detonator. I only need to cut one wire to break the circuit, then we can unsnap it and get it off her. The bad news is the wire is on the inside of the vest which is strapped pretty tight.

"I'm going to lose her if you don't get her out soon," I explained, and he nodded in acknowledgement.

"I'm going to have to pull out her vest as much as I can and try and hook the wire to cut it. But I'm working in a tight space with little light. If I cut the wrong one, we're all going out with a bang," he joked.

I rocked her backwards to give him as much access to the underside of her vest as possible. He lifted the helmet off his head and put it to one side, probably realising that it wouldn't make a difference if the explosives did go off. Holding a pen torch in his mouth, he reached under her to hook the wire.

"Cutting now," he mumbled around the torch as I closed my eyes and held my breath.

CHAPTER THIRTY TWO

Sarah

I woke in a hospital bed to a bombardment of colour. The biggest stuffed Elmer the Elephant toy I'd ever seen was perched on the chair beside me. Every spare inch of the room was covered in balloons, cards, chocolates, and magazines. Groggy and slightly disorientated, it took me a few seconds to realise what I was looking at.

"Are you really here?" I asked, my voice sounding painfully cracked and broken. I was sort of fuzzy and a little out of it, but I could feel the tears running down the side of my face. The rush of pain at the thought that he might be some drug induced mirage, was acute.

"Don't cry Buttercup," Tom said, perching to sit on the edge of my bed. "I'm real." I shook my head in denial as my stupid, confused brain scrambled to sort out fact from fiction. As though he sensed my distress, he reached for my hand and laid it against the side of his face. Offering me solid proof of his existence.

"You died," I argued, still crying.

"No love. I took a couple of hits to the chest, but I was wearing my body armour. I'm bruised up pretty good, but still here. I promised you a runny egg sandwich and I fully intend to deliver."

I closed my eyes as I finally accepted that he was real, letting my palm memorise the heat of his skin and the bristle of his stubble. It was a touch I would have given the world for when I thought he was dead, and I intended never to take it for granted again. I moved slightly and winced, as my body reminded me just how badly it'd been abused of late.

"Don't try and move. If you need something, just ask and I'll get it for you."

"Water?" I asked, and he reached for the glass on the table beside me, bringing the straw to my parched lips. Each long, slow sip was heavenly. With his free hand, Tom tucked a wayward strand of hair behind my ear, and gently wiped away my tears with his thumb. He looked down at me with such love and sadness that my heart was breaking.

"I still can't believe you're really alive," I croaked, as he returned the water to the table.

"I feel the same way. When I think of how close I came to losing you-." He sounded so lost and broken. My throat hurt too much to console him, so I reached out for his hand, and he enveloped it between his own.

"Nan?" I whispered, and fear flooded my veins as I

realised she might still be in danger.

"Don't worry. She's safe and sound. We got her out and she holed up with a friend. I called her from the waiting room while you were being treated, she wanted to come down but I told her you needed to rest and to wait a few days. Which probably means that she's completely ignored me and is on her way."

I smiled, knowing he was probably right. The tears had finally stopped, but I felt strangely vulnerable and more than a little out of it. My eyelids were drifting slowly shut and I fought to keep them open, not wanting to miss a minute of our time together.

"It's okay Buttercup," he said, leaning forward to kiss me gently on the forehead. "You're on a lot of painkillers so you're bound to feel a little tired and groggy and after what you've been through, I think you deserve a little rest."

"I don't want to waste time sleeping," I admitted, still fighting against my body.

"Sar, we have all the time in the world, I promise. You need to rest and you'll feel better when you wake up."

"Lay down with me?" I pleaded. The look on his face as he ran his eyes over my body told me everything I needed to know about how battered and broken I looked.

"Please."

I scooted over and he perched precariously on the side of a bed not built for two people. Carefully manoeuvring himself around the wires that were attached to various parts of my body, he wrapped his arms around me and settled me into his chest. The sound of his strong heartbeat all the lullaby I needed.

"I love you, Buttercup," he whispered, moments before I drifted blissfully to sleep.

———

Tom was half right. When I woke for the second time I felt nowhere near as drugged up or out of it, but my entire body hurt like a son of a bitch.

"You are a hard woman to kill," said a voice from the chair beside me. I turned to see the smiling face of Simon Masterson.

"Are you sure they didn't succeed, because I'm pretty sure this is what death feels like," I replied. The trials and traumas of everything I'd been through echoed in the pain that radiated through every part of my body. He sat up and pressed a call button on the wall behind me.

"Where am I, and what have you done with Elmer?" I knew I was in a hospital, though I no idea which one.

"Who's Elmer?"

"My elephant. He was sitting there," I explained.

"Do you mean that awful monstrosity over there," he replied disdainfully, pointing towards my beloved cuddy toy that had been tossed on a bag in the corner.

"He's not monstrous, he's awesome."

"You are a strange girl Sarah. And in answer to your question, you're in a private room at the Royal London

Hospital," he replied. "You're back under SAS protection, but more to preserve your anonymity than because you're in any real danger."

"So what happened? The last thing I remember was being forced into an explosive vest and dragged into a room full of angry terrorists."

"So the CliffsNotes version," he said, helping himself to a few grapes from an overflowing bag on my side table. "SAS stormed the building and the bomb squad deactivated the vest so we could airlift you here. The bullet wound in your side missed every major organ, but you lost so much blood it was touch and go there for a while. You had a lot of people worried. All of the terrorists were killed, the bioweapon was recovered and I'm getting a promotion," he said, continuing to gorge on my food.

"Tom's alive, isn't he?" I asked. I knew in my heart that I hadn't imagined it, but hearing him confirm it was reassuring.

"He is. Telling you he was dead was apparently Davies's idea to get you into witness protection."

"Where is he?" I asked, desperate to see him again. Hold him. Start our happily ever after.

"He's been at your bedside for days, but he ordered me to 'sit my skinny arse' here and wait for him to get back. Apparently, he and Hunter Jackson are running an errand together."

"An errand. With Hunter Jackson," I said, my voice

filled with disbelief.

"I was as surprised as you are. But don't worry, they'll be back soon. Besides, you have three anxious SAS boys and one irate and slightly scary lady outside, all waiting for you to wake up, so I don't think you'll be short of company until Tom gets back."

"What's going to happen now?" I asked.

"That, is entirely up to you. Did you know that your Aunt was assassinated?" he asked. I shook my head no. Perhaps there should have been some sense of loss that the last of my family was dead but honestly, all I felt was relief.

"Vasili Agheenco shot her when he abducted you. He was probably tying up all loose ends before making a run for it."

"Do you know where he is?" I asked, anxiously, as memories of what he'd almost done to me came flooding back.

"Don't worry. We know exactly where he is and he's being handled. You'll never see him again."

"And the Company? With Aunt Elizabeth being dead, what will happen to all the people who depend on it for jobs?"

"You amaze me Sarah. Your face looks like you've gone twelve rounds with Mike Tyson and you're worried about how some guy you've never met will pay his mortgage." My hand rose automatically to my face, and I winced as I felt the cuts and swelling there.

"It's fine," he said. "You'll be back to normal in no time."

A nurse strode into the room, and reached across me to turn off the call button.

"It's good to see you awake. How are you feeling?" he asked me.

"I've been better," I admitted, with a pained chuckle.

"Well let's check your blood pressure and get you some water, then I'll sort you out with some pain killers. The doctor will be along to check on you shortly." I let the nurse do his tests and dutifully downed the painkillers he gave me, but when he left the room I reminded Simon what I need to know.

"Tatem Shipping?" he rolled his eyes at my tenacity.

"I'm no expert but the market dropped slightly all over when news of the attempted bioweapon attack broke, although shares in Tatem Shipping are holding for the moment. I don't know what will happen now that you've lost the Russian money, but hopefully you'll have enough time to do what you need to secure jobs for the people who work there." I nodded gratefully, satisfied that I'd have time to do what was right by the employees of the company before starting a new life with Tom.

"Thank you," I said, sincerely. "For everything."

"Miss Tatem," he replied, reaching for my hand and kissing the back of my knuckles. "It was an absolute pleasure."

EPILOGUE

"They're here," I murmured, kicking Hunter's ankle. Near soundlessly we moved into position. The day was relatively mild, but the slight breeze carried with it the rumble of a distant convoy. Adjusting my posture carefully, I pulled the 228 calibre L96A1 rifle tight into my shoulder and pressed my eye to the Schmidt and Bender telescopic sight. A crackle indicated that Hunter had activated his throat mic.

"Call 'em as you see 'em," I said.

"Target sector bravo deep. We have two, make that three, Land Rovers heading our way," he murmured quietly.

"Range it."

"Nine hundred and fifty yards and closing. Wind three quarter value."

"Ready," I said, indicating I had the shot lined up.

"Whenever you are," he replied.

Taking a deep breath, I held it as I gently squeezed the trigger. The gun popped, and the recoil bounced it against my shoulder as a bullet, a single bullet, flew through the air with the majesty of an arrow of justice. Vasili Agheenco, his terrorist payment firmly in his back pocket, was fleeing the country. At least he was until I put a hole between his eyes. His sleek black car swerved and careened into a barrier, flipping it in a crash that would have been fatal if he weren't already dead. With the final combat mission of my career a success, we hauled arse. In less than an hour, it would be like we were never there. When we were back on the road, I could finally relax, knowing it really was well and truly over.

"You think you can handle retirement, old man?" he asked me. The guy still pissed me off most of the time, same as Masterson, but I'd never forget that he was willing to take a bullet in order to save Sarah, and that gave him enough brownie points for me to tolerate his shit. At least for a while.

"I'm running the counterterrorism training programme at Hereford," I replied. "It's hardly fucking retirement."

"No more active duty." His tone suggested he hated the idea.

"Yeah, well, I'll remember your bitching when I'm enjoying a Sunday morning in bed with my girl and you're squat shitting in the middle of a jungle somewhere."

"Spoken like a true old man. Maybe I'll start thinking like that when they put me out to pasture," he joked.

"Well, princess, enjoy the spotlight as Alpha Team A group commander. Your time as my understudy is over."

"Fuck you," he said, but it was good-natured. In the end, we all got what we wanted, courtesy of one of the most successful operations in SAS history. At some point, there would likely be medals as well, but none of that mattered to me. The only thing I cared about was lying in a hospital bed. And five hours later, I got my reward.

She was asleep when I arrived. So I sat there, brushing a few stray hairs out of her eyes and taking comfort in the peaceful look on her face as she slept. Eventually, her eyelids fluttered open and she smiled.

"So, I guess I'm stuck with you now then, huh?" she said, reaching across to tangle her fingers in mine.

"Suck it up, buttercup," I replied, gently raising our joined hands to kiss the back of hers. "You're stuck with me forever."

ABOUT THE AUTHOR

R.J. Prescott was born in Cardiff, South Wales, and studied law at the University of Bristol, England. Four weeks before graduation, she fell in love, and stayed. Ten years later, she convinced her crazy, wonderful, firefighter husband to move back to Cardiff where they now live with their two equally crazy sons. Juggling work, writing and family doesn't leave a lot of time, but curling up on the sofa with a cup of tea and a bar of chocolate for family movie night is definitely the best part of R.J. Prescott's week. Her debut novel, *The Hurricane,* became a *USA Today* best seller and was a finalist in the Goodreads Debut Novel of the Year. She loves to hear from her readers so contact her at:

Website: http://rjprescott.com/

Facebook:

https://www.facebook.com/rjprescottauthor/

Twitter: https://twitter.com/rjprescottauth

Instagram: https://www.instagram.com/r.j.prescott/

Keep reading for a sneak peak of The Hurricane!

PROLOGUE

Cormac O'Connell

I felt like a total fucking creeper as I leaned, with my hands in my pockets, against the lamppost, and stared at her through the cafe window from across the road. For weeks now, I'd found myself in the same spot, wondering when I was going to grow a pair of balls and talk to her. Man, this girl was fucking perfect. At least that was what I'd built her up to be. I wasn't sure I could handle the disappointment if she was anything less.

I tilted my head to the left as she walked from the kitchen with a pot of coffee. I didn't want to lose sight of her. Even in that shitty uniform, she was gorgeous. The first time I saw her, I thought she was hot. Then again, every girl I fucked was hot. But this girl was something else. She was beautiful, and there hadn't ever been much of anything in my life you could call beautiful.

Her blond hair was tied back in one of those messy knots that she always wore to work. Loose, I knew it was long, thick, and curly at the ends. I was getting hard as I imagined her straddling me, that hair cascading down as I fisted my hands into it. Jesus, now I was standing on a street corner at 6:30

a.m. with a hard-on. It was official. I was definitely a creeper.

Just then Danny said something funny, and they shared a laugh. Danny was an old man, and I was still jealous. What I wouldn't have given to have her smile like that for me.

She blushed as she glanced around with those beautiful blue eyes, suddenly self-conscious that someone might have seen her laughing. She never did anything to draw attention to herself, which made her the complete opposite of pretty much every girl I'd ever met. Even from here, I could tell she didn't have any makeup on, but she didn't need it. Her skin was flawless, and her plump, pale, pink lips were edible. I was sure a good kiss would darken them up. If I had my way, I'd find out soon enough.

Her cheekbones were a little hollow, which wasn't surprising given how tiny she was. I had at least a foot, and over a hundred pounds on this girl, and I realized how uneasy my size might make her. She was nervous and skittish, so I was probably going to scare the shite out of her. There was fuck all I could do about it, though. It's not like I could have made myself any smaller. Maybe if I waited until she left then sat down before she came back, I wouldn't seem so big.

Despite her size, she had killer legs that went on for miles, and a little hourglass dip at her waist that made me want to wrap my hands around it as I kissed her.

I shifted my weight to the other foot, willing my erection back down before some arsehole walked by and got the wrong idea. To make matters worse, I was fucking freezing. I'd left my hoodie at the gym, thinking it would help my cause to show off my body. It was pretty much the only thing I had going for me. Instead, I just felt like a fucking eejit, knowing that it was too cold for anyone but a total poser to be walking around in a T-shirt. It was the sort of thing that Kier and I would take the piss over. He'd be laughing his arse off if he could see me now.

Emily.

I whispered her name as I rolled it around on my tongue. I heard it yesterday when one of the other waitresses called out to her. It suited her. I thought once more about bottling it and heading back to the gym when she turned and walked toward the kitchen. This was my chance to sit next to Danny before she came back.

Fuck it.

Shoving my hands in my pockets, I headed across the street. I had no idea how much my life was going to change from the minute I sat down at that table.

CHAPTER ONE

Oh, my God, I am so late! I ran down the street, my heart pounding. The early morning commuters trying to make it into the office were oblivious to my plight as I dodged in and out of people. My thin summer shoes offered nearly no protection against the bitter bite of the frosty morning. By the time I opened the back door to Daisy's Cafe, my teeth were chattering and my fingers were stiff with what I was sure was the onset of frostbite. I had no idea what I was going to do when winter really set in. I was barely scraping together enough money for rent and food, let alone having to worry about gloves and a winter coat.

"Mornin', Em." Mike, the owner, smiled as he turned the bacon over in the pan. For the last few weeks, I'd been pulling extra shifts at the cafe and then studying when I got home. I thought I could handle it, but after waking up at my desk half an hour ago, I knew I was wrong.

I wasn't surprised that Mike didn't seem mad. I'd never been late for a shift before, and more often than not, I was the last to leave. Daisy's had heating, after all. Heating and company. Two of the things I was in need of most at the moment.

"Sorry I'm late," I mumbled to Mike. I avoided making

eye contact and raced to hang up my coat and tie my apron. Tapping down the pocket, I made sure I had my pad and pencil and quickly scraped my hair back with one of the elastics kept permanently around my wrist. Wrestling it into a messy bun, I weaved through the kitchen and grabbed a pot of coffee.

I passed Rhona who'd been at Daisy's since the doors first opened.

"Slow down, love," she said with a warm smile. "You just need to do the refills and take the order for table two." She breezed into the kitchen without waiting for a reply.

Daisy's was one of the only cafes around that offered unlimited tea and coffee refills with a meal, which meant the place was usually packed for breakfast. After running around topping up coffees, I said hello to Danny as he sat down at his usual table. We chatted for a bit and, promising him a fresh pot, I headed to the kitchen to pass Mike the order for table two.

As I walked back out, I froze. Sitting next to Danny, and glancing at me over the menu, was hands-down the hottest guy I had ever seen. His nose had a slight crook in it, which made me think it was once broken, but that was the only flaw in his otherwise perfect face. Razor-sharp cheekbones, tanned skin, and dark hair added to the beauty that seemed completely at odds with his stature. If it weren't for the broken nose, he could be a model, but I knew that whatever this man did was dangerous, because everything about him exuded violence. I had no idea who he was, and the fact that he was sitting with Danny should have eased me, but it didn't. My internal alarm was going off big time. From the set of his shoulders, to the sheer size of him, he looked like nothing but trouble. Whoever he was, it looked like Danny was raking him over the coals about something.

Danny was a small, wiry man, who couldn't have been much younger than seventy-five. The deep grooves in his face and leathery skin spoke of hard living, but he was no frail pensioner. Mike was twice the size of Danny, but even he was a little bit scared of him. From my very first shift at Daisy's, he'd strolled through the door a few minutes past opening, plonked himself in an empty booth in my section, and beckoned me over—which soon became our morning ritual.

But that first day was different; I'd been absolutely petrified of everything and everyone. Most regulars had gravitated toward the other girls' sections, wary of the new girl messing up their order. Danny had no such compunctions, though. He'd sat straight down and called out, "Hey, sunshine, come and get me a cuppa coffee. I don't bite."

Shaking like a leaf, I filled his cup and, by sheer force of will, avoided spilling the scalding liquid all over his lap. If he noticed my nerves, he'd never said anything. He rattled off his order then unfolded a crisp, clean newspaper and read silently until I brought out his breakfast. When he was finished, I removed his plate and refilled his coffee.

"Thank you, sunshine," he said, without smiling and

without looking up from his paper.

Things went on that way for a few weeks, and when I finally stopped shaking, he spoke to me. It was never anything too personal, just remarks about the weather, questions about school, and what I thought of my professors. In the beginning, I did my best to find one-word answers, but just over a year later, Danny was the closest thing I had to a friend.

I wanted to run and hide in the kitchen. But hiding wouldn't do me any good, it never did. Ten horrific years of my stepfather, Frank, knocking me around had taught me not to speak unless spoken to and not to make eye contact. Whenever I felt threatened, those were the rules I fell back on.

Moving quickly through the tables, I wiped down a couple, gathered up a few dirty dishes, and after dropping them off at the kitchen, I could procrastinate no further and headed to Danny's table.

"Two full fried breakfasts please, sunshine," Danny croaked, with his usual scowl. If he ever did smile at me, I was a little worried that his weather-beaten face might crack.

Lowering my eyes, I gave him a small nod but didn't reply. It was our usual routine, and he was familiar with it. Without asking him, I filled up his coffee cup, and my hands trembled. It had been months since that happened, and I knew if I had to ask Danny's companion if he'd like coffee, my voice would crack. I turned toward him with the coffeepot in my hand, and my eye caught on the sleeve of his white T-shirt. The biggest biceps that I'd ever seen strained the seams, and beneath, the edge of a tattoo was visible. It looked like a series of intricately woven Celtic designs. From what I could see, the artwork was beautiful.

"O'Connell, do you want coffee or not?" Danny snapped at him. I flinched at the sharpness of his tone, but he did, at least, save me from speaking.

"Yeah, sure," the guy replied lazily, almost bored. I shook badly again, and I was sure that I'd spill it, but I didn't. Gathering up their menus, I all but whispered, "I'll be back with your order soon," and fled to the kitchen to hide. The guy's eyes were boring a hole in my back as I walked away.

Ten minutes later, their order was done. Taking their warm plates through to the cafe, I placed the identical breakfasts down in front of them and escaped.

"You keep your eyes off that, boyo. That one's not for you," I heard Danny warn quietly.

Danny was born and raised in Killarney, Ireland, and I very much doubted that the forty years he'd spent here in London had softened his accent much.

"Why was she shaking so badly?" the man Danny had called O'Connell asked in a deep, husky voice with a slight Irish lilt that was just about the sexiest thing that I had ever heard.

Danny sighed deeply before answering. "You probably scare the shite out of her. That one's special, but she ain't for you, so you'd best mind yourself and leave her to her business. Now, stop looking after something you can't have and think about what I said, 'cause if we have one more conversation about you drinkin' and fightin', you eejit, then you and me are gonna have words!"

The rest of the conversation was lost on me. The idea of Danny threatening this mountain of a man with anything would be enough to make me to smile, if he hadn't mentioned the fighting. Truth be told, you only had to look at O'Connell to know that he was dangerous. It was hard to tell how tall he was, but by the way he was crammed into that booth, I'd guess he was big. Broad shouldered and ripped, he looked every inch a fighter, but it was that relaxed, almost bored, indifference about him that sold the package. He could take care of himself, and he knew it.

A few more of my regulars made their way over to my section, and after doing my rounds with the coffee and rushing back and forth with orders, I realized that the seat across from Danny was empty. I let out a deep breath and began clearing the table.

"Give my compliments to Mike," Danny told me, as I stacked up the plates.

"Sure, Danny," I replied. "Can I get you another coffee?"

"No, thank you, sunshine. My bladder control is not what it used to be, and I'm gonna find it hard enough to get back to work as it is."

This was more information than I needed to know. I was

sure that he threw it out there just to get a rise out of me, and I humored him by rolling my eyes.

"Make sure you wrap up warm, then." I gestured toward his coat and scarf on the bench. "It's bitter out."

I dealt with ringing up his check, and before he'd even closed the door behind him, Katrina Bray was up in my face. With her shirt pulled tight against her impressive cleavage and a skirt rolled higher than her apron, she stomped her way toward me.

"What the hell was Cormac O'Connell doing in your section?"

I gave her the one-shouldered shrug. "I have no friggin' clue, and you're welcome to serve him next time," would be my response of choice, but I kept my mouth shut. Katrina was the last person that I needed to start an argument with.

"You have absolutely no idea who he is, do you?"

She obviously deduced this for herself, given the vacant look on my face. Without waiting for an answer, she flounced off in a cloud of cheap perfume. Rhona, having heard the whole exchange, shoulder bumped me on her way back to the kitchen.

"Go on, girl. 'Bout time that madam had a bit of competition, and once upon a time, I wouldn't have minded a piece of that boy, myself. I wouldn't be turning a blind eye if I was twenty years younger."

"Need some help?" I motioned to the dishes in her hand, trying to change the subject. It had completely escaped her notice that I was neither flirting, nor being flirted with. I was no expert, but I was sure that you actually needed to talk to someone to start a relationship.

"No thanks, love, I've got it. Your section is getting pretty full."

She nodded back toward the cafe. Seeing she was right, I hurried back to take orders. People were pretty slow about coming into my section to begin with, but once they saw me waiting on Danny every day, they slowly started drifting over. The breakfast and lunch shifts flew by, punctuated by evil looks from Katrina. I guessed from her attitude that O'Connell was on her hit list and she hadn't scored with him yet. Which would put him in the minority, from what I heard.

When Katrina wanted a guy, he usually didn't offer much resistance. She had nothing to worry about from me, though. If O'Connell came in here again, she was welcome to him. However good-looking the package, I didn't need that kind of trouble in my life. It wasn't as if he'd ever give me a second look anyway.

By the time my shift ended, I was glad to be heading to class. Waitressing was okay, and it was nice to have some company, but school was where I really lost myself. Getting a place at UCL had been the scariest and most exhilarating thing that had ever happened to me. None of it would have been possible without my former teacher Mrs. Wallis. I had been wriggling around in my seat, trying not to let the chair touch any of the fresh bruises hidden under my sweater when she had approached me. With tears in her eyes, she had told me she knew I had a difficult home life, and as I was nearly eighteen, there was a way of escaping. If I wanted her help, I would have it.

That was the nearest that I ever came to breaking down. Part of me wanted to scream at her that, if she knew, then why didn't she tell social services so they could get me? I think we both knew that would only have made things worse though.

I didn't scream at her or cry, but actually setting out the bare bones of a plan was terrifying. The fear of being caught, and of my stepfather, Frank, discovering what I was doing, had me feeling sick every minute of every day. Using Mrs. Wallis's address, I had applied for university places and identification. When I turned eighteen, I changed my surname legally. I accepted a place studying applied mathematics at University College London, and now, eighteen months later, the only person who could ever connect Emily Thomas from Cardiff, South Wales, with me was Mrs. Wallis, an elderly home economics teacher who was the only person I'd ever trusted.

I'd breezed an access course in accounting over the summer, but my heart was in math. It was clean and pure, and in my world of gray, it was black and white. If I had any chance at building a future, then I needed qualifications.

The dread of being caught was always ever present though. I guessed that Frank was looking for me but getting my degree was worth the risk. If I committed to staying in one place long enough to finish university, I had to keep a low profile. It was my best chance of evading him. So I did what I'd always done. I made no eye contact and never initiated conversation.

It had worked in high school, but university was a completely different kettle of fish. The guys here were relentless. Politely turning down unwanted advances, without causing offense, had become an art form that I'd perfected. It was the safest way to live, but I was lonely. There were days that I desperately wanted someone, anyone, to call a friend. In lecture room three, on that frosty Tuesday afternoon, I got just that.

"This seat taken?"

I looked down at cherry red leather boots with a killer heel and looked up to see that the voice belonging to them liked to coordinate her cherry red hair with her outfit. Clearly I was more than backward when it came to accessorizing. My hair didn't go with anything.

"Um…" I looked around, desperate to say yes, hoping to remain as anonymous as possible. The lecture theater was only a third full, at best, and there was no reason why this girl would want to sit next to me. She wore a denim miniskirt, a fitted black top, and a leather jacket that I would have given my left arm for. With the killer boots and her glossy hair layered artfully around her face, she looked edgy and hot. No wonder half the man-geeks were drooling. My first thought was that she was in the wrong place.

"No," I replied. Could I have been more socially inept? If she was in the right place, it looked like she'd be beating off the guys with a stick, so what better place to take cover than beside the only other girl in the room.

"Nikki Martin," she said, sliding into the adjoining seat.

"Sorry?" I mumbled.

"I'm Nikki Martin," she stated, expectantly awaiting a response.

"Oh, hi," I replied, as I went back to copying down the equation from the projector.

"Oh, my God, you really are one of them," she laughed, teasingly.

"One of them?" I answered, glancing up in confusion.

"The freaks who only speak in numbers and have no social skills whatsoever."

"Wow, rude much?" Oh, my God! I've never been confrontational, ever, but with this girl, it just slipped out.

She laughed again, probably at the look of sheer horror on my face. "So the kitten has claws. You know, you and me are going to get on just fine."

I had no idea what to say to that. This girl was like a beautiful steamroller.

"Okay, a name would be good about now, unless you want me to call you Mathlexy all term."

"Mathlexy?" Yep, I was getting good at repeating everything she said back to her as a question.

"I can tell you're a math fiend by the stack of

handwritten notes you've got there, and you're the sexiest thing this lot has probably ever seen."

She gestured around the lecture hall, and I wasn't convinced that the guys would actually wait until the end of class to pounce on her. The wide-eyed looks of disbelief, appreciation, and finally hunger reminded me of starving hyenas, eyeing up their appetizer. I giggled at the image and snorted through my nose at the absurdity of the name. Snorting was neither sexy nor attractive.

"Emily McCarthy," I offered up in return, hopeful of rejecting that ridiculous nickname before anyone heard it. The last name was new. I'd only had it for a year, and I was still getting used to it. But I figured that keeping my first name wouldn't hurt. Emily was a pretty common name, and people got suspicious if you didn't answer to your name when called because you didn't know it.

"Well, it's nice to meet you, Emily McCarthy," she answered.

By the end of the lecture, I had three sides of crisp clean notes, and Nikki had half a page and some lovely heart and floral murals.

"What's your next class?" she asked, as we were stuffing things into our bags.

"I don't have another one for a couple of hours," I replied. "I was just going to the library to study."

"Perfect, I have a couple of hours free. Let's go and grab a coffee. My treat."

She looped her arm through mine and all but dragged me out, clearly not caring about my plans.

Latte, espresso, tall, fat, mocha, grande. The board in front of me laid out the endless possible taste sensations, and I agonized over my decision. I loved coffee, but on my budget, regular coffee at Daisy's was about as good as it got. So if this was my treat for the month, then I was going to make the most of it.

"Come on, Em," Nikki moaned, "I'm growing old here!"

"A cappuccino, please," I ordered quickly. The barista handed me my drink, and I pulled out the chair next to Nikki.

She took a long sip of her coffee, sighed deeply, and turned to me. "So...the whole social hermit thing. Is it just for a term or are you committed for life?"

ACKNOWLEDGEMENTS

To Mr P, the love of my life and my greatest supporter. Without you, there would be no more words to write. You and the boys are my entire world and I will never, ever take for granted how lucky I am to have married my best friend! Jack and Gabriel, you are both growing up so fast, but every day you show me what wonderful men you will one day become and it makes me prouder than you will ever know. Being your Mum is, and always will be, the greatest thing I have ever done. Every time I nag you to do your homework and remind you to clean you room, remember it's because I love you! To Mum and Dad, who always support and encourage me whenever I have a crazy idea. Thank you for always having faith that I can do anything I set my mind to do if I work hard enough.

Lauren-Marie, I have no idea where I'd be without you to organise, guide and support me. Your friendship means the world to me and I can't thank you enough for everything you do. To say that you are worth your weight in gold is an understatement of epic proportions. The next year is going to be a good one and I can't wait to make loads new and wonderful memories with you!

To my wonderful friend Maria. Thank you for being so patient with me when I disappear for weeks at a time to write, and thank you for always being there to share a cuppa with me when I'm done. You are kind, supporting and selfless and our friendship means the absolute world to me.

Marie, exchanging ideas on this book has been so much fun and I have loved so much working on this together. I don't think either of us ever thought when we were painting walls and chatting about Gateway that we'd ever be here, but I'm so glad that we are. Thank you always for your friendship and support and for re-introducing me to a love of romance that will never die.

To Nicola and Lynsey. Every time I lose faith in myself, you always give it back to me. No matter what you are going through, or how low you might be feeling, you take life by the balls and keep moving forward and I love you both for constantly giving me the confidence I need to send my books out into the world. Nic, I would be lost without you. I can never hope to repay everything you do for me, but I will never take your friendship for granted. You are the ultimate Wonder Woman! Lyns, my only regret is that we don't live closer so I could squish you in person on a regular basis! Thank you so much for all of your support and encouragement. No matter what, you are always there when

I need you.

Clare, Lorayne, Steph and Sarah. Two years ago we were strangers, now I couldn't live without you! You guys keep me sane and laughing even when I'm so tired I can barely string a sentence together! Clare, between the snacks to keep me going and your amazing editorial powers I've been spoiled in this book and I have every intention of taking advantage of your mad skills with every book I write! Lorayne, Steph and Sar, you banded together to buy me time when I didn't have any and when I was at my lowest, you rolled up your sleeves and said, 'what do we need to do to get this done?' All four of you are nothing short of legends and I hope you realise you're stuck with me forever. Thank you all so much. I couldn't have finished this book without you.

To the best family in the world, Gerry, Faye, Ben, Boo, Dave, Gareth, Laura, Dan, Sarah, David and Tiffany. You all make me feel that there is nothing I can't achieve, and no matter what, you always love and support me. I feel so lucky to call you all my family.

Every author I know believes they have the best reader group, but I'm positive I do! Prescott's Hurricanes you inspire me! You are supportive, encouraging and always enthusiastic, even when I make you wait even longer for the Driscoll boys. You bring so much friendship and joy to the group that every day I'm reminded why I love writing. Thank you for being such a huge and amazing part of my world!

To Leigh Stone, there aren't words for how awesome you

are!!! Your skills blow me away and you bail me out time after time. Thank you so much for everything you do for me and for your mad crazy skills. I can't wait to work on our next book together because working with you is nothing short of effortless. You know what I want even before I do!

To Emilie from Inkslinger PR. Thank you for taking a chance on me and for all of your great advice. I've had so much fun working with you!

Rachel de Lune, I'm so glad we get to sign together at last! As always thank you so much for the support and for always being on the other end of the phone if I need you.

To Veronica from Hot Tree Editing, thank you so much for your patience and to Sarah from Okay Cover Creations for an epic cover that I am so in love with!

Thank you so much to all of my friends in Bristol, Cardiff and around the world. Conors, Christine, Jodie, Gav, Kerrie, Kevin, Cynth, Amanda, Ruth, Ceri-Anne, Adele, Paul, Bronwen, and all my friends. Your support and encouragement means the world to me.

Over the last few years I've had the privilege of working with and meeting so many bloggers, authors and readers, many of whom have become close friends. To each and every one of you, thank you. Every day I learn something new and every day I count myself lucky for getting to be part of this wonderful, supportive community bound together by a shared love of books.

To you the reader, as always I thank you from the

bottom of my heart. In a sea of books, you chose mine. To know that has made my dream come true.

My final thank you goes to the original Britney Spears for all of his technical help and patience and to each and every member of the Armed Forces and their families. Thank you for your service and dedication. Your bravery and sacrifice is truly humbling.

CPSIA information can be obtained
at www.ICGtesting.com
Printed in the USA
LVHW041616300919
632704LV00003B/547/P

9 781999 903817